MARINA OLIVER

The Glowing Hours

A SIGNET BOOK

SIGNET

Published by the Penguin Group
Penguin Books Ltd, 27 Wrights Lane, London W8 5TZ, England
Penguin Books USA Inc., 375 Hudson Street, New York, New York 10014, USA
Penguin Books Australia Ltd, Ringwood, Victoria, Australia
Penguin Books Canada Ltd, 10 Alcorn Avenue, Toronto, Ontario, Canada M4V 3B2
Penguin Books (NZ) Ltd, 182–190 Wairau Road, Auckland 10, New Zealand

Penguin Books Ltd, Registered Offices: Harmondsworth, Middlesex, England

First published by Michael Joseph 1995
Published in Signet 1996
1 3 5 7 9 10 8 6 4 2

Copyright © Marina Oliver, 1995
All rights reserved

Printed in England by Clays Ltd, St Ives plc

For Christopher, my dancing partner

I owe a great deal to the many books of reminiscences about Birmingham life, in particular the marvellous accounts by Kathleen Dayus: *Her People*, *Where There's Life*, *All My Days*, and *The Best of Times* (all published by Virago); *Old Ladywood Remembered* by Victor J. Price (Brewin Books); *Edgbaston As It Was* and *Memories of a Twenties Child* by Douglas V. Jones (Westwood Press Publications); and *Will You Please Take Your Partners* by Pauline and Bernard Mannion. Of enormous interest also was Paul Derval's memoir, *The Folies-Bergère* (Methuen). I want also to thank the librarians in Birmingham and the Bodleian for their help, my agent Sarah Molloy for her encouragement, and my editors Laura Longrigg and Richenda Todd for their invaluable skills, patience and friendliness.

On with the dance! Let joy be unconfined;
No sleep till morn, when Youth and Pleasure meet
To chase the glowing Hours with flying feet . . .

Lord Byron, *Childe Harold's Pilgrimage*, Canto III

Chapter One

'AIN'T none on yer comin'?'

Nell, poised astride the narrow windowsill, stuffed her ragged petticoat into the red flannel bloomers. She looked over her shoulder. Nine pairs of eyes, some envious, most apprehensive, stared back at her. How defeated they looked, she thought with a spurt of irritation. They were so passive, so unwilling to fight. Little red-haired Amy was the only one ever to show a scrap of spirit, and she'd soon have it beaten out of her. Then she was ashamed of her scorn. They hadn't had any chance to experience a different sort of life. How could they know it was possible to live without endless anger and violence? She was the eldest of the girls, and had only recently summoned up the courage to rebel.

No one spoke, and with a shrug she grasped the rope made from a rough, almost threadbare blanket, tied to the brass bedstead, and swung her leg out. 'Yer'll rue it,' she warned, then hissed, 'Shut winder, mind, Danny,' as she slid partway down the rope. The frighteningly familiar thumps and bangs from the room beneath ceased, and heavy footsteps could be heard staggering up the narrow, twisting stairs.

She made sure her treasured old patch-box of blue Wednesbury enamelling was safe in the belt she had fashioned for it. It was the only item in the house which was truly her own, and she hid it jealously from everyone else. No one would take this away from her. It was her talisman, her good-luck symbol. Then she dropped the last few feet on to the cobbles of the yard. Keeping in the shadows cast by the small houses, Nell ran swiftly towards the alley and freedom. In the dark entry she untied the shabby black skirt she'd slung round her neck, grinning at the picture she must present. She'd been in too much of a hurry to dress fully, just grabbing the skirt and a shawl that was more holes than substance, and for easier movement draping them round her.

Eth had protested when she dragged the shawl from on top of the blankets. 'That's ours, an' we'll be cold,' she whined nasally.

'You've still got a blanket,' Nell retorted. 'I'll be out in cold all night. 'Sides, there's three on yer to keep each other warm in bed.'

She shivered, more with anger than cold, as she struggled into the skirt. She couldn't endure Pa's constant beatings, she thought, tucking in the blouse, which was too small for her now her breasts were full and round, but was the only one she possessed. Finding somewhere else to sleep on the nights he was drunk and belligerent was all she could do. She bent to fasten her boots properly. At least her feet hadn't grown, and the boots her gran had bought her three years ago when she was thirteen still fitted, or she'd be barefoot like the rest.

Wrapping the shawl round her head, she went out into the street. To her left was the pub on the corner of Ryland Street. Half a dozen barefooted children, dressed in miserable apologies of rags, clustered near the door. Old Billy Bickley, who'd lost his legs at Gallipoli in 1916 eight years earlier, was sitting on his makeshift trolley nearby, playing his fiddle, collecting the few coppers folk could spare.

Nell could hear men carousing inside. They were the fortunate ones, with jobs to do and pennies in their pockets. Beneath the gas lamp on the corner Janie and Katie Pritchard waited hopefully, dressed in torn, seedy finery, the gleam of filthy but still bright satin showing through the encrusted dirt. Nell glanced round. If they were working tonight their brother Wilfred would be nearby, lurking in some alleyway, watching. Not to protect them, she knew, more to ensure they didn't escape his clutches and take their miserable earnings away with them. She turned the other way. Wilfred had tried more than once to entice her into his net with promises of untold wealth and a luxurious life.

'You don't mek enough ter get out o' Ladywood, even,' she'd said scornfully.

He grinned, revealing his blackened teeth and spat out a gobbet of phlegm.

'Thass 'cos Oi'm saving it 'til Oi can goo ter posh plice loike 'Andsworth, 'ave a dacent 'ouse, proper accommodation fer blokes wot cum,' he explained ingratiatingly. 'A pretty little wench loike yow, wi' them slanty green eyes an' curves wot mek a fella' look twoice, 'ud be a proper draw. Yow could foind yersen a rich 'un, mek 'im wed yer, p'raps,' he'd added, his sneering disbelief undisguised.

Nell shuddered at the recollection. She'd been safe then, for he'd spoken to her near the main Ladywood Road, and she knew she could outrun him. She had long, supple legs: he was grossly fat and unhealthy. She was well aware that if he caught her in some dark corner she would have no chance of getting away, and no one would interfere in her defence.

There was a full moon, and though September it was still warm. She had a sudden urge to explore further. Instead of huddling down on the stairs leading to the crypt in St John's churchyard, or finding shelter in a garden shed behind one of the big villas in streets at the better end of Ladywood Road, she'd try Monument Road.

It seemed a long way down the narrow streets and alleys. It was light enough to see clearly, and she wandered past some really big houses. But they were not so enormous as the ones to the south of the Hagley Road, which would have stables. At the sudden thought she hugged her shawl closer. Dare she attempt it? Before he died Gramps had been a coachman, and she had no fear of horses. If she could find a snug corner near the animals, with the steamy heat they produced, she'd have a comfortable refuge even in the depths of winter. If not, life would be even grimmer.

She went past Perrott's Folly, over the Hagley Road, and soon reached a street of houses with carriage drives and side entrances. She'd only been here once before. The first few older houses had small front gardens, but no sign of occupied stables. Nell turned a corner and came to the mansions she sought, big Victorian villas set in their own secluded gardens. Sidling along in the shelter of low sandstone walls which restrained rampant clumps of laurel and rhododendron bushes, pausing to draw in deep, refreshing breaths of the clean, pungent aroma, Nell explored. She found one stable in which could be heard the snufflings of a horse. Her hopes soared, but the door was firmly locked and there was no way in. There were coach houses where she could have been comfortable, and Nell took careful note of where these were. In one there were even cushions left in a pile, which would have made a luxurious bed. A couple of former coach houses were occupied by motor cars, and she could have slept in one of these, warm and secure. But Nell had set her heart on finding a refuge where the warmth and companionship of a horse or pony could be had.

At last she found a stable which was occupied and unlocked. There was just an iron bar hooked across the doorway. Nell retreated into a concealing laurel bush while she considered the situation. As long as she could pull the door closed from inside, and replace the bar in the morning before anyone came, she would be safe. From the subdued noises, the clink of hooves against cobbles, a cough and a wheeze, she thought there might be two occupants. The moon shone directly on the door, and she glanced round cautiously. A thick, high hedge protected her from the house and no one there could see her. There was no room above the stable where a coachman might sleep.

She pushed back the long dark plaits which hung to her waist. She hadn't had time to bundle them up as she usually did. Then she took a deep breath and moved forward. As quietly as

4

possible she lifted the heavy bar out of the bracket and lowered it, then carefully swung open the door. It gave a protesting squeak and Nell, nervous, whisked inside the opening and dragged the door to behind her. To her immense relief her scrabbling fingers found a loop of string attached to the wall and a hook on the inside of the door. Once this was secured she stood quietly to let her eyes become accustomed to the dimness, as diffuse moonlight streamed in through a small, rather dirty window.

There were two loose boxes, in which two equine heads were turned curiously towards her. At one end of the small passageway harness hung neatly on hooks, under a range of shelves holding brushes and curry combs, metal polish and liniments. At the other end, the best find of all, was a heap of loose hay. Several horse blankets were folded on a shelf above.

Nell breathed a sigh of relief. Tentatively she stroked the noses of the horses, fed them each a wisp of hay, and took down two blankets. She spread one out on the soft pile, and wrapped the other round her. With a sigh of pure contentment she sank down into a nest more warm and snug than any bed she'd ever known, and for a fleeting moment wished she might live here for ever.

Then the dream was shattered. The door was pulled open as far as it would go. Moonlight gleamed on a knife being used to hack away at the loop of string, and before Nell could disentangle herself from the enveloping horse blankets the string gave way. The door was flung wide open, and she was blinded by the ray of a lantern.

'Yes, madam, to be sure. It can be ready for you by tomorrow. Naturally, madam. At your service. Shall we send it to madam?'

Gwyneth spoke quietly, holding on to her volatile temper with difficulty. What she would give to be able, just once, to treat the customers with the disdain many of them showed her.

'Of course, girl. And this time it had better be exactly right.'

'Haughty piece! She wants it shortened again, she does, and

by less than half an inch!' Gwyneth muttered beneath her breath to her fellow assistant, her vivid blue eyes glaring after the departing customer.

'Shut up! She's watching you!' Lizzie hissed back.

Gwyneth hastily dropped her eyes as Miss Fremling, the manageress of the gown shop, stalked across the floor to her. 'Miss Davis, your hair is appallingly untidy again. Go and comb it, but don't take all afternoon.'

'She'd like to dismiss me if she could,' Gwyneth complained bitterly, walking along New Street with Lizzie at the end of the day. 'I can't help having curly hair! Why does she have to pick on me so much? If I put a step wrong I'd be finished.'

'She wanted the job for her niece,' Lizzie said consolingly. 'I know you're never rude, but when you're annoyed you do sound a bit sarcastic, and your Welsh accent gets a lot stronger. One day she'll try and use that against you.'

'My accent?' Gwyneth gave an astonished laugh. 'She could dismiss me just because of my accent?'

'I've heard her complaining to Miss Sanders that sometimes it's difficult to understand what you say. She might say the customers can't understand, and that would give her a chance to get rid of you.'

'I see.' Gwyneth was thoughtful. 'I hadn't realized it was so — foreign! I thought I spoke more like my mother than my father.'

'Where does she come from?'

'Shropshire, near Ludlow. And she always insisted we had English nannies. But I had to go to school in Saundersfoot. There wasn't any money to send me away to an English school as well as my brothers. I suppose I'm lucky they didn't all speak Welsh there!'

'Don't risk being dismissed! It's been so much more fun since you came to work at the shop,' Lizzie said urgently.

'I won't risk it on purpose,' Gwyneth said fervently. 'I was so very lucky to get the job without any references, and I couldn't hope to be so fortunate again. I'd have to go and work in a factory if I lost this job, and somehow I don't think I'd like that.'

'You wouldn't. It's terribly hard work, they say. Are we going to a dance tomorrow? The Palais or the Tower?'

'The Tower's too big.' She giggled. 'You may never see your partner again if he goes away.'

Lizzie shook her head. 'They'd come looking for you,' she maintained with certainty. 'You're so pretty with your curly hair and big blue eyes and you're always smiling.'

'You don't mention my ruddy complexion and fat cheeks that make me look like a milkmaid,' Gwyneth grimaced, laughing. 'Or that I'm too tall for most men to feel comfortable dancing with me!'

'I hadn't noticed them keeping away because of that! We can change at work and go straight there. Have you finished your new dress?'

'Just the hem to do.'

'That's the third in a month! I'm saving up for another. I saw some lovely material in the rag market, and there are some feathers Miss Fremling threw out. They were broken, but I can sew them on so that it won't show. Quick! There's our tram!'

Lizzie lived further out from Birmingham city centre, near Warley Park and well past Five Ways, but Gwyneth had found a room just off Islington Row. She'd planned to walk to and from work, but after a long twelve-hour day standing in the shop she'd found she was exhausted. It was too easy to catch the tram with Lizzie, which on its outward journey went right along Islington Row. A month later, now she was more used to it, she could have managed, but she enjoyed Lizzie's company and the gossip they were forbidden at work. It was worth the penny fare. Lizzie wasn't really a friend, but she was company, and it was lonelier than she'd anticipated, leaving home.

And she had only herself to spend her meagre wages on, she thought guiltily. Lizzie had to give all hers to her mother, and was allowed only a couple of shillings a week to spend on herself. She had to save hard for a new dress, for she spent half her money on entrance tickets to dances every Saturday.

Perhaps she ought to send some money home to her mother. Then Gwyneth hardened her heart. No, much as she loved her mother she dared not contact her, give any clue as to her whereabouts, or her father would be storming back into her life. That was the last thing she wanted. If getting away from her stern, bigoted father meant she lost her mother too, that price had to be paid. Besides, she'd left home so that she could dance, and to dance she needed the right dresses.

One day, perhaps, she'd write to her mother. Not yet, though. Her freedom was too new and precious to risk. As she entered the doorway of the tall house where her room, right under the eaves, provided a haven, she was humming below her breath the latest tunes she'd heard at last week's dance.

'What was that fearful commotion last night, Andrew darling?'

Kitty Denver smoothed down her dark bobbed hair, looked longingly at the heaped plate of bacon and sausages, kidneys and eggs in front of her companion, and began to nibble as slowly as possible at an almost transparent slice of bread thinly spread with butter.

Andrew chewed hungrily, looking intently across the table. 'What colour is your hair, precisely?' he asked instead.

Kitty laughed. 'Heavens, how should I know?' she said airily. 'Dark brown? But why this sudden interest in my hair?'

He shook his head, and hastily finished another mouthful. 'In some lights it looks red. Yet in others it seems quite black.'

'Dark brown. That covers every variation, unless you're going to say I'm striped or pied. And my eyes are a funny sort of hazel, in case you want to discuss them too. Don't try and change the subject, sweetie-pie. What happened last night?'

'I went out for a cigarette. I was being good, dear coz, knowing how you feel about the smell —'

'Not me; Mama. She's fanatical, and even though she's on the

8

opposite side of the Atlantic, thank God, and long may she stay there, she'd hear about it from Meggy. And that would be the end of your free room and board here, my sweet. But surely you didn't make all that noise trying to light up?'

He laughed. 'You must get old Betts to put a lock on the stable. Some wretched urchin had got in there and was bedding down for the night.'

Kitty's eyes grew round with excitement and Andrew suppressed a grin. She might pluck her eyebrows into a pencil-thin line, wear the latest fashions and try to appear blasé and sophisticated, but when she was in a pleasant mood she could be a good sort, still eager for fun.

'Did you catch him?' she asked. 'What did you do? How absolutely thrilling! Ought we to send for the police?'

'It wasn't a him. I was so startled to see a girl jump up from the hay I almost dropped the lantern.'

'A girl? Darling, what fun. But why did you have a lantern?'

'I'd fetched it and a knife when I realized someone was inside. I heard the door as she pulled it shut. She'd tied that loop of string round the hook, and luckily I could just get the knife through the crack and cut it.'

'What happened? Did she get away? Or are you being terribly wicked and depraved, and hiding her in your room? Didn't you do that at Oxford with some girl? I shall be jealous, darling.'

He laughed ruefully. 'No, that was Paul. I put the lantern down and went to grab her, but she bit my hand, the little devil! And there's no need to chortle like that!'

'You're six foot tall, broad, you played rugger at Harrow, you shot Germans in the army, and you let a child just bite your hand and escape? How simply divine! And you don't want me to laugh!'

'Damn it, she was older than I thought at first. She looked such a child, but when she ran away, I saw she was – er – taller than I'd expected. It startled me.'

'Taller?' Kitty queried mischievously. Surely you mean more

9

buxom? I am certainly jealous! Andrew, darling, you're actually blushing!'

'Don't be a congenital idiot! Do you want more tea?' he asked curtly, going to the sideboard to replenish his plate.

'Stop being snappy! It's not like you. I don't want any more tea. And I do wish you'd eat less!' she added petulantly, her mood threatening to change. 'It's not fair, I eat hardly anything and I can't stay thin, while you eat like a pig and stay exactly the same as you've been for years.'

'You fuss too much. You're too skinny already. Meggy always says I need feeding up when I come here. And it's so much better than any other digs, I have to make up for the beastly food in them.'

'Andrew, darling, don't let's squabble. Tell me more about this girl. Which way did she go? Why the devil should she try to sleep in our stable? That was it, wasn't it? She wasn't trying to steal the horses?'

'She was wrapped up in one of the blankets; I had the impression she was settling down for the night. But she'd vanished completely by the time I picked up the lantern, not even the rustle of bushes to give her away.'

'What was she like?'

He shrugged. 'It's hard to say. She looked very pale, but that could have been the poor light. Dark hair, it gleamed like ebony, no lighter shades such as you have, thick ropes of it hanging down her back. A wide forehead, pointed chin, but I couldn't see many details, just the shape. Almost as tall as you, very thin, and clothes that were ragged and hardly big enough for her. And boots. I know she had boots because she kicked me on the shin, too.'

Kitty giggled. 'What a lark! That's something I wouldn't dare do! Did she say anything? Was she a local girl, or could she have been a gypsy?'

'I don't know. She didn't make a sound. But just in case she has any friends around, take care today. Get Betts to put on a lock. Aunt Cecily would be furious if she thought I wasn't protecting you properly. That's the only reason she and Meggy encourage me to stay here.'

'Her suffragette notions don't extend that far! Men still have the task of protecting poor feeble women,' Kitty mocked. 'Not that you did very well against another slip of a girl,' she added.

He stood abruptly. 'I must go. Rehearsal at nine. And a matinée. Don't expect me back until late – I'll eat out.'

Kitty pouted. 'You're such a bore these days, obsessed with your wretched saxophone. It was bad enough when I was a child, visiting at Grandmama's, admiring my big cousin, and you used to kick me out so that you could practise, but you weren't so madly dedicated then!'

'I have to prove my professionalism,' Andrew said lightly. 'The family were offended enough when I made it clear I would go on the stage whatever they said, but some of the performers think I'm just a dilettante, so I have to prove them wrong too! Besides, I enjoy it, and what else is life for but to have fun and do what you want?'

'You may have fun but I certainly don't! Why, I hardly see you when you come here. Thank heavens darling Timothy is in Birmingham this weekend.'

Saturday was the day Mrs Baxter had the use of the wash house in the court. It was the least popular day, since everyone wanted to clean their own houses for the weekend. She had to take it because they were the last to come to live there. And she'd given up long ago any pretence that she could keep her home as well as her ma had done. Ma hadn't had sixteen kids. Nor had she been reduced to living in a back-to-back slum house with twelve children in just two small bedrooms, and all the water having to be fetched from a tap the far side of the court.

At first she'd tried hard, when they'd rented a through house in Walsall. Then her Albert lost the good job he'd had on the railways, and they'd moved several times, getting nearer to Dudley, with Albert taking less and less well-paid jobs, and the houses they could afford getting smaller and meaner. Two years ago they'd landed here, in Ladywood. Albert found a job as a porter in one of the metal workshops, and so far, despite his drinking, he'd managed to keep it.

She bent to lay the kindling under the copper, and turned as Nell staggered into the wash house with two brimming buckets. She looked pale and tired, and Mrs Baxter wondered where she had spent the night.

'I've fed the kids, but young Ronny's howlin' again,' Nell said briefly, as her mother helped her lift the heavy buckets to tip the water into the copper. 'Shall I bring him out here?'

'I fed 'im less than an 'our since,' her mother said wearily. ''E don't 'ave the strength ter suck. But yer should be on yer way ter work, ducks,' she added. 'Yer mustn't be late.'

'I won't be, I can run, so I've time to help yer carry a couple more buckets in here, Ma. An' I'll help clear up this afternoon.'

'Yer's a good wench, Nell.'

When Nell had to go at last, fearful of being late to her job operating a press in the same factory where her father worked, Mrs Baxter stood, her youngest child clasped to her sagging breast, and looked after her wistfully. Saturday again. It was the worst day of the week, and not only because it was washday. It was backbreaking work, heaving the buckets of water about, thumping the dirt out of the washing with the dolly, then lifting it all out and rinsing and mangling, finally draining the water and tidying up. All the time she had to try not to make more holes and tears in the worn, shabby fabrics. She could cope with hard work, she'd been used to it all her life. But she dreaded Saturday most of all because it was the night Albert went to the pub.

He couldn't usually afford to go more than once a week, not since they'd moved here. On Saturdays he went regularly, and drank until he was convinced he was boxing champion of Birmingham. He'd been a fine figure of a man when she'd married him; now he was flabby and coarse. She'd come to dread the nights he went boozing. It was a blessing if he came to blows with a neighbour, or a mate down at the pub. Then he'd roll home either too battered to want to do more than crawl into bed, or so pleased he'd won he went to bed happy. The first was better for her, as then he didn't want her body; and she could endure it when he was happy. It was when he'd been deprived of a fight that he took it out on her or the kids. Like last night when he'd found a shilling in the gutter on his way home, but being Friday none of his usual cronies had been in the pub. She thought she ought to have got used to beatings, she'd had so many. They still hurt though, especially when he wielded his belt instead of just his hands and feet. It was the kids she was afraid for, Nell in particular.

Albert hadn't wanted her to come home at first when Gran Perry died. He'd called her stuck up, with her swanky voice and finicky ways. Then he'd got her a job with his own employer, and her wages reconciled him to her presence. To begin with she'd answered him back and he couldn't abide that. She'd soon learned not to and taken her own way of avoiding him. Albert might be too drunk to count his children on those nights when he went into the bedroom and whipped them, but she knew Nell wasn't there. One day he might realize it too. She didn't dare ask her daughter where she went, in case Albert beat it out of her. She couldn't betray Nell if she didn't know. She just prayed, if there was any God left, that He would watch over Nell and keep her from evil company.

When Kitty strolled down to the stable she found Betts, the gardener and coachman, already fixing a stout padlock to the door.

'Dunno what's a'comin', folks get so bold,' he grumbled, taking off his flat cap and scratching his almost bald head. 'It's a mercy Mr Andrew dain't set stable alight, messin' about wi' lanterns.'

Kitty absentmindedly agreed as she gave the horses their daily apples. The horse blankets were still lying on the heap of hay, and she reached for them. A tattered shawl slid to the floor, and after she'd folded the blankets Kitty picked it up.

'She must have left this,' she remarked to Betts, who grunted and looked disparagingly at the shawl. Originally knitted from black wool, it was thin, ragged and full of holes. Someone had made an attempt to darn the worst holes with different coloured scraps of wool, but as Kitty handled it more threads gave way. It was long past being usable.

'Burn it,' Betts advised. 'It'll be crawlin' wi' lice.'

Kitty shuddered fastidiously and held the shawl away from her. She walked to the end of the garden and was about to throw it on the bonfire pile when she paused. The intruder, whoever she was, had owned this, and the chances were she hadn't anything else. A rare compassionate impulse attacked Kitty and she turned away.

Thoughtfully Kitty wandered back. The girl would never dare come to ask for the shawl, but she might steal back secretly and try to find it. Kitty strolled on towards the garden in front of the house. Where could she leave it? Eventually she draped the shawl over a bush in the shrubbery just inside the front gateway. Anyone trying to hide from view of the windows would be likely to see it, but no one on the carriage drive could. And it was hidden from the road by the sandstone wall.

'I'm clemmed! That shawl belonged to all on us!'

'It's still warmer than downstairs, with no coal and nothin' else fer the fire,' Nell replied, yawning.

'It 'ud be warmer still if you 'adn't took that shawl!'

'Oh, Eth! Stop moaning!' Nell muttered. 'I'm tired. Let me get ter sleep.'

'Yer shouldn't 'a' spent all last night out then,' Eth said self-righteously.

'I'd rather sleep in the gutter than let 'im beat me again. How can yer stand it, Eth?'

Nell, lying precariously on the outside of the narrow bed, felt her sister shrug.

'What else can us do? Pa's allus got drunk an' when 'e gets mad as well 'e comes an' leathers us.'

'We could leave. Now you've got a job too we could find a room somewhere, like Ned and Bert did. Danny and Sam said before they went out they'll go now Sam's working, soon as he's saved a few bob. The other lads are gettin' bigger, there ain't room fer four o' them in a bed now. Nor for us. And the two little 'uns will soon be too big for that mattress on the floor.'

'Nell, don't leave me!' Amy, lying top to toe between her older sisters, sat up suddenly. 'Tek me with yer, please! I couldn't bear it if yer weren't 'ere!'

'You're too little, police 'ud send yer back. An' lie down, Amy, yer mekin' it wus!' Eth grumbled 'It's bloody cold wi'out that shawl! Yer shouldn't 'a' took it!'

Nell sighed with exasperation. 'I'll go and look fer it tomorrow. I know where I dropped it. Eth, why won't yer get away with me?'

'Shurrup, you lot! Let rest on us sleep!' It was Norman, the youngest of the four boys who slept in the bed behind the curtain which divided the already small room into two.

Nell couldn't sleep despite her weariness. She had crept back to the familiar churchyard and huddled down in the shelter of a buttress after her adventure in the stable. She was too wary to stay in the Edgbaston area, in one of the other places she'd found, in case a search was begun. It was the frustration of her position which irked her most, though, and she fretted at Eth's acceptance of it. The older boys were going, but she knew she couldn't survive on her own. She didn't earn enough. She needed Eth, the only other girl old enough to have a job.

Could she run away? Would it be possible to get out of Birmingham, where Pa could never find her? But she'd never been further than Sutton Coldfield, and he'd guess she might go there. He'd found her there last year when she'd run away before. Nell thrust away thoughts of Sutton. If she began to remember her gran and the lovely green countryside and the peaceful park with its beautiful trees and open spaces and tranquil pools she would cry, and that served no purpose. Gran was dead; she had to look after herself. And, whether Eth came with her or not, soon she would get out of this hellish slum.

Chapter Two

KITTY brushed her hair vigorously until it shone like silk. Then she slipped on her newest dress, straight and simple in heavy pale yellow satin, with slightly deeper-coloured fringes in layers from the shoulders to the knee length skirt. Her satin shoes with the instep strap had been dyed to match. Leaning close to the looking glass she carefully outlined her mouth with bright red lipstick, emphasizing the rosebud shape, then patted on powder to dry it. She looked discontentedly at her nose, wishing it was fractionally shorter. She considered it marred what was otherwise an acceptably pretty face. Then she shrugged. It didn't seem to deter men; she could attract any she chose. Perhaps that was why all the girls she knew seemed jealous and unfriendly. More powder on her cheeks and nose, half-a-dozen gold bracelets pushed high up one bare arm, a lavish spraying with her latest apple-blossom perfume, and she was ready. She picked up her pearl-embroidered bag and lacy gloves and went downstairs. Meggy, grey hair scraped back in a bun, thin lips almost invisible in her lined face, waited in the hall. Her once upright figure was old and bent now she was in her late fifties, but her voice was sharp as she held out Kitty's fur coat.

'Put this on. You're not decent in that dress, showing yer arms and legs like a hussy.'

'Meggy, it's the fashion. And I don't need a coat, it's still warm and I'm going in a motor,' she protested, while allowing Meggy to help her into the long enveloping coat.

Meggy had been with them since the age of thirteen. She'd started as a tweenie at Kitty's grandmother's country house near Warwick, risen to be cook, and when her mother became involved in the suffragette movement in London, had gone to keep house for her.

'I didn't want her to come, I couldn't afford to pay her nearly as much as your grandmother,' Kitty's mama had once explained when she was exasperated with Meggy. 'I actually dismissed her a couple of times, but short of throwing her and her boxes out into the street there was no way of getting rid of her.'

Kitty knew exactly what her mother had faced. Meggy never took no for an answer, she ignored all protests until the other person, weary and probably by now late for half-a-dozen appointments, gave in. Kitty, as a child, had screamed and thrown tantrums to no avail. Now, though she made token protests, she had learned to give in at once. She could always take the coat off once out of sight of the house.

A moment later there was a toot on a motor-car horn, and Kitty ran down the steps, Meggy looking after her with a mixture of reluctant pride and more open disapproval. Kitty scrambled into the car, leaned over to kiss the young man driving it on the cheek, then turned and grinned back at Meggy.

'Was that for my benefit or Meggy's?' the Honourable Timothy Travers asked languidly.

'Hers, of course. I wanted to see whether her mouth would turn down any further. Stop round the corner, there's a darling, I must take this frightful coat off.'

'It's only a few hundred yards,' he remarked, but obligingly stopped so that Kitty could wriggle out of the heavy coat and stow it in the dickey seat.

'The car's divine, especially the two-colour design. Is it new?' she asked.

'I've had it a month or so. It's fast, does sixty on the flat.'

'But it's a Morris, isn't it?'

'Yes, an MG Super Sports. They've only just begun to build them.'

'You have a nerve, darling, bringing an Oxford car to Birmingham!'

'These will be the rage soon, you'll see.'

Their destination was one of the large houses on the Calthorpe estate. When they arrived there were already a dozen motor cars parked in the drive and Timothy tucked his neatly into a space and scrambled out over the door.

'Come on, old girl. I can hear the music already.'

A four-piece dance band was playing in the large drawing room, where the carpets had been taken up to make a dance floor. Several couples were already revolving, and Timothy immediately whisked Kitty on to the floor. Two hours later they sat together in a large conservatory which had been turned into a dining room, eating small cakes and sipping champagne.

'You dance superbly, darling,' Kitty said, licking cream from her fingers. 'I hadn't done that outside spin before. I'm beginning to realize there's a lot more to it than most people think.'

'Most people just walk round and do the occasional jig, and think they're experts.'

'I suppose in the old dances everyone could follow those who knew it, you were either in teams and they'd drag you through the figures, or you were following everyone else round the room. In modern dancing each couple is on their own. If you try to watch anyone else you fall over your partner's feet.'

'I hadn't liked to mention it,' Timothy murmured, and Kitty flicked a dollop of cream towards him.

'We ought to practise together. When can you come?'

'There's only this weekend. I have to go back to London on Monday. I'm sailing to South Africa for a few weeks.'

'South Africa?'

'The pater's uncle out there wants to see me. He lost his son in the war, and wants to inspect me to see whether he'll leave me his ill-gotten gains.'

'Timothy! How simply divine! Is he filthy rich?'

'I expect so. He owns a diamond mine, or a gold mine, I forget which. He was the black sheep, you know, a remittance man, and was packed off there years before I was born. The next thing we hear, he's richer than a bank. It made the pater's old man furious to know his kid brother was richer than he was, able to buy up the family acres if he wanted to. He died still complaining.'

'Goody for you. Go and pay lavish attention to the old rogue, and make him give you a gold mine or two to be going on with. I'll have to find another dancing partner though.'

'Unless you wanted to come with me?'

Kitty glanced at him, startled. She and Timothy had been friends for a year, since they'd met at the London house of one of Kitty's aunts. He visited Birmingham every few weeks, either to stay with friends or on business at one of his father's smaller estates to the west of the city. Usually he came to see her and they enjoyed one another's company. Never before, though, had he suggested anything other than friendship. She wondered precisely what he was suggesting now. She couldn't see Timothy getting married.

'I think I'll wait and see whether you inherit, darling,' she replied lightly.

'Right ho! I'll send a cable if I do. Mind you, the old chap's still hale and hearty, probably good for another twenty years.'

'The dancing. Let's try the tango, I've never mastered it properly, and I'd love to show off like some Argentinian gypsy.'

'Tomorrow then? Or would Meggy object on a Sunday?'

'What if she does? She's my servant. Anyway, it's her day off, she won't know. She'll go to her sister's as usual. Come in the afternoon, and if Andrew's in a good mood we'll get him to wind up the gramophone.'

'There isn't a single man here who can dance properly!' Gwyneth complained to Lizzie. 'They all seem to prefer walking on my toes.'

Lizzie giggled and tossed her neatly shingled blonde head. 'I don't come here to dance,' she confided. 'I think I've clicked.

See that big feller over by the band? The one with the green waistcoat. He wants to walk me home. Lives in Harborne. Got a good job, he's a carpenter, working on some of the new houses in Bourneville.'

Gwyneth nodded. It seemed as though half the people in the hall came just for the opportunity to meet each other. She came to dance. From the time she could toddle she'd wanted to dance.

'I wonder if it would be worth going to a proper class?' she mused.

'Why bother? They sometimes have professionals here to demonstrate the new dances, and you can watch the others.'

I want much more, Gwyneth thought. Lizzie just didn't understand how much more there was. I want to know the proper steps, I want a partner who can dance them with me, do something more exciting, more satisfying than at the dance halls.

Nell woke with a start. Had she been dreaming? No, it came again, a high, piercing scream. This time it was followed by a ferocious bellow which sounded like Pa, and other angry male voices.

'I'm frit!' It was Amy, clinging to her arm and hiding her face against Nell's shoulder.

'That's Ma yellin',' Eth said, her voice trembling. ''Er don't never do that, even when 'e 'its 'er.'

'It sounds like Danny. I'm goin' ter see what's up,' Nell whispered, though in the noise beneath them no one could have heard her voice. 'Amy, stay with Eth and Fanny, they'll look after yer.'

She slipped on her skirt and crept to the door. One hinge was broken, so she had to ease it open carefully.

'Let me goo first,' Benjy said behind her, but Nell shook her head and he didn't persist. He was twelve, but thin and weedy, and one blow from Pa's fist would send him right across the room.

Nell crept down the steep, crooked stairs, Benjy at her heels, his hand on her shoulder. From the kitchen came a series of thumps, interspersed with pleas to stop it from Ma. The gas mantle shed a soft glow over the room, and as she paused at the bottom of the stairs Nell took in the scene instantly. Danny was sprawled across the table, a long cut on his cheek oozing blood. Fifteen-year-old Sam stood before him, valiantly but vainly trying to fend off Pa who was laying about him with his belt, while Ma crouched beside the sink dressed in nothing but her old petticoat, her lank grey hair awry, shaken out of her usual apathy as she alternately wept and begged Pa to stop.

'Shurrup, woman!' Pa flung over his shoulder. 'I'm not 'avin' me own sons wakin' me up wi' their carryin's-on, defyin' me! I'll teach 'em 'oo's boss!'

'Yer've killed our Danny! Look at 'im, 'e's not movin'! 'E's dead!'

At that moment Danny groaned and tried to heave himself off the table, but succeeded only in slithering to the floor in a heap. Sam glanced round as Danny's limp arm knocked against his leg, and with a yell of triumph Pa dropped the belt and waded in with his fists, catching the distracted Sam on the chin. Sam staggered, caught his foot in the orange box doing duty as a stool, and fell heavily to the floor. Before anyone could move Pa was bending over him, kicking him viciously as Sam curled up in a vain attempt to escape the blows. At last Pa, panting from his efforts, stepped back.

'That'll larn yer both not ter defy me!' he snarled. Danny and Sam lay still, and Nell couldn't tell whether they heard or not. 'An' stop yer blartin', woman!' he added angrily. 'Leave 'em be! Do 'em good ter lay there all night. Gerrup ter bed!'

Nell turned and hastily shoved Benjy up the stairs in front of her. 'Hurry! Yer don't want him beatin' you too!' she urged, and Benjy, suppressing his frightened sobs, complied.

When the sounds from their parents' room ceased, and even Ma's stifled sobs had stopped, Nell crept out of bed again. She hadn't bothered to remove her skirt before scrambling in and hushing the others into silence.

Cautiously she crept down into the kitchen. Danny was

sitting in Pa's chair, a wet rag pressed to his cheek, while Sam crouched on the orange box, clutching his stomach and groaning.

'Can I help?' she asked quietly. 'Why was Pa so mad at yer?'

Danny glanced at her. 'We'm all right, just cut an' bruised,' he replied wearily. 'But that finishes it, we'm off the minute we can gerra room somewhere.'

'Why was he mad?'

'We brung a couple o' gals in, thought 'e was safe in bed,' Sam said, and groaned.

'That was a daft thing ter do,' Nell said sharply.

'Where else can us goo? It's cold ternight, an' they ain't got anywhere,' Sam complained.

'Go ter bed, Nell. An' thanks, yer a good 'un,' Danny said. 'We'll be up soon as we'm fit.'

Emily Baxter sighed. She'd only been asleep five minutes. She eased herself slowly out of the sagging bed, careful not to disturb Albert. After the fight he had taken her roughly, but swiftly, then turned his back and dropped straight into a deep sleep. But Ronny's feeble wails might disturb him and he'd be mad enough to thrash her.

She staggered across to the small mattress where Ronny and little Joan slept, and picked up her youngest son. Sitting with her back to the wall, her skirt wrapped round them both for warmth, she held the baby to her breast. For a few moments he sucked eagerly, then his sickly wails began again. Her shoulders drooped. She'd suspected it for some time, that her milk had gone. Ronny was puny; he was not thriving. Although nine months old he hadn't begun to sit up by himself, let alone crawl. In one way that was a blessing, for he wasn't always under her feet, but she was desperately afraid he'd soon follow her other two little ones who'd died. Somehow, these days, she didn't seem to have enough milk as she'd had with the others.

They couldn't afford cow's milk. Then she straightened her

back. She'd find the coppers somehow. And she'd take him to see that new doctor at the clinic. She'd heard he was kind.

Meanwhile Ronny would have to make do with a rag soaked in sugar water. Rocking him gently, aware that he was far too small, she crept down the stairs to find some sustenance for her baby.

Only a couple of the families in the Baxters' court went to church, to the Wesleyan chapel down towards Broad Street. Most of them were only too glad of the chance to lie late in bed, sleeping off the excesses of payday.

It was quiet when Nell slid out of bed and crept, boots in hand, down the stairs. After the previous night's row everyone else was asleep. There was some scummy water in a bowl in the corner sink, which the others would use for washing if they thought about it, or Ma remembered to nag them, but she preferred the fresh tap water out in the yard, even when it was freezing cold.

She seized the rough towel hanging on a nail. At least it was still quite clean, having been washed yesterday. The only soap they had was the strong green block used for the clothes, but she felt lucky to have any at all. One day, she promised herself, she'd have soft, perfumed soap which lathered easily.

In the empty, quiet yard she filled a bucket and carried it into the wash house. There she quickly stripped off her clothes and carefully hung up her belt with the treasured patch-box. She pinned her hair on top of her head, then soaped her body all over, shivering as she upended the bucket to rinse herself. A fierce rubbing made her skin glow; then, with a grimace of distaste as she saw how grubby they were, she climbed back into her clothes. How could she keep clean when she had no clothes other than those she stood up in, and even had to sleep in her underthings? She had to borrow her ma's old dress when she wanted to wash her own, and could only do that when it wasn't in one of the pawn shops in Monument Road.

She shrugged as she took the bucket and soap and towel back

into the kitchen. One day she'd leave. Even if Eth wouldn't come with her she'd find a way. Then she'd have all her money to spend on herself, to buy a change of clothes, to get good soap. Most of all she'd have space to herself.

With a sigh Nell recalled the difficulties as she used the almost toothless old comb and braided her hair. She had no money, her wages were all given to Pa. She couldn't get a room of her own without her employer, and therefore Pa knowing where. She'd have to find another job, secretly. Yet as she looked now she couldn't expect any respectable employer to take her without references. She couldn't get references without her father knowing. It seemed utterly hopeless. She would, however, find a way.

There were just a few crusts in the kitchen, which the babies needed more than she did. She could probably scavenge some discarded apples behind the shops in Monument Road. It was fortunate Ma was paid by the day when she went scrubbing for her ladies, or they'd never have anything to eat. The boys were good, bringing their wages home, but her father demanded of their mutual employer that Nell's wages were given to him, and she doubted whether Ma saw more than a few coppers. She was lucky. She found half a loaf of yesterday's bread in the gutter, and it wasn't very muddy. For a moment she thought of taking it back home, but the temptation and the gnawing hunger were too great. As she wandered on in the bright sunshine she tore off rough chunks and stuffed them greedily into her mouth. After the cold night it was a lovely September day and she'd go a longer way round towards the house where she'd lost the shawl, approaching it from another direction.

In this wealthier part of the city many people were driving or walking to church. Nell felt a sudden nostalgia for the small squat-towered Holy Trinity church where she had worshipped with her gran, and loitered amongst the gravestones until the last stragglers had entered. Then she crept through the door and huddled into the corner of the pew, making herself as small and inconspicuous as possible. When they sang one of her favourite hymns, though, she joined in without thinking, and more than one head turned to see where the pure clear soprano voice came from.

Suddenly aware of the interest Nell clamped her mouth shut, and as soon as the congregation bent forward again in prayer she slipped out of the door and hurried on her way. It had been foolish, forgetting herself like that. She could have got into dreadful trouble. People who lived in these big houses didn't appreciate ragamuffins from the slums singing in their churches.

When she got to the house with the stable she looked round cautiously, but there was no one in sight. She darted through the gateway and plunged into the shrubbery, but was so eager to get to the back of the house she didn't notice the shawl Kitty had placed for her.

She didn't have to get close to see that a new lock had been fixed to the stable door. If her shawl was still inside she couldn't get to it. Her shoulders slumped. Eth was right, it was cold without even that pathetic extra cover on the bed the four older girls shared. When winter came it would be much worse. Only as she turned away did she realize that the haven she had been so excited about, the warm bed she had looked forward to on those nights when fear of her pa's violence drove her out of her own home, was no longer within her reach.

She went back through the shrubbery, head bent dejectedly. Unless news of her escapade had been spread about the district, and everyone else had made their coach houses and sheds secure, there were still other places where she would be comfortable and warm. They didn't have the horses, though, and Nell saw with sudden clarity it was their companionship she craved as much as their warmth. She blinked back sudden tears. She was being ridiculous, mourning something she'd never had. She threw back her head proudly and saw, draped on a bush in front of her, the shawl.

'Oh! Thank God!' she exclaimed, and reached for the familiar, once despised but now precious object. She lifted it gently from the bush, taking care not to snag its fragile threads, and with a smile of delight twisted it round and over her head. She crossed her arms, her hands on her shoulders, and then jumped with surprise and fear.

'This time you won't get away so easily,' a deep masculine voice said in her ear as large hard hands covered her own and grasped her wrists.

Chapter Three

NELL fought ferociously, but this time Andrew was ready for her. Despite her backward kicks and attempts to bite the hands which held her imprisoned she was helpless in his grip, her arms crossed in front of her and his large muscular body pressed tight against her back.

'Little wildcat!' he commented coolly. 'All I want is for you to calm down and tell me what you were doing in our stable the other night.'

Nell redoubled her efforts, in vain. Suddenly she slumped in his arms and went totally limp. As Andrew, startled, relaxed his grip she wriggled free, and leaving her now utterly ruined shawl in his hands fled for the drive.

Andrew reacted instinctively, hurling himself after her in a flying tackle reminiscent of his schooldays. They sprawled together in the loamy soil, Nell pinioned beneath him with the breath driven from her body. Before she could move Andrew ripped away the shreds of the shawl which clung to him, seized both her thin wrists in one huge hand, and then lay triumphant, looking down at her with a grin on his face.

Panting for breath Nell was forced to study the face so close above her own. It was handsome, was her first irrelevant thought. He had smooth dark hair at the moment flopping across a wide brow, and grey, deep-set eyes which twinkled in amusement.

There was a decided cleft in his square chin, and another above his wide mouth.

'You've ruined my shawl!' she gasped as soon as she could speak.

'It wasn't worth saving. Don't worry, I'm sure we can find you another. If you tell me why you were in the stable, that is,' he added. 'Come on, it's useless trying to get away from me. You might as well spill the beans.'

'Let me get up then. I've no breath to talk with a great lump of lard on top of me.'

He laughed, and taking care to hold on to her tightly eased both of them to their feet. Nell pulled tentatively but gave up at once. He'd been ready for her and she knew she was beaten.

'Come on, walk,' he ordered, and led the way towards the drive and up to the house. Nell perforce went with him, half afraid she would be punished for her earlier trespass, half eager to see inside this mansion. At the same time her mind was marvelling at the casual way he'd offered to provide her with another shawl. Then mentally she shrugged. Such gestures meant nothing to rich folk such as he must be. Pa was always ranting about how wealthy the factory owners were.

The front door was open and Nell had a confused impression of huge pale rugs underfoot on a highly polished wooden floor. Intricately carved bannisters rose beside a flight of wide, shallow stairs, and plain white walls surrounded her, with just one painting of startling colours and indecipherable shapes. Then she was thrust unceremoniously into a small room at the back of the house.

There was a girl a few years older than Nell lounging on a settee. Elegantly tall and slim, her bobbed hair and make-up impeccable, she wore a pale pink satin dressing gown and held a glass in her hand. She was nibbling olives from a huge bowl beside her.

'Andrew! For heaven's sake, darling! What the devil's this?' she asked sharply.

'This, Kitty, is our nocturnal visitor, come back to explain herself.'

Nell glowered at him. 'I came to get my shawl, which I left here, and which you've ruined!' she corrected him angrily, then trembled at her temerity at speaking to one of the Edgbaston swells in such a way.

'And you shall have another, I said so. But only when you've explained. Would you like some coffee? Or a drink? I see Kitty's already started on the cocktails.'

Nell gave him a startled look. Whatever else she'd expected it wasn't to be offered cocktails. Girls from the slums were not treated as visitors by the gentry.

'I – please could I have one of them?' she asked hesitantly, gesturing towards the bowl of olives. The smell, strange though it was, had made her mouth water.

Kitty sat up suddenly. 'Are you hungry?' she demanded, her plucked eyebrows shooting up almost into her shiny dark bob of hair.

Wordlessly Nell nodded. Kitty smiled at her, suddenly decisive. This was intriguing, a change from the usual monotony of life. 'Then you need something a bit more filling than these. Andrew, Meggy left our lunch on a tray. Be a darling, go and get it, and make some coffee.' She rose to her feet and crossed the room to a small walnut bureau. Opening the top she abstracted a biscuit tin, and came back to offer it to Nell. 'I keep it there because Meggy, my housekeeper, disapproves of eating between meals. But I'm trying to diet, to lose weight, and I get so terribly hungry!'

She really meant it, Nell could see. How friendly she sounded, and how tempting the biscuits looked.

'I'm usually hungry,' Nell replied simply, taking a biscuit. She forced herself to eat it as slowly as she could.

Kitty grinned at her. 'Sit down beside me and tell me about yourself.'

Nell looked doubtfully at the settee, upholstered in pale cream brocade. 'I'm much too dirty,' she protested. 'My clothes weren't clean before but it didn't help when your – he – knocked me down.' She stole a look at Kitty's hand, but she wore no wedding ring. Perhaps the handsome man, Andrew, she'd called him, was her brother or boyfriend. He didn't seem to be her husband.

'Is that what he did?' Kitty seemed amused. 'We'll see about cleaning your clothes after you've eaten. Do sit down. I've been thinking of getting the covers done again, I'm utterly bored with the white look, so don't worry about making them dirty. And you don't have to be polite; you can eat the whole tinful if you want. But maybe you should go easy on these, they are rather rich. Are you quite starving?'

Nell sat gingerly on the edge of the settee, took another biscuit and shook her head. It was so strange to be here in a rich man's house, a much larger house than any she'd ever been inside before, and be treated as a normal human being.

'Not really. I found half a loaf on my way here. It's just there's so many of us at home, there never seems enough to go round.'

'So you have a home. We wondered. We thought perhaps you didn't have anywhere to sleep. That was why you came to the stable, wasn't it?'

'Partly.' Nell hesitated. Ought she to explain about her pa's vicious temper to these rich folk? She compromised. 'It's crowded at home. I sometimes can't bear it so I get out and sleep wherever I can find a shed or something. But I wanted to be with horses. They're warm, and company. That's why I looked for a stable.'

'You must live nearby. In Ladywood perhaps? Oh, good, here's Andrew. Put the tray on this table, darling, and we can all reach it. Lovely, ham and beef sandwiches, and cheese and tomatoes. Have as much as you can manage, there's far too much for us. And then we can talk.'

Nell lay back in the hot water, foaming hillocks of bubbles heaped around her body. She must be dreaming. She hadn't

31

known such luxury existed. She'd heard of bathrooms, of course, and at school had even known a couple of girls who had indoor water closets at home instead of having to use communal privies at the end of the courts, but she'd never imagined them to be like this.

Ruefully she readjusted her ideas. Instead of the tin bath and stone sink of her imagination, and the odorous pit like the one which, as small children, they'd all been terrified of falling into as they balanced on the wooden seat, here was a porcelain palace. The bath was enormous, shiny white and surrounded by a wide shelf of polished mahogany. It perched on elaborately carved legs which looked like the claws of some huge animal, and she dreaded to think how many buckets of water it would have needed to fill if there hadn't been, miraculously, both hot and cold taps. The washbasin was similarly huge, and both it and the lavatory pan were decorated with pale pink and blue flowers.

Kitty had turned on the taps, thrown lavish handfuls of bath crystals into the steaming water, scenting it and producing the foam, and pulled two enormous white fluffy towels out of a cupboard.

'Take as long as you want. Wash your hair, too. I'll be sorting out some clothes for you, so come along to my room when you've finished. It's the one I showed you at the top of the stairs.'

As she began to unbraid her hair Nell remembered the hard green soap she'd used that morning, and the promise she'd made herself that one day she'd have better. Well, this wasn't hers, but now she knew what it could be like she was even more determined to achieve a small part of this luxury, one day, however hard she had to work and however long she had to wait. With renewed vigour she washed herself all over, lathered her hair and then lay back again in the water until it began to cool and her flesh became wrinkled.

Reluctantly scrambling out she wrapped herself in one of the towels, and marvelled at the effortless way the water disappeared.

No heaving heavy buckets outside, and dragging the tin tub out when it was empty enough to move. She rinsed her hair in the washbasin and rubbed it as dry as she could.

At last she had no more to do. She had to leave this incredible room. Nell glanced with a shudder of distaste at her old skirt and blouse, which however hard she tried she could not keep clean, and the underclothes she shrank from touching now that her body was warm and clean and fragrant. Kitty had promised her some clothes. Wrapping the towel more firmly about her she went along the passageway to the room the other girl had indicated. The door was open and she could hear Kitty inside, singing tunefully as she opened and closed cupboard doors. Nell tapped hesitantly on the door.

'There you are! I began to worry you'd slipped away down the plughole! Come in, let's sort out some underthings first. What about these?'

'But – they're far too good to give me!' Nell protested, backing away yet with an unconscious hand stretched out towards the flimsy silken garments Kitty was holding.

'Nonsense! And anyway I haven't any other sort, and these are at least a year old. Try them on. You're thinner than I am but that doesn't matter.'

Nell slipped into the camisole and drawers and petticoat. They were so thin she felt naked still, but they caressed her body gently and as she moved slightly there was a whispering accompaniment.

'That's perfect,' Kitty gloated. 'Now I've sorted out some things that might be suitable. They're on the bed. Try them on.'

It was impossible to resist. Nell swallowed her qualms. All they owed her was a shawl that was so tattered no one else would have given her a halfpenny for it. Even Ma had stopped trying to pawn it. Yet Kitty was so eager, and genuinely seemed to take pleasure in giving away her clothes, she could not refuse. She tried on gowns softer and warmer than she'd known existed, but knew she mustn't give way to temptation. She wouldn't be allowed to keep them.

'If I could have just this skirt, and a blouse?' she said at last regretfully.

'You must take more than that!'

Nell shook her head. 'Pa would take them away from me if I have more than I can wear,' she explained reluctantly.

Kitty was unconvinced, and Nell had to give more details than she wished about her family. Kitty was shocked, but finally accepted Nell's assurances that one outfit would have to be enough.

'But you must take this coat, it's nice and warm,' she insisted. 'And look, what about this hat? It's the same shade of brown, although it's not very fashionable now with a brim and feathers. Still, you could take the feathers off. And you must have some gloves, no outfit is complete without gloves.'

Nell surrendered to the magic of the moment, and bemused at the sheer volume of discarded clothes on Kitty's bed, agreed.

'That's enough! If you can't tango now, Kitty, you never will,' Andrew declared, and took the record off the gramophone.

'Thanks, old chap. She's utterly inexhaustible. After last night too, I expected to find her prostrate today.' Timothy, tall, slender, thin-faced, heaved a great ostentatious sigh and flung himself down into one of the armchairs they'd pushed to the side of the drawing room. Kitty came and perched on the arm, mockingly fanning him with a newspaper, and stroking back the overlong lock of blond hair which had fallen over one eye.

'Weakling,' she chided. 'Let's have a cocktail, Andrew. I fancy a Side Car. Meggy left something in the slow oven for dinner, but it's too early yet.'

'Tell me about your mysterious visitor,' Timothy said as Andrew filled the cocktail shaker. 'You actually asked her to lunch? Wasn't that rather — well, unnecessary? One doesn't hobnob with the proletariat.'

'Even you'd have felt pity if you could have seen the way she was eyeing the olives, and doing her desperate best not to gobble the biscuits,' Kitty replied slowly. 'She was so thin! I know its fashionable, but this was pitiable. And when she was cleaned up and wearing my clothes she was amazingly beautiful!'

'You lent her some of your clothes?' Timothy was shaken out of his usual languor. 'Kitty! What the devil will you do next? A girl from the slums borrowing your clothes? You'll have to burn them!'

'She didn't have nits or lice, if that's what you mean,' Kitty retorted. 'Darling, don't fret. I gave her my clothes, her own weren't fit to wear, and they were much too small for her. Besides, Andrew practically tore them off her.' She looked mischievously across at Andrew, who was scowling at her remark. 'I wanted her to take more but the foolish girl wouldn't accept them.'

'You know she said she daren't leave them lying about or her mother would either pawn or sell them,' Andrew said quietly. 'She had just the clothes she stood up in, and they were almost threadbare.'

'Surely she could have found somewhere to hide them. Everyone has somewhere,' Kitty said.

'From what she said, and she was so apologetic that her clothes weren't clean, she wasn't even able to wash them because she didn't have anything else to wear while she did so,' Andrew reminded her.

'You'll have to burn the ones she left,' Timothy insisted, a grimace of distaste pursing his lips.

'I can't, she took them away. Said her next sister would be glad to have them.'

'Ugh! How revolting! I can't understand why people tolerate living like that!'

'Perhaps they should all join the trades unions, old boy,' Andrew chuckled. 'You'd like that even less.'

Kitty leapt angrily to her feet and interrupted him. 'Timothy, don't be such a boring snob! I've never heard anything like it before, but she can't help it. Her father's a drunken sot, her mother's browbeaten and defeated, and so would any woman be after having sixteen children in twenty years! Fourteen are still living, and all but two of them in a tiny back-to-back house no bigger than this room!'

'If that's what you believe.' Timothy shrugged. 'I'm not interested enough in how the peasants live to argue with you. It's much too boring.'

'I do believe her. I've never seen those awful houses, and I truly can't imagine what they're like, but Mrs Cartwright next door works at some Mission in Hockley and she's told me how dreadful they are. Besides, someone so beautiful couldn't tell lies. She had a heart-shaped face, and green eyes, and they slanted a little, and her chin was pointed. Her hair was so thick and long it almost made me regret I'd cut my own. Andrew, wasn't she lovely?'

'She looked a hundred times better after you'd made her have a bath and put on some of your old clothes,' he agreed slowly. 'And she had the sense to choose good warm ones, not finery which would have been quite out of place in her home.'

'She'll be on your doorstep begging every week,' Timothy prophesied gloomily.

Kitty shook her head. 'I'm sure she won't. I had a dreadful job to make her accept anything but a new shawl and she only took that to replace the one Andrew tore to shreds when he rugby tackled her in the shrubbery.'

Timothy grinned, his long, lean face lightening and his hazel eyes suddenly filling with amusement. 'Rolling in the bushes, Andrew? Tearing the clothes off a poor working gal? Not your usual style, is it?'

Andrew laughed self-consciously and explained. 'So we owed her a shawl. Kitty, I've only just realized. She spoke quite well, didn't have much of a Birmingham accent.'

'I asked her about that. She lived for most of her life with her mother's parents, who were, it seems, several classes above her father. She went to a school in Sutton Coldfield and was taught to speak properly.' Timothy looked sceptical, and Kitty frowned at him. 'You're being beastly, Timothy! Don't say another word! You won't turn me against her. She was beautiful and gentle. I could do a lot with her, I know.'

Timothy laughed. 'Somehow, my dear Kitty, I don't see you as a female Professor Higgins creating a beautiful swan out of your ugly duckling.'

'She was far from ugly, old chap,' Andrew said quietly. 'There was something about her, I'm not sure what . . . She was vulnerable and wary, ready to vanish at the slightest hint of danger. If you ever get the chance to see her, even in her old clothes, you'll be shaken out of that complacency of yours!'

'Don't argue, boys. Now, darlings, let's have dinner. Shall we eat in Meggy's kitchen? She won't normally allow me to — says it's slumming! Oh dear! What a dreadful thing to say. I don't suppose poor Nell has anything half as good in her home.'

Nell eased her sore shoulders as she hauled on the lever of the press, but even the pain couldn't dim her glow of triumph. She still had the good serge skirt and the neat white poplin blouse, as well as the hat and thick woollen coat. She'd spread that on the bed in the hope of keeping it out of Pa's clutches. Now she could really begin to look for another job. She had respectable clothes in which to go for interviews. You weren't respectable without a hat and gloves.

Pa had been surly when she'd returned the previous afternoon. 'Where've you been?' he demanded as she slipped through the door. 'And what the bloody 'ell's that on yer back?'

Since she couldn't tell him the truth she chose to say nothing, and all hell had been let loose. He'd ranted like a madman, and the rest of her brothers and sisters had slid out of the kitchen, the younger ones escaping into the yard to cower out of sight, the older ones to walk the streets until his anger was exhausted. She and Ma were left to face him alone. When he'd done accusing her of selling her body for useless finery, and punched away her mother who tried to defend her, he'd ordered her to give him the clothes.

'They'm far too good fer you!'

'My old 'uns are too small! If yer takes these away I'll march down Ryland Street naked, and tell folks yer thieved 'em off me!'

For a moment she quailed, thinking she'd gone too far. It had been a silent but intense struggle, but he must have seen she meant it, and he still had a shred of pride left. He slumped in his chair in front of the feeble fire. The remains of the old fishy crates Danny brought home from the fried-fish shop where he worked glowed feebly, giving out just enough heat to boil a kettle.

It had been too easy a victory. By the time the rest of the family crept back in to snatch slices of bread and dripping, all they had for tea, he was simmering with frustrated fury, and found the excuse he needed when four-year-old Betty dropped her piece of bread on the cracked, dirty floor slabs and began to wail.

'Yer pushed 'er!' he promptly accused Nell. She was sitting on the upturned orange box next to Betty who was standing beside the deal table to eat her tea.

It was patently untrue, but no one dared to remonstrate. His small eyes gleaming maliciously, Mr Baxter stood up, slowly undid the wide leather belt which held up his patched trousers, and ordered Nell to bend over in front of him. She glanced towards the door but there were too many people in her way. Before she could reach it he would be on her, and defiance would make him more vicious.

'Tek off that fancy blouse first. Yer can find another, an' that'll mek a bob or two at 'Annah Clark's in Broad Street. 'Er teks better stuff than Ma West.'

With a shrug and a scornful smile Nell complied as slowly as she dared, but when her pa saw the silk camisole she wore beneath he went berserk. Nell bit her tongue, suppressing the cries of agony induced as the strap, with the hard steel buckle, landed time after time on her back and shoulders.

It was fortunate for her he still had enough sense of what was right not to order her to lift her skirts. She didn't think she could have borne the humiliation of having her bare bottom whipped in front of all her brothers and sisters. Her main concern was to rescue the blouse. When he'd had enough and slumped, exhausted, into the chair beside the fireplace, she snatched up the blouse and escaped outside to the wash house. There she stripped off the silk camisole. It was ripped to shreds, streaked with blood, and utterly ruined.

Ten-year-old Amy crept out to where she huddled in the wash house. 'Nell, are yer 'urtin' much?' she whispered.

Nell swallowed the tears she had allowed to fall. 'I'm sore,' she admitted. 'I wish I could reach me back ter wash off the blood.'

Amy, who worshipped her eldest sister, shyly took her hand in her own little ones. 'I'll do it,' she offered eagerly. 'I'll be right gentle, I promise.'

And she had been. Pa had taken himself off to the pub, hoping to find a mate to treat him. Amy fetched a stub of candle and some rags, and in the feeble light of the candle and the glow from the gas lamp in the yard she helped Nell soak off the dried blood. She even insisted on going to beg some ointment from Mrs Jenkins, a childless widow who lived in the next court and often comforted them when they were hurt.

The bleeding soon stopped, and Nell could safely put on the precious blouse. By morning her back ached abominably. It was small consolation that Eth, Fanny and Amy, who shared her bed, lavished extravagant praise on the thick shawl and coat she had brought home, and refrained from asking a single question about how she had obtained them.

Chapter Four

Dᴜʀɪɴɢ the next week at work Gwyneth grew more determined to look for a school which taught modern dancing. She'd
go on her own now Lizzie had found herself a man. Lizzie was
going dancing again on Saturday with her new boyfriend, the
carpenter she'd met at the dance hall.

'I feel bad about it,' she said on Monday as they walked to
the tram. 'It's as if I'm deserting you.'

'Don't be a fool!' Gwyneth tried to reassure her.

'But I do. Tell you what, I'll ask George if he's got a pal.
Perhaps the next week we'll make up a foursome.'

'No, don't do that. Not until you know him better and are
going out regularly,' Gwyneth warned and Lizzie looked thoughtful. It wouldn't do to presume or be too forward and risk
losing George. He was a catch, if she could hold on to him.

Back in her room Gwyneth forced herself to examine her
motives. She really did want to learn to dance properly. She
always had, but her father's refusal to allow her to go to classes
as a child, indeed his utter condemnation of secular singing and
every form of dancing as the works of the devil, had soured
their relationship all her life.

She also didn't want to be put into the position of making up
a foursome with George and any of his friends. She found them
brash and crude. Was she being snobbish? Was she judging too
hastily on the acquaintance of just a few minutes after the dance

on Saturday? They had chatted outside the ballroom before separating, and perhaps George and his friends, with their broad jokes and winks and nudges, had been embarrassed, and shown off to cover it up. It wasn't just that she hadn't particularly liked them; if she went with Lizzie it would become a custom, difficult to break, and she didn't want to spend her very limited free time that way.

By Wednesday Gwyneth had convinced herself her reluctance was not due to snobbishness, but a genuine desire to learn properly. One of the problems of being the rebellious daughter of a minister was the constant need to examine everything she did in case it was uncharitable, selfish, or in some other way wrong. She'd been chastised for such faults so often it was second nature to worry about them.

She'd escaped from all that. Now she could please herself. Wednesday was her half-day and she'd seen some advertisements for dancing schools, so she looked at the ones near the city centre. One in Broad Street took her fancy. 'The Bliss School of Stage and Modern Dancing', the notice outside the house proclaimed. 'Proprietors: Frank and Edwina Bliss'. As she hesitated the door opened and a group of girls and young men emerged. They looked cheerful and contented. Gwyneth watched them disappear down the road and took a deep breath. Nervously she smoothed down her unruly hair. Then she knocked firmly on the door.

Mr Bliss was charming. Perhaps he was a bit too smooth with his thickly brilliantined hair and small dapper moustache, and Gwyneth didn't like men to smell of old English lavender, but he was businesslike. He showed her the room he called the studio, which was really the two ground floor parlours of the house knocked into one big room, with a piano in the corner and rows of pegs along one wall.

'We don't dress up. They are not social dances we organize,' he explained in his slightly clipped, pedantic manner. Gwyneth wondered if he were French, but she didn't think so, despite the occasional French words he slipped into his speech. 'Wear a light, comfortable dress with plenty of room to move. Keep one pair of well-fitting shoes just for dancing, and bring a bag to keep them in and change when you get here. That's what the pegs are for, to hang up your coats and hats and outdoor shoes.'

'I'd like to do theatrical dancing too, Mr Bliss,' Gwyneth said diffidently. 'Is it difficult?'

'Not if you have talent and discipline. But I do not allow just anyone to join the stage classes. I need to know their potential first. Then, if I approve, they can come to a beginners' class and try out.'

'I understand, Mr Bliss.'

'I'm training troupes of girls like my friend John Tiller does. With the new Ciné Variety theatres there's a great demand for good chorus girls, many opportunities for dancers with talent. Would you like to earn your living in the musical theatre?'

'Oh, yes,' Gwyneth breathed. If only she could! 'I can sing too,' she told him.

'Good. Girls have to have all sorts of talents to succeed on the stage. It's not easy. It demands dedication and hard work.'

'I'll work as hard as anyone,' Gwyneth declared, her eyes shining.

'Then I will see you on Saturday afternoon. It's the only time I can fit you in, there's such a craze for dancing now and so many people want to come.'

Gwyneth hardly listened to Lizzie as the following Saturday approached. She was quite uninterested in the other girl's excited speculations about George, and worries about how far she should let him go if he wanted to kiss her after the dance. All she could think of were her own plans for dancing classes. After she had seen Mr Bliss and arranged for her lessons she could barely wait for Saturday afternoon to arrive, and Miss Fremling took her aside more than once to warn her to pay more attention to her work.

When she arrived, eager and excited, ten minutes early for

her lesson, Gwyneth soon saw that Mr Bliss's remarks about the craze for dancing were true. A plump maid, who was no more than fifteen, neat and pert in her black dress and frilly white apron, let her in.

'The first lesson ain't – isn't finished yet, miss,' she said breathlessly. 'You'll 'ave ter wait in the passage.'

Gwyneth didn't care. She was too interested in the photographs of dancers which lined the walls of the passage. Studying these in the rather dim light which came from a small window at the back of the house, she tapped her feet in time to the piano music coming from the studio.

The maid opened the door several more times, and when the early class finished the passage was crowded with girls and young men. Gwyneth smiled shyly at them, and a few smiled back, but no one spoke until the earlier class emerged. Then it was only to apologize and ask pardon repeatedly as the incoming class pressed through the outgoing throng, eager to get into the studio and not waste a minute of their precious hour.

Mr Bliss was waiting, and greeted them all gravely. 'This is your first lesson, ladies and gentlemen, so I explain my method. First we talk a little about important principles of dancing, then Edwina and I will demonstrate a few simple steps, after which you all practise alone. Finally you try them out with partners, and Edwina and I will come round and make sure you are doing them correctly. You understand?'

They nodded, glancing at one another nervously.

'Very well. To be good dancers you must always have the body correctly balanced. If you do not you will look awkward, you may even fall over.' There were some giggles from one or two of the girls. 'Precisely. You also need a sense of rhythm, to follow the regular beats of the music and to be able to keep in time. It is important that the music is played in the correct time, or tempo. The music for some dances has three beats to a bar, like the waltz, which we are going to start with today.'

'I thought we'd never get away from just walking round saying "one, two, three," over and over again!' a pretty blonde girl complained as she and Gwyneth walked away together.

'But it worked! I could feel myself doing it better by the end,' Gwyneth said eagerly. 'Couldn't you?'

The other shrugged. 'I thought I could do it before I came, but having to remember all the names of the steps and think which foot to start on made it all much more complicated.'

'I found that helped. And it was a lot better knowing what your partner was going to do instead of waiting to see which way he pushed you, and then him starting off on the wrong foot and shuffling around out of time with the music!'

'I don't know. I thought we'd get on to proper dancing sooner. I want to learn the latest steps. If we don't do a lot more next week I don't think I'll waste my money. I'd rather go to a real dance.'

'My mother used to say you couldn't run before you walked, and I suppose dancing is the same. You have to practise the basic steps first.'

They reached the side street which led towards Gwyneth's lodgings. As the other girl waved goodbye and walked away Gwyneth found her thoughts turning relentlessly towards her home and especially her mother. She was doing what she wanted, but it was lonely all the same. She wondered how her mother was getting on without her. Was she worried, or angry? Ought she to send a letter to tell them she was safe and well, with a good job and a respectable room? No, it was too soon. And when she did send a letter she must somehow arrange for it to be posted away from Birmingham, so that they would not be able to trace her. Having tasted freedom she had no intention of ever relinquishing it to go back into her father's dour, joyless control.

A week later Nell had the chance she'd been looking for. The previous evening her father had been enticed into the boxing ring behind one of the pubs in Hockley, boasting that he could knock out the professional who was challenging all comers. Instead, he'd been knocked clean out of the ring on to the cobbles and was carried home by his mates. Apart from a mammoth headache he had twisted his ankle, and once put to bed declared he would stay there and be waited on for a change.

When it was dinnertime, Nell went to ask if she could speak to Mr Forster, who owned the factory.

'Well?' he snapped at her. He was a short, tubby man with bristling white eyebrows and a ring of hair surrounding a perfectly bald patch. In the long brown apron he wore all the time, even in his office, he was just like the picture of a monk her gran had shown her in a book.

'Please, sir, will you give me my wages in future, and not give them to my father?' she asked boldly.

'What! Of all the cheek! Young lady, you are under age and fortunate to be working here. I only gave you a job because your father said you were a good worker. If he chooses to look after your money to prevent you from wasting it that's his business, not mine.'

'But *he* wastes it!' Nell burst out, furious at this injustice. 'He never gives me a penny for myself!'

Mr Forster looked her up and down, his bushy eyebrows raised. 'Then how do you manage to come to work dressed in good quality clothes that must have cost many times what you earn during a week?'

'I was given them!'

'Yes? And who would be foolish enough to give away clothes of that quality to someone like you? What did you have to do for them, my dear?'

Nell glared at him. His eyes had suddenly grown smaller, like a pig's, and a fat tongue slid out of his mouth and wetted his fleshy lips. Her shoulders sagged. He would never believe her, and probably all sorts of damaging rumours would be spread if she tried to explain. Besides, it was clear he didn't intend to agree to her request about her wages.

'I did nothing. Someone damaged my old clothes and wanted to help,' she said quietly, and turned to go.

Outside the office she leaned for a moment against the wall

and closed her eyes. It was ironic that her good fortune in being given these beautiful clothes had caused the beating she'd received, and might lead to unpleasant gossip. She shivered as she recalled the look in old Mr Forster's eyes. She'd have to watch out for him, the old goat!

'Are you feeling unwell?'

She swung round quickly, but it was only Tom Simmons, one of the office clerks. He'd been in the same class as her oldest brother Ned until he'd moved to King Edward's School at Five Ways. He lived in a better part of Ladywood, a big house in Alston Street. She'd heard his father was some sort of high-up official in the railwaymen's union, and often went to other cities making speeches, even meeting the Ministers in Parliament.

'I'm all right, thanks.'

'You look very nice in that blouse and skirt.'

'Thank you. I must go, I've still got to eat my dinner.'

One slice of bread and dripping didn't take long to eat, but she knew that if she stayed her fury with both her father and Mr Forster would boil over. It would be wiser to say nothing. By the time she was walking home her anger had become a dull ache of resentment. When Tom fell into step beside her she knew she wouldn't tell him. He might think the worst of her too. Tom, however, was obsessed with a different idea.

'I wondered, Nell – can I call you Nell? After all, Ned and I were once good friends. Would you do me the honour of coming to the Lyric with me tonight? They have a good programme.'

Nell looked at him in astonishment. He'd never paid her any attention before beyond a casual greeting. Was this the result of good clothes?

He was good looking in a slender, bland way, with curly brown hair, wide cheekbones, good teeth and a ready smile. Most of the girls had, at one time or other, been eager to attract his attention, though as far as Nell knew he'd never shown the slightest interest in any of them.

She was tempted. It didn't commit her to anything, and she

hadn't been to a picture palace for more than four years. She and her grandmother had often gone until Gran got too arthritic to walk as far as the New Picture House down by the Ebrook. Suddenly she made up her mind. At home they'd all be bad tempered because Pa would be yelling down the stairs or thumping the bedroom floor demanding impossible delicacies. She would take the opportunity of a little harmless enjoyment.

'Thank you, Tom. That would be nice.'

'Do you have to go home to tell them first? If not, we could have a bite to eat and still make the second showing.'

'I don't need to go home,' Nell declared. They'd scarcely notice whether she was in or not. And whatever Tom meant by a 'bite', it would surely be preferable to the watery stew which was all her mother could ever afford.

Gwyneth found herself doing everything in waltz time. She moved round the shop in a daze, humming under her breath all the waltz tunes she knew, oblivious to the stares of the customers who watched, bemused, as she one-two-threed her way across the floor towards them.

'Gwyneth!' Lizzie hissed to her as Miss Fremling emerged from the cubby hole she called her office.

'What? Oh, yes, thanks. Thanks, Lizzie,' Gwyneth muttered, and turned her flushed cheeks towards the customer who had just entered the shop, accompanied by a tall man.

Gwyneth smiled brilliantly, and as she saw one of her most valued customers respond in like manner Miss Fremling changed her own frown to a muted smile of approval. The smile grew a mite less frosty when she saw that Mrs Mandeville selected no fewer than four gowns to try on.

'I wonder if they're too short?' Mrs Mandeville asked anxiously.

'Shorter skirts are the fashion this year, Mother,' the man said encouragingly. He shot a conspiratorial smile towards Gwyneth, and nodded slightly. 'Try them on and see how young you look.'

She laughed. 'I'm not a girl still, Paul dear. I don't want to appear foolish.'

'You're so tall and slim, madam, they'll look very elegant on you,' Gwyneth said, sincere in her praise. The woman must have been at least fifty, but she still had a slender, upright figure and shapely legs.

Gwyneth caught the look of approval in the young man's eyes, and felt her cheeks grow warm. He was amazingly handsome, in a rugged sort of way. His face was strong. Yes, that was the word. His features were bold, his chin square and his eyes dark and keen under light brown, slightly tawny-coloured hair. She noticed his hands, well cared for, with long, powerful fingers.

'Paul dear, I don't want to keep you waiting. You have to visit the Colonel. If he approves of you he'll tell lots of his friends to come to you. Your practice will soon be thriving.'

'I'll go now, and you'll be ready when I get back. I'm sure the young lady can keep you occupied.'

'I've just returned from a visit to Australia. My sister, you know, is living there,' Mrs Mandeville explained to Miss Fremling after he left. 'I'm out of mourning for my husband now and I need some new gowns for the winter. I decided to stay with Paul while I came to see what you had. You usually have the best in town, far better than in Kenilworth, and I don't fancy going all the way to London after the long journey home. And I haven't the slightest idea what is fashionable here. I depend on you to advise me.'

'Miss Davis will help you, and if you need any advice with regard to alterations I will be pleased to assist.'

When Mrs Mandeville had departed, having chosen a total of six gowns, Miss Fremling was so delighted her frown was completely banished for some time.

'She was actually arch when she told you off for dancing in the shop,' Lizzie giggled as they walked to the tram.

Gwyneth laughed ruefully. 'Thank heaven for Mrs Mandeville! And her son. He persuaded her to buy the extra ones, you know, when he came back for her. He said she was invited to several houseparties before Christmas, and would need plenty of gowns.' She sighed. 'I wonder what it's like to stay in really big houses, with proper ballrooms, and dance at private parties?'

'For goodness sake! What's got into you, Gwyneth? You can't talk about anything else but dancing these days!'

'But it's so exciting! Lizzie, there's so much more to it than I thought, and Mr Bliss is a very good teacher. He and his wife do demonstration dances at places like the Tower. She's very pretty, slim and tall, with a very elegant blonde bob. Are you sure you don't want to come to my classes?'

Lizzie laughed. 'Not me! I don't call it fun to spend an hour walking about a small room in time to music, and have to pay to be shown how! Besides, at a proper dance you get closer, if you know what I mean.' She giggled. 'Gwyneth, promise you won't tell anybody?'

'Tell anybody? Tell them what? Tell who?'

'Promise!'

'If you want me to. Though I don't know anybody you do apart from at work, so I'm not likely to.'

'George — asked if he could kiss me on Saturday,' Lizzie whispered, looking round to make sure no one was eavesdropping.

'Oh. Did he? What did you say?' Gwyneth tried to summon up some enthusiasm for what Lizzie clearly regarded as an earth shattering event.

'I let him. Gwyneth, you don't think I'm fast, do you?' she asked anxiously. 'I know I only met him two weeks before, but he's such a gentleman, he wouldn't take advantage, honestly he wouldn't.'

'I'm sure he wouldn't. Was it nice?' she asked after a pause, since it was clear Lizzie had much more to say.

Lizzie sighed ecstatically. 'It was wonderful! He put his arms round me, gently, almost as if we were dancing, then he placed his lips on mine! I could hardly breathe! I opened my eyes just a bit, and he was looking at me so – well, so lovingly! I felt just as if I was one of those vamps in the pictures!'

Gwyneth stifled a giggle as her unruly imagination set to work. She couldn't afford to offend Lizzie, who was the only friend she'd made so far in Birmingham, but she did think it was a dreadful fuss about a simple little kiss. She was sure she wouldn't get so excited if a man kissed her. It wasn't as if George could be compared with Ronald Coleman or Rudolph Valentino. She wouldn't want men like that to kiss her, anyway, she thought suddenly. She'd prefer a man less smooth, with a firm chin, and hair the colour of the lions she'd once seen when they'd stayed in London with her aunt and visited the zoo. As she realized she had just drawn in her mind a picture of Mr Mandeville, her cheeks flamed. Fortunately Lizzie was absorbed in her account of her exact feelings during every single second the kiss had lasted, and hadn't noticed either her abstraction or her blushes. Gwyneth managed to utter suitable remarks until the tram came, and was thankful it was so crowded they had to sit apart.

How she would love to dance with him. He looked a very capable man – surely he would be able to dance well. Then she shook herself angrily. Mrs Mandeville had ordered her gowns to be sent to her son's house in one of the most select roads in Edgbaston; she was just a shopgirl. The likelihood of their ever dancing together was remote. She wouldn't even think about it again. She would concentrate all her energy, or at least what she had left over from her job, into learning as much as she could about dancing so that she could soon transfer into a stage class. Then she might escape from the toil and dreariness of her present job into a world infinitely more attractive and glamorous. And one in which, her inner voice persisted, she might attract the attention of Mr Mandeville.

Andrew realized he wasn't playing with his normal verve and enthusiasm and the knowledge infuriated him. He didn't allow anything to come between him and his playing. He'd seen the rest of the band glance at him occasionally in a puzzled manner. They knew his attention was not as singlemindedly on his music as it normally was.

He couldn't forget that girl or her face with the big green eyes that held such a wary expression. It made him feel she'd be off like a startled fawn at the slightest intimation of danger. He recalled the snub nose which he'd had the craziest desire to kiss, and the wide cheekbones, and the delicious mobile lips from which her gentle, musical voice had issued. It was incredible that she could produce so many different sounds. When they'd eaten and she'd relaxed Kitty had persuaded her to demonstrate the accent her family used. Nell had then switched into broad Scots, saying she'd once seen a comedian when her grandmother had taken her to a pantomime and had been fascinated by his voice.

She could make a living on the music halls with impersonations. For a moment Andrew had a glimpse of life as it might be, Nell travelling up and down the country with him, playing at the same theatres, going back at night to shared lodgings.

By the time their act was over he was in a filthy temper. Nell wasn't there and it was not probable that he'd ever see her again. Nor was it like him to yearn for a particular girl. They were easy to attract, and just as easy to relinquish. When one of the other performers, the magician's assistant, smiled invitingly at him as he passed her in the corridor on his way to the dressing room, he stopped and spoke. Five minutes later they left the theatre together, and Andrew did his best to forget Nell.

Kitty paced across the room. She was bored. Timothy had departed to South Africa. Andrew was somewhere in the Potteries and it might be several weeks before he returned to Birmingham. In the meantime life was dull, and she had no prospects of excitement for days.

She wished she knew how to contact Nell, the waif Andrew had brought to her. It had been exciting, something different, meeting her, and more than that, she had liked the girl and felt sympathy for her. Nell had been so pathetically grateful for a few old clothes. If only they'd been the same class they could, Kitty felt sure, have been great friends. Nell would surely not be so fickle as the rest of her so-called girlfriends. She had no friends in Birmingham, she thought fretfully, just acquaintances. Her best friends from school were either married, living in London (or in one case California), and somehow they never bothered to keep in touch.

'This is ridiculous!' she chided herself. 'Don't moan about having no friends, go out and make some, right here!'

With renewed vigour she sat at the small bureau in her sitting room and drew a sheet of scented writing paper towards her. After letting the ink dry on the pen nib several times while she chewed the other end, she gave a satisfied nod and began to make a list of all the young people she knew in Birmingham. She sat back eventually and considered the result of her labours. It was her twentieth birthday soon. She'd hold a dance combined with a treasure hunt and supper. Twenty people would be the right number, enough for real competition. It would fill the big drawing room, yet not be so many Meggy would refuse to cook for them.

Rather guiltily she wondered whether she ought to consult Meggy first, then briskly shook her head. If Meggy objected she would bring in caterers. She simply would not allow her mother's housekeeper, however much an old and valued servant, to dictate to her what she might do.

Carefully she pruned the list until she had selected the most appropriate young people from her Birmingham acquaintances. She hesitated when she came to Paul Mandeville. He was older than her crowd, and more serious, despite the reputation he'd had during the war for daredevil exploits, and the medals he'd won for bravery, but she had known him all her life. She shrugged. If he refused there were others. She could at least try.

'Meggy, I'm going to see Maisie and Fleur,' she called into the kitchen an hour later, and whisked out of the house before Meggy could question her.

It wasn't far to the Carpenter house in Vicarage Road, and

soon she and the two sisters were giggling as they elaborated on Kitty's plans.

'If you make up the list of what we have to find, Kitty, you won't be able to compete,' Fleur said suddenly. 'It simply wouldn't be fair.'

'Bother! I hadn't thought of that. And we absolutely must have equal numbers of men and girls for the dance.'

'Let's ask each man to suggest one object, then it will be fair,' Maisie suggested.

'We'll make them vow not to cheat, not to collect them first.'

'Can we go anywhere in Birmingham to find them? We have to set the rules beforehand.'

'We can't have too wide an area. Let's decide on some boundaries, and then you can help me write the invitations and tell them the rules.'

'And we can post the letters today, that's plenty of time for next Saturday.'

'Plenty of time to get a new dress, you mean, Maisie,' Fleur laughed excitedly. 'What about music, Kitty? Will you have records or a band? It's utterly beastly Andrew isn't here to play.'

'But if he were playing his saxophone you wouldn't be able to dance with him,' Maisie pointed out rather sharply.

'Oh, no.' Fleur pouted prettily. She'd once been told it made her look adorably helpless, and ever since she'd practised every day in front of her dressing-table mirror.

'I mean to ask someone I know who plays the piano. We can have records as well,' Kitty interposed quickly. She was well aware both sisters had fallen for her cousin when they'd met him two weeks earlier, and that he thought them silly and empty headed. She hugged the knowledge to her. Thankfully his absence meant they couldn't squabble over his imagined preferences. They were inclined to be dramatic, and sulk if they felt neglected. How she wished her London friends were here instead. She would nonetheless create some fun and ignore Fleur's tantrums.

*

Nell resisted as Tom changed direction and tried to steer her into a shop doorway. He'd destroyed her mood, as he had last week when he'd first tried to embrace her. She was too absorbed reliving the magic of the music hall they'd just been to at the Empire. In particular she was recreating the exciting dance routines performed by a dozen girls dressed in glittering costumes and tall feathered headdresses.

'No, Tom,' she said firmly. 'I told you before I didn't want to be mauled.'

'But Nell, I love you! I love you so much!' Tom protested and Nell sighed.

'You can't!' she said sharply. 'We've only been out together three times.'

'I've watched you every day at work, since the first time,' he told her. 'Can you possibly care for me, just a little?'

'I like you,' she said slowly. 'I don't know what love is.'

'Liking's enough. It will turn to love, I know it will. Oh, Nell, I want to shout it aloud, tell everyone, I'm so happy! When can we be married? We can live with my parents, and you needn't ever work again in that awful press shop. Mother is delicate and needs help, and I know they'll both adore you.'

Nell struggled to stem the enthusiastic tide. 'Hold on, Tom! I didn't say I wanted to marry you!'

'But – you said you liked me?'

His bewildered and slightly offended tone would have been laughable in other circumstances, Nell thought. She suppressed her mirth and gathered her wits together. 'It's too soon. I don't know!' She hastened to soothe any damaged pride.

'I'd have thought marriage to me, and the comfortable home I can offer you, would be better than that hovel you live in now! You wouldn't have to work again, you could have nice clothes, good food, and a woman to do the rough!' he elaborated, offended.

'I know, Tom, and I'm honoured, truly I am, but it wouldn't be fair to marry you unless I loved you properly. I don't know you nearly well enough yet,' she added.

'Then we must get to know one another quickly,' he said, and she was relieved to hear the indulgent tone creep back into his voice. 'Next week I'll take you dancing. There's more time to talk than at the pictures.'

Nell's thoughts had swung back to the chorus line at the theatre again and she almost laughed. That wasn't what he meant, but for a moment she imagined herself up there on a stage, dancing in front of thousands of people, dressed in those marvellous brightly coloured clothes. She'd seen nothing like them since her grandparents had taken her to the pantomime at the Theatre Royal when she was a child. She oughtn't to encourage him if he was beginning to get silly notions about love, but she'd loved dancing as a child, yet had never been in a dance hall. She wavered. The temptation to experience it was overwhelming, yet it was impossible.

'Tom, I don't have anything suitable to wear.'

He laughed indulgently. 'That's what every woman says!'

'But in my case it's absolutely true!' she snapped. 'All I have in the world is the blouse and skirt I'm wearing now, the same as I wear every day to work. You know old Forster gives Pa my money, so I never have anything to spend on myself. Even if I had any finery it would be whisked away to the pawn shop as soon as I took it off! I'd be lucky to find these clothes waiting for me when I got back, even.'

'Nell!' He was appalled. 'That's dreadful! I hadn't realized it was as bad as that. Then why don't you get out of it by marrying me?'

'I can't change my family,' she said wearily. 'But I can avoid making a mistake I'd have to suffer the rest of my life.'

'Marrying me wouldn't be a mistake.' He was offended again. He did seem to take offence terribly easily.

Nell sighed. 'Tom, don't you understand? It could be a mistake, that's all I'm saying. You might regret it too. And it's far too soon even to think about it anyway.'

'You can trust my judgement, Nell. A man always knows best.'

'Rubbish! Like my father? And why have they given women – some women – the vote?'

He was silent for a while and she thought she had annoyed him. As they passed under the lamp on the corner he stopped and faced her. 'Nell, I still want to take you dancing. I've had an idea. I'm sure my mother would lend you something. She's only an inch or so shorter than you are. You could come to our house and change.'

Nell's eyes gleamed. She'd never seen ballroom dancing except on films, and she longed to go. Could this be the answer, the beginning of a new life? She realized suddenly that for the past two years she had simply endured the horrors life had thrown at her – her gran's death, the appalling conditions at home, the dirt and the poverty. She'd been like a leaf, swirled about by whatever wind blew. Now she'd fight back. She'd do all she could to enjoy some fun, to get away from her dreary, grinding existence.

'But what would she think?' she asked hesitantly. His mother would no doubt find it very strange to be asked to lend her clothes to her son's girlfriend. 'I wouldn't want her to – well, to imagine things!'

'Leave it to me!' he said confidently. His mother denied him nothing. He was the only child and he could tell her of his plans. She would welcome Nell without making her feel in any way uncomfortable. His optimism soared. He was certain he would be organizing their wedding by Christmas.

Nell had reached the entrance to their court when she heard running footsteps behind her.

'Nell, wait fer me!'

She turned, startled. It was Amy. 'What on earth are you doin' out so late?' she demanded as her sister, panting, stopped beside her.

'I climbed out the window. I wanted ter ask yer summat.'

'Amy, you're too young to go roaming the streets alone,' Nell chided her. 'You could ask me whatever it is in bed.'

'No I couldn't. It's a secret, an' Eth would tell Pa, mean ol' cow!'

'Amy, you mustn't call Eth that! She's not so bad if you don't make her cross.'

'Is! Nell, wait!' she wailed as Nell made to move on.

'It's cold standing here, Amy.'

'Yer wasn't cold when yer were with Tom Simmons,' Amy said petulantly.

Nell swung round to face her. 'Have you been spyin' on me?'

'No! I just follered yer. I saw which way yer went, an' waited till yer come back. Nell, yer won't marry 'im, will yer?'

'No, of course not,' she said sharply. Yet who could tell when life at home would become so unbearable she might be glad to take that escape. Since the fight Danny and Sam had scarcely ever been in the house except to sleep, and they pointedly ignored Pa, despite his jibes about their lack of fighting ability and crude aspersions about their supposed lack of other manly attributes. They spoke only when absolutely necessary to Ma, and at night Nell could hear them whispering together behind the curtain.

'If yer do, let me live with yer instead of at 'ome,' Amy said in a rush, and clung desperately to Nell while her thin body was racked with sobs.

'Amy, hush, luv!' Nell tried to soothe her.

'I 'ates it there! Nell, it's 'orrible! Pa's gettin' wus, and you'm the only one what luvs me!'

'Ma loves you,' Nell said, feeling helpless. 'Amy, pet, I'm not going to marry Tom, but even if I did you couldn't come to live with me unless Pa agreed. The police would make you go back, you're too young to leave home.'

'Yer could make 'im say it was all right!' Amy began to weep again.

'Amy, it won't happen. And in a few years you'll be at work, earning money, and able to leave home.'

'I wish it weren't so long ter wait,' Amy sniffed. 'Promise, Nell? If yer do marry 'im?'

'I promise, if I ever marry Tom, but that's very unlikely.'

It satisfied Amy a little and Nell persuaded her to dry her eyes, and then went into the house first to make sure Pa had already gone upstairs and it was safe for Amy to creep up to bed. She hadn't realized her little sister felt so unhappy. Ought she to accept Tom and persuade him to talk to Pa? Surely if Pa thought he had one less mouth to feed he might let Amy go? Then she shuddered in revulsion. She'd seen too much of the difficulties her mother faced to want to fall into the same trap. Even for Amy's sake she could not condemn herself to a lifetime of marriage to Tom – or anyone.

Chapter Five

'MOTHER, I don't want to leave you alone, you don't visit me very often,' Paul said at breakfast.

'You have to have a life of your own, Paul,' Mrs Mandeville said firmly. 'You've worked far too hard the last few years, and if you have no social life I'll never have any grandchildren.'

He laughed. 'I'm busy setting up a new practice! Are you matchmaking? You've never before suggested that Kitty Denver would be an acceptable daughter-in-law!'

'And I'm not now. She's far too flighty, she wouldn't suit you at all. Accepting her invitation to this party she's organizing would not give anyone the wrong idea. It's not as though you'd be alone, you're not even likely to be paired with her for the treasure hunt. You can be sure she has someone else in mind to partner her.'

'I've no desire to go chasing all over Birmingham looking for pointless objects, just to give Kitty something to occupy herself.'

'No, it is rather silly. Though I recall you used to indulge in worse things when you were a medical student!'

'That was reaction against the war!'

'But I thought it was the suffering you saw that made you decide to be a doctor?'

'It was, but we also needed to forget the horrors. I'm a staid, qualified doctor now. I have to be a model of propriety.'

'You still need to relax. I feel responsible for Kitty in a way, while her foolish mother flaunts herself in New York. Even in Australia we heard stories of her goings-on.'

'I know you used to be friends with her mother, but how does that make you responsible for Kitty?'

'Not friends, exactly. We took part in a few marches together, but I was never involved in that particular set, and certainly never indulged in throwing bricks at windows or chaining myself to railings. Most undignified.'

'One day you must tell me all about your disreputable suffragette past,' he said, grinning at her.

'I was older than she was, you see, and our parents had been good friends. I tried to keep an eye on her, as much as I could. I would be happier if I felt you were keeping a friendly eye on Kitty since her mother doesn't seem to think it her duty.'

'But you'll be left alone.'

'It wouldn't be a tragedy. Actually, Paul, I was wondering whether I might invite some of my old friends who still live in Birmingham to visit me one evening?'

'A dinner party? Of course, but shouldn't I be here to host it for you?'

'They're all terrible old fogies, darling. And many of them are your patients and would only plague you for free advice on their gout or rheumatism! I'd be much more comfortable if I knew you weren't sitting there bored out of your mind!'

'You'd prefer I was bored silly amongst Kitty's friends?'

'You'll accept?'

'Since you clearly have plans for some sort of assignation I won't spoil it for you. I'll go. But I shall be home on the stroke of midnight, so make sure you copy Cinderella!'

'And I'll be coming to stay with you again soon, and perhaps we'll go to the pantomime like we used to do, years ago. I'll make you have some fun! I'd enjoy it too.'

Nell lay in bed wishing she had someone to confide in. Eth, just two years younger, would have been the natural person to share secrets with, but it would not do. Apart from Eth's snide suggestions and unconcealed jealousy about the good clothes she'd been given, the years she had spent living with her grandparents had erected an unscalable barrier between the sisters. Amy was the sister she felt closest to, but Amy was only ten, too young to know anything about love and marriage. And even mentioning Tom would be likely to provoke another storm of weeping such as had occurred that night Amy had lain in wait for her.

Nell sighed, and turned over carefully, trying not to wake her sisters. The bed was far too small for the four of them, even sleeping top to toe, and if she woke Eth her sister would be complaining for the rest of the night.

She forced her thoughts away from the dancing. That had been revelation enough, the vast, brilliantly lit Tower ballroom and the gowns and enthralling music. After watching the others for a while she'd been impatient to try for herself, knowing she could do as well, and so it had proved. She'd danced a lot as a child, improvising steps, and Tom was a good dancer; soon they had been whirling confidently about the ballroom. Nell felt totally at home there. What bothered her was her obligation to Tom and Mrs Simmons.

'Come in, my dear.' Mrs Simmons had been welcoming when she'd presented herself at their large house, one of a pair with a good garden at the back.

'Mother has two dresses for you to choose from,' Tom said when Nell had been shown into the front parlour. He eyed her consideringly. 'Yes, you're much the same height, and though you're a little thinner they should fit well enough.'

'Come and try them on, Nell dear,' Mrs Simmons urged. 'You haven't much time before you need to leave.'

The dresses had been laid out in the spare bedroom and Nell had no hesitation in choosing the plain, straight one in a dark pink taffeta rather than the fussy white lace with dozens of frills. Both were too large, but Nell not only preferred the plain one, she knew the style disguised the poor fit better.

'It's longer than the fashion this year,' Mrs Simmons worried. 'Perhaps you can use the other one next time.'

'It's beautiful and I'm so grateful to you,' Nell said.

'Look, try on these shoes. I think they'll fit. They're white, they'll go with either dress.'

The shoes were produced, carefully wrapped in tissue, and Nell slipped them on. They were a fraction too large, but when Mrs Simmons stuffed the toes with cotton wool they fitted better and the straps over the instep were tight enough to keep them in place.

As she handled them Nell was suspicious. 'These are new. They haven't been worn.' Had Tom bought them specially? She hesitated, then reminded herself the shoes were a loan, not a present. He couldn't be misled into thinking she'd accepted such a personal gift from him.

'Oh, yes, you see they were too small for me,' Mrs Simmons said swiftly.

Nell glanced down at Mrs Simmons's neat, delicate feet, but she could hardly call her a liar, and she did so desperately want to go dancing. She nodded. 'It's very good of you.'

'I want to please our Tom. It's time he found himself a nice lass. You do like him, my dear, don't you? He's told me such a lot about you.'

'He's very kind,' Nell managed to say.

She felt guilty. Tom was thoughtful, and it was plain his mother would be kind to anyone he chose to be his wife. She would have a much easier life with Tom than she would married to someone like her father. Was that all that mattered?

Then the thought of her mother, struggling to make a home of sorts for her large family, made Nell shudder. Marriage meant children, and the necessary intimacies which produced them. She would never want to do that with a man, and supposing she could bring herself to endure it, there wouldn't be room even in Tom's big house for many children as well as his parents.

She couldn't take advantage of Tom's fondness for her any more. What he had shown her, though, had stiffened her determination to get away from home, to make some money for herself, and to acquire clothes in which she could learn to dance. She turned over once more and racked her brains for ways of achieving this now overriding ambition.

'There simply isn't a single imaginative item of treasure in this boring old list!' Kitty complained, struggling into her fur coat.

Paul Mandeville laughed. 'We don't have the advantages of London — we can't steal a busby from the guards outside Buckingham Palace, or ashtrays from the Savoy!'

'You wouldn't do that even if you could,' Kitty teased. 'You're far too much the upright citizen these days, though your mother was hinting at what a devil you used to be.'

'Don't believe her! But I mean to enjoy tonight. What have we to find?'

'A programme from the Theatre Royal, a tram ticket from the Ladywood tram, a bottle of Greenwood's mineral water, some Kunzle cakes, a menu card from Endersby's Hotel, a copy of *Antic Hay*. There's absolutely nothing here we can't get just by walking in and asking, buying or picking up out of the gutter!'

'Then let's start.' They went outside and scrambled into his car, a big Sunbeam tourer. 'Where first?'

'Endersby's. They say Mrs Endersby is a darling, but by the time she's been asked for ten menu cards she might be just a little bit annoyed.'

'She's too kind for that, as well as beautiful and talented. Every man in Edgbaston is wildly envious of Mr Endersby for finding her first.'

'A paragon, in fact,' Kitty said dismissively.

'You'll like her. It's amazing, women adore her too.'

Kitty raised her eyebrows disbelievingly, but did not comment. She hadn't known any woman equally admired by both men and her own sex.

'I'll book a table and take you there for dinner next week,'

Paul suggested as he drove out and swung towards the Hagley Road. 'It can be my birthday present to you.'

'Really? Oh, that's fabulous! They have dinner dances in their new ballroom. Right, Endersby's first, then we can go into the city centre. I know Meggy has some mineral water, we can collect that when we get back.'

'If that's allowed, my mother has a whole box of Kunzle cakes, she bought them for tea tomorrow, never can resist them when she's near their shop at Five Ways.'

'Simply any method is allowed in treasure hunts,' Kitty declared, 'short of actually stealing something.'

'I'm sure *Antic Hay* is at home too. She always reads the new novels, and that's been out for over a year. I believe she left it at my house when she went to Australia.'

'We'd better make sure while we're in Edgbaston, then if she didn't we can be thinking where else to go while we collect the other things.'

Almost an hour later they returned, to find they had just been beaten by Fleur Carpenter and Terry Rance, a young army officer on leave.

'Strategy,' he crowed, as Kitty and Paul ran in through the front door.

Fleur giggled. 'We saw Maisie actually grubbing in the gutter near the tram stop! We pipped her home and snaffled all the mineral water so that she couldn't get any there. And *Antic Hay* and all Mother's Kunzle cakes. She'll be utterly furious!'

During the next half-hour the other teams straggled in, and after Terry and Fleur had been ceremoniously presented with their prize, a magnum of champagne, they trooped into supper, watched benignly by Meggy.

'I can't make it out,' Kitty confided to Maisie, having soothed the other girl's ruffled feelings at what she considered the base advantage taken by her sister to spoil her own chances.

'What do you mean?'

'Meggy. She prepared all this without a murmur. Well, only a token grumble and saying she needed a couple of girls all day to help. And now she's looking positively smug.'

'It's because of Paul,' Maisie replied. 'She approves of him and probably thinks he'd keep you out of mischief. He's rich, too, and though he doesn't need to work he does, he has what she'd call a proper job.'

'You think she's trying to pair us off? But I'm not sure I would marry him and I'm certain I wouldn't want to marry a doctor. He's fun, that's all.'

Gwyneth was astonished, then delighted when Mr Bliss told her, after just a couple of lessons, that she could join his stage class.

'You have an extraordinary talent and the ability to learn new movements quickly,' he'd explained. 'You must stay in the modern class, but I think you can catch up in the stage class too.'

Stage dancing, Gwyneth found, required far more stamina than modern ballroom dancing. 'It's not the steps, they're easy once you get the idea, and if you can keep in time,' she explained to Lizzie. 'The steps of the foxtrot are much more complicated. You just need more energy. I seem to be hungry all the time now, and the girl in the room below mine is always complaining about the noise when I practise.'

'I wouldn't like to practise every day like you do.'

'I must catch up. Mr Bliss is planning to send out a troupe of girls to the local theatres soon. I might be good enough to be in it.'

'But what about your job here?'

'I'd have to give that up.'

Lizzie stared at her, aghast. 'Gwyneth! You wouldn't! How could you live? Are dancers paid enough? What about the times you aren't working?'

'I'd be paid more when I was working, but some of the time I'd get nothing. I need to save as much as I can before then. Miss Fremling has said I can stay late and help with alterations.

I can earn a bit more doing those, and I have enough clothes to last me, I won't waste my money on them like I used to.'

'You'll be so tired.'

'I know, but dancing is an exhausting life. Mrs Bliss was telling me she always feels tired. It's worth it, and I have to train myself to manage.'

'I couldn't do it.'

'How's George?' Gwyneth asked. Somewhat surprisingly Lizzie hadn't mentioned him this morning. She knew they'd been going out for the day yesterday on the new motorcycle combination George had acquired.

Lizzie flushed. 'We've quarrelled,' she said briefly, and her eyes filled with tears.

Before she could say more Miss Fremling approached. 'Miss Davis. If I might have a word with you?'

Gwyneth followed apprehensively into the small makeshift office, wondering how she could have offended. To her astonishment she discovered she had not.

'Would it be possible for you to stay behind tomorrow evening and do some of the alterations then?' Miss Fremling asked.

'Yes, of course,' Gwyneth replied.

'And ... Miss Davis, you've been with us for almost two months now. I was uncertain at first, but you've settled down well, in fact I've come to rely on you more than I can the others.'

Gwyneth blinked. This was totally unexpected. 'Thank you,' she murmured.

'And so,' Miss Fremling went on, 'I feel I can trust you. As you know, I normally remain behind for an hour making up the books and checking stock in the evenings. The cleaner is also here during that time, and I lock up after she's gone. I cannot do that tomorrow, I have an engagement — that is to say an important appointment.' She's actually blushing, Gwyneth told herself with inward amusement, and wondered just what sort of appointment could affect the stately Miss Fremling in such a way. 'Could I trust you to supervise the cleaner? She's new but I'll show her what to do tonight. Make sure you lock up very carefully afterwards.'

'Of course. I'm honoured to be trusted,' Gwyneth said.

Miss Fremling became brisk, swiftly demonstrating the locks Gwyneth had to see to. Then with a curt nod she dismissed her. It was dinnertime and Lizzie was eating her sandwiches in the tiny space behind the stockroom which served as a kitchen.

'What happened?' Gwyneth demanded, squeezing on to a stool beside her.

Lizzie gulped. 'He – We went up into the Lickey Hills. We walked over the hills, and he – George – well, he wanted to go further than I did, and he was so angry. Said I'd led him on, was a tease, no better than a tart! He stormed off and I had to find my own way home. I'll never forgive him!'

'Never mind,' Gwyneth said, feeling inadequate. 'No harm's done, and there are plenty of men who would respect you, who'd never want you to do wrong.'

'But I love him!' Lizzie wailed. 'Why did he have to spoil it all?' She soon calmed down and returned to the shop, but refused to say any more when they walked to the tram. 'I just want to forget. Tell me all about the stage dancing. How many girls are there in a troupe? Perhaps we could go and see a music hall one day, maybe the Tiller Girls will be here soon, and one day you'll be famous like them and travel all over the world.'

Chapter Six

'NELL, luv, will yer be at 'ome tonight?'

'Not till late, Ma.'

'Yer pa's been askin' where yer've been.'

'Keeping out the way,' Nell said brusquely. 'I must go, or I'll be late fer work.'

Mrs Baxter sighed. Nell had changed, and she couldn't decide whether it was due to the new clothes she'd somehow obtained or the beating her pa had given her because of them. She was quieter and she rarely came home before ten, later on Saturdays. Perhaps she'd found herself a lad. Mrs Baxter hoped so, for Nell's sake.

Then she paused. She'd been just seventeen when she'd married Albert, only six months older than Nell was now. He'd been such a catch, she'd thought then. He'd come to Sutton Coldfield to work as a porter on the railways, and was a big, strong young man. He was full of plans for becoming a guard, and then perhaps even a driver. He'd swept her off her feet, urging marriage within a month of their meeting. Her parents had at first refused, and relented only when she'd said that if they didn't agree she'd run away and live with him without marriage. Perhaps it wasn't wise to be wed so young. Perhaps her folk had known better than she had, in her impetuous desire not to lose her first suitor.

Might Nell make the same mistake? Yet surely she'd choose

more carefully. And almost anything would be preferable for her than staying here with her pa, for he was getting more vicious every year as disappointment at the ruin of all his dreams overcame him. Yes, for Nell an early marriage might be good. The sooner she could escape the better. If her lad had a good job he'd be able to afford a house, there were plenty to rent at only a few shillings a week. Then she'd be safe from Pa.

He seemed to have been more careful since the night he'd whipped Nell. He still came home drunk on Saturdays, but appeared to retain enough control to stop beating the others. If only it would last! But she knew Albert better than that. Perhaps he'd had a fright. Nell had glared at him with such scorn, he'd seemed abashed after it was over.

Nell, unaware of her mother's speculations, went to the factory. At last she had taken a step towards a new life. It would not be with Tom Simmons, for she was determined never to make herself dependent on any man. Instead she'd found another, part-time job. It would take months, but she would have some money of her own, enough eventually to take a room and then look for a job away from her father's place of work, so that she could keep all her earnings. She'd already made another pocket on her belt to keep the coins beside her precious box. And once she could afford to pay for dancing lessons, she could look forward to freedom.

She slipped away after finishing work at the factory, thankful it was on the city side of Ladywood. As she'd discovered yesterday she would have to run most of the way to get to Corporation Street in time. She was breathless when she reached the shop, and hardly able to speak when a dark, pretty girl scarcely older than herself came to let her in.

'I'm Nell Baxter, the cleaner,' she gasped.

'Come in. Miss Fremling can't be here tonight. I'm Gwyneth Davis, I work here. Do you know where everything is?'

'Yes, thanks, miss.'

'You're out of breath. I've just made a pot of tea. Would you like some?'

'I oughtn't to,' Nell said slowly, but licked her lips. She'd had nothing since a crust of bread and dripping for breakfast; there hadn't been anything to spare for her dinner after Pa had been given his, and she'd refused to take the last slice which was all the babies and her mother had until Mrs Baxter received her money from that day's cleaning job. Thank goodness the ones old enough for school could get the free breakfast provided there. Without that they'd surely starve.

'Of course you must. There's a full pot, plenty for us both.'

As Nell busied herself with the broom, sweeping the floor and then kneeling to polish the linoleum, she watched Gwyneth turning up the hems of two gowns, stitching swiftly. The other girl was humming to herself, her foot tapping the floor in time.

'That tune, I heard it at the Tower,' Nell said suddenly. 'Oh, I'm sorry, miss, I shouldn't have spoken out of turn.'

Gwyneth looked up eagerly. 'No, do talk. And don't call me "miss", it makes me feel so old! It's boring doing hems, and must be worse polishing floors. You go dancing?'

'I've only been once, but I'm going again as soon as I can afford a dress and some proper shoes.'

'I go to classes now. I want to learn properly. I'm starting stage dancing too.'

'Like on the music halls?'

Nell was staring at her in astonishment, and Gwyneth laughed, embarrassed. 'Yes. Why not?'

'I thought you had to start that sort of dancing when you were little,' Nell said slowly. 'My gran said I should have been a ballet dancer, I was always dancing and doing handstands when I was a kid.'

'You do for ballet, but stage dancing's much easier. If you can keep in time to the music and learn quickly it's very simple.'

Nell bent over her polishing, her mind in a whirl. She didn't speak again until Gwyneth, glancing at the clock, folded up her work and announced it was time to go.

'Put the things away. You've been polishing that bit of linoleum for the past ten minutes.'

'Oh!' Nell laughed, disconcerted. 'I was dreaming.'

'About dancing? Would you like to have lessons?'

'Yes, but I'd never earn enough to pay for them, not for ages.'

'You will if you want it enough.'

Nell put away the polish and the cloths, fetched her coat and waited with Gwyneth while she locked the door and checked it. Some day she might become a dancer. It was a fantastic thought, one she could scarcely comprehend. She walked slowly, absorbed in the possibilities which had opened up for her. She should have asked Miss Davis where she might find a teacher. She'd been very friendly, unlike most shopgirls who looked down on other workers. But it was too soon. First she had to earn enough money to escape from home.

'I am utterly, madly bored!' Kitty declared.

Maisie suppressed her irritation. Kitty was fun, but also often exasperating. 'I don't see how you can be,' she replied after a moment, concentrating on smoothing her rouge powder with a brush. 'You don't have parents forever asking where you've been and with whom, and forbidding you to pluck your eyebrows and use lipstick.'

'My dear mama may be in America, but you can be sure Meggy tells her absolutely everything I do!' Kitty said petulantly. 'Actually, even if she were here I don't suppose she would care frightfully. She didn't care enough to marry my father, whoever he was.'

'I think that was fearfully brave of her,' Maisie declared. 'If I were ever in such a position I'd die!'

'Not if you were enjoying it.' Maisie looked blank. 'The position, silly. The one you have to get into before you can conceive a bastard!'

Maisie flushed a painful red, her natural colour vying with the harsher scarlet of the rouge.

'Kitty! You shouldn't talk like that!'

Kitty shrugged. 'Don't be so dreadfully bourgeois! It's almost 1925! Everyone talks about sex now.'

'But they didn't when your mother had you. Has she really never told you who your father is?' she added after a minute.

'I doubt if she knew herself. She and her friends lived in Chelsea amongst the artists, and free love was the fashion. Orgies in studios when they weren't in Holloway or chucking themselves under racehorses.'

'Then your father might be someone famous!' Maisie was awed at this new idea.

'Or he might have been a docker or a groom! They weren't fussy, you know, Mama and her friends. For them free love and equality meant lifting their petticoats for any man who took their fancy.'

'She kept you. She didn't try to hide you.'

'She had her own money, or I might have finished up in Dr Barnardo's home in Moseley, or worse. Forget it, Maisie. I try to. I'm not proud of being a bastard.'

'You're so pretty your father must have been someone handsome.'

'I said forget it! I'm bored.'

'I wouldn't be bored if Paul Mandeville took me to dinner,' Maisie commented. 'But he never looks at me. Was it fun?'

'He's fun for a while, but when I wanted to drive out to the Lickeys afterwards he said he had to be up early the next day. So terribly ancient!'

'He works.'

'Yes, and that's boring too! I wish Andrew or Timothy were here.'

'Andrew works. When does he come back to Birmingham?'

'Playing a saxophone isn't work! He doesn't need to do it. It isn't serious. I don't know when he'll be back. In a few weeks, I think, when his band comes to the Theatre Royal. He never lets me know, says I can look in the theatre advertisements, as if I could be bothered. You can if you're interested. What shall we do today?'

'Let's go into town and have lunch. Then I want to do some Christmas shopping. And I saw an advertisement for a new compact, different compartments for powder and rouge and lipstick. Someone might have it.'

Kitty shrugged. 'If you want to. I might see if there's a new evening gown I like in Lewis's. It's much more fun to have it straight away instead of waiting ages until a dressmaker's finished it. By then I don't like it.'

Soon they were walking down the Hagley Road, having decided they needed some exercise.

'I've never been to Endersby's Hotel,' Maisie commented as they passed the long white-painted elegant building.

'Shall I suggest to Paul that he takes you on Saturday? Instead of me?'

'Kitty, you couldn't!'

'I could, but I don't think I'll be so self-sacrificing! Even Paul is better than no one.'

Nell insisted that Tom left her well before they reached her court. Even though it was dark now the street lights were good in the main roads. She didn't want prying neighbours speculating on where she'd been on a Sunday afternoon. She was angry with herself, knowing she ought not to have accepted Tom's invitation to tea. His parents had been kind, but Mrs Simmons had dropped some heavy hints about it being time Tom found himself a nice girl and settled down, and Mr Simmons had been jocular, insisting on kissing her when they left.

'You don't object to a fatherly kiss, do you, lass?' he'd boomed, clutching her shoulder so firmly that she'd had to submit.

She would make excuses next time, she vowed. She didn't want Tom, but had felt an obligation to Mrs Simmons and had let herself be persuaded. Taking a girl home was a declaration, and she wasn't at all ready for it. She had other ambitions now.

As she turned into the court she heard a strangled sob. Their one lamp was out again, but she could see someone huddling down outside the door.

'Who's there?' she called sharply, and suddenly two wet, bitterly cold hands clasped her own.

'Nell! We'm frit!'

'Benjy? Norman? What on earth's happened? Why are you so wet and cold?'

Norman's teeth were chattering so hard he couldn't speak, but Benjy stammered out an explanation. 'We was playin' by paper mill. Norm fell in canal. I 'ad ter jump in ter get 'im out!'

'Come in right away, and take off those wet clothes!' Nell snapped, but as she moved towards the door they hauled her back.

'Pa! 'E'll kill us! 'E said we weren't ter play there no more!'

'Go in the wash house then, and I'll bring you a towel!'

Luckily Pa was snoozing in front of the fire. Nell was able to take the thin towel out to her brothers, and despite their muffled protests rub them dry.

'Rub your hair now, and I'll see if I can get something for you to wear.'

All she could find were an old pair of working trousers Danny had discarded when he changed into his best ones before going out earlier in the day, and the old skirt she'd brought home from Kitty's house.

'I'm not wearin' gal's things!' Norman protested indignantly, feeling braver now he was dry.

'Then go in naked!' Nell said exasperatedly. 'All you've got to do is sneak past Pa — he's asleep — and get into bed. When he goes up to bed I'll spread these out in front of the fire, and hope they dry in time for school!'

Sometimes Paul was quite fun, Kitty admitted to herself a few days later when they were once more sitting in the spacious restaurant of Endersby's. Andrew had told her of the escapades Paul had indulged in during his years in the army and as a student, but she'd seen little of this lighter side. It was certainly a *coup* to have him as her escort. He seemed to know every other diner, and Kitty was aware of several envious looks from girls dining with their families or less handsome men.

When they were drinking coffee a tall, distinguished-looking man came across the room towards them. He wasn't much older than Paul but there were slight wings of grey in his dark hair.

'Paul, it's good to see you again. Marigold said you'd been in the other week. How is your mother?'

'Disliking the English winter after her trip to Australia. Have you met Miss Denver? Kitty, may I present Mr Richard Endersby?'

They exchanged a few polite remarks, then Paul asked where Mrs Endersby was. 'I thought she was usually here on Saturdays?'

'She is, but it's young Harry's first birthday tomorrow and she had the preparations for that to see to.'

'Is he a year old? It seems no time since Diana was born.'

'She's fourteen months older. And Dick is already nine. It's hard to believe.'

'You haven't a dance this evening,' Kitty interrupted. She thought only women talked about their offspring in such doting, sentimental tones. 'I thought you had one every Saturday?'

Mr Endersby turned towards her. 'Not tonight, but they will be regular from next week. I've hired a new band but they couldn't start tonight. They are so good I thought it was worth waiting for them, and I trust you'll agree.'

'We must come if you recommend them,' Paul nodded.

'Do you have anyone to demonstrate the new steps?' Kitty asked eagerly. This was more interesting than talk of babies.

'Actually, I'm letting a dancing school have the ballroom several times a week. The proprietors want to run more classes, both modern ballroom and stage dancing, where there is more room to practise. They will give occasional demonstrations on Saturdays. They seem very good.'

'Shall we come again next week?' Paul asked when Mr Endersby had moved on to speak to some other guests.

Paul was finding the task imposed on him by his mother more enjoyable than he had expected: Kitty could be as delightfully charming as she was often irritatingly perverse. It was doing him good to have some social life, he knew. He ought to go out more, though he never wanted again to sink into the whirl of pleasure he'd enjoyed as a student. It was odd. Although the suffering he'd seen during the war had originally inspired him to become a doctor, he could now rarely bring himself to recall the details. For years he'd been haunted by the memories of desperately mutilated men, limbs blown away, guts torn from their still-living bodies, screaming for relief no one could provide. He'd thought the stench of gas, mud and entrails which had clung to him, transferred from the bodies of the poor wretches he'd carried to safety, would never go away. They'd deserved the medals, not he. They had endured ordeals no one should be asked to undergo while he had acted from pure instinct. And the end had come, he knew, just in time for him. If he'd been forced to serve four whole years he doubted if he'd have retained his sanity, even had he survived. His wildness during the time of studying had been a way of forgetting, of filling every minute so that he had no leisure to remember the horrors of the trenches.

He dragged his attention back to Kitty, while mentally reassuring his mother that he was never likely to lose his heart to her.

'It might be amusing,' she said now. 'I wonder what sort of stage dancing they teach? I thought one had to start as soon as one could walk to do ballet.'

Pa had, as usual on Saturdays, rolled home roaring drunk. Nell lay tense, poised for flight, but he staggered no further than the room where he and Ma slept in the sagging iron-framed bed, with the babies on a mattress on the floor, and within minutes she heard him snoring loudly. She relaxed. She'd been prepared to go, but she felt guilty these days at leaving Amy to face Pa without her. Now she wouldn't have to make that agonizing choice. She was half asleep when noisy footsteps on the stairs brought her wide awake, sitting up in bed while Eth clutched her arm nervously.

'It's Danny an' Sam, blast 'em! They'll wake Pa!' Eth grumbled.

'They sound drunk too,' Nell muttered. 'They haven't come home drunk before.'

In fact, since the fight with Pa, they slept out of the house more often than not. She'd never asked where, but from sly hints Sam dropped she suspected they'd found a couple of girls who welcomed them into their beds.

'Bloody women! Dunno their own bleedin' minds,' Danny was saying as he staggered up the stairs.

'Mek 'em learn! Mek all bloody women learn!'

Their voices were slurred, and Nell could hear their boots scraping on the stairs, and the dull thuds as they crashed from side to side of the narrow staircase. Whichever one was in front kicked the door, and it slewed open on its single hinge, as drunkenly askew as they were. For once the lamp in the court outside the house was lit, and Nell could see the two boys clinging to each other, swaying precariously. Waves of beer and onion fumes wafted before them into the small room, and Nell felt like retching.

'Be careful, you'll wake Pa!' she said sharply.

'Oo, lissen ter posh Nellie! Thinks 'er's too good fer us,' Danny jeered.

'Mek 'er learn!' Sam suddenly thumped his brother on the shoulder 'Women! Learn 'em 'ere! We don't 'ave ter bother wi' shtuck-up judys loike that pair o' drabs in Sandpits. Know what I'm thinkin', Danny boy?'

'Women? 'Ere? Sam, you'm a bloody geniyus! Why should us 'ave ter goo out in cold when we've got women 'ere? Eth fer you, an' pretty little Nell fer me! Eh, Amy an' Fanny, an' rest on yer, out!'

Eth began to whimper, but Nell stood up to face her brothers as the younger ones scuttled past, Norman helped on his way by a kick from Sam. Amy herded in front of her the two little girls, Lily and Betty, who were wailing with fright after such a rude awakening.

'You're blind drunk, and talking obscene rubbish!' Nell stormed at them, trying not to show how frightened she was. Frightened? Of her own brothers? She was often frightened of Pa, but never before had any reason to believe her brothers might harm her. But they were too incapably drunk to know what they were doing. She looked round for a weapon, but there was none. Sam had already pushed Eth down on her bed, and was tearing at her ragged petticoat, while Eth sobbed and pleaded with him to stop.

Nell circled in the small space available as Danny lunged towards her. She dragged at the curtain which divided the room into two, and as it fell it impeded him for a precious moment. Taking her chance she stooped and reached under the bed for the heavy chamberpot. Danny had been stretching out for her and overbalanced as she bent down, and she had time to stand up, raise the chamberpot in both hands, and bring it crashing on to his head. She didn't wait to see whether he was knocked out, but grabbed the largest piece of the ruined pot and advanced purposefully on Sam. He, heedless of all but his need to control Eth, had torn her underwear into shreds and was struggling to unbutton his flies.

'Get out of here, or you won't ever be able to do anything to a girl again!' Nell threatened, grabbing him by the shoulder.

He staggered and rolled off Eth, who scrambled swiftly as far away from him as she could and cowered against the wall. Nell brandished her improvised weapon, and as Sam stretched out his hand to try and take it from her she slashed down at his arm.

'Next time it'll be somewhere a lot more painful!' she threatened.

'Yer rotten bleedin' cow!' he gasped as blood began to pour from the wound.

For some time Nell had been vaguely aware of shouts from the other room and now, with a moment to pause, she realized it was Amy screaming at Pa to wake up and save Nell. Then she heard Pa's voice and he came staggering through the door.

'Yer've killed Danny an' nearly crippled me, yer blasted bitch!' Sam said viciously, but to Nell's relief Danny began to groan and rolled over on the bed where he'd fallen.

'Wassamarrer?' Pa asked. He was almost as drunk as the boys.

'They was goin' ter mek us –' Eth stopped. Even in this extremity she couldn't quite bring herself either to believe or speak about what had so nearly happened. Instead she burst into tears and clung to Nell.

'Gerrout! Don't ever come back 'ere again!' Pa roared, and as Sam, holding on to the gaping tear in his arm, stared stupidly at him, Pa took him by the shoulder and bodily threw him down the stairs. Then he turned to Danny, who was sitting groggily on the bed holding his head and groaning.

'Albert, don't 'urt 'em!' Ma was wailing, but Pa took no notice and heaved an unresisting Danny to his feet and through the door.

It was then he noticed the mess of broken pottery and worse on the bed.

'An' who did that?' he demanded angrily. 'Who's ruined a dacent mattress an' blankets? An' a good pisspot!'

'It were Nell, Pa,' Eth whimpered. ''Er was stoppin' Danny from –' Again she dissolved into tears, and Pa glared at Nell.

'I'm tekin' me belt ter you, me gal. It's time you learned 'oo was boss.'

He turned to go downstairs, where there was a considerable commotion as Ma berated the boys while she tried to stem the bleeding from Sam's arm, and Sam, by now sober and afraid of what they had tried to do, urged Danny to get on with it and come quick.

Nell didn't dare trust that Pa would be diverted, nor that he would listen to her explanation. He hadn't had a fight tonight and would take out all his spleen on her. Within seconds she was out of the window, and then running as fast as she could away from the court. She had to avoid her brothers too, now. Even if, when sober, they felt ashamed of what they'd tried to do, they might still want to retaliate.

'Oh, it's you, I hoped it would be! Thank goodness. I'm late, I just couldn't run, and Miss Fremling said she'd dismiss me if it happened again.'

Nell was panting as she hung up her coat. Then a bout of coughing made her double up in agony, and it was some time before she could catch her breath. Gwyneth guided her to a chair and fetched a glass of water.

'Sit down and drink this. You don't look fit to be at work anyway, you're feverish.' She looked concerned. Over the past two weeks she'd talked with Nell several times, and found she had more in common with her than she did with Lizzie or any of her fellow pupils at the dancing school.

'It's just a cold. I'll be all right. I must be. I can't afford to be ill.'

'Here, I bought some buns, have one with your tea.'

Nell licked her lips. They looked good and she was hungry. 'I oughtn't. You're always buying me cakes, but I can't pay you back.'

'I don't want payment. We're friends, aren't we?'

'How can we be? We're different.'

Gwyneth laughed. 'What do you mean?'

Nell shrugged. 'You've been to a good school, your father's a minister, while I live in a slum.'

'That has nothing to do with it! Where we live or what our fathers are doesn't matter a scrap. I like you, Nell. Isn't that enough?'

There was something about Nell which made her special. Gwyneth suspected her life was very hard, more from what she avoided saying than the few details she revealed. When she was relaxed she could be amazingly funny, as on the occasion when she had mimicked an elderly bespatted gentleman who had been staring at them through the glass of the door, and when he'd seen them looking at him had scuttled away in haste, getting hopelessly entangled between his walking stick and umbrella.

Nell smiled. 'Thanks,' she said shyly, then caught sight of the clock. 'Oh, I haven't time for tea, I'm late already. I'll keep you late if I don't finish on time.'

'It doesn't bother me.' She poured out the tea and handed Nell the cup. 'Why do you have to run to get here on time?'

'I don't finish in the factory till half past seven, much later some nights if the foreman's being nasty, and I have to be here by eight. I always have to run some of the way.'

'You do another job all day and then work here every evening?' Gwyneth was horrified. Nell hadn't told her this. Nell nodded, holding the cup in both hands to warm herself. She shivered and leaned her head back against the wall. 'But you're ill! Do you have to work so hard?'

'I need to earn enough money to get away,' Nell admitted. 'But it's taking such a long time! Sometimes I think I'll never do it.'

'Get away? From where?'

'Home.'

Gwyneth frowned. 'That's two of us. I ran away from home too. But if you have a job in the daytime as well as here surely you can afford to rent a room somewhere?'

Nell shook her head wearily. She was feeling utterly drained. Doing two jobs was more exhausting than she'd imagined, and by the time she got home at night it was long after ten. It was all she could do to drag her feet up the stairs and collapse into bed. These days she slept so heavily not even the tossing of Eth or the snoring of the boys kept her awake. She hadn't even had the energy to think about the fight on Saturday, though she had felt a mild surprise that Pa hadn't commented on her disappearance. Perhaps Ma had distracted him. Eth was being difficult and wouldn't tell her anything, but Amy knew only that Pa had gone to bed after throwing out the boys and barring the door.

After she'd escaped through the window Nell had spent the night huddled in a leaking storage shed behind a shop in

Monument Road. She'd been too tired to try and find one of the refuges she'd seen on her first foray into the wealthier district, but it had been a bitterly cold night, with a touch of frost, and by the morning she had been stiff and aching, her chest constricted as if with tightly tied ropes. Two days later it was difficult to draw breath and her legs didn't seem able to obey her instructions to move.

'I must scrub this floor. It's so dirty after all the rain.'

'You've plenty of time. Of course, if you don't want to tell me I won't pry, but perhaps I can help.'

'My boss gives my wages at the factory to Pa,' she explained. 'I don't have any for myself except what I earn here. He doesn't know about this job.'

Gwyneth stared at her in amazement, both her anger and compassion stirred. 'That's monstrous!'

'I need to save enough so that I can pay for a room while I look for another job,' Nell went on. 'I can't stay there, you see. But it'll take months, and if I lose this job I may not be able to find another in the evenings.'

'And if you come straight here you haven't had time to eat since dinnertime. No wonder you're so thin!'

Nell shrugged. She didn't see any point in telling her new friend that she rarely had more for dinner than a crust of dry bread and a half-rotten apple thrown out by the shops.

'I must get on.'

Half an hour later she looked up, startled. Gwyneth had on her coat. 'Is it time to finish? I must have been asleep. I've only scrubbed half the floor!'

'I want to slip out for a few minutes. It's early yet. Lock the door after me and let me in when I come back.'

'Won't Miss Fremling mind? You could get into trouble.'

'Miss Fremling has other things to think about. I saw her with a man on Saturday, and I believe she's with him on the nights she asks me to stay here. She's much more human these days, too.' Gwyneth giggled. 'Will you be all right on your own?'

Nell nodded. It crossed her mind that she could easily steal and sell some of these expensive gowns to raise the money she needed, and she wondered whether Gwyneth had considered the possibility. She went on scrubbing mechanically, too weary to know how long the other girl was gone. When the tap came on the door she jumped nervously, then saw Gwyneth carrying a small parcel and went to let her in.

'Here, hot pies for both of us,' Gwyneth said, 'and I'll make some more tea. Stop that scrubbing now, you've almost done and it won't take long to finish.'

The aroma made Nell feel faint, and she had to make a tremendous effort to move towards the table where Gwyneth was setting out plates and knives and forks. As the hot flaky pastry crumbled and the thick brown gravy oozed out, she sighed and lifted a forkful of vegetables towards her mouth. Ten minutes later every crumb had gone.

'I haven't had food like that since I lived with my gran,' Nell said, and suddenly burst into floods of tears. 'I didn't know people could be so kind!' she sobbed as Gwyneth, alarmed, sprang up to put her arms round the younger girl's shoulders.

'Nell, don't cry! You're all right now! Here, use my handkerchief. Let's have a cup of tea.'

'I'm sorry,' Nell whispered. 'I'm so sorry. Thank you. Just look at the time! I won't be finished till midnight, I'm so slow today!'

'You'll sit there while I finish for you,' Gwyneth ordered. 'You aren't fit to do such hard work, and afterwards I want to tell you my plan.'

'I'm so glad I came to the classes with you, Kitty. I wish you would too, Fleur,' Maisie said as they walked down the Hagley Road towards Broad Street.

'I prefer to go shopping,' Fleur said, tossing her head.

'Leave Fleur alone if she chooses to be standoffish,' Kitty said cheerfully. 'I think Mr Bliss is a very good teacher and we will be having the benefit, Maisie, it's Fleur's loss. Let's all go to the Tower on Saturday. I want to practise in a big ballroom.'

Maisie giggled, then shook her head. 'We couldn't, Kitty! Not a public ballroom! Mother wouldn't permit it!'

'Don't tell her you're going.'

'But — we always have to say where we're going and with whom!'

A few minutes later Maisie stopped to speak to an old school friend and Fleur drew Kitty aside.

'I'll come to the Tower,' she whispered. 'But don't tell Maisie, or she'd give me away!'

Kitty grinned at her. 'No fear! Good for you, Fleur! You've got heaps more spunk.'

Fleur preened. 'Did you know Maisie wants to go to the stage classes too?'

'Maisie? Stage classes? What a hoot!' Kitty laughed. 'Don't say I told you, but she can't even do the waltz properly. Does she fancy herself in a chorus line?'

'I don't know. She'd never be permitted to do it, so I don't see why she wants the bother of extra classes.'

'Perhaps she's fallen for Mr Bliss! He thinks he's the very devil of a fellow!' Kitty almost doubled up with laughter. 'Saturday, then, where shall we meet? Quickly, Maisie's coming.'

Chapter Seven

'WHAT is the difference between the brush and the hesitation? Miss Baxter?' Nell bit her lip. She'd been concentrating so hard on memorizing the order in which to put her feet for the feather step, and when to use contrary body movement, she'd forgotten Mr Bliss's habit of barking questions at his students.

'Oh. In the hesitation there's more of a pause when you bring one foot up to the other, before moving it on again.'

'And the weight?'

'You don't change from the first foot in either.'

'Good! And the chassé?'

'You can change weight from one foot to the other after they're brought together.'

'We will demonstrate. Come.'

Nell looked apprehensive. It was the first time during the six weeks she'd been attending Mr Bliss's dancing classes that he had singled her out for demonstrating to the others. She was the newest pupil, and only Gwyneth's determined coaching had made it possible for her to join the class at all.

Afterwards, as she waited for Gwyneth's more advanced class to finish so that they could walk home together, she reflected on how much she owed her friend. They had by now become very close, drawn together by the fact they both had fathers impossible to live with, but also by their obsession with dancing. She had been on the verge of despair, thinking she could never scrape together enough money to leave home, when Gwyneth had made her incredible suggestion the night Nell had nearly collapsed in the dress shop.

'There's a room free where I live,' she'd said when Nell's sobs had finished. 'It's only a small one next to mine, not much more than a cupboard, but there's a bed and a table. I'm sure my landlady would let you have it for three or four shillings, even half a crown.'

Nell was making swift calculations. 'I've saved just over a pound. That would be enough for rent and food and coal for two or three weeks, until I could get another daytime job.'

'You already have this one. Your family know nothing about it?'

'No, or he'd soon take the money from me.'

'Where is your money? Do you have to go home for it? And what about clothes?'

Nell shook her head and smiled faintly. 'I don't have any other clothes. As for my money, I have to keep it with me or someone else would find it and steal it.'

'Then let's finish here and go and see my landlady. It will be good to have a friend.'

Nell felt qualms about leaving Amy, but hung on to the idea that only if she got away could she ever help her little sister. By the time they reached Gwyneth's lodging house and arranged for Nell to take the room she was shivering uncontrollably, incapable of thinking properly. Gwyneth made up a fire in the tiny grate, and aired one of her own warm flannelette nightgowns before it.

'Take your clothes off, they feel damp, and get into this, then straight into bed.'

The following day Nell was scarcely able to move, and for several days Gwyneth was on the verge of calling a doctor. What had she done, she wondered, persuading a girl she hardly knew to abandon her home and job? But she liked Nell, was horrified by her story, and her plight made her determined to help. After all, she thought wryly, her father was always preaching about giving succour.

Nell soon began to recover, though, with the good food and the warmth Gwyneth provided. By the end of the week she was fretting to begin looking for a new job.

'Miss Fremling will have sacked me by now,' she worried, as she and Gwyneth sat in front of the fire on Sunday afternoon.

'No, she won't. I told her you were ill and offered to do some of the work until you were well enough to go back. She let me sweep and dust, and though the linoleum isn't polished like you kept it it's still presentable.'

'I must find something in the daytime.'

'What did you do before?'

'I worked a press, stamping out the metal shapes for buttons.'

'Do you want to do that again? Isn't it hard work?'

'It's easier with the power presses, but they're dangerous, you have to watch them every second or they could chop your hand off. I was so tired the last few weeks I was thankful I didn't have one of them.'

'There are lots of small factories, and I've seen notices outside advertising for girls and women. I suppose they pay them less than a man. The unions aren't interested in fighting for women's wages.'

'I won't go back to Ladywood, someone would recognize me and tell my pa. I might try somewhere in Hockley, in the jewellery workshops.'

'You could work in a shop. You speak well, and Miss Fremling says that's the most important thing. Why don't you have the same sort of accent as most of the people round here?'

'Oi can talk loike folks born in Brummagem!' Nell said with a slight laugh. 'Or like you, girl, with your lovely lilting Welsh voice that sounds like music, do you see. And actually, darling, I think your accent is simply terribly divine!'

Gwyneth laughed. 'How on earth do you do it?'

'In the first place I wasn't born here, we lived in Walsall. That's really the Black Country, the accent's slightly different. When I was three my grandparents took me to live with them. I nearly died. I caught diphtheria, and Ma had Sammy and Eth by then, with Benjy on the way, as well as my three older brothers. They might all have caught it. They, my grandparents, lived in the country, in Sutton Coldfield, and after I got better I was still not strong so they kept me.'

'But surely they were neither Welsh nor spoke like the gentry?'

'No, but somehow I can imitate anyone. Gramps was coachman to a very rich family, and they often had foreign friends to stay, Americans and French, mainly. I used to listen to them, and Gramps encouraged me to try and copy how they spoke. He liked me to sing and dance for him, and pretend to be different people. It made him laugh, though Gran used to be annoyed, said it would get me into trouble.'

'Why did you come home?' Gwyneth asked gently.

'Gramps died three years ago, and though Gran was allowed to stay on in the cottage she seemed to have given up trying. Six months later, just before I was fourteen, she went to put some roses on his grave, came home and went to bed early. The next morning she didn't call me for school and when I went into her room she was dead. Pa came and fetched me home. They'd moved around a lot, but he'd just got a job in Ladywood. I was old enough to go out to work and he wanted my wages. Not me, I was just another mouth to feed.'

'Poor Nell! But you could work in a shop. I'm sure Miss Fremling would give you a good reference. She's not such a battle-axe as she makes out. I think she's like that just to make herself appear tough.'

Two days later Nell obtained a job in a bakery. It wasn't as clean as Gwyneth's gown shop, with the flour and the crumbs and sticky cakes, but it had the enormous advantage that she was allowed to bring home left-over bread and pies, and this was usually enough to provide both girls with at least one meal a day.

She was earning enough to give up the evening job, pay rent for her tiny room, and buy cheap clothes from the Bull Ring market. When Gwyneth discovered Nell was swift to learn the dance steps she was herself practising, she persuaded her to join Mr Bliss's classes. Within two weeks Nell was allowed to join the stage class too. She was ecstatic, and several times the lodgers on the floor beneath complained at the noise as the two girls practised together.

'Take no notice,' Gwyneth laughed. 'Soon we'll be able to give up the shops and become real stage dancers. I've got tickets for the pantomime, only shilling ones in the gallery, but we can look at a real troupe of dancers. It's my Christmas present to you. Now let's go through that routine again.'

'Girls, watch the way I turn out my knees while I point my toes together,' Nell instantly said in a superb imitation of Frank Bliss's rather precise, clipped tones, and waddled across the room with her arms supporting an imaginary partner. 'Now kick, higher, higher, higher! Miss Davis, be careful of the light bulbs! We can't afford to replace any more!

'Oh, Frank,' she breathed in Edwina's soft West Country burr. 'Give them a rest! They'll be collapsing from exhaustion, littering the floor, and we won't have time to carry them all out of the studio before the next class!'

'Stop it!' Gwyneth gasped, doubled up with laughter. 'I can't breathe properly!'

Nell was such fun, she thought later as she lay in bed. She'd never had a sister to share jokes with, and her father had considered them too good to mix with the villagers, so she rarely played with their children outside school. It had been a good day when she'd suggested Nell came to live in the same house.

'My dear young lady, I only take experienced modern ballroom dancers into my stage classes,' Frank Bliss said yet again, trying to keep his patience. Some of these upper-class girls with their imperious voices and absolute confidence seemed to think they could order everyone about.

'You don't know how experienced I am,' Kitty replied. 'Won't you let me show you?'

She darted across to the gramophone and began to wind it up. As the music filled Endersby's ballroom she came back, smiling seductively as she sidled close to him. Frank shrugged. She was slender, yet shapely, and it wasn't often such a haughty young piece was actually begging to be taken into his arms. He didn't need to pull her close. She moulded herself against him, and he had to remind himself he was supposed to be testing her dancing skills. They swayed to the tune of a waltz, and when the music changed into foxtrot rhythm Kitty altered step without faltering.

'Don't you want to teach me — other things?' she murmured, lifting up her face to his as the music came to a close.

'Perhaps, soon,' he muttered, breaking away from the tantalizing attraction of her perfume. 'You are very good — a very good dancer, Miss Denver, and after you have been in the ballroom class for a few more weeks you will almost certainly be competent enough to join the stage class. The elementary one,' he added cautiously.

Kitty suppressed an irritated sigh. Instead she looked up through her long silky eyelashes, and placed one of her slender hands, the nails painted a delicate pink, on his arm. 'I don't want to wait,' she said huskily. 'Perhaps if I came to your house for private lessons I would be ready for the stage class sooner?'

He resisted temptation. There were far too many people in his house. 'It wouldn't be convenient, I'm afraid,' he said curtly. 'I have an increasing number of classes now I am using this ballroom, and I don't give private stage lessons, just a few for special students who want extra ballroom tuition.'

'I'm sure it would help if I had extra tuition in ballroom dances,' Kitty suggested. He tried to move away but her clasp on his arm tightened and she swayed towards him. 'You could come to my house. There's never anyone there except our housekeeper. My mother's away, and we have a very good gramophone.'

He capitulated, but there was a look in Kitty's eye he distrusted. He dared not be caught alone with her. There had been enough of that sort of trouble when he'd been teaching in Bristol. 'We'll see. Suppose you join the stage class here on Wednesday afternoons? On probation, as it were? After a month we'll discuss it again and see whether you are able to keep up with the others. They've all had more lessons than you have.'

'But probably not as much – experience,' Kitty said sweetly. 'Thank you, Mr Bliss. I won't forget your kindness.'

'You're going to join the stage class?' Maisie was almost incoherent with fury.

'Why not, if Mr Bliss thinks I have talent?' Kitty drawled.

'You're no better than I am, and he wouldn't let me join!'

'Maisie, you can't be as good! Kitty's brilliant! She had all sorts of people admiring her at the Tower again on Saturday, and always had dozens of partners to choose from,' Fleur put in.

'The Tower? You didn't go to the Tower, Fleur!' Maisie exclaimed, distracted.

'Oh, don't be stuffy!' Kitty retorted. 'Why shouldn't she if she wants to?'

Maisie turned on her. 'Because if she gets entangled with your sort, Kitty Denver, she'll soon be no better than you!'

'What exactly do you mean by that?' Kitty asked, her eyes glittering.

'It's not fair you get into the stage class and I don't! I'm as good as you are, better, in fact, so why did he choose you? Did you offer to go to bed with him? Blood will out, I suppose!'

'Kitty, you didn't, did you?' Fleur was astounded.

'How else could she get such favouritism?' Maisie demanded, her face mottled red with fury.

Fleur instinctively drew away from Kitty, and looked at her in horrified fascination. Kitty shrugged her shoulders.

'I did nothing of the sort. Fleur, we were going shopping for some new shoes. Shall we be off?'

Fleur gazed unhappily at her. 'I – I'm sorry, Kitty, I have a headache. I'd better lie down.'

*

'You have a pretty dress and you ought to try it out at a dance,' Gwyneth declared as she finished sewing on the fringe of long red tassels to the edge of the dress.

'I've never before had anything so beautiful! You've been so good to me!' Nell exclaimed. She recalled the over-large dress Tom's mother had lent her, and cringed as she thought how unfashionable it had been. Yet at the time she had been so pleased to wear it. She truly wasn't being ungrateful, it had been kind of Mrs Simmons to lend it to her, but now, as she walked to and from her new job in the centre of Birmingham, she saw how really fashionable women dressed.

'Let's go to the Palais on Saturday.'

'That's in Monument Road, it's too near where I used to live,' Nell said swiftly.

'Of course, I'm sorry. I forgot.'

'If anyone I knew saw me, and told Pa, he might find me.'

'Are you still afraid? He couldn't make you go back home.'

'No, I suppose not,' Nell said slowly. 'It's so fabulous, like waking up from a nightmare, to be free. But I'm sure he'd try to force me back.'

'We won't risk it. We can go to Tony's, by the Hippodrome.'

For the first hour of the dance Nell floated in a dream. Neither she nor Gwyneth lacked partners, but most of them had only a rudimentary idea of the proper steps and stumbled round the floor more or less in time to the music.

Despite this Nell was in a cloud of happiness. For the first time in her adult life she felt she looked attractive. Instead of the outgrown rags she had worn until her adventure in the stable, and then the clothes Kitty had given her, she had something made especially for her, something new, something she had bought with money she had earned. She held her head high, and had no need of cosmetics to brighten her eyes and make her cheeks glow. Then the bubble burst.

'I thought it was you! Even though you've had all your lovely hair cut off into this ugly shingle style.'

She swung round, her hand covering her mouth to suppress the cry of dismay. 'Tom!'

'Where on earth have you been, Nell?' Tom demanded, in his agitation grasping her arm until his fingers bit into the soft flesh and Nell cried out to him to let her go.

'I found a room, and another job,' Nell told him, looking round for Gwyneth, but her friend was talking to a group of people at the far side of the ballroom.

'A well-paid one, by the look of this fancy dress,' he said sternly. 'It must have cost a great deal.'

'My friend made it for me.'

'Made it? What friend? Are you sure you don't mean a man friend, and he bought it for you?'

'No I don't! I met Gwyneth at work, and have a room in the same house! How dare you suggest something disreputable!' Nell flared.

Tom was instantly contrite. 'Nell, I'm sorry! I've been beside myself with worry, not knowing what had happened to you. I've been thinking all sorts of dreadful things. But you're looking well, better than before.'

'Thank you. How is – everybody?'

'Your pa nearly went mad when he realized you'd gone, and he couldn't find you. He discovered we'd been out together, and came round to our house, demanding we give you back to him. Luckily my father was there and threatened to call the police if he didn't go away.'

'Tom, I'm sorry! I didn't think he'd care whether I left or not, apart from losing my wages.'

'He felt you'd made a laughing stock of him, I suppose. But after a week or so he calmed down and went round trying to convince everyone you'd run off with all his savings. No one believed him, naturally, they know he hasn't two pennies to rub together after he's been in the Ryland Arms or the Turf.'

'What about Ma, and the little ones?' Nell asked quietly. 'I do feel bad about not telling them where I live, but if they knew he'd very likely beat it out of them. Ma always said it was wiser not to have secrets if we didn't want him to find out about them.'

'She's probably right. I don't know how she can bear to stay with such a brute!'

Nell shook her head sadly. 'What can she do? There's nowhere for her to go, and how could she possibly manage on her own with all the children to feed? He couldn't always have been like this. Surely not, or she couldn't ever have loved him!'

At that moment Gwyneth returned, and Nell introduced Tom as an old friend.

'Oh, dear, we hoped to avoid Nell's old friends,' Gwyneth said cheerfully. 'You won't peach on her, will you? You won't tell her father where she is?'

'I don't know where she's working or living,' Tom said stiffly, 'so I can hardly give her away. Besides, I'm not working at the same place as he is now.'

'Good. It's best you're kept in ignorance, then you can't tell anyone accidentally.'

'I am capable of holding my tongue!'

'Yes, of course, Tom,' Nell reassured him. 'Where are you working now?'

'I've obtained a post with the Railway Union, the same offices where my father works. Nell, I must see you again, I still meant what I said.'

'I hope you didn't tell him where we live, he looked a sanctimonious prig!' Gwyneth muttered as they walked along Corporation Street.

Nell laughed slightly. 'No. I said I might go to the dance most weeks. Poor Tom. He means well, and he was kind to me. He took me out several times, and he wanted to marry me. It would have been a way out, but somehow I simply can't bear the idea of being married, especially to Tom.'

'Marriage is a trap, and with him you'd have regretted it more than with most!'

'At least I can always be grateful to him for taking me to my first dance. If he hadn't, perhaps I'd never have got the courage to escape. Now I can't imagine life without dancing.'

Chapter Eight

'ANYONE home? Kitty! Meggy! I'm back.'

Meggy came out of the kitchen as Kitty hurtled down the stairs and threw herself into Andrew's arms.

'Why didn't you let us know?' they both demanded, and Meggy began to fuss about airing his bed and cooking a proper meal for him, while Kitty wanted to know where he had been and how long he was staying.

'As a matter of fact, I shall be in Birmingham for a longish time, so I mean to find somewhere, a small apartment, where I can stay. I can't impose on you and Meggy for months,' he said after Meggy had returned to the kitchen and Kitty had gone to the drinks table and mixed a Stinger.

'Why on earth not? I'm bored with no one else living here.'

'Perhaps, but while it might be acceptable for me to stay here for a week or two when I've an engagement at one of the theatres in Birmingham, living here for months would not exactly enhance your reputation, my dear cousin.'

'What reputation?' Kitty asked sharply. 'Do you really think a bastard with no known father and an absentee mother who's an ex-jailbird suffragette has any reputation to lose?'

'You are yourself, Kitty, not what your parents were.'

'Oh yes? Tell that to the stuffy old matrons in London who warn their daughters I'm contaminated, and refuse to invite me to their parties, and dirty old men old enough to be my father who think I'm like my mother, ready to jump into anyone's bed! Maybe one of them is my father!' she added bitterly. 'Why do you think I bury myself here? At least I have a few friends here in Edgbaston who don't turn up their noses at me.'

'You exaggerate, darling. But that's beside the point. I shall be working. Some friends and I have formed a dance band, and I can't have Meggy sitting up all hours every night waiting for me to come home.'

'A dance band? Andrew, how simply marvellous! So you won't be dashing all round the country playing at different theatres every week. Where will you be playing? At the Tower? Where?'

'At Endersby's ballroom, actually, for three nights a week. And possibly at tea dances too. They are becoming very popular, and Mr Endersby plans to increase that side of the business. He means to open ballrooms at some of their other hotels, and if they are successful maybe separate dance halls too. As well as playing in the band I will be advising him. And we will be playing at private functions at the Grand and the Botanical Gardens.'

'I've joined a dancing class at Endersby's,' Kitty said eagerly.

'You? But you can dance very well already. Why do you need to go to classes?'

'Not ballroom dancing, though I mean to keep those classes on too. There's an enormous amount I don't know, and new steps being invented all the time. As a matter of fact, darling, I'm doing stage dancing too.'

'Stage dancing? Kitty, you can't! That would completely ruin your reputation!'

'Why do you have this sudden interest in my reputation?' she demanded angrily, stamping her foot. 'I'll do what I like, and I won't be preached at! You're only my cousin, not my brother! At least Mama didn't saddle me with that horror!'

'It's precisely because you have neither father nor brother, and a totally feckless mother, that I feel some responsibility towards you,' he said, angry in his turn. 'Don't you want to make a respectable marriage? Or do you mean to go the same way as your mother? It's neither a happy nor a satisfying life, as I'm sure she'd tell you if she loved you at all!'

'Get out!' Kitty suddenly lost her temper completely and screamed at him hysterically. 'I *was* planning to marry you, but if all you can think about is conferring respectability on me by the generous gift of your precious name, then I don't want you!' She threw herself down on the floor, beating her fists into the thick rug.

Andrew stared down at her in bewilderment, then shrugged. 'My name happens to be the same as yours,' he said mildly. 'Even if it weren't, though, and even had we not been cousins, I would never have considered bestowing it on you. You are fun to be with, Kitty, except when you're in a tantrum, but when I marry it will be to someone quite different.'

As he turned to leave the room he met Meggy at the door.

'Your room's ready, Master Andrew, and I'll have dinner on the table in half an hour.'

'I'm sorry, Meggy, I can't stay. Look after Kitty, would you?'

'Please, can you tell me the way to the ballroom? Oh, Miss Denver, it's you!'

Kitty swung round and cried out in delight. 'Nell! It is Nell, isn't it? You look so different with your hair cut. What are you doing here at Endersby's?'

Nell smiled shyly back at her. 'I'm going to one of Mr Bliss's stage classes.'

'So am I! What a marvellous coincidence. It's this way, down this corridor. There's an outside entrance, but this way is quicker. I've often wondered what happened to you. You're looking better now, not so thin.'

'I ran away from home. It was only possible because of you and the lovely clothes you gave me,' Nell explained. 'I was respectable enough to get a job, so I could save some money, and then I met Gwyneth, and she helped me run away from home, and to join the classes. I've never stopped being grateful to you.'

Kitty beamed. 'You'll have to tell me everything. There isn't time now, but we'll have a pot of tea and some cakes afterwards. Can you stay?'

Nell nodded shyly. It was daunting enough having to enter such a magnificent hotel as Endersby's, now Mr Bliss held some of his classes here, and even more so to contemplate sitting in one of the rooms having waiters bringing tea in the elegant silver and china they surely used. But she'd promised to wait for Gwyneth who was in the later, more advanced class, and with Kitty to show her how to go on she knew she would not be nervous.

Afterwards they chatted away eagerly, Nell telling Kitty all about Gwyneth and her new life. She repeatedly stressed that it would never have happened without the clothes Kitty had given her, and Kitty glowed with the remembered satisfaction of being generous.

'Did you know Andrew is going to be playing here, at their dances?' she said suddenly.

'Andrew? Your cousin? No, it's the first time I've even been here. Is he staying with you?'

Kitty frowned. 'No, he flew into a pet when he heard I wanted to go on the stage, and stormed out. I haven't seen him since. He says it will damage my reputation, the idiot! Why he can do it but not me he didn't wait to explain!'

'I don't see why you shouldn't if you want to,' Nell declared. 'It's supposed to be a different world now, with more chances for women. But does Andrew think all women on the stage are – well, disreputable?'

'I suppose so. Silly man. Golly, is that the time? I must fly. See you next week.'

'Nell, it's time you bought a new hat.'

Nell looked ruefully at the one she was trying, yet again, to make more fashionable. She stuck it on her head and began to pull faces at the mirror. 'I can't get it right! I've taken off the feathers and cut off part of the brim, but it still doesn't look like those gorgeous cloche hats we saw in Greys. Like the ones in that film.' She struck an attitude, clasping her hands in front of her and looking beseechingly at an imaginary partner.

'You can afford something now.'

'Not from Greys!'

'Well, no, perhaps they are a bit expensive. But we could go to the Co-op. They're bound to have the Clara Bow style. One in velvet would look nice.'

Nell felt ungrateful to be discarding Kitty's gift, but the hat really was so old fashioned she now felt dowdy in it. She marvelled at herself. Only six months ago she'd been thankful to have anything, however ragged, to wear. Now she could afford to be particular, actually to consider style and fashion.

'Come on then! Before I change my mind!'

'I think our luck has changed,' Frank gloated as he and Edwina walked home from Endersby's one frosty night. 'It's so much better working the good classes in the ballroom, and Mr Endersby is prepared to rent it to us for another day.'

'And you have several bookings for The Bliss Blondies. That was a good name for the stage troupe.'

'Yes, that side is going well too. Gwyneth Davis was disappointed not to be included, but she's much too dark. I promised her I would soon be able to get a troupe of brunettes together.'

'Her young friend Nell Baxter might be good enough, she's a natural in the stage class and has worked very hard to learn the steps,' Edwina suggested. She had a soft spot for Nell, recognizing in the girl someone from a similar background to her own who had the talent to escape.

'Possibly, and that haughty Kitty Denver could be good if she paid more attention, though she hasn't the same strict grounding as the others. It doesn't mean so much to her, and I'm not sure she understands how hard a life it can be on the stage.'

'I doubt if she'll stay. But why not put her in to start with, and by the time she gives up, if she does, you'll have someone else to take her place. Could you manage with a line of ten?'

'For the bookings at the smaller theatres it would be better. Eight might be enough, sometimes, and I might even try to devise a speciality act with the three of them. They can all sing well.'

'And Nell is a marvellous mimic. I overheard her entertaining the other girls one day, she'd been to a review at the Empire and was showing them some of the acts.'

'Let's promote Nell and Kitty to the advanced stage class and watch them, see how they work together. We could put them in a longer line first, then decide about something smaller after they've had a few professional engagements.'

The opportunity for a professional booking came sooner than he or Edwina had hoped. After just a few lessons with the enlarged stage class Mrs Endersby asked to see Frank.

'I hope you don't mind,' she said when he was seated in her office drinking coffee, 'but I've been watching the girls. My husband and I are planning a special series of dinner dances with entertainment for the guests during dinner. It would be a longer programme than the normal exhibition dances you and Mrs Bliss do. I wondered if some of your girls would be able to perform too. Just half a dozen of them, since the ballroom is not very large with tables set out all round.'

He put on what he considered his irresistible smile and smoothed his moustache. Mrs Endersby was very young and very lovely, with her deep golden hair, bobbed in the latest style, and her almost ethereal air which often misled people into underestimating her considerable business acumen and iron determination. He'd heard stories about how she had built up a chain of hotels during and immediately after the war, when for some reason her husband had been detained in Germany. She couldn't have been more than a girl then, and she didn't look more than twenty now, despite her three children.

'It would be a wonderful experience for them,' he said slowly.

'I will pay the appropriate fee, both for you and the girls,' Mrs Endersby went on. 'Our new band is so good we want to do something different to display their talent, but solos by the boys would not be varied enough. Would you think it over and next week we can discuss your suggestions?'

'This is the answer,' Frank said exultantly that night as he and Edwina lay in bed. 'We spread the word, get some of the theatre managers to come and see them, and bookings will be flooding in! And I've thought of another name, The Bliss Beauties. Tomorrow we'll work out a really special routine for them. And we'll have to hire someone to design costumes. This is no time for economies, we must have the best!'

'You can't leave the troupe now, Kitty!' Gwyneth said persuasively. Through Nell she'd come to know Kitty well, since the three of them had developed the habit of going to the Kardomah café after classes, where they talked about dancing, the films they saw, and their dreams of life on the stage.

'I can if I choose to! And if that dreadful girl Jane tries to make fun of me once more I shall!'

Edwina sighed. 'Kitty, she was just angry because you missed that step. You started off on the wrong foot.'

'I couldn't help it! I've only done that sequence once before!'

'That's the problem,' Gwyneth said slowly. 'You're very good, Kitty, but you've had less practice than the rest of us, and it's not surprising you don't remember it all straight away. Can we go through it out of class sometime?'

'I'd like to do it too,' Nell said eagerly. 'I don't know it as well as the rest do, and I made some mistakes today. And we've only got a week before the performance. That has to be perfect.'

'Isn't the studio empty sometimes now there are so many classes at the hotel?' Gwyneth asked Edwina. 'Would Mr Bliss permit us to use it? Just the three of us? That would be enough to practise the routines. We could use a gramophone, we wouldn't need the pianist.'

'I'll arrange it. When can you all come?'

'As soon as possible, and every time the studio is free. Is that all right with you, Kitty?'

Kitty forced herself to smile. She didn't want to leave the stage troupe, it would give Maisie such pleasure. She knew she could be as good as the others if only she had time.

'Thanks, Gwyneth!' she said. 'You're a real friend, not like some people I know! We'll show them!'

The tables were all crowded. Discreet advertisements of the new venture at Endersby's Hotel had ensured a flood of bookings from the wealthy residents of Edgbaston, and many more from the suburbs. Paul Mandeville was there with his mother. He had, somewhat reluctantly, agreed to join her because his uncle and cousin Felicity were also staying with him for a couple of nights.

'I'd rather not,' he protested when his mother booked the table. 'There's so much illness about at this time of year I prefer to spend my spare time relaxing at home.'

'You spend too much time at the free clinic,' she chided gently. 'I know you're needed there, but your private work is growing fast. If you overwork and become ill, what will happen to folk then?'

'I'm not ill, just tired.'

'And you could do with a change. Besides, what would Felicity think if you didn't come?'

'Why can't her fiancé come? I thought they were all travelling up to Yorkshire together.'

'Apparently he's gone ahead, and William and Felicity decided to visit us on the way.'

Fortunately his cousin was a good dancer, and Paul began to enjoy himself. He'd always liked Felicity, who was only a year younger than him. As children they had fallen into many scrapes together, and he was pleased she had finally decided to settle down. Her doting widowed father had despaired of her during the past few years as she flitted from one boyfriend to another, refusing to take any of them seriously.

She confided during their dances that Freddie was quite different, charming, handsome and intelligent, and that he adored her. Paul was amused, hoping the unknown Freddie could live up to his reputation, and as they watched the entertainment Richard Endersby had devised he could hear Felicity whispering eagerly to his mother, no doubt telling her the same thing.

The band played a medley of popular songs from musical shows, many of which, like the recent hit *Stop Flirting*, with the sensational new dancers Fred and Adèle Astaire, had been seen at Birmingham theatres. Then Andrew Denver had his solo, and Paul sat up and concentrated. He'd known Andrew years ago. They'd been in the same regiment, and after the war had gone around with the same girls, been to the same parties. He was aware that Andrew played the saxophone, but imagined he was merely amusing himself, since he was already rich and had no need to work. From the first few soaring, glorious notes he knew this interpretation had been wildly inaccurate. Andrew now was a complete professional, dedicated, intense, and talented way above the average.

'Oh, boy! He's fantastic!' Felicity whispered as a storm of applause erupted. 'I wouldn't like to have to follow that!'

'They don't look too eager,' Paul agreed, watching the somewhat straggling line of girls waiting just beyond the small platform where the band sat.

There were half a dozen of them, shuffling their feet and coughing nervously, dressed in a shimmering rainbow of colours.

'Marigold Endersby tells me it's their first time dancing in public,' Mrs Mandeville said softly. 'They are pupils of that rather smooth little man, the dancing master who rents the ballroom for classes.'

Andrew had returned to his place, and the band played a fanfare. Paul watched as the girls straightened up, smiled nervously, and holding on to the shoulders of the girl in front, moved in a swaying waltz time on to the ballroom floor. Frank had taken Edwina's advice, something he didn't often do, but in this aspect of their work she was growing very confident and he respected her views. She had an instinctive flair for devising routines, and strongly resisted his original notions, saying they were far too complicated and difficult for inexperienced dancers. She also rejected his suggestions for costumes.

'These girls aren't used to being half naked. If they have to worry about showing their legs and whether ostrich feathers will fall out of their hair they won't concentrate on the steps,' she pointed out. 'It can be just as effective if the dresses are pretty and the routine simple. Besides, it's for a classy audience, men and women, and we don't want any Edgbaston worthies being offended or embarrassed. They aren't dirty old men looking for high-kicking lovelies and sexy thrills.'

As she led the line of girls Gwyneth, who had been involved in some of the planning, was heartily thankful for Edwina's firmness. All dark haired, the girls looked wholesome and pretty in knee-length white satin dresses. Gauzy, multi-coloured squares of material floated cornerwise from the shoulders and more were sewn to the loose, dropped waists.

They all wore white satin headbands, and their short bobbed hair gleamed. White silk stockings and white satin shoes completed the attractive picture, and as a ripple of applause came from the audience Gwyneth knew it would be a success.

They used basic ballroom steps, first linked as a line, then twirling free, coming together in a bewildering pattern of twos and threes as they wove their intricate maze. The coloured material floated around them and added to the kaleidoscopic effect, and when they ended by forming a line, hands linked behind one another's waists, and high-kicked their way off the ballroom floor they were followed by a storm of applause.

'We've done it! We're proper dancers!' Kitty gasped. 'Nell, who could have imagined it? We are dancing in the same troupe!'

'And only six months ago I was sneaking into your stable to find a bed for the night!' Nell laughed. 'I can hardly believe it!'

'Hush, girls! Mr Denver is playing again,' Frank hissed, and herded the excited girls into the small room where they had changed. He shut the door.

'Well done, girls. You were very good indeed. Now please listen carefully. Mr Endersby has agreed that you may accept invitations to dance if you wish. We would not permit it with every troupe, but I have assured him you are all sensible young ladies. He knows you won't abuse the permission, but he agrees with me that it would help to promote both the ballroom and the dancing school if you talk about them to his guests.'

Not all the girls relished this prospect, and between them Kitty and Gwyneth had to persuade Nell and one of the others that they would be able to manage. When Andrew's second solo was finished, and the band struck up once more for ordinary dancing, Frank led the girls back into the ballroom.

Kitty, who had not been too nervous to look about her and note which of her friends were present, seized Gwyneth and Nell by the hand and made straight for Paul Mandeville's table.

'Mrs Mandeville, Paul, how lovely to see you! Don't you think Andrew is clever? Did you enjoy the dancing? I've brought my special friends Nell and Gwyneth to be introduced.'

'I had no idea you wished to be a stage dancer, Kitty,' Mrs Mandeville replied, rather disapprovingly, and introduced her brother and niece. By the time Kitty turned round to her friends she found only Gwyneth, looking pale and bereft. She glanced further, to see Nell, clasped in Paul's arms, being whirled about the room.

Chapter Nine

'Do you want to go?' Gwyneth asked. They were sitting in Gwyneth's room eating their evening meal.

'It's rather a cheek, isn't it, mixing with her rich friends?'

'She has invited us.'

'I know. I suppose it might be fun. It's a lovely house.'

'How do you know? You didn't tell me Kitty had invited you to her home before. I know she's very friendly, not at all snobbish, but we haven't known her for more than a few weeks.'

'She didn't.' Nell shook her head and laughed, rather shame-faced. 'It seems such a long time ago, and I've left that life behind me now, thanks to you, and earlier, thanks to Kitty.'

'Tell me. It sounds intriguing.'

Nell explained about that momentous night when she'd hidden in the stable behind Kitty's house, which had changed her life.

'When I went back for the shawl Andrew caught me. They were so kind and helpful. They didn't care a bit about me being a ragamuffin from Ladywood. They fed me, and Kitty gave me that good blouse and skirt, and the hat and coat. It was only because of them I got the job in the shop and met you.'

'That was kind of her! But she didn't say anything at class.'

'She is kind. I suppose she didn't want to embarrass me. But while you had your classes we talked and she asked what had happened, how I met you and managed to pay for lessons.'

'So you met Andrew too,' Gwyneth said slowly. 'He'll be at the party, he's Kitty's cousin. So will that good-looking doctor who whisked you away from us at Endersby's. I met him once before. He came into the shop and persuaded his mother to buy lots of new gowns.'

Nell flushed slightly. 'I didn't realize you knew him. He's known Kitty for years, he said.'

'He was certainly attracted to you. Did you like him?' Gwyneth demanded, rather tense. Paul Mandeville had danced with her too, but only out of politeness, she was sure. He'd been abstracted and spoken hardly at all.

'He was very pleasant, but we only danced together twice. I didn't have a lot of time to get to know him,' Nell protested.

She had in fact been so bemused at finding herself dancing with such a handsome, distinguished-looking man in one of Birmingham's most prestigious hotels she'd scarcely noticed what he'd talked about, and couldn't recall a single one of her own remarks. She hoped he hadn't thought her a complete fool.

'So we'll go to Kitty's party on Saturday. She said something about an old friend coming back from abroad. Timothy, I think she said his name was. That's the reason for it.'

'I thought it was to celebrate our first public performance. I know the rest of the troupe have been invited.'

'It will do that too, but from what she says Kitty doesn't need an excuse for a party. We'll think about dresses later. First we ought to practise that new set of steps. Mr Bliss is hoping to get us an engagement at one of the local theatres next week, they've been let down by another act.'

Gwyneth wound up the old gramophone they had bought with the money from their performance at Endersby's, and they began to practise the routine Edwina had devised especially for them. Mr Bliss had been pleased with their performance, saying Nell had become so good she and Gwyneth were to perform a few more elaborate steps during the routine, with the less skilled girls in the background. It was a great help that they could practise every evening when they came home from their daytime jobs.

Five minutes later there was a heavy knocking on the door. 'Miss Davis! Miss Davis! Am yow theer?'

Gwyneth grinned across at Nell as she stopped the gramophone. 'Another complaint! Coming, Mrs Price,' she said, raising her voice.

She opened the door and a large, red-faced woman, arms akimbo, marched into the room. 'It ain't good enuff, yow gals, kickin' up yer legs an upsettin' dacent folk wot wants ter sleep!'

'It's only nine o'clock, Mrs Price,' Gwyneth said placatingly, glancing across at the small alarm clock beside her bed. 'No one can be asleep yet, and you know we have to practise, but we'll be done soon, I promise.'

'Yer'll be dun roight now! Oi'm a'tellin' yow, no more bangin' an' thumpin'. Oi runs a dacent 'ouse, an' Oi'm not 'avin' yow lot in it no more! Out yer goos, next wik, sharpish. An' that's me last werd!'

She left, banging the door, and the two girls stared at each other, suddenly frightened. Nell sank down on to the bed. 'What on earth shall we do?' she asked, a note of panic in her voice.

Gwyneth sat beside her. 'We'll look for somewhere else.'

Nell gulped. She'd never had to find herself a room — Gwyneth had suggested this one — and she had no idea how to set about it. Suddenly she realized how ignorant she was still about the world. 'How do we start?' she said, feeling helpless and inadequate.

'There are advertisements in newspapers, and shop windows, even in the houses where there are vacancies. Don't worry,' Gwyneth tried to reassure her. 'Maybe we can find somewhere on the ground floor, where we won't disturb anybody underneath. Cheer up, Nell, we've got two days and all next week to do it. It may not be so cheap, but we could share. There are plenty of rooms. We won't be homeless, and soon we'll be travelling all over the country, dancing at lots of different theatres. We'll be looking for places to live in lots of new towns. This is a sort of rehearsal.'

'Fleur! It's been ages! How are you? I haven't seen Maisie at the classes recently.'

Fleur turned slowly away from the counter where she had been looking at some gloves. 'Kitty?' she replied coolly. 'Maisie has enrolled in a good, respectable dancing school.'

Kitty laughed. 'Is she still holding a grudge about my being put into the stage class? Come on, Fleur, forget it! Maisie won't ever be good enough for the stage. You said as much to me that night we went to the Tower. I'm having a party tomorrow, and you haven't said whether you're coming. Do come! Andrew will be there. He's back in Birmingham for some time now.'

'No, thank you, Kitty. We have better – I mean other plans for tomorrow.'

Kitty frowned, but before she could reply Fleur swept away, her head held high and her eyes averted. The salesgirl, who had been an interested audience to the short exchange, sighed and began to replace the gloves in the drawer, avoiding Kitty's eye.

Kitty stared after Fleur in angry amazement. She hadn't thought the girl had enough spirit to snub anyone. Well, that would be the last time she spoke to either of the Carpenter sisters! They were jealous cats! But then, she supposed sisters would always support each other in the end. There were plenty of other people who were glad to be friends with her, who appreciated her! Nell Baxter, for instance, made it obvious she admired her looks, and was almost embarrassingly grateful for those clothes. Nell was, she suddenly thought, a sort of protégée, and even though she came from a dreadful background that wasn't her fault. She behaved and sounded like everyone else, and she was much friendlier than the Carpenter sisters or her other girlfriends. So was Gwyneth, and she'd been enormously helpful about extra practice. Kitty knew it was necessary to prevent the indignity of being told she was not good enough, which would have allowed Maisie to crow. She was good enough, but she'd started much later than the others. To her surprise it had been fun, too, just the three of them together. They laughed at the silliest things, and had even begun planning speciality dances for three. Kitty smiled to herself. Perhaps friendships amongst the bohemian theatre people would be more satisfying than with people she had known until now.

'Nell? Nell, wait fer me!'

Nell swung round, startled, then held out her arms as Amy came rushing across the Hagley Road, dodging the trams and causing a horse pulling a coal wagon to shy nervously.

'Amy! You nearly got run over!'

'I thought it was you! I've missed yer so much! Oh, Nell, Nell!'

She didn't seem able to go on, and instead burst into tears. Nell drew her towards a low wall surrounding one of the big houses and made her sit down, then she took out a handkerchief and mopped up Amy's tears.

'Ma thought yer'd been killed, went ter the hospitals. Then 'er said yer'd been sold by summat called white traders. What's them, Nell?'

Nell closed her eyes. How thoughtless she'd been! She just hadn't imagined the agony Ma would have felt at her sudden disappearance. And she knew that in spite of it all Ma loved them. It wasn't her fault she couldn't stand up to Pa and protect them from him.

'I – I didn't mean to make you worry,' she said after a pause.

'Why didn't yer tell us where yer was?' Amy asked.

'I was ill at first, and I couldn't say goodbye,' Nell explained. 'A friend helped me. Afterwards I didn't dare to, in case Pa came after me. I wanted to see you, Amy, and Ma, truly I did, but I won't come back, and I don't want him to know where I am. Nor Danny and Sam.' She shivered at the recollection. 'Have they been home since?'

Amy shook her head. 'Pa's bin madder'n ever since yer went.

Danny an' Sam never came back. It sent 'im up wall. 'E chucked 'em out, but 'e still wants their money.'

'I wouldn't have thought it paid for more than their food,' Nell said slowly.

'Pa said we'll 'av ter go and find a cheaper 'ouse. I don't want ter leave me friends at school, nor Suky in next yard.' Amy was miserable. School and her few friends must be the only pleasure she had in life, Nell thought, feeling guilty that her own life was now so enjoyable.

'I don't suppose he will. There can't be many houses in Ladywood let for less rent,' Nell tried to reassure her.

'You'm speakin' all posh,' Amy commented, her tears having dried up.

Nell laughed, a little self-consciously. 'I'm used to talking like this now. You know I always could imitate anyone else. My new friends all talk like this, so I do as well.'

'It's smashin'. I'd like ter do it an' all.' Amy smiled shyly at her sister. 'What are yer doin', Nell? 'Ave yer got a job? Yer must 'ave, ter buy nice clothes. An' where d'yer live? Can I see yer sometimes?'

'Don't worry about me, I'm earning plenty and I've got a nice room,' Nell said quickly, wondering whether she would still have a room by the following week. 'Tell Ma not to worry, I'm fine.' She reached into her pocket. 'Here's half a crown. Take it straight to Ma. I'd send more if I could afford it. Don't let Pa know. I don't want him finding out and coming after me.'

'I won't! Nell, ta ever so! Shall I wait 'ere an' see yer again?'

'You'd better not,' Nell said cautiously. 'He might wonder why you were here. But look, he's usually dead to the world Sunday mornings. Come to Perrott's Folly and if I can I'll be there. But promise you won't let anyone else, not even Ma, know? If it stops being a secret he'll beat all of us.'

Amy shuddered. 'Pa beats us lots more now. 'E said 'e'd kill yer if 'e found out where yer was. I wish I could run away too, an' I will when I'm older!'

*

'Dick! What are you doing here? You are not supposed to be in the hotel.'

Dick, his eyes still gleaming, turned guiltily to face his father. Richard Endersby felt the familiar stab of regret that he had missed his son's first few years because of the war. Although he was dark while she was fair, he was so like Marigold, with his blue eyes and delightful smile.

'I was listening to Mr Denver playing. Father, may I learn to play the saxophone?'

'You made a dreadful fuss when you had to have piano lessons.'

Dick hung his head. 'I know, but that was different! It wasn't fun.' He became animated and bounced up and down in front of Richard as he tried to explain. 'Mr Denver let me have a go, blowing into the mouthpiece. He was telling me all about Adolphe Sax who invented it. Did you know it's the air vibrating in the tube which makes the sound? The sound comes out differently depending on the size – I think it's the size, but he used longer words – of the space?'

Richard suppressed a grin. 'If it isn't another of your enthusiasms, that vanishes the next day, we'll think about lessons. But you'll have to do piano too.'

'I don't mind that if I can play the saxophone,' Dick offered generously. 'Thank you! I will work hard, I promise! Do you know they used to use it in army bands, and they even put it into proper orchestras! Now may I go home and tell Mother?'

'I feel so guilty about leaving Amy in those conditions.'

Gwyneth nodded sympathetically. 'Was it really so dreadful? You've never told me many details.'

'I was too ashamed, I suppose,' Nell replied slowly. 'Because I'd lived with Gran for so long, I never really knew the others. Eth was jealous, and I can't blame her. She had to put up with Pa's beatings a lot longer than I did! Amy was different, somehow. I felt closer to her, like a real sister.'

'I never had a sister, and I don't think it's the same with

brothers. I never felt I could confide in mine, anyway, though we got on well enough. But you can't do anything about Amy. It will help her to know you're still near her.'

'I felt dreadful when she said how worried Ma was. I've been so selfish, thinking only of my own wants.'

Gwyneth shook her head. 'You may be able to help Amy later on, when we're famous dancers and earning fabulous amounts of money! You wouldn't help by going back home.'

Nell shuddered. 'I know, and I couldn't bear that now I've escaped once.'

'You know, we're like sisters now,' Gwyneth said brightly, attempting to cheer Nell up. 'Did you ever want an older sister?'

Nell smiled. 'Sometimes, especially since Gran died. I used to think it would be more bearable if I had someone to confide in, ask for help. You've certainly been like a sister in that way! Now we ought to get ready for the party. I never thought, that day they caught me in the stables, that I'd soon be going to a party there with half of Edgbaston!'

'Ma! Look! 'Alf a crown! Fer all of us.'

Amy rushed through the door, which hung crookedly on its rusty hinges. She skipped across to where her mother sat beside the small table, listlessly attempting to sew up a triangular tear in eight-year-old Norman's trousers. He was sitting, glowering, on an upturned orange box, as near to the small fire as he could get without scorching his bare skinny flanks.

'Amy, luv! Where on earth did yer get so much money?'

'Our Nell! Ma, yer should 'ave seen 'er!'

'Nell? My God, Amy, yer not making this up, are yer? Did yer really see our Nell? Is 'er all right?'

'Course 'er is! Right as rain! Looked a real lady, posh as the Queen!'

'You ain't never seen the Queen,' Norman said scornfully, turning so that his other side got the benefit of the meagre heat coming from the flames.

'Neither 'ave you, so you don't know what 'er looks like, so there!' Amy shot back at him. 'I've seen plenty o' toffs down in the 'Agley Road. That's where I seen our Nell, Ma!'

'Did 'er tell yer where 'er was livin'? 'As 'er got a proper job?'

'I dunno. But next time I'll ask 'er.'

'Next time? Yer knows where ter find 'er? Why didn't yer say?'

'Nell said not ter let Pa know.'

The stairs door crashed open.

'An' yer pa says yer'll tell 'im straight off, or I'll leather yer till yer yells fer mercy!'

Amy screamed, and as her father came towards her turned to flee. He would have caught her if her mother hadn't jumped to her feet and collided with him. As Amy fled along the yard and through the alleyway she could hear her father's roars of fury and the beseeching cries of her mother.

Sobbing wildly, she pressed her hands over her ears long after she was hundreds of yards away, so far that it was impossible to hear. But she had lost all reason, and fled along Ledsham Street, turning blindly along St Vincent Street, until she came to Sandpits. Instinctively she avoided the brighter patches where the lights from the pubs spilled out on to the pavements, and the doors might open to let out roistering men. For a moment she rested, panting for breath, clinging to the wall round the old gardens. If she could climb in there she might be safe, she thought, but the railings were too high. Wearily she staggered on, barely aware of the groups of boys and girls who paraded up and down making loud comments about each other. They ignored her, even when at last, too exhausted to go further or to care if Pa caught her, she sank down on to a pile of rubbish outside a shop, sobbing and shivering inconsolably.

Chapter Ten

THANKS to Gwyneth's skills <u>with</u> her needle she and Nell had elegantly suitable gowns for Kitty's party.

'The simpler the better,' she declared, and fashioned sleeveless, short-skirted, dropped waisted dresses in plain satin, apple green for her and a deep rose pink for Nell, both with long black fringes suspended from shoulders and waist.

Kitty was wearing an elaborate silk dress with handkerchief hem, in dark blue. Three ropes of pearls dangled almost to her waist and another strand was twisted through the bandeau she wore low on her forehead.

'Darlings, your dresses are divine! Come in and meet the gang!' she greeted them, and within seconds they were surrounded by what seemed like hundreds of people.

Nell afterwards worked out that there were no more than thirty or so guests in the big drawing room, where the carpet had been rolled back and a trio of musicians was playing dance tunes, but they were all talking or laughing so loudly the noise was overwhelming.

Before she could obey her first instinct to flee, Andrew Denver appeared beside her. 'Nell, you look wonderful!'

'Better than the last time we met here?' Nell said breathlessly, and he laughed, seized her by the waist and swung her round as the musicians struck up a lively polka.

She lost track of the men she danced with, and the cocktails she was given. Through caution she usually deposited the drinks, barely tasted, on some table or window ledge as soon as she decently could. Nevertheless, by the time Kitty announced that supper was ready in the dining room across the hall Nell had lost all her shyness and felt she was floating on air. She'd been so nervous of meeting Kitty's wealthy friends. Gwyneth, who had mixed freely with all sorts of people since her childhood because of her father's position and her brothers' schoolfriends, reassured her.

'Your accent is as good as theirs now, so they'll never know where you come from,' she insisted. 'They'll accept you without thinking.'

Nell hadn't been so sure, but it had proved correct. No one was interested in where she came from, only in her present life on the stage. The men all wanted to flirt, while the girls were eager to hear all about the supposed glamour. Gwyneth had encouraged Nell to mimic some of the characters they had met, and she suddenly found herself blossoming under the admiring attention.

She still had enough sense left to realize that one man she had expected to dance with had not approached her at all; he did not even appear to recognize her. Finding herself next to Gwyneth as Kitty swept them towards the buffet Nell caught her arm. 'Is Paul Mandeville dancing with anyone?' she asked.

'Yes, I've danced with him and so has Kitty. Why?'

'I – nothing.'

'If you were wondering why he hasn't asked you, it's probably because no one can get near you with all the men clamouring for dances,' Gwyneth laughed, and Nell blushed.

'There are more men than girls,' she said hurriedly.

'Yes. Kitty knows how to organize parties for her own benefit. Have you met Timothy?' she added.

'No. Isn't he the man the party is supposed to be for? The one who's been abroad?'

'Yes. He's nice. Come and be introduced.'

The Honourable Timothy Travers was deeply tanned, and his

straw-coloured hair was even longer than usual. He smiled lazily at Nell when she and Gwyneth walked across and pulled up some more chairs for them.

'Come and tell me all about this mischief Kitty's been getting into while I haven't been here to look after her,' he drawled languidly.

Gwyneth raised her eyebrows slightly. 'Mischief?' she queried swiftly. 'You call stage dancing mischief?'

'It's hardly what you'd expect a girl like Kitty to get involved with, is it?' he replied.

'Exactly what sort of girl would you expect to get involved with it?' Gwyneth asked softly, and Nell tensed. She'd heard that tone before, when Gwyneth had berated one of the men lodging in their house, who had tried to steal a kiss on the dark stairs.

To her relief Timothy laughed. 'I wasn't trying to be insulting,' he assured her. 'I know you are a dancer. I simply didn't expect Kitty to have enough determination to do all the necessary practising, that's all.'

'Oh.' Gwyneth let out her breath slowly. 'I see.'

'Yes.' He turned to Nell. 'And I believe you're a dancer too? Kitty pointed out her two best friends, and I could hardly forget such stunning beauties. It's Nell, isn't it? Will you dance with me afterwards?'

They spent almost an hour together, dancing and then sitting in one of the small parlours. Timothy talked enthusiastically about his recent visit to South Africa.

'I may go back there soon. It's a beautiful country and it's given me a taste for travel. I've a fancy to visit Australia now. Hasn't Paul Mandeville's mother just come back from there?'

'Yes, I think so. Some months ago. Are you really going?' Nell asked enviously. Until now she'd hardly imagined herself ever going to London. To hear someone talk so casually about visiting the other side of the world was odd.

'One day I will. But the sea journey is so tedious,' Timothy replied. 'I think I'd rather wait until they can fly us there. Now they've managed to cross the Atlantic we ought soon to be able to do more than just hop across the Channel to Biarritz or Le Touquet. How about coming with me?'

'I've never thought about going anywhere except England,' Nell said honestly. 'And I simply can't imagine what it would be like flying in an aeroplane.' She knew he wasn't serious, this was the sort of joking conversation Kitty's upper-class friends indulged in.

He pulled her to her feet as the band started playing a tango. 'Can you do this? I spent a whole afternoon trying to teach Kitty the basic steps. Yes, you're good. If your stage dancing is successful perhaps The Bliss Beauties will be going to Paris or even New York.'

'Really? I'd never thought of that!'

'Why not? The Tiller Girls are in Paris, at the Folies-Bergère.'

'But I thought —' Nell stopped in confusion, and a slow blush stained her cheeks.

Timothy held her closer as he whirled them into a reverse spin and oversway. 'You thought the Folies-Bergère was a less than respectable place, yes?' he asked, grinning down at her.

Nell nodded as she slowly came upright.

'They do have nudes,' he said in a matter-of-fact tone, 'but it's all very tasteful, and the English dancers are more heavily chaperoned than they are in this country. They live in a hostel run by an English parson, and what could be more respectable than that?'

'I just want to dance,' Nell said firmly, and he laughed in delight.

'It's hard work, dancing. I wonder whether Kitty might prefer to be a showgirl or a nude?'

'Surely not,' Nell protested, aghast at the idea.

'She needs constant admiration without making a great deal of effort,' he said disapprovingly.

Soon afterwards he went to fetch a drink, saying Nell looked hot, and as she waited Andrew strolled up to her.

'You look as if you could do with some fresh air. Shall we go and visit your friends in the stable?'

'Timothy is fetching me a drink,' she replied, shaking her head.

'You needn't mind him, it's far more important to keep the musicians happy.'

'Aren't you playing at all tonight?'

'Tonight I'm off duty, I'm enjoying myself. Especially when I'm talking to you.'

'Hands off, old chap! Your drink, Nell. Shall I send this interloper about his business?'

Timothy's tone was light, but he put a proprietorial arm round Nell's shoulders and stood beside her, facing Andrew. The latter grinned back at him.

'Make the most of your opportunities, Timothy! Unless you come and work as a waiter at Endersby's I'll have Nell all to myself on the nights she's working there.'

'Are you doing more shows there, Nell?' Timothy asked. 'I heard how successful the first one was. I wish I'd been back in time to see it.'

'It depends on whether we have theatrical engagements. Mr Bliss may use other girls, he has quite a few in his classes who are ready to form troupes. But if we're in a Birmingham theatre he'll sometimes arrange for us to come back to Endersby's afterwards,' Nell explained.

'And you'll be doing two shows a night? Won't that be hard work?'

'It's normal, lots of troupes rush off to do performances at the ciné-variety theatres in between ordinary stage work.'

'You should complain. Form a union and demand better conditions. Besides, if you're worked so hard how can you have the energy for pleasant little suppers afterwards with your admirers?'

Andrew chuckled. 'She won't need to, Timothy, she'll be permitting the equally hard-working musician to escort her home!'

Nell told herself firmly that such bantering was meaningless, the normal sort of friendly teasing she'd noticed before with Kitty and her upper-class men friends. There was no harm in it, it was fun, far preferable to Tom's heavy-handed gallantries.

It wasn't the sort of conversation Paul Mandeville employed. It was almost midnight before he walked across the room and, with a brief smile at Timothy, who seemed to have attached himself permanently to Nell's side, held out a hand to her.

'Come and talk to me for a change.'

By now they were dancing to a gramophone, and the more lively dances had given way to the slow foxtrot. Many of the dancers, finding the steps too difficult, had taken the opportunity to visit the buffet for more food and only half a dozen couples circled the floor in time with the dreamy music.

'Kitty says you might be doing an act in the music hall next week. Will it be the same as the one at Endersby's?'

Nell shook her head. 'We've changed it a lot. Some of it's similar, but we can't do exactly the same moves on a stage facing the audience. In the ballroom we had people all round us. Mrs Bliss is very clever at working it all out.'

He seemed interested in the details, unlike Andrew who, despite his music, frankly admitted he liked to dance but hardly knew the names of the dances, just went with the music as he saw fit. Nell discovered that Paul understood and appreciated some of the technical problems.

'Where do you come from?' he asked after a while. 'Sometimes I think I can hear the Birmingham accent in your voice, at other times you sound more like your friend, the Welsh girl.'

Nell bit her lip. 'I can't stop imitating everyone,' she admitted. 'I come from Birmingham, at least I lived in Ladywood for two years.'

'Ladywood? I do a clinic there twice a week. Do you still live there?'

'I'm not sure where we'll be living after next week. Our landlady is throwing us out because the other tenants complain about us practising. Gwyneth and I have been looking for a couple of rooms all day, but we want to stay together, and we need space to practise. Gwyneth says we're bound to find somewhere, but I can't help worrying.'

'She's right, you'll soon find rooms. Where did you live before Ladywood? Have you any family there?'

'I lived with my grandparents in Sutton Coldfield, until they died,' Nell explained, avoiding the latter question.

'Sutton? I often went there, I had a schoolfriend who lived in the town, between the station and Sutton Park. I used to love riding there.' The dance ended, and Paul drew Nell to sit beside him on a settee. 'Do you ever go back?'

Swiftly Nell shook her head. 'I want to, yet I know it would upset me,' she confessed.

'Were you so happy there?' he asked sympathetically.

'It was heaven,' Nell breathed, and the combination of his understanding and the longing to return to that life brought sudden tears to her eyes. She blinked fiercely and sniffed. 'I – I'm sorry,' she gasped.

'You'll go back one day,' Paul prophesied, and Nell found his handkerchief pressed into her hand. 'Don't worry, no one's looking,' he added softly, and Nell saw that he'd moved to shield her from the rest of the room. 'Come and dance with me again,' he said as Nell shyly handed back the handkerchief.

She complied. He was so tall and held her in such a close, comforting clasp she had to tilt her head back to look at him. He talked easily about the days he had spent in the Park, with his friend and other boys from the town. In summer they had swum in the pools, some winters they'd been able to skate, but whether they had been swimming, skating or riding they always seemed to be having a race or contest of some kind.

'We were crazy,' Paul said with a sudden laugh. 'When I think of the dead trees we climbed and the thin ice we trusted to hold us, and all the other stupid pranks we indulged in, I'm amazed we all survived; particularly when the army used it for a training site. We were shot at more than once, venturing on to firing ranges, having idiotic bets about how close we could come to the soldiers without being spotted. Good training for when we became soldiers, I suppose,' he finished soberly.

By the time the party ended Nell knew that instead of being afraid to return she was now looking forward to revisiting Sutton. It would hurt, knowing her grandparents were no longer there, but she could face it without the desire to turn back the clock. They had been the best years of her life, but she had to go on, and now she knew she could. The worst days were behind her and a shining future beckoned.

'Where do you live, child?'

Amy was shivering so badly her teeth were chattering and she was totally unable to reply.

'It's no good, Flora. She looks terrified to me. Let's take her home for the night, then if she can't talk to us in the morning we ought to pass her over to the authorities.'

'Help me lift her. Gracious, she's so thin! Skin and bone! It's a wonder she's alive.'

'Poor mite. She's probably been scavenging off the street stalls. It's possible her parents have died, I suppose. That could account for her fright.'

Amy tried to tell them she had parents and a family, but the words just would not come. They formed all right inside her head, but couldn't get through her teeth, which for some odd reason were clamped hard together, so hard the only noises she could make were frightening whimpers.

'Can you manage, Sibyl?'

'Yes, she's no weight at all. Smithers, get the rug out of the motor.'

'Yes, Miss Dawson.'

'Perhaps if we wrap her up she'll stop this dreadful shivering. What time is it?'

'Almost midnight. How fortunate you spotted her lying here. Let's get home, we'll be able to do something in the morning.'

*

It was a small theatre, and the dressing rooms were tiny. The largest was reserved for the comic who topped the bill, much to the disgust of the more experienced performers.

'All he needs to do is change his jacket! I can't see why he should have the largest room when the rest of us have to share!' one of the Singing Twins complained. 'There'll be four of us sharing one dressing room!'

'Think yourselves lucky!' an elderly man, a juggler, replied. 'I'm wi' the three acrobats, the tenor, half the Dancin' Duo, as well as Mick and his bloody monkeys! There ain't room to even swing one o' the blasted critters!'

The eight Bliss Beauties, huddled together in the auditorium on the following Monday morning as they waited for the Master of Ceremonies to arrive, looked apprehensively at one another. None of them had ever seen a theatre dressing room, and Mr Bliss had not explained much at their final rehearsal on Saturday, just told them to be on time.

'Edwina will make sure your costumes are there. She'll be able to sort out any problems, but the stage manager will show you where to go. Do as he says, he knows you're new to all of it.'

'It's as well we didn't know,' Gwyneth muttered when they were eventually herded into a room about ten feet square, with two rickety-looking chairs, one poorly lit mirror and a small washbasin. Their costumes were in a large wicker basket which took up a great deal of the floor space, but apart from a couple of hooks there was nowhere to hang them. 'We'll have to take turns standing up, let alone changing.'

'Thank goodness we're not in pantomime, with lots of changes,' Kitty said, determined to be optimistic. 'I shall put on my make-up at home. It will be easier than crowding round that ghastly flyblown mirror.'

'It's the performing that worries me.'

'But where is Edwina? She's supposed to be here! Looking after things!' Nell was suffering from a sudden attack of nerves. It had seemed easy, dancing in the ballroom at Endersby's. They were used to practising there, the musicians were familiar, and the hotel staff friendly. Many of the chambermaids had been frankly envious of the glamorous life they assumed dancers led, and the guests had been attentive and appreciative.

Here, though, they were the least experienced of the acts appearing. From snatches of overheard conversation they realized some of the other performers seemed to know one another, or at least have heard of their fellow artistes. They grumbled incessantly about the facilities and the management, and seemed to delight in telling stories of horrors to which they or others had been subjected by hostile audiences. Being booed off stage seemed the least awful fate which could await them.

Nell had begun to appreciate that much of the success of their act depended on her and Gwyneth. The rest of the troupe were no more than adequate, good enough for a line, capable of keeping in step, but without the particular verve and extra talent which could make them stand out as special. And she wanted so much to be extra special.

She'd been thrust into doing the solo spot and more complicated steps with Gwyneth, and began to doubt her ability to succeed. Gwyneth had been dancing for longer than she had, and was by far the most talented of Mr Bliss's pupils. The routine demanded a pair, and while she thought she was better than the other girls she was far from convinced she was anywhere near the quality of Gwyneth.

Her fears increased. The dusty backstage atmosphere, the smells of grease paint, canvas and size, sweat and, inexplicably, sour cabbage, made her nauseous. It was a relief when, finally dressed in their costumes and with make-up applied, they were summoned from the overcrowded, stuffy little dressing room on to the stage for the rehearsal.

The relief did not persist for long. In the wings it was freezing cold, and stage hands and technicians bustled about, shouting incomprehensible remarks to one another and cursing volubly at anyone who got in their way. The old hands waited, snug in fur coats or thick shawls, riposting with laughter and quick retorts to the abuse they received. The acrobats were doing handstands in the only large space available, while the Dancing Duo swore at them as they tried to practise their steps, dodging the flying feet as best they could. Nell and the others huddled miserably in a corner until it was time to start.

This was delayed again and again as new problems were discovered to do with the lighting or the special effects, and it was an hour after they'd been called before the first run-through started.

'At least we're first on, we can go after we've done our turn,' Kitty muttered. 'That is, if my feet unfreeze and I can manage the steps without shivering my way off the edge of the stage.'

They had not previously rehearsed on the stage. It took several false starts as they got used to the distance they needed to cover on their entrance, spread out more when the producer complained they didn't fill the stage, argued with the musicians who were playing the music too slowly, and had to move further forward to be properly within the best lighted area. By the time they'd completed their turn two of the girls were near to tears, Kitty was almost bursting with rage, and Gwyneth was in the mood to have a furious row with Frank Bliss.

'Either he or Edwina should have been here!' she fumed as they changed out of their costumes. 'They're supposed to know about the problems, and it's up to them to find solutions, not me!'

'I can't go on again!' a girl named Kathy wept. 'It's too humiliating! Did you hear them saying some of the audience threw rotten tomatoes if they didn't like the acts? I don't think I want to be a dancer if it's going to be like this.'

'It won't always be like this,' Nell soothed her. She didn't feel like going on again at the moment, but for just a few minutes, when it had finally been going smoothly, she had glimpsed the power and the magic of doing something really well, of capturing the imagination of an audience, being absorbed into a world of music and colour and movement. They could not manage, however, if one of the girls walked off in a huff.

'I'm going straight to Mr Bliss. I'll sort things out,' Gwyneth promised. Her temper had cooled swiftly, as it usually did, and she realized she had to cajole the nervous girls through these first vital few days.

'Shall we all come?' one of the waverers asked.

'No need.' If they did, Gwyneth knew, she would have less chance of making Mr Bliss listen to her, for it would all be exaggerated and he would merely retaliate with anger. 'Nell can come. Bring warm coats for this evening, and get here early so that we can change one or two at a time.'

Kitty was looking worried, and as Gwyneth and Nell left she followed them. 'Gwyneth, can we have an hour's practice before tonight?'

'Come to the studio now. I know it's free.'

Kitty was unusually subdued. She rarely admitted to mistakes. 'I know I muffed some of the steps. I'm terrified of letting you all down.'

Gwyneth realized how difficult such a confession had been, for Kitty rarely thought of anyone but herself. She smiled encouragingly. 'It's only practice you need.' Later, as the three of them were in the studio she was relieved she had been correct.

'Imagine you're a horse in that high-stepping sequence. You know how they pick their feet up and seem to let their ankles go loose. Do it like that, but don't relax, point your toes straight down.'

Kitty concentrated. 'Oh, it's easy now I can think like that.'

'And when we're moving sideways to the left, on that step you missed, Kitty, at the very end as we turn to move back, take two steps on the left foot, hop, keeping your right knee up and swinging your body round. Then you'll be on the proper foot, balanced ready to reverse smoothly. Let's try it. That's it! Good! I knew you could do it!'

'Mother! What's brought you home? Why didn't you send to tell us you were coming?'

Cecily Denver tossed aside the magazine she was reading and looked at her daughter. Then she gave a deep sigh. 'What a nuisance you are, child! Getting yourself into all sorts of mischief.'

'I'm not!' Kitty was genuinely puzzled. 'What sort of mischief?'

'This wretched dancing, of course. How could you be so idiotic? It will ruin all your chances of a good marriage! Why you couldn't have been satisfied with one of the men who wanted you last year I don't know.'

'You're a fine one to talk about getting married!' Kitty flared, throwing herself down into a chair opposite her mother. 'It didn't matter so much to you!'

'No, and perhaps it was a mistake. At least you'd have had a man to control you.'

'You mean my father? Are you going to tell me who it was? If he wanted to marry you why the devil did you refuse him?'

'That wasn't what I meant, and stop trying to avoid the real question. Tell me about the dancing. How on earth did you get involved?'

'It's perfectly respectable, Mother. I started to go to modern ballroom classes, and the people who run the school also run stage classes. I thought it would be fun! Life's pretty dreary sometimes, you know, all alone in this house, with no one but Meggy to look at.'

'You'll have to stop.'

'No! Mother, we have the first proper professional performance in a theatre tonight! It would ruin it for everyone else if I couldn't do it! Anyway, who sneaked on me? Was it Meggy?'

'Don't blame her. She didn't say a word. It was Andrew who wrote to me and informed me that I was neglecting my duties as a fond parent.'

'Andrew! But he — he's on the stage himself! How could he!'

'I imagine it's because he's on the stage that he knows what it is really like, and wants to prevent you from ruining your entire life. It's still different for men, despite all we've fought for. They can still do lots of things we can't. Luckily I was planning to come to France, but it's most inconvenient to have to come via Birmingham.'

Kitty begged and stormed and pleaded, eventually gaining her mother's permission to continue with the week's engagement.

'I've never known you want to do anything which demanded hard work and commitment,' she said wearily at last. 'Since it is arranged, you'd better do it for this week. But no longer. And as you haven't the wit to keep out of mischief by yourself, I shall have to provide you with a chaperone. I can't stay, I'm going to Manchester on Wednesday for a couple of days, then to Nice for a month or so, and after that probably back to California. I'll see whether Cousin Maud can come. She'd no doubt jump at the idea of a comfortable home away from her wretched sisters. I know she's always saying Harrogate doesn't suit her.'

'Cousin Maud? Mother! You wouldn't! She's the most tremendous bore, she never stops wittering on about nothing! And she smells of camphor!'

'Yes, but what else can I do? You are too irresponsible to be left alone, you never take any notice of Meggy, and even Andrew can't control you.'

'I don't want Andrew to control me!' Kitty ground her teeth. 'I'll never forgive him for this! For the very first time in my life I've found something I enjoy doing, and he's trying to ruin it for me.'

'Albert, you ought ter go ter police,' Mrs Baxter said timidly. 'Our Amy ain't been 'ome fer two days now.'

'Shut yer gob, woman! Bloody wench'll turn up when 'er's 'ungry.'

'But 'er's only a little 'un. Albert, I know summat's 'appened. I can feel it in me bones.'

'That's what yer said when Nell scarpered, an' yer was wrong. 'Er's doin' well fer 'erself, an' never a thought fer us, selfish bitch!'

They were alone in the kitchen. The younger children were in bed, subdued because of the row which had erupted on Saturday after Amy had appeared with news of Nell and the half-crown she said Nell had given her. The older ones had vanished as soon as their father had come home, roaring drunk for the third night running, having spent the half-crown at the Ryland Arms. Only Mrs Baxter, emboldened by her fears for both her missing daughters, had stayed to face him.

'Nell's a good 'un, 'er wouldn't 'ave gone if you 'adn't beat 'er.'

'Don't be so bloody daft! They're likely fleecin' fellers what can't get it fer free!'

'Albert, our Nell's not like that, 'er isn't!'

''Ow d'yer know? Where can 'er get 'alf-crowns from, honest like? Tell me that, eh? Jus' tell me that!'

'Nell's a good gal. It were you drove 'er away from 'ome, an now you've gone an' sent little Amy after 'er, she's most like killed by now!'

'Fer God's sake, woman, lay off!'

'If 'er's not back by mornin', Albert, I'm goin' ter police station in Ladywood Road, an' askin' if they've found 'er.'

'You go anywhere near bloody coppers an' I'll break every bone in yer body! Then yer'll be feelin' summat in 'em, that yer will!'

Paul Mandeville glanced round suspiciously as he walked to the box office. Why on earth had he succumbed to that crazy urge to visit this obscure little fleapit just to watch a music hall, something which normally bored him to tears? He hadn't done anything so impulsive for years. At least he would be unlikely to be seen or recognized by any of his friends or patients.

Then he realized that as well as the wealthy residents of Edgbaston he had patients from the Ladywood clinic who might well be attracted to this sort of entertainment. He pulled up his white silk scarf, thankful that it was a cold night, and snapped down the brim of his hat over his eyes. Feeling rather foolish he tried to roughen his accent as he asked for his ticket, insisting on a seat at the side where he would be unlikely to be seen from the stage.

As he sat watching the very mixed but sparse audience arrive he tried to analyse his motives. His mother had been disapproving of Kitty's dancing ambitions.

'It will send her the same way as her mother, you mark my words,' she had confided in him after Felicity left to join her fiancé.

'Not all dancers are immoral and disreputable,' he protested.

'No, of course not, but think of the sort of life they lead, moving about, living in dingy lodgings, open to all sorts of temptations. It would be surprising if a girl of Kitty's breeding didn't soon tire of the constant practising and look for an easier life. And when a girl displays her legs and wears almost nothing, it's as good as saying she's for sale.'

He could not delude himself that he was here to watch over Kitty's morals, though. For one thing he could not be constantly on guard. For another, he doubted whether he would have the slightest influence over her if he did make any protest.

It was the other one who intrigued him, the shy, fawnlike one who was so hauntingly beautiful.

Her story, as much as he had heard, was a strange one. How could she appear so untouched after life in those dreadful houses? Then he remembered she'd spent years with her grandparents in the countryside. He wanted to know why. He wanted to talk with her again. He wanted, he realized with a sudden revelation that was a mixture of delight and horror, to know her much better than he'd ever before known a woman.

It was to see Nell make her stage début that he'd come to this wretched little theatre. And yet he knew he would never tell her. He would creep out as unobtrusively as he'd entered, and hug to himself the memories of Nell dancing.

'Beginners please! That means you lot!'

'Cheeky devil!' Kitty's voice was high with nerves. Perhaps her mother was right, this wasn't all fun. Yet most of the time she enjoyed the companionship of the troupe, the dancing itself, and was looking forward to the admiration of the audiences such as she had experienced at the show at Endersby's.

'Come on, girls. Mrs Bliss is ill, so we're on our own. Let's prove to everyone out there just how good we can be!' Gwyneth said encouragingly.

'We'll be so good they'll beg us to go to London, and Paris, and even New York!' Nell added.

She and Gwyneth both knew how desperately nervous the other girls were, how much they needed encouragement. Even the sophisticated Kitty had been complaining about feeling sick ever since they'd arrived at the theatre for the opening performance. They had to hide their own nervousness and pretend they felt no apprehension, if they were to spur the rest of the troupe through the ordeal.

The Bliss Beauties were dressed, made up, and frantically going through the order of the steps in their heads, since there wasn't room in the tiny dressing room for more than minimal movement.

'Let's go. Remember the changes we worked out this morning, otherwise just let's enjoy being on a real, professional stage at last!' Gwyneth said bracingly. 'It's what we've been working towards for months.'

'And don't miss that change of step again, Kitty,' Jane said, her voice tense.

'It wasn't my fault! You turned too soon!'

'Jane, stop it! We all made mistakes this morning, Kitty made no more than you did, or anyone else, but it won't help to rake them up!' Gwyneth said sharply. 'Don't worry, Kitty, you'll be fine, we all will.'

Kitty, for once nervous, gave Gwyneth a grateful smile. The practice earlier had convinced her she could do it. 'Thanks,' she muttered, and took a deep breath.

In some miraculous fashion the chaos of the morning had been resolved. The backdrops were in place, the orchestra tuning up, the lights blazing. From beyond the somewhat grubby curtain a muted buzz of anticipation could be heard.

'It's real!' one of the other girls whispered to Nell. 'Somehow I never quite believed it would ever happen!'

It was happening all right. Nell was aquiver with nerves. Why had she ever wanted to become a dancer? Or why had she ever wanted to forsake the anonymity of the ballroom for the appalling glare of the stage, and the prominence which ensured every mistake would be noted, commented upon, and probably jeered at?

The overture finished, the name of the troupe, which suddenly seemed quite ridiculous and at the same time presumptuous and fantastic, was being announced, and the music they knew so well could be heard swelling away into the furthest corners of the auditorium.

'Come on! Good luck!' Gwyneth said softly, and only Nell realized how incredibly nervous her friend was.

She's brave, encouraging us and going on when she's a bundle of nerves herself, Nell thought. She knows everyone depends on her. I could never appear so calm and experienced.

There was time for no more reflection, no more nerves. The demands of the dance predominated. The music compelled. And suddenly the steps she had practised so diligently, so painstakingly, were all that mattered. They were there, to be used, to be performed for the pleasure of doing something well and to provide entertainment.

They had been so absorbed by the pressures of the moment that it was some time before the girls realized there were strange noises floating up from the audience.

Whisperings, coughs, the occasional shout, rustlings and laughter, were the unexpected accompaniments of their performance. For a moment, as the first euphoria of actually having got on to the stage without disaster evaporated, the girls faltered, but fortunately this was the moment when Nell and Gwyneth began their speciality dance, and any hesitation was masked by the changes. Gradually, the noises subsided. Nell and Gwyneth smiled at each other with relief as they managed the trickiest sequence, which had been troublesome during the rehearsal. The final moves were completed, accompanied by a soaring sense of delight and triumph.

At last it was over, and to a thin trickle of applause and a few raucous shouts of encouragement the girls kicked their way off stage.

'God, we made it! I thought it would never be over!' Kitty exclaimed, exuberant now they had finished and no disaster had claimed them. She was a success! She could dance, had proved she was good enough to dance on the stage! She seized Nell by the hand and swung her round in a triumphant spin.

'Gerrout the way!'

It was the stage manager, and the dancers hastily stumbled down the stairs towards their dressing room.

'Thank God we don't have to wait around. No palaver like final curtain calls!' Kitty said, throwing herself down into a chair.

'Do you think we'll get bookings in other theatres?'

'There weren't many people there. I could see past the footlights and the theatre was half empty.'

'It's Monday, there's never a good house on Mondays,' one suddenly knowledgeable girl proclaimed.

'Why was there so much noise? It really put me off.'

'Latecomers. I expect the opening act always suffers while people are settling down. At least we weren't trying to sing or tell jokes with nobody listening! But one day, Bliss Beauties, we'll be top of the bill, and they'll all be waiting with bated breath to see us!' Gwyneth encouraged them. 'Now, do you all know where your own costumes are, so that there'll be no muddles tomorrow?'

'If we did have more bookings it might solve the problem of where we're going to live,' Nell said later. The others had all left and she and Gwyneth were finishing tidying up.

Kitty, still in her costume, sprawled in a chair. 'Why? I thought you had rooms near Islington Row?' she asked.

'We do, but we're being thrown out for making too much noise practising, and we haven't found anywhere else yet,' Nell said, the ecstasy suddenly evaporating as once more she began to worry about where they could go.

Kitty looked at them for a moment, then smiled broadly. 'That's easily solved. Why don't you both come and live with me?'

They looked at her, bemused. 'We couldn't!' Gwyneth exclaimed.

'Why on earth not? I have masses of space.'

'But . . . it wouldn't be – well – suitable.'

'I don't see why not. We can work together, do all the practising we like, and no one will ever complain!'

'Kitty, we're not your sort! Your family is rich and important. People would say you'd been imposed on.'

'Absolute nonsense! If it makes you feel better I'll call it a business proposition and offer you rooms in my boarding house! Why not me when you'd be prepared to take rooms wherever else they were available?'

'You'd let us pay?' Nell asked slowly. She was so accustomed to Kitty's insistent generosity when they went out together for a meal it hadn't occurred to her that Kitty might be willing to regard this as a business arrangement.

'If it makes you feel better about it. Darlings, I've got reasons of my own. I don't want to have to give up dancing, and I might have to. This could be a way round it.'

'What do you mean? You can't give up now, Kitty, you're really good after that extra practice,' Gwyneth exclaimed. 'And we need you if we're going to introduce the threesome dances.'

Kitty grimaced. 'My darling mama has descended on me, all of a sudden acting respectable, and insisting I give up dancing and have a ghastly old maid cousin to live with me. I'm sure she'd agree to this instead, especially with Gwyneth being the daughter of a minister! If she knows you are dancing with me she might relent. She doesn't really care, just feels she ought to be seen doing her duty, but I've no doubt she's already regretting the trouble it'll be! Meggy approves of you both, for a start! She said no one else has ever offered to help her clear up after a party. Come and see Mama in the morning? Before she whizzes off to Manchester?'

'I think we should,' Gwyneth said to Nell the following day, after Cecily Denver had, though with some misgivings, approved the idea and agreed to try the arrangement for a couple of months. 'I know Kitty can sometimes be difficult, but we can always move out again if we want to.'

'Her mama won't consider us paying rent. Do we want to feel beholden?' Nell asked doubtfully.

'We'll insist on paying for food,' Gwyneth suggested. 'And we can give Meggy money or presents to pay for the extra work. We have to be practical, Nell. We've neither of us much money to spare, don't forget, and have to rely on what we can earn dancing. We ought to save for the times we may not be working. Let's look on the free board as payment for chaperoning Kitty.' And, she thought rather guiltily to herself, there was more chance of meeting Paul Mandeville again if she was at Kitty's, mixing with her set. This, however, she could never reveal to Nell, and she was herself confused. She'd been powerfully attracted to Paul right from the start, in a way she'd never expected to be to any man. It was for his looks, of course, to begin with. But every moment she spent in his company, and there had, she thought ruefully, been precious few of those, reinforced the attraction. She'd watched him, though, when she could do so unobtrusively. Gwyneth sighed. She didn't want the complication of a man in her life, she told herself firmly. Not yet, she would not consider marriage for years yet. One day in the future perhaps, if Paul were to love her, she might give up her dancing. Then she told herself not to be foolish. Such dreams were pointless, idiotic. Paul would never marry a girl such as she was, a dancer. She banished the regrets as she heard Nell speak.

'May deah gel, the leetle finger of your left glove is not perfectly straight, and your parting has two hairs on the wrong side. It will give the deah boys quaite the wrong impression! They'll think you *easy*!' Nell clowned, in a wicked parody of Cecily Denver's manner, and they dissolved into helpless laughter.

Chapter Eleven

'So you're both running away from your fathers and I haven't got one!'

It was late on Sunday morning. On Saturday Gwyneth and Nell had transferred their few belongings to Kitty's home, danced in both the matinée and evening performances, and attended a theatre party organized for them by an ecstatic Frank Bliss.

'You were superb!' he told them. 'I invited a couple of agents to see you, and we already have bookings for the week after next, and probably for the following month too! We can spend this week polishing the act, for there are still minor problems,' he added more cautiously.

'And we can always improve,' Gwyneth enthused. 'Thank goodness it got better after the first night.'

It had got very much better, and by the end of the week the troupe were receiving genuinely warm applause. Their confidence had increased dramatically and all were eager for another engagement.

Now the three girls were relaxing over an enormous late breakfast, and exchanging details about their lives. Kitty had demanded they told her everything.

'I left home mainly because my father was so bigoted,' Gwyneth said slowly. 'He thought all dancing and all singing apart from hymns were wicked.'

'Don't you miss your mother?' Nell asked softly.

'Yes, enormously. I want to write, but I daren't let her know I'm in Birmingham.'

'I'd like to see Ma too, but Pa would force her to tell him where I was, so I daren't.'

'What about you, Kitty? How long was your mother in America?'

'She went last summer. I was in London for the season, and I think she hoped I'd be married by the end of it, and off her hands. When I showed no signs of getting engaged she left. She said it was for just a couple of months, but I think she's met a new man. She is going back there soon, and never mentioned plans to come home for good.'

Nell and Gwyneth, both used to mothers who, in their different ways, had been completely dominated by overbearing husbands, did not know what to say about these revelations, which they found strange and in some ways disturbing. They'd never before known women who were so independent and apparently uncaring of the good opinion of others.

'Why did you come to Birmingham, Gwyneth?' Nell asked after a slight pause. 'I thought your home was in South Wales?'

'Yes, in Pembrokeshire, near Saundersfoot. They'll have thought I went to Cardiff, or maybe Bristol, because they are the nearest big cities. Or they may think I'm in London. I chose Birmingham just because it would seem unlikely. We don't know anyone here, and I'd never been before.'

'When you tell me about your fathers I'm almost thankful not to have one,' Kitty declared. 'Yours must be frightfully difficult to live with, Gwyneth, but at least he didn't beat you like Nell's did.'

'Both are bad,' Nell said slowly. 'Constant disapproval must be as difficult to bear as beatings and violence.'

'But your mothers put up with it! I can't imagine how any woman could endure the sort of behaviour you've described,' Kitty declared hotly. 'If a man were constantly criticizing me, or punched and slapped me like your father does, Nell, I'd walk straight out of the door and never go back.'

'Leaving your children?' Gwyneth said quietly. 'You wouldn't marry a man unless you loved him, and probably by the time you found out what he was really like you'd have a couple of children to provide for, and no means of doing so on your own.' Kitty didn't appear to appreciate what it was like not to have money.

'Yes, that I can understand, I suppose,' Kitty conceded. 'From what you've said, Gwyneth, your father isn't violent in the same way but he's so much in control! I'm amazed that your mother accepts it, however unreasonable he is.'

'Is that another form of love? She promised to obey, for better or worse, and she regards her marriage vows seriously. Your mother had the courage not to take that way, Kitty, and even though she had you she kept her independence.'

Kitty sighed and absentmindedly poured another cup of tea. 'Surely with the right husbands, who are reasonable and civilized and adore us, we could be married and still independent.'

'I don't ever want to be married,' Nell said vehemently. She had been unusually quiet, leaving most of the conversation to the others, but now she turned to them and spoke in heartfelt tones. 'Love is a trap! Girls imagine it gives them security, but it can't last, and just produces children who in the end are the main ones to suffer! I'm going to make it on my own, without the help of a man!'

'Good for you, Nell! You're so much more confident than when I first met you.'

'It's like waking up from a nightmare,' Nell confessed. 'I was much more sure of myself when I lived with Gran. The last two years at home seemed like a dreadful prison, so awful I didn't know how to fight it. It was enough just to endure.'

'But you've escaped now,' Kitty said soothingly.

Nell nodded. She was determined her future life would be different. 'I have, but my brothers and sisters haven't. That makes me feel guilty, yet there's nothing I can do. The older ones have got away, but with anger. They don't go home any more than I do. And that life has affected them,' she said almost to herself, recalling the brutal behaviour of her brothers. 'The little ones have to endure hell until they can tolerate it no longer! And my mother has to bear it for them as well as herself. I would feel dreadful if I had children who had to suffer. I know my mother feels enormous guilt about what he does to us, but she's so defeated, she can't do anything but wait for death to release her. And there are so many living like that.'

'Poverty doesn't always make people into beasts,' Gwyneth said quietly. 'In the villages back home there were some marvellous people, who'd give up their last crust to help a child or someone worse off than themselves. And they enjoyed themselves, singing, playing games, even though life was so grim.'

'And wealth doesn't make people good or generous. I've seen plenty of horrors in rich families, though not anything like so awful as you've described, Nell.'

'Are we all determined not to marry?' Gwyneth asked after a pause. 'Nell doesn't want children who might suffer. I'm determined no man will prevent me from dancing, and I can't see any husband being willing to let me go on appearing on the stage, especially in those new costumes Mr Bliss was talking about! What about you, Kitty?'

'I suppose I will marry, I've always expected to, despite my mother's example. You see, I don't want to be alone,' Kitty said slowly. 'I want to be independent too, and I know that with the right man it would be possible to be both. I've seen my mother, getting older and more and more absorbed in her campaigns. She doesn't love me or she wouldn't leave me alone so much. That's a form of cruelty too.'

'She's given you all the money you want,' Gwyneth said a little severely. 'She even insisted we didn't need to pay rent.'

Kitty laughed. 'So that you'd feel an obligation and stay with me! She really approved of your common sense, Gwyneth. She'd also begun to realize I could make Cousin Maud's life a misery if I had to give up dancing.'

'At least she let us pay towards the food,' Nell said.

'Of course having plenty of money makes things easier for me,' Kitty agreed. 'But it doesn't hurt her to give it to me. She has to make no sacrifice. Her aunt left her this house, and she has money from a family trust. She doesn't use half her income, even after providing for me and subscribing to her causes. She didn't have to give up a single thing in order to do it.'

'So who's the ideal man who will give you independence as well as love?' Nell asked, pushing her own worries aside and forcing herself to speak lightly.

Kitty grinned and began counting on her fingers. 'I'm not sure I've met him yet. Perhaps some fabulously rich American will see me on the stage and fall desperately in love with me. Or would an Italian prince be more exciting?'

'Or a desert sheik who'd carry you off to his tent?' Gwyneth asked, laughing. 'Isn't there anyone you already know?'

Kitty shrugged, then laughed rather self-consciously. 'I always planned to marry Andrew,' she confessed. 'He's always been my big cousin, I adored him when I was little. And he was such fun, so full of mad ideas! But he's starting to get a bit of a bore, he's so determined to make a name with his saxophone playing. It's the only thing he's ever cared about. On the other hand, we could travel, it could be exciting to be part of the theatre, and I won't stay a dancer long enough to become famous myself, even if I had the talent,' she added deprecatingly.

'You'll not give up?' Nell demanded, alarmed. Was this so recent friendship insecure after all?

'Not yet, until I get bored. I once thought I might like to marry Paul Mandeville, but he's so solid and dependable these days, not like he used to be when he and Andrew got up to all sorts of japes. He never does anything impulsive or adventurous. It would be lovely and safe, but I'm not sure I want life without any excitement. No, I think it will have to be Timothy. He'll have a title one day, and simply pots of money, and we can forever be doing divinely exciting things, spending the winter in the south of France, popping across to Paris or Le Touquet whenever we felt like it.'

'Would you really marry a man for money and a title?' Nell asked, surprised.

'Only if he was absolutely crazy over me! But I'd have to have a rich husband – my mother's trust money stops when she dies, and then all I'll have is this house.' She grinned, then sprang to her feet. 'Come on, let me show you my inheritance. You must have been too tired last night to do anything but collapse into bed.'

For most of the following week The Bliss Beauties polished and refined their routine. They were appearing in a larger theatre next and on Wednesday, when they were rehearsing in the Endersby's ballroom, Frank told them he had negotiated performances for several more weeks at theatres in the towns nearby.

'You're still the opening act, so there'll be no need for you to find lodgings, plenty of time to get back to Birmingham by tram or train.'

'I am not coming back on trams or trains,' Kitty said afterwards as they were changing. 'Betts can drive us.'

'Not in the trap, surely?'

'No, that would take an age and be miserably cold at night. It's still only March. Are you ready? Let's go.' She led the way out of the separate ballroom entrance.

'Then how?' Gwyneth demanded as they walked along the path leading to the front of the hotel.

'I told Mama before she left I simply must have a motor. Betts learned to drive last year when she was at home. She complained the horses were smelly and wouldn't use the trap. She said I could buy one of Sir Herbert Austin's little cars, the ones he makes at Longbridge. I might even learn to drive it myself,' she said excitedly as they emerged on to the carriage sweep in front of the main building. 'It will be terribly cramped with Betts as well.'

'I've never been in a motor,' Nell said enviously.

'Then we'll have to remedy that at once. May I drive you all home?'

'Paul! You startled me!' Kitty exclaimed. 'You shouldn't be eavesdropping, but as it's fortunate for us we'll forgive you!' She smiled brilliantly at him, and stepped towards his car which stood beside the front door.

'At least I didn't hear ill of myself. Kitty, since Nell has never ridden in a motor before, let her come in the front,' he added, and Kitty, with a slight pout, shrugged and climbed into the rear seat. Gwyneth followed and Nell, hardly able to believe what was happening, found herself seated in grandeur beside Paul as he drove the short distance to Kitty's home.

'What were you doing at Endersby's, Paul?' Kitty asked as they started. She had to shout over the noise of the engine and the considerable amount of traffic on the Hagley Road.

'One of the guests was indisposed. Nothing serious, thank goodness,' he replied, turning his head to make himself heard. 'I hear you're staying with Kitty at The Firs,' he said more quietly, so that only Nell could hear.

'Yes, isn't that kind of her?'

'Nell, this is a ridiculously short drive. I'd like to show you what the car can do. Will you come out with me for the day on Sunday?'

'Me?' She was bemused, at first unsure whether she wanted to go. Despite her returning confidence this was different. He wasn't like Tom; he was rich and important. Then she gave herself a mental shake. She'd determined to get the most out of her new life, and here was an opportunity to experience something exciting. He was simply being kind to her.

'Yes, you, and alone. I'd like to get to know you, talk to you. We can start early and have lunch out. You don't have a performance on Saturday, or a Sunday rehearsal, do you?'

'No, but I – I have something I must do, I can't come before ten o'clock.'

'Then I'll call for you at ten.'

Surely, Nell thought with a sudden surge of anxiety, that

would give Amy plenty of time to come to their secret meeting place by Perrott's Folly. She hadn't come the previous Sunday, when Nell had slipped away from The Firs before the others were awake, and waited by the tall tower after which Monument Road had been named. Nell had been telling herself ever since that there was nothing to worry about, Amy might have forgotten, or had to do something for Ma so that she couldn't get away. Nell hadn't been able to wait long, she didn't want to appear ungrateful to Kitty on their first morning with her. But if Amy could come she'd be there before ten, and Nell could enjoy her day out without worrying.

'Where would you like to go?' Paul asked as they set off.

Kitty had first been amazed, then very quiet, finally effusively supportive when Nell shyly told the others about Paul's invitation. Gwyneth had turned abruptly away, saying she felt exhausted, and slowly climbed the stairs to her room.

'It's ages since Paul Mandeville did anything impulsive,' Kitty said. 'Good for you, Nell! You must borrow my fur coat, it can be fiendishly cold in a motor in March.'

So Nell sat beside Paul, wrapped in Kitty's deliciously warm furs, with more fur rugs draped over her legs, unable fully to comprehend what was happening. Firmly she thrust out of her mind her disappointment that Amy had once more not come to meet her. She wondered whether her sister couldn't be bothered, but didn't want to believe that. Something had prevented her from coming. She'd keep on going every week, and would eventually discover what it was.

'I really don't mind where we go. You choose. I don't know anywhere,' she replied.

She would have liked to go back to Sutton, but shied away from suggesting it. She knew it would bring back painful memories, and she didn't want to break down in front of Paul again, who was so much older and so clever, and would probably despise her for weakness. Besides, he frightened her a little. Not in the same terrifying way she was scared of her father, for she knew instinctively Paul could never be cruel. It was more a worry that he would dismiss her nostalgia, as well as her other fears as insignificant, foolish, unworthy. She was nervous enough about doing or saying something which he would find silly or unsophisticated, and which might make him disapprove of her. For some inexplicable reason she wanted to look well in his eyes. He was the most superior being she had ever encountered.

'We'll go to Malvern Hills. I used to spend holidays there as a child, with an uncle. It's a lovely clear day, and from the top we can see right back to Birmingham.'

He turned southwards, and Nell gazed, awestruck, at the enormous houses set in spacious grounds. 'You don't live in a house like these, do you?' she asked after a few minutes.

He chuckled. 'No, my house is considerably smaller. You've never seen them before?'

'I've hardly dared come far into this side of the Hagley Road,' she confessed. 'Just to Kitty's house, but that's near the main road. They don't allow shops and trade, and it seemed too presumptuous just to walk round the streets. Besides, everyone else except nannies drives round in carriages or motors and I'd feel terribly out of place, as though everyone were looking at me.'

'If they were looking it would be because you're so beautiful,' he said lightly.

When Nell stole a glance at him he was staring straight ahead. She couldn't think what to say, so remained silent. It was the sort of meaningless compliment Kitty's friends all used, she decided, though she was surprised Paul behaved in the same manner. She'd thought of him as different. She wasn't at all sure how to deal with compliments from him. Anyway, although she wasn't ugly, her eyes were too big and her nose too small for beauty.

'Have you ever been through Bourneville?' Paul asked a few minutes later. 'We're coming into it now.'

'No. Doesn't it belong to the chocolate factory?'

'One of the Cadbury family built a few houses here in the last century, because the factory was so far out of the city and difficult for his workmen to get to. About thirty years ago they built a lot more, and it was one of the first planned villages.'

'What a lot of space!' Nell exclaimed a few minutes later. 'You could get half a dozen Ladywood courts into just one of those gardens!'

'It's being used as a model for the new estates being built in the suburbs. Soon, I hope, they'll increase the amount of building they're doing and pull down the slums.'

'That would be a dream to most people,' Nell said longingly. 'But if everyone has to move out into the suburbs, they couldn't afford to get to work. The rents would be higher and they couldn't pay tram and bus fares as well as higher rents.'

'They might build blocks of flats, for exactly those reasons.'

They drove on for a while without speaking, Paul wondering why on earth he was burbling on about slum clearance and other tediously boring matters when he had the loveliest girl he'd ever seen by his side, and all he really wanted to do was ask Nell to tell him every single detail about her life. He reflected ruefully on the odd effect she had on him, making him slink, almost in disguise, into a music hall, then ask her out for the day, alone, something he'd never done before with any girl, even Victoria. He felt eighteen again, gauche and uncertain, desperately anxious to impress the girls who had fluttered round the young men in uniform. Those days, before they went to France, had been both exciting and terrifying. They'd heard stories of the pitiful state of the men in the trenches, seen the wounded, mourned the dead, but they'd had no concept of the reality. They were to be heroes and they revelled in the adulation. They knew deep down they might also die, and subconsciously strove to live what life might be left them to the full. They'd been brash and immature but they had become adults within days of reaching the front. He dragged his roving thoughts back to the present and broke the slightly awkward silence as he pointed.

'This is Longbridge. Look, there's Sir Herbert Austin's workshops where they build the cars.'

Nell stared in amazement. 'It's huge! None of the factories in Ladywood are anywhere near as big!'

'No, but Sir Herbert employs tens of thousands of workers. Kitty says she is buying one of the new little cars?'

Nell laughed. 'Yes, she'll have it some time next week. She's very cross not to have it today, as we're dancing at Wolverhampton next week and will have to come home by train until it's here. I wonder whether she'll learn to drive it as she plans?'

'I expect so. Driving isn't difficult, even in a big car like this.'

Soon they were out into real country, bowling along at a great speed. Nell was thankful she'd listened to Kitty's advice and not tried to wear a hat. Paul had the hood down and even the scarf she'd tied round her head kept threatening to break free. She clutched it anxiously whenever a strong gust of wind caught them.

'You can see Worcester Cathedral,' Paul said after another long silence, pointing. 'Shall we stop by the river?'

'It's the Severn, isn't it? My gran once told me she spent a few days here with her gran, and went on a boat. She said they had funny little round boats which don't come more than a few inches out of the water.'

'Coracles. They still have them, and they look dreadfully unsafe, but they hardly ever turn over.'

They walked alongside the river for a while, then Nell shivered despite the fur coat and Paul was instantly solicitous.

'You mustn't catch cold. Come on, I'm planning to eat in a hotel high on the side of the hill, where we can look out of the restaurant window across towards the river. We won't be able to see it, but we'll know it's there.'

Nell smiled shyly at him as he tucked the rugs round her. He had the craziest urge to throw away all caution and discretion and sweep her into his arms. But staid, responsible, eligible doctors with wealthy patients didn't behave like that. They didn't announce they were madly in love with a girl they'd met only a couple of times, a girl from a totally unsuitable background who was earning her living in the rather dubious profession of stage dancer.

He started the car again. Soon they were climbing a steep hill towards the hotel, built of old stone, which, in summer, would be covered in creeper. By now Nell was used to good food, and sufficient of it. She'd never before eaten in a restaurant, though, and gazed round in awe at the quietly luxurious room, with its light-coloured panelled walls, enormous crystal chandeliers, and wide windows with red velvet curtains looped back to each side. They were shown to a window table set right inside a large bay, and she exclaimed in delight at the view stretched before her, seemingly for tens of miles.

'We can see even more from on top of the hills. We'll walk up there afterwards,' Paul promised. 'Shall I order for both of us?'

'Yes, please,' Nell said thankfully. She had caught a glimpse of the menu, and to her horror realized it was in French. How ignorant Paul would have thought her if she'd had to confess the only words she knew were the few she'd seen in the magazines Kitty bought. She didn't think '*Eau de Cologne*' or '*Les Reines des Crèmes*' would be of great value here. Concentrating hard, Nell watched Paul and carefully selected the knives and forks he did from the daunting array of cutlery set before them. To her relief she seemed to make no mistakes, and gradually relaxed, relishing the food and champagne.

'I enjoyed the stage performance,' Paul said. 'Mr Bliss must be a good teacher.'

'I am ze best in ze vorrrld!' Nell mimicked, shrill and staccato, stroking an imaginary moustache. 'Zere is no one 'oo can teach ze dance better zan Monsieur de Blees!'

Paul grinned. 'No false modesty, then? Is he French?'

'I don't think so. He puts on the accent when he's trying to impress new pupils, but then he forgets! To ze left, Mademoiselle, to ze left, I say! Do you not 'ear me, or is it zat you cannot tell ze left from ze right? Mon Dieu, vat 'ave I done to deserrrve such pupils! Now what the devil's the matter, Patsy? I said no one was to disturb the lessons!'

Paul chuckled. 'I seem to recall his house belonged to some-one else a year or so back. Has he been in Broad Street long?'

'No, nor Birmingham, but he never talks about the past. One of the girls who comes from Bristol once asked him if he'd had a school there, and he denied it so crossly he made us suspicious. She – this girl – said there had been some scandal to do with a French dancing teacher. One of his pupils complained that he was trying to make her – well, go to bed with him,' Nell said, blushing slightly, 'and he suddenly vanished, leaving all sorts of rumours as well as unpaid bills.'

'He hasn't tried to force you?' Paul asked with quick concern, leaning towards her.

Nell swiftly shook her head. 'No, nothing. He may not be the same teacher, and anyway I'm not pretty enough to tempt older men.' She grinned mischievously. 'Not like Kitty.' She assumed a deep, plummy voice. 'This is your very first professional engagement? I can hardly believe it, my dear child! You show such talent, such flair! But there are many pitfalls awaiting the unwary. I feel it my duty to warn you. You will allow me to give you a little supper, perhaps, and I can teach you all about this mad, crazy theatrical world we inhabit. Such innocence and purity as yours must be protected, and it would be an honour to take on that role.'

Paul was laughing. 'Who on earth was that?'

'The tenor.' She trilled a few notes, slightly off key. 'He fancied himself in heavy opera, but even without knowing any operas I could tell he was never quite right! I know the orchestra wasn't first class, but at least they played in tune, and he so often missed notes, or came in late. And I'm convinced he made up the words when he forgot them! He really fancied his chances with Kitty, too, but she went all haughty, called him her good man, and made him fetch us all cups of tea.' Nell giggled. 'At least I won't have that sort of problem!'

Paul doubted it. She was enchanting, with her eyes sparkling, bubbling with laughter as she recounted absurdities, a delicious smile playing on her lips. It was all he could do not to reach across the table and claim those lips for himself. Firmly he made himself concentrate on the meal.

Afterwards they drove further up the hill, curving round until they emerged at the top and, as Paul had promised, could see an enormous distance. Below them the woods and fields lay in patterns, criss-crossed by roads and cart tracks, and a long way off they could see an occasional gleam where the river showed through gaps in the winter trees.

'We mustn't stay long, it's cold and will soon be dark,' Paul said, and Nell wondered if she'd imagined the tinge of regret in his voice.

'It's been a wonderful day. Thank you,' Nell said when Paul stopped the car outside The Firs and jumped out.

'It's been wonderful for me too. Will you come with me again?' he asked as he helped her down. 'In the summer we can really enjoy the countryside.'

She smiled, tremulous and delighted. 'I'd love it. If you really want me to.'

'I want —'

His words were cut short as the front door opened and Kitty came running out. 'At last! We thought you'd never get back! Paul, come in and have supper with us, Andrew's here, and Timothy as well.'

Paul shook his head, explained he had work to do before the following day, an article he was writing for a medical journal, and drove away. Nell turned towards the house, still in a dream.

'Andrew's coming to see us tonight, and will drive us home in his car,' Kitty announced as the three girls were changing at the Wolverhampton theatre on Monday.

'I didn't know he had a car,' Gwyneth said.

'He's just bought one. A Vauxhall tourer. I don't know why he wants such a big one, since he lives just a few minutes by tram away from Endersby's and hardly ever plays anywhere else, but it's lucky for us.'

The entire troupe felt like old hands now. 'This dressing

room is so much bigger and better equipped, thank goodness,' Gwyneth said when they were told where to go.

'And that was Belle, one of the Singing Twins, she recognized us,' another girl marvelled.

The morning's rehearsal had gone smoothly, and some of The Bliss Beauties had felt confident enough to crack jokes with the stage hands as they waited in the wings. They were still the first on the bill, and had to endure the interruptions of latecomers, but by now they knew this was normal and didn't allow it to distract them. Although a larger theatre than the previous one, it was fuller even on Monday, and the applause the girls received was more than merely polite, it was warm and enthusiastic. The manager beamed at them as they ran down to the dressing room, and detained Gwyneth briefly.

'He said he'll definitely give us regular bookings!' she announced as she whirled into the dressing room. 'We're made, girls! The Bliss Beauties are on their way!'

Andrew was waiting for them in the narrow street outside the stage door. 'You were absolutely fantastic!' he enthused, leaping down from his large car to hug them each in turn. They chattered excitedly all the way back to Edgbaston, and Andrew joined them for the supper Meggy had prepared. 'Chorus lines are all very well, but you're all talented enough to do better than that,' he pronounced when they were sprawling round Kitty's sitting room afterwards. 'I've had a few ideas, can I come and talk about them tomorrow?'

'Not too early!' Kitty groaned. 'It's midnight now, and we working girls have to get our beauty sleep! God, to think I used to go to bed at dawn and never notice, and now I feel utterly grim by midnight!'

Chapter Twelve

Amy hated the place they brought her to. She'd begun to trust Miss Flora and Miss Sibyl, though she'd been too frightened to speak to them. Then she'd been taken to a big house with lots of other children, inspected and prodded and talked at by lots of different ladies and gentlemen, and after weeks, so many she couldn't remember, taken to an even bigger house. She didn't even know where she was, except that it was a long train journey from Birmingham, a place called Barkingside. Now, even when she wanted to speak, she couldn't. Sometimes she thought it had been a good job she hadn't been able to speak. Scared and miserable as she was at this place they called Dr Barnardo's, although she hadn't seen a doctor called that, just a man they called Dr Meredith, she knew she would be utterly terrified if they forced her to go back and face Pa, even though the children called her 'Dummy' when the grown-ups weren't around. She was well fed and they didn't beat her, but she missed Ma and Nell so fiercely it was far worse than one of Pa's beatings, and occasionally she wondered if it might be better to tell them who she was. But there was nothing she could do, for try as she might she couldn't speak now.

'I want to do something different. I'm getting bored playing in the same place all the time. You can all dance, and all sing,' Andrew said enthusiastically. 'We can create a bigger act, singing and dancing and musical solos. It would be sensational!'

They were in Kitty's drawing room, trying out various songs.

'You mean a complete bill?' Gwyneth asked doubtfully.

'Gwyneth has a lovely rich contralto, Nell and Kitty are sopranos. You are all good but different, and blend together well. A couple of the chaps can sing too.'

The girls looked at one another. 'I'd like it,' Kitty said after a while. 'It would be fun.'

'But I want to dance,' Gwyneth said slowly. 'We've only just started in a troupe, and anyway I'm not sure I'd enjoy doing all the rest.'

'Don't you enjoy singing?' Kitty asked.

'I prefer dancing.'

'What about you, Nell?'

'I'm not sure. I don't know anything about singing, and I don't know whether I'd like to be doing special dances all the time, though I'd like to try acrobatic dancing – I used to love doing handstands and cartwheels. It's more . . . comforting to be in a line.'

'There's no need to decide now. You have several weeks in theatres in Birmingham or near by, we can talk about it and think about some preliminary ideas, and then see if they'll work.'

'Mr and Mrs Bliss have been so good to us, and got us these bookings, I'd hate to let them down,' Gwyneth said.

'You can't stay with them for ever, they don't expect that, and it will be months before we're ready. You can give them notice, and surely he's doing so well now with lots of new classes he wouldn't find it difficult to replace you in the line. He'll have to get used to doing that. The girls don't stay in the same troupe for long, usually. They get other offers, move into better known troupes, like one of John Tiller's, or leave to get married. And if it's a success it will be good for the Bliss School when people know you were trained there.'

'We'll see. We've only just started dancing professionally,'

Gwyneth warned. 'Best not look too far ahead until we're sure we're being successful with the troupe.'

'It's not broken, just a severely strained muscle, but it means you won't be able to dance for several weeks,' Paul said.

'But I've so little money saved, I have to work!' Nell protested, and gasped as Paul bound up her swollen ankle.

'You don't need to pay me anything, Nell, so don't worry about that,' Kitty said swiftly.

'If you try to dance too soon you'll injure yourself so badly you'll never be able to dance again,' Paul warned.

'What will Mr Bliss say?'

'Gwyneth has gone to see him now so that they can decide who replaces you for next week's booking,' Kitty told her. 'Thank goodness it happened tonight, we've Sunday to rehearse with a new girl.'

'You've all been so kind! You and Gwyneth even carried me off the stage without the audience noticing!'

'That was Gwyneth's quick thinking, and you'd finished your solo dance anyway, so it looked planned, and we could go on without you for the rest of the act.'

Nell chuckled suddenly. 'The stage manager was so bewildered when you threw me into his arms and danced back on to the stage! He didn't know whether to throw me back on too.'

'I don't think I'd have minded being carried down to the dressing room in his arms! He was rather divinely big and strong,' Kitty giggled.

'At least he didn't make you walk on it,' Paul said to Nell, but she thought he looked angry.

Kitty drew closer to the fire and put on some more coal. 'Brr! It's freezing cold tonight, I was shivering before we went on,' she said. 'I was glad to start dancing to warm up.'

'Do you practise before you go on?' Paul asked.

'Practise? No, there's never enough room.'

'I don't mean do your routine, all together. Doing steps, warming up gradually, getting your muscles ready, loosening them, so that when you start to dance properly it isn't too much of a strain on them. Hasn't Mr Bliss ever told you to do that?'

'Not before a stage performance. In classes we start with simple exercises first.'

'If you don't warm up there's always a risk of this sort of injury. Does Mr Bliss pay you when you're not working in the theatre?'

'He's our manager. When we all had to give up our jobs in order to rehearse, before the first engagement, he paid us for the week of the rehearsals. That's half what we get when we're performing. He takes some of that, as his fee for managing and training us. It's instead of us paying for classes, and the usual system, he said.'

'Then it was his negligence in not telling you to warm up that caused the injury. He should pay you at least the rehearsal rate.'

'I never thought of that,' Gwyneth said slowly. 'If I go and complain, Paul, will you come with me and tell him, as a doctor, you advise it?'

'Of course.'

'He wouldn't like it to be known amongst other theatrical people that he doesn't take proper care of his troupes.'

'And he should pay you at least the rehearsal rate if you are injured.'

'That would be a relief,' Nell said. 'I really would feel better if I could at least pay Kitty. She's already helped me so much.'

'Now get to bed, it's late and you must be in pain. Can you manage to hop, or shall I carry you upstairs?'

'I'll manage,' Nell said swiftly, blushing at the idea of him carrying her. 'Kitty found this walking stick somewhere, and I can use that.'

'Good. Then don't put any weight on that foot. I'll come round tomorrow and see how the swelling is.'

'Poor little Nell!'

It was Sunday afternoon, and she was alone with Andrew. He

and Paul had both appeared at The Firs during the morning. After lunch, when Kitty and Gwyneth had to go to rehearse the new line for the engagement the following week, and Paul was summoned to another patient who had fallen from a horse, Andrew said he would stay and keep Nell company.

'The swelling has gone down a lot, it's not very bad,' Nell told him. 'I just won't be able to dance for a while.' Nor go and see whether Amy had tried to meet her, she thought guiltily to herself.

'Then I've a suggestion to make. Whenever I'm not playing at Endersby's, I'll take you to the theatre. We can study as many different acts as possible to get ideas for our own.'

She protested, but he brushed aside all her objections. Nell was so tempted by what she regarded as pure pleasure rather than the work he insisted it would be she soon agreed.

'Good. I'll go home and see what next week's programmes are. I'm not playing tomorrow, so I'll get some tickets.'

'But how on earth shall I manage to walk there, and climb up all the stairs?'

'I have the car, so we won't have to walk far. If you can't manage I'll carry you. And I'll get a box so that you can put your foot on a stool, if that's what Dr Paul recommends.'

'It's very good of you to take so much trouble.'

'Trouble? Nell, it's a heaven-sent opportunity to get to know you better. Don't you realize it's what I've wanted ever since I caught you that day in the shrubbery?'

'You can't expect me to swing that heavy handle?' Kitty said disbelievingly.

'Darling, be sensible! It's the only way to start the motor,' Timothy replied.

'But it's heavy!'

'Not as bad as you imagine. Come on, try it.'

'I have my new dress on.'

'And when you go driving you'll always have good clothes on. You can keep it out of the way.'

Reluctantly Kitty climbed down from the driving seat and took the starting handle in a fastidious grasp.

'Start at the top, push down, and then as it comes up this side pull sharply.'

Kitty gave it a tentative push. 'It's too big,' she announced with relief, standing up.

'It's better if it's big – more leverage.'

'Oh, this is impossible! How the devil can you expect me to understand these mechanic's expressions!' Kitty was examining her hands in horror. 'Just look what you've made me do! There's a smear of oil on my glove, and it will get on my other clothes!'

Timothy, bored, grasped the starting handle and with a swift turn brought the little Austin Seven to life. It purred with satisfaction. Kitty beamed at Timothy and settled herself once more behind the wheel.

'You'll have to learn one day,' Timothy said as he climbed in beside her.

'Pooh! I'll find someone to do it for me.'

'Even if you are stranded on a lonely country road, at night, in the rain, with no one in sight?' he asked sceptically.

'Why on earth should I ever be on some miserable deserted road?'

'You do plan to travel the country appearing at theatres,' he reminded her.

'Yes, but Gwyneth and Nell will always be with me. I'm sure they'll understand about leverage, and be happy to do it. After all, I shall be providing the motor.'

'Nell has a sprained ankle at the moment,' he reminded her, 'and she always looks too fragile to me even to be dancing.'

Kitty glared at him. 'It's always Nell! Paul's besotted with her, and Andrew's like a puppy with a bone, planning all these frightfully stupid theatre trips! As if she needs to watch everyone else when we can do it perfectly well already!'

He shrugged. 'Don't be so ridiculous, Kitty. It's quite possible you might be on your own. What then?' he persisted.

'There'll always be someone,' she replied airily. 'Now show me what to do next, darling Timothy. I can't wait to drive it properly.'

An hour later she steered, somewhat uncertainly, back through the gateway of The Firs.

'There! Thanks, darling, you can hop down now. I'll go out on my own for a few minutes. I know what to do.'

'No.'

'What do you mean?'

Timothy ran his hands through his already ruffled hair and sighed. 'You aren't safe yet, darling. It was providence that you missed the tram in the Hagley Road, and you have to give way to horses. You almost ran down that baker's trap.'

'Stupid man! Anyway, I paid him for the damned loaves he dropped off when he swerved so idiotically. He should have stacked them more carefully.'

'And next time it might be a child. Do you imagine you'll be able to buy off the parents?'

'Some of them might be glad to get rid of a few extra mouths!' she said bitterly, her face white with anger, but after a moment she shrugged and opened the door. 'Come and have a cocktail.'

'Why did you want me to teach you?' Timothy asked as he followed her into the house.

'You're the only one with the patience to put up with me,' she admitted, grinning, and turned to kiss him lightly on the cheek. 'Dear Timothy! What would I do without you?'

Nell was giggling unrestrainedly when finally she was settled in one of the boxes at the Theatre Royal.

'Andrew, the fuss! I might have been a princess!'

'You are my princess,' he replied lightly. 'Now you're sure you have enough cushions under that leg? Paul would slaughter me if I damaged it, and Gwyneth has threatened all sorts of revenge if I delay your recovery. She says no one else can do the special routine with her.'

'Hush, it's starting!'

For the next hour she sat entranced, watching the stage. Andrew divided his attention between the performers and Nell. In the six months or so since he had caught her in the shrubbery she had changed in so many ways. She wasn't so thin, now that she had proper food, but she still had that slender, waif-like beauty which caught at the heart. Her smile was enchanting, shy and fleeting, yet brilliant in its quality. Too often, though, she seemed absorbed in her own reflections, withdrawn and sad. It was as if she was in another world.

In other ways, she had blossomed. The small defiance she had shown when he had captured her had, he suspected, been uncharacteristic and sparked by the terror consuming her, as well as despair at losing that deplorable shawl. Now she had much more confidence and often voiced her own opinions strongly, particularly if they were to do with dancing. She seemed to have an instinctive flair for what was the best, and privately Andrew considered that in time she could be even better than Gwyneth.

At the interval she turned shining eyes towards him. 'That was wonderful! But surely we could never hope to be as good!'

'We will be. You are already better than those dancers,' he reassured her. 'They just look good because they have elaborate costumes – lots of glitter and feathers. In theatre, Nell, it's the outward appearance that's most important. Provided, that is, the performers are averagely competent.'

'That doesn't apply to your playing,' she said slowly.

'Not so much, perhaps. But it still sounds better if the player shows confidence. A superb musician who hesitates can sound worse than someone who plays on and covers up mistakes. Dancing in a troupe it's enough to keep together and look good. We'll have to be a little better in our new act, but with plenty of practice we will be.'

At the end he insisted on carrying her out to his car, parked nearby. She was more conscious of the stares of other theatre-goers than she had been on their arrival. Then it had been amusing to have the theatre management carving a path through

the crowds, ushering her in as if she were an honoured guest.
Now, making their way to Andrew's car and the intimacy of the
drive home, she felt uneasy clasped tightly in his arms. His face
was so close to her own she could feel his breath on her cheek.
She shivered suddenly and his arms tightened about her.

'Cold?'

'A little, yes.'

'It could be frosty tonight. Here we are. Can you stand while
I unlock the door?'

'I'm able to hop, or walk with a stick,' she reminded him
with a nervous laugh.

'But how inelegant! Not at all the way a dancer should be
seen. There, get in. We'll soon be warm.'

He helped her in, solicitously tucked the rugs about her, and
climbed into the driver's seat. For a moment he sat looking at
her in the light of the street lamp, and then gave a slight shrug
and set off for Edgbaston.

Meggy was waiting for them in the hall, and pursed her lips
when Andrew carried Nell in.

'Are the others back yet?' he asked cheerfully as he set her
gently on her feet.

'No, Master Andrew, you know perfectly well they won't be
home till near midnight. Even later if Miss Kitty bamboozles
Betts into letting her drive that pesky motor. She ain't fit to be
let loose with such a contraption. Now, Miss Nell, up to bed
with you, you look worn out.'

'I am tired,' Nell admitted.

'It was too much for you, an evening at the theatre just a
couple of days after you sprained your ankle. I'll help you up
the stairs. There's no call for you to stay,' Meggy added curtly
without turning round, and behind her back Andrew grimaced.

'Dear Meggy! Cerberus in person. I'll see you tomorrow,
Nell. I've arranged for some more tickets.'

'I'll never be able to do it!' Gwyneth sighed. 'There are so many
things to remember all at once!'

'It will get better,' Timothy reassured her.

They were sitting in the Austin Seven, at an isolated spot at the top of the Lickey Hills. Gwyneth, with many false starts and mistakes, had driven Kitty's new car from Edgbaston.

'Kitty mastered it at once,' she said, a trace of envy in her voice. 'She's already driving by herself. I don't seem to have the least idea. I'd be terrified to be left on my own, and I make such terrible noises I'm afraid I'm wrecking the car.'

'Of course you aren't. But I'll drive now.'

'Thanks. Heavens, I'm stiff!' she exclaimed as they changed seats. 'It's much harder work than dancing for several hours.'

'It's just because you aren't relaxed. Look, we're quite near my father's house. Let's go there and have something to eat.'

'But – won't he mind?' Gwyneth asked.

'He won't be there. It's really no more than a large farmhouse, which he inherited from a distant cousin who was killed in the war. He has a farm manager who lives in part of it, and his wife acts as housekeeper for my father, who uses the house just for flying visits to Birmingham. It's where I stay when I come up here.'

'I don't think I ought.'

'Gwyneth, it's nearly time for lunch. We couldn't drive back to Edgbaston quickly, but after you've relaxed you might feel able to try driving again.'

'Will I ever learn to drive?'

'Of course you will. It's like learning to ride. The second time you get on a horse it feels so much more familiar you can concentrate better on other things.'

Gwyneth nodded. 'Yes, that's true. We had an old pony at home and I was terrified the first time my brothers made me sit on him. Next time I wondered why it had seemed so frightening.'

'Driving is the same. Soon you'll be even better than Kitty. She's too impatient to be really good.'

'She wasn't very happy to lend me her car.'

'She soon agreed when I promised to fetch you home from

Dudley next week. Anyway, she has both Paul and Andrew to keep her company today.'

'Yes,' Gwyneth said in a small voice. She couldn't help but see how Paul looked at Nell, the concern and tenderness in his eyes as he checked her sprained ankle. Fiercely she commanded herself to forget her dreams. Paul was always pleasant, as he was to everyone, but he barely noticed she was there. She hadn't the slightest hope of attracting his attention while Nell was around. She doubted he would notice her even if in some miraculous way Nell were out of reach.

The first tug of attraction Gwyneth had felt on seeing him had, if anything, intensified as she came to know him better. He was handsome, of course. That had been the first thing to strike her. From the stories Kitty and Andrew told, he had been as crazy as they were when he was young. It sounded as though he'd never refused any bet, however hazardous, and Andrew frequently hinted at the many female hearts lying strewn in his path, while claiming he was bound to secrecy about Paul's early amatory exploits. Now he was calm, thoughtful, considerate, and an exceptionally dedicated doctor, caring intensely for all his patients whether they were rich aristocrats or filthy paupers.

She smiled wryly to herself. He was so very different from her father. She had inherited her own fiery temper from him, although she never held grudges like her father did. If anyone displeased him, he was stern and unforgiving. He professed to care deeply for the welfare of his flock, but Gwyneth had over the years become cynical. He was more concerned with whether they obeyed his injunctions than whether they sinned. Real sinners, those who disobeyed him, were turned away condemned. She shook herself slightly and tried to concentrate on Timothy's explanation. It looked so easy when he did it.

'Here we are,' he said shortly, and turned off the narrow lane they had been following on to an even narrower farm track. Over the brow of a small hill she could see a tall, twisted chimney, and as they crested the rise she gasped in delight.

'It's beautiful! It's bigger than a farm, surely?'

'I suppose it was once a manor house, but it is really no more than a large farm. It's always been called Manor Farm. It dates back to Tudor times, though most of it was rebuilt about a hundred and fifty years ago.'

It lay in a shallow bowl, with no other houses in sight. The main part of the house was long and low, white painted and facing south, but behind there was a straggling wing of higgledy-piggledy roofs, above uneven walls of great black beams and red bricks in a variety of herringbone patterns. Scattered nearby were stables and farm buildings, barns and cowsheds, and a wide crescent of trees just bursting into leaf sheltered the entire farmstead from northerly winds.

'Welcome home,' Timothy said softly as he drew to a halt in front of the house.

He was proud of the house, Gwyneth realized. After introducing her to Mrs Sankey, his housekeeper, who promised a meal ready in half an hour, he took her to inspect the main rooms.

'It was my great-great-great-grandfather who did most of the building. He'd married the owner's daughter, a second marriage for him when he was in his forties, and he was by all accounts a doting husband. She wanted the latest fashions, and was completely indulged. Some of the rooms are far too grand for what is, after all, no more than a farmhouse, but she wanted to pretend she had a miniature Stoneleigh Abbey. See how the rooms in this part all lead into one another, like a suite of state banqueting halls!'

'The ceilings are incredible!' Gwyneth gasped, gazing up at them. 'I love that moulding and the paintings.'

'Even the cherubs?' Timothy asked mischievously. 'My cousin's wife was a real prim Victorian, she tried to make him paint over them, said they weren't decent. Fortunately he refused to let her do it, and she had to be content with slinging a false ceiling of plain material underneath to hide them from the affronted gaze of her guests.'

Gwyneth laughed. 'It would have been wicked to have ruined

them,' she agreed. 'Thank goodness we have a more sensible attitude now.'

'I'm glad you agree. I've asked Mrs Sankey to set lunch in my own sitting room. It's far too formal in the big dining room Father uses when he comes here.'

He took her arm and led the way upstairs to a suite of rooms at one end of the front wing. A fire had been hastily lit, and Mrs Sankey was laying a small circular table by the window. 'Soon be ready, Master Timothy,' she said cheerfully. 'Lucky we had a big Sunday roast today, plenty for all of us. And rhubarb pie to follow, the first picking. With fresh cream. Shall I bring some wine?'

'Yes please. Champagne, I think.'

She eyed Gwyneth with interest as she left the room, and was soon back with the first course, a tureen of delicious leek soup, and a bottle of champagne. 'Enjoy your dinner,' she said cheerfully as she left the room.

'She's nice,' Gwyneth commented.

'A little too inclined to think I'm still a ten-year-old up to mischief!' Timothy replied with a grin, opening the champagne and filling the glasses. 'To you, Gwyneth, and your success!'

The meal was delicious, but substantial farmhouse fare, and Gwyneth had to be coaxed into eating the big helpings of pie Mrs Sankey brought.

'She'd be offended, and it really isn't heavy,' Timothy urged. 'Have the last of the champagne with it.'

She seemed to have drunk a great deal, Gwyneth thought hazily as she lifted the glass. Concentrating on driving, then the food and wine, much more of both than she was accustomed to, had made her sleepy, and when Timothy suggested they moved to sit on a deep settee beside the fire she was happy to agree.

'I'll build up the fire, it's getting cold outside,' he said, and Gwyneth nodded.

When she woke it was dark, the room was lit only by firelight, and Timothy's arm was around her shoulder.

'A real sleeping beauty,' he murmured, and bent to kiss her on the lips.

Gwyneth, still muzzy, didn't move. Timothy pulled her closer, and she blinked and looked round. 'It's dark.'

'It is. You slept for ages, you must have been very tired. It's too dark to drive home. We'll have to stay here tonight. Fortunately my bed is a big one.'

For a moment she didn't understand. 'But there must be several spare bedrooms,' she began, and then struggled to sit up, trying to push him away. 'Timothy!'

'Timothy!' he imitated her. 'Darling, don't be coy. We can't let this opportunity slip, can we?'

'I'm not going to share your bed!' she declared, by now fully awake. 'And it's perfectly possible to drive in the dark, there are lights on the car. You showed them to me. How else could we get home from the theatres?'

'Gwyneth, my lovely girl, it's useless, and you know it. I won't be ungenerous.'

'You could give me this house and its entire contents but it still wouldn't be generous enough!' she snapped, trying to jump to her feet.

'You won't get away,' he drawled, holding her down with ease.

'You damned useless men think all you have to do is wave money under a girl's nose and she'll fall on her back for you!' Gwyneth raged. 'No, I tell you, and if you don't let me go I'll scream the place down!'

'Temper, temper, now. Mrs Sankey will be in her own part of the house, and those walls are thick. I told her we'd let ourselves out, and she knows better than to interfere. It's not the first time she's turned a discreet eye.'

'And you think you'll make me one of your paid whores! You have a damned cheek! You may be stronger than I am, and you may be able to rape me, but if you do, I promise the whole of Birmingham will know about it the minute I get back!'

'And your father?' he asked quietly. 'Such an outrageous fuss would bring him hot-foot from his Welsh valley, surely? If only to rescue you from the jaws of hell.'

For a moment Gwyneth was still. Then as Timothy relaxed his grip, thinking he'd won, she stamped the sharp heel of her shoe down on his instep, and as he gasped with pain wrenched her hands free and boxed him soundly on both ears. She was up and had whisked through the door while he was still too startled to move. To her relief she saw the key and pulled it out of the keyhole, slamming the door and managing to lock Timothy in just as he began to tug at it from the other side.

'I could leave you here,' she panted. 'As you said, Mrs Sankey wouldn't hear you.'

'Gwyneth, you little devil! Let me out!'

'Only if you promise not to even touch me again.'

'Puritan! How was I to know you weren't like all the other dancers?'

'Which other dancers? How many have you tried, Timothy? How can you be so sure they're all as immoral as you are?'

'Here, that's below the belt!'

'One law for the rich young man, eh?'

'Stop fooling, Gwyneth, and let me out. I've no intention of trying to touch you now! I'd rather bed with a tiger!'

'I don't trust you. Perhaps I should go and give Mrs Sankey the key? Tell her what you wanted?'

'You little devil! Open the door, do you hear!'

'I hear. And thank you for the driving lesson, by the way. I think I'll be able to get back home by myself!'

Chapter Thirteen

Mrs Baxter dragged herself up the rickety stairs. It was all too much for her. Thank God, since Amy had disappeared, Eth had been more helpful, and had said she'd bring something home for supper. Her children were good to her. At least, the ones left at home were. Benjy had a part-time job delivering coal, and even little Fanny, just past her twelfth birthday, had insisted she went back to bed.

'I'll go and clean at Mrs Tolley's,' she'd said firmly. 'Yer'd only fall in 'oss-road an' get run over, way yer lookin'.'

'But yer should be in school,' Mrs Baxter protested weakly.

'Yer can write me a note fer tomorrow. That way, no truant officer'll be after us.'

'The little 'uns?'

'Mrs Jenks from next door'll look after Ronny, an' keep an eye on t'others in court, an' give 'em a crust if they start yellin' before I'm 'ome.'

Emily knew she shouldn't, it was wrong to expect the kids to look after her, but she felt so ill she didn't really care. All she wanted was to fall into bed and sleep away her aches and pains and the misery which hadn't left her since Amy's disappearance so many weeks ago. It had been bad enough when Nell went, but Nell was old enough to look after herself. So long as nothing dreadful had happened to her, Nell could manage alone. Amy was still a child. She might be dead, but somehow her mother knew she wasn't. She seemed to feel the child calling to her, but she couldn't hear clearly. Amy was trying to tell her something, asking for help, but she didn't know what she could do, how she could help her baby. All sorts of terrible things could have happened to her, and she'd never know.

She mustn't think about it. Visions of the dreadful fates which might have overtaken the child just caused her to shake uncontrollably. Yet she couldn't push the thoughts away; on they came, relentless.

When Fanny came home late that afternoon her mother was lying half in, half out of bed, the thin blanket on the floor. Her skin was blue with cold, for there was no fire in the house and there had been a fierce wind blowing that day.

'Ma! Oh, Ma, wake up!'

Fanny tried to rouse her mother, but it was useless. Mrs Baxter breathed noisily, and moaned, but she did not open her eyes.

Sobbing with fright, and unable to lift her mother back into the high bed, Fanny eased her down on to the thin mattress where the two babies slept. She had some obscure notion that people ought to lie flat, or they might drown in their own vomit. Ma had been sick, she noticed, when she calmed down enough to look around the room. She'd better clean that up. Pa would be angry. But it would be hours before Eth or Pa came home. And Ma needed help. Eventually Fanny, greatly daring, made up her mind. She would go to the clinic and fetch one of the nurses. At least she could ask them what to do. And she knew that if folk really couldn't afford to pay, they sometimes gave away medicines. They'd given Ma some for Ronny, and he'd got better.

'Poor Timothy!' Kitty howled with laughter as she led him through into her small sitting room. 'We made Gwyneth tell us what had happened last night when she staggered in. It was a miracle she managed to get the motor here in one piece, she was so angry.'

'Little devil! I climbed out of the window in the end. Too shaming to let the Sankeys know I'd been bested by a mere slip of a gal! At least she'd left the key in the door and had the decency not to tell them.'

'But how did you get here? Surely you had to ask someone to drive you?'

'Not likely! I got back in and opened the door, then I skulked in my own room until morning. The Sankeys keep out of the way, when I have guests —'

'When you take a girl home, you mean,' Kitty interposed, grinning.

Timothy ignored her. 'They couldn't hear the car from their side of the house, and by the time they came round this morning they'd have thought we'd left. I had to walk to the station and take the bally train.'

Kitty chortled. 'What a comedown! But Timothy, it's hilarious! Fancy Gwyneth having the guts to lock you up like that.'

'She led me on. How was I to know she wasn't like all the other dancers?'

'Like me too?' she asked sweetly.

He laughed. 'No, of course not. You're different, Kitty, you're not the same class as those girls. They're looking for wealthy husbands, most of them, and if they can't manage that they usually accept a wealthy lover.'

'I don't believe Gwyneth wants either,' Kitty said musingly. 'She might accept a husband, if she fell in love, but never a lover.' She struck a pose. 'She is wedded to her art! Of course, if the lover were someone in the theatre, someone who would be useful for her career, pure dear Gwyneth might consider it worth her virtue. I truly believe she would kill for her dancing — when she was in a temper. Not normally.'

'Well, I'm finished with her! It was a scaly trick, and I am not amused. Where is she?'

'She's gone to talk to Mr Bliss. She said she had some ideas about new routines, but I think she knew you'd be coming and wanted to avoid you.'

'Of course she knew I'd be fetching my own car! And I'm not surprised she wanted to avoid me!'

'Poor Timothy, you really don't understand the working classes, do you? Poor but honest! What you need is a girl from your own background, someone who would understand you.'

'We've got bookings for the band in London for several weeks, Nell,' Andrew said. 'I have to go next Monday.'

'Oh, that's good! But what will Mr Endersby say about your leaving?'

'Richard understands. He has another group in mind. When we've done this tour we may come back for a while – his new ballroom in the Stafford hotel is due to open in a month or so.'

'What about the act we were planning?'

'That's at an early stage yet. We can discuss it on Sunday. Gwyneth has lots of ideas, even though she still doesn't know what she wants, and you can work on those while I'm away. The real snag is that I won't be able to take you to any more theatres after tonight.'

'But I'll be dancing again soon, perhaps the week after next. My ankle is almost strong enough. I think I could dance on it now, but Paul won't agree – he says I might do permanent damage if I dance too soon.'

'He's right, it isn't worth risking. So this is to be our last outing together for the time being.'

'I have appreciated seeing all these marvellous acts,' Nell said quietly. 'They've given me lots of ideas.'

'Me too,' Andrew murmured. 'Ssh, the second half's starting. But afterwards we'll celebrate, shall we?'

Nell wasn't sure she wanted to be alone with Andrew after the show. He was adopting a possessive air which disturbed her. Even though it was now perfectly possible for her to walk unaided, he insisted on supporting her with his arm round her waist, and seemed to take every opportunity to touch her.

It wasn't just that he was being solicitous. When she caught his gaze on her she was aware of the intensity of feeling in his eyes. Several times she had been expecting him to kiss her, but at the last moment he had drawn away. Nell didn't want his kisses. She still shuddered at the recollection of Tom's attempted embraces. She forced her attention back to the singer on the stage. This was pointless speculation. She didn't want anyone's kisses and she wouldn't accept them from Andrew.

When the show was over, however, and Andrew drove to the Grand Hotel where he had booked a table for a late supper, she did not protest. It would have been churlish and it did not commit her. She looked around in awe. Apart from Endersby's and the hotel where she had lunched with Paul she had never seen such magnificence. The enormous chandeliers cast a brilliance over everything, and all the well-dressed people looked as though they dined in such splendour every day. Briefly it crossed her mind to wonder what her mother would say if she knew. She thrust the thought aside. It was too painful to recall the squalor in which the rest of the family lived, the brutality and filth which surrounded them. Since her injury had prevented her for weeks from trying to meet Amy at Perrott's Folly, even her favourite sister would have given up on her.

'Nell, my dear, to us!' Andrew said as he raised his champagne glass towards her.

She looked at him doubtfully. 'The new act?' she queried.

'More than that. Nell, you must have realized how I feel about you. I think I knew that first day. I love you, Nell.'

Quickly she shook her head. 'No! You mustn't! It's not suitable! Besides, I don't want to marry, I want to dance!'

He looked at her quizzically, and his lips twitched. 'I won't be difficult, I promise. I just wanted you to know. Now let's be comfortable and talk about other things, and enjoy our last evening together.'

Kitty was pacing up and down her sitting room when Nell came in. 'Where on earth have you been? The show must have finished ages ago!'

'I'm sorry, I didn't know you needed me. Andrew took me out to supper. He's going away next week, on tour.'

'It's not me that wants you, it's Paul! He's been waiting here for hours.'

Nell saw Paul then. He'd been sitting in a chair partly concealed by the open door, but now he stepped forward and took her hands in his.

'Nell, come and sit down. I discovered today that your mother is very ill.'

'Ma? Ill? Paul, I must go to her straightaway, there's no one to look after her!' Nell exclaimed, trying to free her hands from his grasp.

'It's far too late, she'll be asleep. Nell, she's being cared for, your sister Eth and little Fanny are being very good, and one of the nurses from the clinic goes in every day.'

'What's the matter with her?'

'Sit down. You can see her tomorrow, it's all arranged. We don't know what's wrong exactly, she has a high fever, and has been unconscious for much of the time, but she is a little better now. She's badly undernourished, of course, but I think this is more a fever of the brain than the body, she's so desperately worried about Amy.'

'Amy? Why? What's the matter with her?' Nell was trembling with anxiety, and Paul had the greatest difficulty not to take her in his arms to soothe her.

'She disappeared several weeks ago. No one knows where she is or what became of her.'

'Amy gone? Oh no! Then that's why she didn't come to meet me!'

Nell stared at him in horror, and tears gathered in her eyes. Paul gestured to Kitty, who shrugged and left the room. Then Paul did gather Nell into his arms and as she struggled to suppress her sobs he held her close.

'Tell me,' he said gently when she had regained some control.

'I met her one day, in the Hagley Road. It was about the time we came to live here with Kitty. We said we'd try to meet each Sunday morning by Perrott's Folly. But she didn't come, and then I hurt my ankle and I couldn't go. Did she – did she think I'd forgotten her?'

'I don't know. I've only seen your mother once, when the nurse asked me to go in this evening. I realized from the names it must be your family. I talked for a while with Eth, but that's all I know.'

'Pa? Did you see him? Was he there?'

'No. He was drowning his sorrows. It seems he's drinking more than he used to, though Eth didn't know where he got the money.'

'I must go back and take care of her.'

'No. She doesn't want that. She was quite rational when I saw her, and I told her you were well, and what you were doing. She's insistent that now you have escaped — those were her words — you must not go back. She's content to know you are safe, and to see you sometimes.'

'She's just saying that. Paul, I must go now!'

'No, you must sleep now. I understand your father has threatened violence if he sees you. I've brought a sleeping draught you must take tonight, and I will come with you in the morning.'

Nell protested, but in vain, and she realized that it would be quicker to take his medicine and know she could see her mother in the morning than argue all night. She fell asleep bitterly condemning herself for having left home, and by so doing driving Amy into terrible unknown dangers.

Nell hurried into the court. Despite her worry about her mother and Amy, the breath caught in her throat at the nauseous reek which assailed her nostrils. She'd forgotten how foul it was in these small, enclosed spaces where the sunshine rarely penetrated. The mingled smells of rubbish, smoke, dirty washing, rancid fat and rarely cleaned privies made her gag, and she marvelled that so short a time before she'd lived here and scarcely noticed.

Paul was beside her, and as she reached the door to her home he took her hand in a comforting grip. Fanny had been watching for them and dragged open the door.

'Nell! Oh, Nell!' she cried, and threw herself into Nell's arms.

'It's all right, Fanny. Give over, I'm back now. Where's Ma?' Nell asked, moving into the kitchen and looking round her at the familiar chaos. The younger children sat, unnaturally quiet, in a huddle on the floor, and Nell went to hug and kiss them all in turn.

'In our bed. Eth's with 'er. The nurse said she wasn't to be with Pa or the little 'uns, an' she made the boys move in with Pa. Eth an' me sleep on the floor, so's we can 'elp 'er in the night,' Fanny explained in a rush.

'Let's go upstairs. You first, Nell,' Paul said.

She smiled at Paul tremulously and, hugging Fanny to her, climbed the stairs. Ma was propped up on pillows, pillows which hadn't been there before, and there were clean sheets and a good thick blanket. But Nell hardly saw them as she ran to bend and kiss her mother. 'You look so thin!' she exclaimed. 'Oh Ma!'

'Nell, luv!' Mrs Baxter was too weak to sob but tears oozed from between her closed eyelids as Nell cautiously hugged her.

'I didn't mean to worry you when I went away,' Nell said quietly.

'I know, ducks. If I'd known 'e'd 'ave beat it out of me, so it were best yer didn't tell me. Amy said yer was all right.'

'Amy?' Nell asked hesitantly.

Mrs Baxter turned her face away and gestured feebly to Eth. 'You tell 'er.'

'It were after yer giv 'er that money,' Eth said. It was the first time she'd spoken, and she didn't offer to kiss Nell, but stood at the other side of the bed as if distancing herself from her sister.

'Go on.'

'Well, 'er came 'ome, all excited, an' told Ma 'er'd seen yer, all posh like a bleedin' toff. Pa 'eard and 'e frit 'er, an' 'er ran off. That's it.'

'Did you go to the police?'

'Pa didn't let Ma go.'

Nell buried her face in her hands for a moment. It was too much. What had become of her little sister? 'I should have told her where I was living. Then she might have come to me.'

'You know very well your father would have made her tell him,' Paul said quietly. 'How are you today, Mrs Baxter? You look a little better.'

'It's your medicine, doctor. An' seein' Nell.'

'I'm staying here to look after you now, Ma,' Nell declared, but both Mrs Baxter and Paul shook their heads. Her mother spoke first.

''E'd kill yer,' she said simply. ''E blames yer fer the lads goin', losin' the wages they brung 'ome, an' Amy. Yer mustn't stay 'ere.'

'She's right, Nell, it would make matters worse. Send money or food, or clothes. Your mother can say she was given them by the Mission. And I've spoken to your father and threatened him with police action if he beats any of the family again. I don't think he'll take it out on them.'

'I don't want yer back, luv. Now yer've found summat better, keep it. Fer my sake.'

It was some time before they could persuade Nell that it would make things worse with Pa if she tried to come back, but at last she shrugged. 'I'll come and see you when I can, when Pa's safely out of the way.'

'And I'll make arrangements to bring anything you like, letters or food or money,' Paul said. 'Now we'd better go.'

A week later Nell once more visited her mother, and found that she was much better. Reassured over that, though still desperately concerned about Amy's fate, Nell promised to come as often as she could.

Later in the afternoon she and Gwyneth went to see Mr Bliss, and discuss how Nell, her ankle strong again, could resume dancing with the troupe.

'I shall need lots of practice,' Nell said, worried. 'Paul says I mustn't do too much for the first few weeks, but I can begin to dance the less strenuous routines.'

'That means no speciality spots,' Frank Bliss said with a sigh. 'Gwyneth is excellent by herself, but so far we've found no one good enough to partner her. I think you'd better just come to join as many classes as you can next week.'

'That would help me start,' Nell nodded.

'You must try to be ready for the stage the following week. In three weeks the Beauties are due to have their first engagement in Stoke-on-Trent. They'll have to stay in lodgings, and I know Edwina would be happier if you were with Gwyneth to help take care of the girls.'

Nell raised her eyebrows, but did not comment. She was less apprehensive now at the idea of finding lodgings in a strange town than she had been when she'd met Gwyneth. In fact, she thought with inner amazement, she was confident over all manner of new things, from dining in expensive restaurants to talking with important people. Yet she hardly thought she was capable of supervising the dancing troupe, many of whom were a couple of years older than she was. She said as much to Gwyneth when they were back at The Firs, drinking tea and indulging in some Kunzle cakes Kitty had bought the previous day.

'It's not age that matters,' Gwyneth said. 'The Tiller Girls have "Head Girls", but Mr Bliss hasn't got a name for us, he doesn't want to look as though he's copying them too much.'

She lapsed into silence, and as Nell's own thoughts had swung back to her family, they sat for some time without speaking. Eventually Nell roused herself.

'Have you seen the new costumes Edwina's designed?'

'Yes, they're a lot more glittery than any we've had before. And I love those saucy little hats!'

'And such short skirts! I felt quite embarrassed when I tried mine on,' Nell said with a slight laugh.

'If we mean to be successful we'll have to get used to showing so much leg! They are a gorgeous shade of red, perfect for us with our dark hair.'

'At least they are quite modest at the top. I suspect Edwina's breaking us in gently, taking off a few more inches in a different place with every new costume!'

'Then I hope she stops soon! I'll go and see what Meggy's left for dinner,' she offered.

'Kitty is out with Timothy, and said they wouldn't be back.'

'I wish her luck with him,' Gwyneth said bitterly.

'He's still not forgiven you,' Nell said. 'You hurt his pride, I think.'

'He hasn't spoken to me since. Are all men the same? Why should they assume that because we perform in public, we're ready to leap into bed with any man who deigns to ask us? And think it an honour to receive his attentions!'

'I'm sure not all men do,' Nell replied quietly. 'Andrew and Paul would never suggest it.'

'More's the pity!' Gwyneth muttered, but so quietly that Nell didn't hear.

'Did you like Timothy?' Nell asked hesitantly. She wondered if this was the reason for her friend's unusual lack of sparkle.

Gwyneth looked at her for a moment without replying. Then she turned away her face. 'Yes, I did like him,' she said in a flat voice, and to her surprise discovered it was the truth. She had liked him, and if Paul were not around, she knew she could have fallen for him. 'Not enough to become his mistress, though. No man will ever mean more to me than dancing.'

Gwyneth and Kitty were doing a matinée, and Nell had been to one of Mr Bliss's classes. Afterwards she walked along Ryland Street, buying good quality beef and vegetables in shops which before she had never hoped to patronize. Pa would be at work, so this was a good time to go and see how Ma was. She had almost reached the corner when someone called her name, and she froze in horror. She ought not to have come in broad daylight! Someone would tell Pa.

Slowly she turned, and to her relief recognized Tom Simmons running towards her. 'Tom! You frightened me. Why aren't you at work?'

'I'm on my way to see someone. Nell, I've been trying to find you for weeks, but it seemed as though you'd vanished.'

'No, I'm still living in Birmingham.'

'Where? Who are you living with? Nell, you must tell me. I feel so helpless when I don't know where to begin to look for you.'

'Why should you want to?'

'Look, here's a tea room. Come and have a cup of tea with me, and tell me how you are. You look well . . . and prosperous,' he added more slowly. It had suddenly occurred to him that if Nell were doing well for herself she would be less inclined to accept his proposal. He'd thought long and hard about whether he still wanted Nell as his wife. There could be all sorts of scandal he didn't know about, which might emerge in the future and be of considerable embarrassment to a rising young union official. Yet the lure of Nell's slender body and delicate features persuaded him there was nothing that could be bad enough to make him give her up. He avoided answering while ordering the tea and some scones, then began to ask Nell more questions. At the crucial moment an innate caution told him that he must make sure, discover all he could, before possibly making a fool of himself.

'How are your family?' he began. 'Are you on your way to visit them?'

'Ma's been ill,' Nell replied briefly. 'Tom, please don't tell Pa you've seen me. He doesn't know I come to see Ma, and if he did he'd think they knew where I live, and try to beat it out of them.'

'I'm no tell-tale,' Tom replied stiffly. 'Besides, I don't work at Forster's any more, so I never see him.' For a while he was diverted into telling Nell about his new position, and how he had actually been to London the previous week to talk with some of the leaders of the miners' union. 'They are all very concerned about the bad situation in the mines. The agreement reached last year has failed, because there's a slump in coal prices and no profits. We're afraid the owners will try to wriggle out of it. However, I doubt if anything can happen during the summer. And I'm learning Russian!' he added importantly.

'Russian? Why on earth should you want to learn Russian?' Nell asked, astonished.

'The British Trades Union Congress has been holding talks with the Red International of Labour Unions, and the Russian union leader Tomsky spoke at the Congress last September. I hope to be there this year, and understand him without having to wait for a translation.'

'I see. Have you become a Communist, Tom?'

'Of course not, but we have to talk to Russia, persuade the Government how important a country it is.'

'Yes, I suppose so. Tom, I must go, I haven't much time to spare. Thank you for the tea, and it was nice to see you again.'

'Don't go. Tell me what you are doing. What sort of job do you have now?'

'I'm a dancer. On the stage. I'm one of The Bliss Beauties.'

He was appalled and showed it. 'Nell! How could you!'

'There's nothing wrong with it,' she insisted defensively.

'It's wrong, Nell, immoral and shameless to display yourself on the stage, and for a girl as young as you to live away from her family. They need you, even more now, it seems, with your mother ill. You should give it up before you become corrupted.'

'I won't give it up, and I won't live at home. I'm going on tour anyway.'

'You're much too young to be travelling the country. It's just not decent. You could get into all kinds of difficulties in that sort of situation.'

'Pa never thought for a second of my welfare, Tom! And I'd much sooner get into the difficulties you suggest than go home to be beaten every time Pa got into a temper! Not that I'm likely to become a whore as you seem to think!' She rose impetuously to her feet, knocking the last remaining scone to the floor as her sleeve swept the table. 'Thank you for the tea, Tom!' she snapped, but to the top of his head for he had bent to try and save the scone. No doubt he'd have to pay for it if it fell on the floor, Nell thought contemptuously as she almost ran out of the teashop. How boring and pompous he sounded, an old man already. How could she ever have imagined he was pleasant!

Paul finished earlier than usual at the clinic. He looked at his watch. There was time before dinner to visit a couple of his private patients. Suddenly he knew he wouldn't. He had no serious cases to attend to, they could all wait until tomorrow.

He drove to The Firs. It was Saturday and Nell would be alone, since Kitty and Gwyneth had a matinée. He would say he had come to see how her ankle was coping with the dancing classes she'd resumed. Then he felt quite foolish. Why should he need to make an excuse? Even if he didn't genuinely wish to make certain she was not putting too much strain on her ankle, he didn't need to pretend to himself he was going to visit her for any reason but his own pleasure.

She was in Kitty's sitting room, mending some of the white stockings they wore on stage. As Meggy showed him in and offered to bring tea Nell smiled up at him, and his heart turned over. She was so incredibly lovely. And causing him to behave in quite uncharacteristic ways, he mused with inward laughter. It was almost like being an irresponsible student again, he felt so young. Right from the moment he'd met her in Endersby's ballroom, and without even asking her had whisked her into his arms and on to the dance floor, she had bewitched him. She was the first girl he'd taken out for years, and he would never have slunk into that dreadful theatre to watch anyone else. And though he took his work in the Ladywood clinic very seriously, and contributed generously to charity, he had not previously involved himself with a patient to the extent of providing sheets and pillows and blankets from his own house as he had for Mrs Baxter.

'I've come to see how your ankle is,' he said abruptly, and Nell looked at him, puzzled at his tone.

'It's quite better, thank you. After the first class it felt more tired than the other leg, but not sore, and by the second day not even that.'

'I'll have a look at it though.'

Obediently she raised her leg on to the small footstool he brought across the room, and he prodded and flexed the ankle. Then he smiled at her, and she was relieved. It was the normal, friendly Paul again.

'I didn't know anyone had so many pairs of white stockings,' he said, sitting down beside her.

Nell laughed. 'I offered to darn all the others. They don't need them anywhere except Birmingham. We discovered that from some other dancers. Elsewhere they use a sort of white paste which is a lot cheaper than stockings. Only Birmingham has a law which forbids bare legs on stage.'

'You mustn't let Kitty take advantage of you,' he warned. 'She's thoughtless.'

'She's been very kind to us. Besides, I have nothing else to do.'

'Let me teach you to drive. I'll give you your first lesson after we've had this tea.'

'You?'

'What's so strange about that?' he demanded, both amused and affronted by her look of astonishment.

'I'm sorry, I didn't mean to sound rude. It's just that only Timothy has offered to teach us, and I couldn't because of my ankle. Besides, Kitty's taken the car.'

'I meant in my car. I know it's a lot bigger, but it really isn't any more difficult to control.'

Nell's eyes were shining. 'Would you really? Oh, Paul, that would be absolutely divine, as Kitty would say! I think after that quarrel Gwyneth had with Timothy he's forgotten he said he'd teach me too.'

'Would you feel safe with him?' Paul asked, grinning. He'd much enjoyed the story of Timothy's discomfiture.

'Oh, he doesn't want me,' Nell said dismissively. 'He tried not to believe he was attracted to Gwyneth, he thinks far too much of his name and position to get involved with a girl from the lower orders. But she's so beautiful and lively he couldn't help himself, I suppose. I wouldn't be nearly so tempting, a skinny little girl from the slums.'

At first Tom was furiously angry when Nell walked out on him. He wouldn't put up with such treatment. She was a slut and he wouldn't give her the satisfaction of knowing she'd meant anything to him. He'd ignore her. Then he began to recall her smile, which made him feel warm all over, and her slender yet enticing curves, so tantalizing under the straight dress she'd been wearing. He had to admit he wanted her. If he could rescue her from this life of depravity she was heading for, he would have achieved something more important than merely securing her for himself.

He soon discovered that The Bliss Beauties were appearing in a small theatre in Walsall, and on Saturday he went there on the train in time to secure a ticket for the evening performance. Despite himself and although he wondered why Nell was absent he was impressed by the performance, especially the dark, vivid girl who did the solo spot. He began, very faintly, to discern the attraction the music and the movement must have for Nell. By now the Beauties had progressed to opening the second half of the show, and fortunately for Tom they didn't leave the theatre immediately after their performance, as they usually did. When he pushed through the crowds afterwards to find the stage door, down a narrow, odorous alley, he was directed by a jovial doorkeeper to a large room at the side of the stage.

He'd come to try and discover what had happened to Nell. He hesitated in the doorway. It seemed as though a party was in progress. The performers, most of them still in their stage costumes, were mingling with a crowd of people, talking loudly and drinking wine. Then a waiter stopped and offered Tom a glass from a tray, and Tom moved towards one of the dancers who was standing nearby.

'Hello, I thought you were very good,' he said stiffly.

Kitty turned towards him, her eyes slightly frosty. 'Thank you,' she replied, and began to move away.

'I was hoping to meet Nell here, Nell Baxter,' Tom said hurriedly.

Kitty turned round slowly. 'Nell?' she asked. 'Are you a friend?'

'Well, yes. I've known her for years. I was at school with her brother. Until I went to King Edward's,' Tom stammered, determined to emphasize at the same time his familiarity with Nell and his own better schooling. 'Are you a friend too?' he ventured.

Kitty eyed him thoughtfully. He might be useful. She was feeling disgruntled at the attention Nell was receiving from the men she had previously considered her own property, and if she could turn the tables and make Nell jealous it would give her some satisfaction. Besides, he was quite good looking in a rough sort of way. She smiled, so brilliantly that Tom blinked.

'How long is it since you've seen her?' she asked, linking her arm in Tom's and drawing him to the side of the room.

'Earlier this week, Wednesday afternoon, when she went to visit her mother,' Tom replied, bemused at the closeness of this girl, with her cut-glass accent and overpowering perfume.

'Didn't she invite you to the party I'm having next week?' Kitty asked.

'Party? No, she didn't say anything.'

'Poor Nell, she must be shy of asking her old friends to the house. She lives with me, you know, but I cannot persuade her to treat the house as her own. Do come, next Sunday, about eight. We'll dance. We working girls can only see our friends on Sundays, every other day is devoted to our art.' Kitty smiled provocatively, mentally listing the people she could invite to this impromptu party.

She gave Tom the address, and Tom managed to suppress his astonishment. Fancy Nell living with the nobs! Then, as he walked slowly back to the station, his anger began to rise. What on earth had Nell done to be accepted in such circles? He would most certainly be attending that party, and this time she wouldn't avoid him.

Chapter Fourteen

N ELL had enjoyed her first driving lesson, once she'd overcome her awe at sitting behind the wheel of such a large car. Paul had taken her to some of the wide, empty roads on the Calthorpe estate and once she had mastered the basics her confidence grew rapidly, though Paul insisted she mustn't drive for too long the first time.

'I plan to drive out to Kenilworth tomorrow,' he'd said as she drew up with a flourish outside The Firs. 'Come with me and you can try it out in some of the country lanes.'

'Kenilworth? Where the castle is?' she asked. 'I've been reading about that in one of Kitty's books.'

'And you'd like to see it, no doubt? So you'll come? Let's make an early start, and it won't be too much out of our way to go through Warwick. Then you can see another castle, this time not a ruined one.'

Now there was no chance of meeting Amy, Nell was happy to start at nine. She had wondered if her little sister might still be going to Perrott's Folly, hoping to see her, but she had been the previous two weeks, and there had been no Amy. After hearing how the child had vanished from home, she knew there was little likelihood that Amy would be able to come, even if she was still alive.

Hastily she thrust that thought aside, it was too painful. She knew it was foolish, but she couldn't help blaming herself. If she hadn't given Amy the money her sister wouldn't have run home and blurted out that she'd seen Nell. Then Pa wouldn't have been mad and frightened Amy so much that she'd run away. For several nights after she'd heard this story Nell had been unable to sleep. Every time she was about to drop off a vision of her sister would float before her eyes, and Nell would torture herself imagining the dangers which Amy might have encountered. Paul had commented on the shadows beneath her eyes, and forced her to confess her worries. Then he'd insisted she took a sleeping draught for a few nights, to banish the nightmares.

When Nell quietly let herself out of the house and went to meet him as he pulled into the drive, he smiled cheerfully at her. 'I imagine Kitty and Gwyneth are still asleep?' he asked.

Nell jumped in beside him. 'Yes, there was a party last night, they were late back. Kitty said to tell you she's planning one at home next Sunday, and hopes you can come.'

'What is she celebrating?'

'Kitty, doesn't need an excuse to throw a party. Though I think Andrew will be here that day, and she wants to invite some of the theatre people. We are getting to know quite a few acts now, we've appeared on the same bill together several times already.'

'Tell her I'll be happy to come. And thanks. I'll drive to begin with, then you can take over when we come to a quiet bit of road.'

For an hour they spoke little apart from Nell's questions about cars and Paul's explanations and instructions. He was, she decided, immensely patient, and that must be why she was finding it so easy. Gwyneth had confessed that after her solitary and hair-raising drive back to Edgbaston from Timothy's house she never wanted to drive again, but Nell was sure that with Paul as a teacher she would find it quite easy.

Soon afterwards they reached Warwick and parked in the main street. They walked to look at the ancient town gateways, and Nell stared in amazement at the castle, spread out on its cliffside for what seemed like miles along the bank of the river.

'It's huge! Is it bigger than Windsor castle?'

'I doubt it, but I don't really know. It's one of the best preserved medieval castles in England. Not in the least like Kenilworth, which is little more than a few walls on the top of a hill.'

They returned to the car and set off for Kenilworth, along peaceful country roads filled with the sound of birdsong, where the verges were covered with primroses and other spring flowers. Driving into Kenilworth Nell stared in awe at the ruined sandstone keep, rearing gaunt fingers up to the sky.

'I can imagine an army fighting here,' she said slowly.

'Yes. Now look in front, round this bend.'

Nell glanced at him, but he was smiling to himself. As they rounded the bend they came to a stream which flowed across the road, and she gasped then laughed as he drove straight into it.

'Aren't you afraid of getting stuck?'

'No, the ford's shallow enough at the moment, though it's in a dip of the road. It can get too high to pass. I used to love driving through as a child. I just wanted to share it with you. Now we're going to visit my mother for lunch. She lives in a house just off the High Street.'

'Your mother?' Nell was suddenly apprehensive. 'Is she expecting us – me?'

'Yes, I telephoned her this morning. I often drive out to see her on Sundays. She moved here after my father died, saying she no longer wanted a big house to run, and I suspect to leave me on my own. She wouldn't have wanted to feel her presence restricted my life in any way, and when – if – I'd married, she would have gone anyway.'

Nell was quiet as he found his way through narrow lanes and eventually drew up outside a small but elegant Georgian house. She wondered apprehensively what Mrs Mandeville would say when she realized that her son expected her to entertain a girl from Ladywood, and to make it even worse, a stage dancer. The only time she'd seen his mother had been after that first performance at Endersby's, and she'd had the impression then that the older woman had disapproved of them, not quite liking the fact that Paul had danced with her.

Mrs Mandeville was affable, however, kissing Paul and greeting Nell with a sunny smile, and leading them right through the house to sit in a sunny conservatory which had been added to it half a century before.

'Even though it's May it's too cold to sit outside, but we can have sherry in comfort, in the sunshine. I spend every sunny morning here, it does my old bones good to feel the heat. Tell me, how is Kitty? Has she tired of this stage dancing yet?'

Nell gradually relaxed and answered Mrs Mandeville's questions about Kitty, the theatre, and the castles she'd seen that morning. A pretty maid served them with lunch, and afterwards they sat in a delightfully feminine drawing room where the walls were covered in decorative tapestries and water colour landscapes.

'You can see how I spend my time, my dear,' Mrs Mandeville said, gesturing to the paintings. 'I paint in the summer, and work at the tapestries in the winter.'

'They are lovely,' Nell said. 'May I look more closely?'

'Of course. Does your mother have similar hobbies?'

Nell was thankful she had risen to her feet and had her back to Mrs Mandeville. She hadn't meant to be cruel. She couldn't know where Nell came from, or that her mother hadn't time or money for the decencies of life, let alone hobbies of the sort Mrs Mandeville and her class took for granted.

'Mrs Baxter has a large family, she is very busy,' Paul said smoothly, and Nell flashed him a glance of gratitude. It wasn't a lie, but she shrank from having to explain her circumstances to this elegant woman. Mrs Mandeville, she surmised, was a good fifteen to twenty years older than her own mother, yet she looked much younger. That was what poverty and excessive childbearing did to women.

It wasn't, Nell told herself, that she was ashamed of Ma. Then she paused. Wasn't she? Hadn't she often wished her mother would be more assertive, stand up to Pa, especially when he beat the children? Was that a form of shame? And she would hate it if Mrs Mandeville were to go into her old home. She was becoming a snob. That was what living with Kitty and meeting her wealthy friends, mixing with men like Paul and Timothy, had done to her.

She was subdued on the drive home, and Paul, imagining she was tired, insisted on driving and left her to her own thoughts.

'I'll see you at the party next Sunday,' he said briefly when they reached The Firs. 'Sleep well, my dear.'

It had been decided that Nell would not rejoin the troupe for another week. Then she would have a week before the engagement away from home. Once more she went to see Ma, while Pa was at work, to find Mrs Baxter much improved, sitting up in bed and complaining that she felt well enough to get up and do something.

'Yer fancy docter won't let 'er,' Eth said resentfully as Nell went down to the kitchen ready to leave. 'An' 'e sent Fanny back ter school, made me stop off work ter look after Ma. 'Tain't fair! I don't get me wages, an' if I'm off much longer I'll lose me job an' all!'

'Eth, I'm sorry! Look, I brought ten shillings. That'll help, and keep some of it for yourself to make up for what you've lost. Ma used to let you keep a shilling each week, didn't she?'

Instead of being grateful Eth was outraged. 'Lady bloody Bountiful! I don't want yer blood money! Yer thinks yer can live with yer fancy friends, an' givin' us a couple o' bob'll pay us off!'

'Please yourself!' Nell said angrily. 'Let Ma have it, she'll be grateful!'

'Yer drove Danny an' Sam away, an' Amy ran off because of yer bleedin' money!'

'That's not true! It was before I had any money! Danny and Sam were drunk, but they should never have tried — what they did! You were as frightened as I was, and as glad not to have them here!'

'Well, they've gone, they're no 'elp with Ma. An' Ned's gettin' wed, 'e ain't got no time neither.'

'Ned? Getting married?'

'Next week.' Eth had relapsed into her normal sullenness after the brief show of bitter anger. 'Gal from up Lozells way. Me name's Florence,' she said, mimicking a refined accent. 'Won't let us call 'er Flo like everyone else. 'Er's breedin', but they was waitin' fer 'ouse near where 'e works. 'Er dad's on railway, an' got our Ned a job porterin' at New Street,' she added proudly. 'Yer needs someone ter speak fer yer ter get on railways. Ned says 'e'll 'ave chance ter be shunter next year.'

'Tell Ned I'm pleased for him,' Nell said quietly. 'And cheer up, Eth, Ma looks a lot better and you'll be able to go back to work in a few days.'

Although he wore his best dark grey worsted suit with his new double-breasted matching waistcoat Tom looked and felt out of place in Kitty's drawing room. He knew he was stiff and uncomfortable. It wasn't as if he were overdressed, because several of the men wore dinner jackets. Nor was he underdressed; a few of the more bohemian sported velvet smoking jackets. It was just, he thought with an unaccustomed flash of insight, that they all seemed much more at home in their clothes.

Nell looked ravishing in a virginal white satin dress, trimmed with pale blue ribbons, a matching blue bandeau round her head. Then Tom felt a blush stain his cheeks as he realized that the skirt was above her knees. How could she! It was positively indecent, and when she was married to him he would forbid such disgusting clothes.

She seemed quite at home amongst the swells, too. When he'd been shown in Nell had been at the far end of the room, in the midst of an animated group of young men and girls. She seemed to be joking with one of the men, and the others added occasional comments, laughing all the while. She hadn't looked his way, and he'd felt a slow stirring of resentment. She ought to have been aware of his presence. She must have known Kitty had invited him, and should have been waiting to greet him and introduce him to her friends.

Then he forgot Nell as Kitty swooped down on him, called him 'darling', and led him swiftly into another room where a long table was laid out with the sort of food Tom had seen only on cinema screens.

'Champagne?' Kitty asked, and pushed a brimming glass into his hand. 'Drink up, Tom, you're way behind everyone else, and need to catch up or you won't enjoy the party.' She seized a plate, rapidly filled it with elegant bite-sized morsels, and took Tom's arm to drag him towards an armchair set inside a deep bay window embrasure. 'Sit down,' she ordered, pushing him into the deep chair and then, rather to his horror, perched herself on the arm with her toes tucked under his knees.

Her skirt was even shorter than Nell's, he realized, and gulped, trying to look away from her knees so close to his face. Kitty laughed at his expression, and leaned forward to slide something in between his unresisting lips. It was food, but he had no idea what as he chewed on it, and swallowed hastily as she waved another portion before his eyes.

'Drink,' she commanded and, mesmerized, he obeyed. Somehow she had a bottle within reach, and his glass was never more than half empty. 'Tell me all about yourself,' he heard her say, softly and intimately.

By the time she led him back to the drawing room, where they were dancing to jazz records, and melted into his arms, Tom had almost forgotten Nell. This was a dream. This beautiful, exciting girl, an aristocrat whose grandfather had a title, was clearly besotted with him. He moved in a trance, oblivious of everyone else, and when Kitty took his hand and led him out of the room, along a short passage, and into a much cosier sitting room, he went unresisting. When she shut the door and turned to him, smiling and lifting up her lips enticingly as she stepped close, it was perfectly natural to fold her in his arms and bend to kiss her.

*

'How did you know it was my birthday?' Nell demanded. They could never afford to celebrate birthdays at home, and since her gran died she'd hardly even thought about it.

Paul laughed. 'Your mother mentioned it the last time I went to see her. I've brought you a present, and I hope you'll come out with me tonight. I thought we might go to the cinema. The West End has a restaurant, we could have dinner afterwards.'

'Thank you,' she said shyly. 'I'd like that.'

'Aren't you going to open your present?'

Nell blinked back sudden tears. 'I've not had a birthday present for three years. Thank you Paul!'

She carefully untied the coloured ribbon and unwrapped the paper to reveal an oblong box, with the name of one of the most exclusive stores in Birmingham on it. When she opened the lid there were several layers of tissue paper, and then she lifted out a square-cornered leather handbag. In shiny black leather, it was hand tooled, and the frame was silver. In one corner the initials EB were entwined in silver. She lifted shining eyes to gaze at him, entranced.

'How did you know my real name was Eleanor?'

'Your mother again, Nell. Look inside.'

Slowly she twisted the catch and opened the lid, and gasped again. Inside the handbag was fitted out as a small dressing case, or vanity bag, with chunky cut-glass bottles with gold knobs, a gold compact, and two lipstick holders.

'I hope it might be useful for your stage make-up,' Paul said quietly.

'It's absolutely wonderful! But I mustn't accept! It's too much!'

'It's a small part of what I'd like to give you, Nell. I must go now, though. I'll call for you tonight.'

Before she could protest again he had gone. She carried the bag up to her bedroom and sat looking at it for ages before she could force herself to lift out the bottles, and then she discovered that they contained various lotions, creams, and powders, as did the compact and the lipstick holders. A tiny perfume bottle nestled amongst them, and even two tiny tablets of soap. Nell recalled that day which had changed her life, when she had vowed to buy perfumed soap for herself, and suddenly she began to weep, but whether from sorrow or happiness she could not tell. First Kitty, now Paul was being so generous. Why did trade unionists like Tom always condemn the rich?

She dressed with care for the evening, having bathed using one of the tablets of soap, and sprayed her body with the perfume. When Paul arrived, looking distinguished in his dinner jacket, she was ready.

She never could recall what film they saw that evening, nor what they ate, for she floated in a cloud of enchantment. When Paul drove her home she turned to him impulsively as he halted in front of The Firs.

'I'll never forget this birthday, it's been the most wonderful of my life!'

He smiled down at her. 'The first of many we'll share, I hope,' he murmured, and to her astonishment bent to kiss her fleetingly on the forehead.

Nell's return to the troupe was tiring for her, but produced no ill effects. For the week's performance at Stoke-on-Trent the three girls found rooms in a large old house near the theatre, and Nell's fears about her ability to find somewhere to live were finally banished. She was, she knew, far more worldly and sophisticated now than when she left home.

For the following month they toured towns in Staffordshire and Derbyshire, and by the end of that time Nell had resumed the speciality spots with Gwyneth. They became used to travelling late at night on Saturdays, returning to Edgbaston for what was supposed to be a day of rest each Sunday.

It rarely happened that way. Kitty, with a secret smile, would vanish in the car soon after a late breakfast and not return until midnight. Nell and Gwyneth were left to work and plan with Andrew, as they devised the new act which was to include them all.

'Where the devil does Kitty go to?' he asked on the second Sunday. 'I've driven all the way from Bristol to sort things out, and how can we if she's not here?'

'She doesn't tell us where she goes,' Nell explained. 'She says she's no good at thinking up new ideas, and anyway isn't good enough to dance on her own.'

'She'll have to stay and practise when we've got it all sorted out. We need the three of you for the singing, and some of the dance numbers. I've been talking to some of the hotels in the towns where we've been playing, and I think we could do business with them, in the same way as at Endersby's. They like a brief show during the interval at dances, or during dinner, but it's a nuisance having to arrange with several different acts. One of the new men in the band, the second alto sax, can do conjuring tricks, and I've been working on a comedy routine with him. What I suggest is one long combined act of singing and dancing with the band, which we can offer to the music halls, and a more detailed, separate set of turns as a complete show at hotels and dance halls.'

They spent hours discussing routines, the girls trying out various ideas and learning the songs Andrew wanted to include. He'd discovered a talented young lyricist who was willing to write songs for them, and Andrew composed some of the tunes, including a signature tune for the group. When, after a month, Andrew said he was appearing for two weeks in Blackpool and would not be coming to Edgbaston the following weekend, both Gwyneth and Nell heaved secret sighs of relief.

'But after that you'll have to be here too, Kitty, or I'll find someone else,' Andrew threatened. It was Monday morning, just after breakfast, and he was about to set off on the long drive to Blackpool.

Kitty pouted. 'I'm not at all sure I want to carry on with this dancing,' she replied petulantly. 'It interferes too much with having fun.'

'Let me know by Saturday week,' was all Andrew said, and with a wave drove away.

'Let's have a party next Sunday,' Kitty proposed as they shut the door and went back to have another cup of coffee. 'We'll be performing in Birmingham the following week, and after all this travelling that's something to celebrate!'

She disappeared to write invitations, and Nell went to visit her mother. By now Mrs Baxter was much better, and had insisted on going back to her cleaning jobs.

'Yer nice doctor didn't want me ter go,' she told Nell, 'but we needed the money. I'm a lot better now, but I do wish I knew where our Amy is.'

'Have you still not been to the police?' Nell asked. 'Even after all this time, they might be able to help.'

'But they'll think it odd I didn't go at once. 'Sides, yer Pa'd go mad, 'e don't 'old with talkin' ter coppers.'

'Shall I go?'

Mrs Baxter shook her head. 'No, luv. It ain't no use. Yer Pa'd find out yer've been comin' 'ere, an' 'e'd kill me!'

There was nothing Nell could do, and she had to leave soon, for they would be setting off for Worcester immediately after lunch. That was where they'd paused on the first time Paul had taken her out, she thought as she walked back towards the Hagley Road. A reminiscent smile curved her lips. She'd been so terrified of doing something wrong, of using the wrong knife, but she needn't have worried. He'd been so kind, so thoughtful.

When she heard his voice she thought for a moment she was imagining it, still deep in her memories, but then there was a touch on her arm and she turned to find him smiling down at her.

'Nell! I knew it was you. How are you? When will you be performing in Birmingham again so that a busy doctor can come and see you?'

She explained, and knowing that Kitty would be bound to have invited him, shyly asked if he would be coming to the party on Sunday.

'Indeed I will. But have you had any chance to practise driving?'

Nell shook her head. 'No, Kitty says she doesn't feel confident enough to teach me, and her car is different from yours.'

'Then spend Sunday with me and you can have another lesson. Is nine o'clock too early?'

'No, and thank you. I'd like that.'

Once more Nell sat in Mrs Mandeville's conservatory. This time the doors were open, and the shades protected them from the July sunshine. Paul's mother had welcomed her with a cheerful smile, and during lunch seemed genuinely interested in how she was progressing with the driving lessons.

Paul set down the delicate Spode coffee cup, and rose to his feet. 'I'd better go now.'

'Thank you dear. I told Mrs Waters you wouldn't mind popping in to see her. She swears you are the only doctor who understands her constitution.'

'Or the only one who's prepared to tell her she eats too much!' he said with a laugh. 'I'll be back soon.'

'And I'll show Nell the garden while you're gone. I'm very proud of my roses this year,' she went on after Paul had crossed the lawn and passed through a small gate set in the hedge. 'Let's go this way first.'

'They are lovely, and the scent's so strong!' Nell marvelled, bending to sniff at a glorious white cabbage-like bloom.

'My favourite flower. Victoria liked them too.'

'Victoria?' For a wild moment Nell wondered if she was talking about the old Queen, then told herself not to be silly.

'My god-daughter. The only child of a very dear friend. You may have seen her portrait, Paul still has the painting that was done of her on her seventeenth birthday. He keeps it in his study at home. She and Paul were going to be married.' Nell opened her mouth, but found she couldn't speak. Fortunately Mrs Mandeville had moved on. 'He hasn't got over her death yet. She died, you know, a few weeks before their wedding. Her horse took fright at something and bolted with her, and before anyone could reach her they had fallen over a cliff. So tragic, and Paul was there too, he had to try and help her. She died in his arms. It's several years ago now, he wasn't even qualified. They were both so young, but so very much in love. I hope one day he'll get over it.'

She walked on, and clearly didn't expect any comment. She began to talk about the other plants, some of which Nell remembered seeing in her grandparents' garden, and Nell was able to reply with reasonable calm. Poor Paul, she was thinking. What a terrible thing to have happened. It must be devastating to lose the person you loved. As they turned back towards the house Mrs Mandeville smiled brightly at her.

'My dear, don't tell him I told you. I don't expect he'll have mentioned it to you, he hates speaking about Victoria. But he can't mourn her for ever. One day he must look for a wife. I just pray he will find a suitable girl, one who can support him properly, understand his work, be a hostess for him. He needs someone from his own background, someone who understands his kind of life. He has the potential to make a great name for himself, if only he has the right kind of wife.'

Chapter Fifteen

Nell was quiet on the drive home, biting back almost every remark she thought of making. She couldn't find anything which wasn't connected with the dreadful loss Paul had suffered, and was terrified of letting drop what Mrs Mandeville had told her, and reviving his misery. Fortunately Paul decided she must do most of the driving, and took her silence to be concentration.

'You are doing really well,' he praised her when she came to a halt outside The Firs. 'Next time you must drive a little way by yourself, knowing you are on your own is an enormous boost to confidence. I'd better go home and change. I'll see you at the party.'

Gwyneth was climbing the stairs when Nell went in, and Nell followed her up to her room.

'Did you have a nice time?' Gwyneth asked.

'Yes, thank you,' Nell replied slowly.

'I saw you come right up to the house. You seem to be doing well.'

'Paul's such a marvellous teacher. Perhaps you should ask him to teach you?'

'No!'

'Gwyneth, are you still frightened?'

Gwyneth shuddered. 'I'll never forget driving home in the dark, knowing that any minute I might tip over into a ditch, or get a puncture and not have the slightest idea how to change the wheel.'

'Paul once said that if you had a fright, you needed to face up to whatever it was that had scared you as soon as possible. If you didn't, it became more and more terrifying.'

'I'm sure he's right, but I won't go crawling to him begging favours!'

'I don't think he'd be offended, Gwyneth, he's so nice.'

'Are you falling for him?'

Nell laughed. 'Of course not! A man like Paul would never want someone like me! I just like him, he's kind and friendly, he doesn't frighten me like Timothy does. And that's not because of what he tried to do to you, I was a bit frightened of Timothy before, he always seemed so . . . I don't know, so superior, and he knew it.'

'He likes you.' She couldn't drop the subject, painful though it was. Gwyneth had watched Paul's growing friendship with Nell, and fought to suppress her own longings for him. Yet it was like a scab, unhealed, and she had to pick at it all the time to make the pain sharper.

'Paul? Not like that. Besides, I'm not suitable for him. Did you know he was engaged and his fiancée died just before the wedding?' She had to discuss it with someone. Kitty probably already knew, she'd known Paul for years, but somehow Nell didn't want to talk about Paul to Kitty.

'Paul? Engaged? Did he tell you?'

'No, his mother mentioned it. The girl was thrown from a horse, and she says he's never got over it. I feel so sorry for him. It must be even worse than not knowing what's happened to Amy. At least I can hope she's safe somewhere.'

Gwyneth crossed to the wardrobe. 'I'm sure she will be, Nell. But look at the time, we'd better get changed. Do you want the bathroom first?'

Tom was wary. Tonight was going to be tricky. He had to find time to talk to Nell without Kitty becoming suspicious. He'd half planned to miss the party, then persuaded himself he could carry it off. Kitty was the hostess, after all, she must pay some attention to her other guests, and that would give him a chance to talk to Nell. It would look odd if he didn't. Kitty couldn't possibly object.

The sheer dazzlement which had held him in thrall for weeks was beginning to fade. At first he had been bewildered, then astounded, to have an upper-class girl like Kitty literally throw herself into his arms. Then for a time he had forgotten Nell completely while Kitty made it plain she wanted nothing more than to be with him. Each Sunday she had driven them to some isolated spot in the countryside, produced a picnic basket and a bottle of wine, and asked for nothing more than a few kisses and to be told the story of his life. He'd begun to feel no end of a swell fellow.

'You don't seem very fond of me, Tom,' she'd pouted the previous week when they'd finished eating and were drinking the last of the wine.

'But of course I am,' he protested.

'Then show it, darling,' she demanded, lounging back on the rug and stretching out her hand to pull him down beside her. 'You're not afraid of me, are you?' she whispered in his ear.

'Of course not.' He tried to sound confident, and since his hand had somehow come to rest in the vicinity of her breast, and she didn't seem to have noticed, he ventured to stroke her gently. Her reaction startled him.

'Ah, Tom! That's nice! Do it again!'

He swallowed hastily, but he did it again. Kitty rolled towards him and he found his hand trapped between their bodies as she pressed hard against him. After a while she moved away and sat up.

'It's no good here. Tom, I know a very discreet little hotel, in Lichfield. We'll be home much earlier in a fortnight, when we're in Birmingham. We could get there late on Saturday night and have two nights together. Wouldn't that be utterly divine? If I give you the telephone number, can you book a room, for Mr and Mrs Simmons?'

Alarm bells had begun to ring. Tom had been out with few girls until he took out Nell, and he'd been rather shocked at the abandoned way Kitty kissed him. Women shouldn't behave in such a forward manner. They should leave it to men to initiate what love-making they considered appropriate. It was exciting, true, but he didn't think it was quite nice, with open mouths and tongues all tangled up. It did odd things to him, evoked sensations he'd always been taught were wicked. And he wasn't at all sure he wanted to spend a weekend in a hotel with Kitty masquerading as his wife.

For one thing, it was inevitable that someone would discover it. That would be disastrous for his career. Equally important, he wasn't at all confident that he could become the sort of lover Kitty clearly expected. The coarse descriptions he had overheard from his male friends, to which he had listened in sneering contempt, somehow didn't sound appropriate for Kitty. One of Tom's inflexible rules since his early teens had been to prepare himself thoroughly for everything he did, but he wasn't at all sure how this principle applied now.

He hadn't booked the room for the next weekend. He'd make some excuse, say he had to go to London on union affairs. And then if only he could get Nell to listen to reason they would both be free of the spell Kitty seemed to have cast over them.

Luckily Kitty was busy introducing some of the dancers she'd invited to the party to a couple of men when he arrived. He recognized them from his visit to the Walsall theatre and the party afterwards. He smiled at Kitty, and slid round the group on his way to find Nell.

She was talking to a tall, bronze-haired man who looked slightly familiar, and her Welsh friend Gwyneth was there too, with a tall, fair, languid man who had 'Eton' written all over him. Tom hovered nearby, hidden by a thriving aspidistra.

'Paul, I'm sure that if you gave Gwyneth just one lesson she'd get over this stupid fear,' Nell was saying.

'I'd be delighted, of course.'

'Nell! You mustn't ask Paul, he doesn't have enough time,' Gwyneth protested, blushing furiously.

'If I go down on my knees and apologize humbly, and vow never to take you near Manor Farm, will you come with me?' the languid fellow drawled.

Tom saw Nell turn to look at him in surprise, then swing round to stare at Gwyneth when the latter, after a slight pause, laughed and put her hand on the last speaker's arm.

'If that's a promise, Timothy, I'll accept. Thank you, Paul, but I don't think I could face driving a different car just yet.'

Gwyneth and the man called Timothy moved away, and Tom hastily stepped forward. 'Nell, hello.'

'I'll see you later, Nell,' Paul said, and Tom was left in possession of the field.

'I have to talk to you, Nell. Is there somewhere we can go where we can be private?'

'Ma? Is she worse?' He didn't reply, but turned away and walked towards the dining room. It was too early for the guests to be there at the moment, and they could be sure of a few minutes alone. 'Tom, what is it?' Nell demanded, following him in. 'Is it Ma?'

'Only indirectly, Nell. As you know, I haven't really approved of your actions, but I can understand how the glamour of the stage has attracted you. However, you've been performing for four months now, and I'm hoping you are ready to consider my proposal more seriously than last time.'

'Your proposal?'

'Yes, of course,' he said impatiently. 'Nell, I once asked you to marry me. I am repeating that offer. I have a better job now, one with more prospects, and I can say without boasting that I hope to rise to a much higher level in the union. I want you to share my life. I know you have been helping your mother with some of the money you have earned, and while I cannot undertake to offer to support your family, you will not find me ungenerous or censorious if you choose to spend some of your pin-money helping them.' There was a prolonged silence. 'Well, what do you have to say? You look surprised, but you need not be. You must know I have cared for you and still do, despite everything.'

Nell took a deep breath. 'Thank you Tom, I am flattered, but no.'

'No? Nell!' For the first time his voice held a shred of emotion. 'Nell, you can't mean that!'

'I'm sorry, Tom, but I do. I — respect you, but I don't want to marry anyone. Now I must go and see whether Kitty needs any help.'

Before he could move she had whisked out of the room. Tom began to follow, and then realized the futility of it. A slow, burning anger swelled up inside him, and he blundered into the hall, out of the house, and began to walk blindly towards his home.

As they were dancing in Birmingham this week they had planned a rehearsal for the afternoon. Gwyneth, apprehensive, had gone for her promised driving lesson with Timothy.

'If you insist on an unearthly hour in the morning, I doubt he'll have the energy to rape you,' Kitty said in a brittle tone.

Kitty for some reason was in a foul temper and had refused to lend Gwyneth the Austin. Nell took care to keep out of her way. She spent some time down in the stables, which she liked to do when she was disturbed, remembering her first visit there.

She stroked the horses and nodded in sympathy as Betts muttered complaints that now Miss Kitty had this pesky motor the horses were growing fat.

'Only get out when Meggy goes ter shops,' he muttered. 'Miss Kitty don't even ride 'em now, and 'er used ter spend all 'er time ridin' when 'er was a nipper.'

Nell wished she could learn to ride, but it was an impossible dream. She could recall being lifted on to the back of a plump pony one day, when Gramps's employer had once been visited by a family with children who had brought their own ponies to ride in the Park. And she had occasionally, when Gramps had been safely out of the way, scrambled on to the back of Monarch, the huge carriage horse who was also, at harvest time, called on to help bring home the hay.

She was returning to the house half an hour later when, with an ominous coughing noise, Timothy's car rolled through the gateway. Nell ran towards the sound and was in time to see Timothy lifting Gwyneth down from the passenger seat. The car looked a wreck, its nearside light smashed, and the running board buckled. Elsewhere the paintwork was heavily scratched, and Timothy had difficulty in closing the door.

'Gwyneth! What on earth's happened? Are you hurt?'

'She's not hurt, just shocked,' Timothy said swiftly. 'Go and get Meggy to put some hot-water bottles in her bed, and see if you can get hold of Paul. She needs something to calm her nerves.'

Gwyneth was sobbing convulsively, clutching at Timothy's arm as he carried her into the house. Nell fled to the kitchens, and while Meggy busied herself with filling hot-water bottles from the kettle always kept simmering on the stove, tried to telephone Paul. She'd only used the telephone once before, but she knew Paul's number, and was soon asking for him. To her immense relief he replied and said he'd come round at once. She went to help Gwyneth into bed, and before they had settled her Paul was with them.

'No damage, just shock,' he said cheerfully. 'Here, take this, and after a sleep you'll be as right as rain.'

'The performance, tonight!' Gwyneth whispered.

'See how you feel when you wake up,' Paul replied. 'Now be a good girl, drink this, and you'll be better all the sooner.'

'I'll sit with her,' Meggy offered, and Paul smiled his thanks. Gwyneth's eyelids were already drooping, and he gently steered Nell out of the room.

'Let's go and find out what happened. I saw the car as I came in.'

Timothy was pacing to and fro in Kitty's sitting room, and Nell suddenly realized Kitty was absent. 'Where's Kitty?' she asked, but neither of the men knew.

'Probably gone shopping,' Timothy said brusquely. 'How's Gwyneth?'

This sounded quite likely, Kitty always went shopping when she was out of temper, and she'd been unaccountably touchy this morning.

'She's all right, don't worry. After she's slept she'll be quite back to normal,' Paul said reassuringly. 'Sit down, Timothy. What happened?'

'It wasn't her fault! She was doing quite well, but we were coming along Metchley Park Road when a child suddenly ran across in front of us. He came from nowhere, just appeared from behind the hedge. I thought he'd had it.' Timothy took out a large handkerchief and wiped his forehead.

'And?' Paul prompted.

'She reacted so fast I didn't even see! She swung the car over, and we finished up halfway through the hedge! The child had vanished, and I had the devil of a job to get the damned motor back on the road. Luckily it was still working, though it began to sound odd as we got closer to The Firs. But I thought she'd fainted, and she was trembling so badly I was terrified! She isn't hurt?'

'Not at all, though she might have nightmares for a while,' Paul said cheerfully. 'I'll make her stay in bed for a day or so. The new act the girls are planning with Andrew should take her mind off it. And Timothy, do your best to get her into a motor as soon as possible. If yours has to be off the road for long borrow mine.'

'When do you think she'll be able to dance?' Nell asked, her mind turning to immediate problems now she was reassured that Gwyneth wasn't hurt.

'Not tonight, she'll be exhausted from the effects of shock. I'll see her again tomorrow.'

'Then I'd better go and tell Mr Bliss, and decide how we

reorganize the troupe. Thank goodness we have a rehearsal this afternoon.'

'You can do a solo dance,' Edwina said firmly.

'But I've never done one before,' Nell protested.

'Everyone has to start sometime. And you are very good, but you've always felt yourself overshadowed by Gwyneth. Change into your practice clothes and we'll run through the one you've been learning. I think that with a few cuts you could do it tonight. And then we'd better make sure Gwyneth's costume fits you, it's different from the rest.'

There was little choice. The Bliss Beauties were becoming known for the variety of their speciality dances, but these had nearly all been performed by Nell and Gwyneth together, or the older girl alone. Now Nell had an intensive hour of practice, and for the first time had to cope with a huge headdress of ostrich plumes which gave her little time to worry about the scanty nature of the rest of the costume, cut in a deep V to her waist at the back, and with only minuscule straps holding up the front. She just had time to rush home to see how Gwyneth was before going to the theatre for the run-through.

Kitty had not reappeared at The Firs, and Timothy, having made arrangements with a garage on the Hagley Road for his car to be collected and taken away for repair, was still pacing up and down in the small sitting room.

'She'll be all right,' Nell said softly.

'I know, but I want to see her. I'll wait until she wakes up.'

'Tell her Mrs Bliss has reorganized the dancing, so that she won't worry. And give her my love.'

Kitty seemed to be her usual cheerful self when Nell reached the theatre, and full of concern for Gwyneth.

'You're sure she wasn't hurt?'

'Paul said not.'

'And do we cut the solo spot?'

'No. Mrs Bliss says I've got to do it.'

'You? But Nell, are you sure you can? You haven't done it before.'

'I know, and I don't want to do it in the least, but Mrs Bliss insists. She says it's one of the things that makes the troupe different, and there's been publicity in the papers about us. It will be bad for us all if I don't. I've been rehearsing with her.'

'It'll be worse if you make a mess of it.'

She didn't however. Nell received genuinely warm applause for her solo performance, and she and Kitty drove home in jubilant mood, full of relief that the performance had gone well.

'Nell was wonderful!' Gwyneth enthused the following Sunday morning. Andrew had arrived late the previous night, and was having breakfast with the girls. 'I was still feeling quite feeble, and she did the solos all week. She had a special mention in the *Post*!'

'I wish I'd seen it. Perhaps we can include it in our act. Now, I've been making more enquiries, and the north is a good place to start. If you think we're ready we can get a few bookings next month, in Blackpool and Manchester.'

'So soon?' Nell gasped.

'We have to start sometime.'

Nell had heard those words before. Edwina Bliss had given her the confidence to do the solos, and that had been all right after her first moments of panic. This would be too.

'How long are you in Birmingham?' Andrew went on.

'Another two weeks, at different theatres,' Gwyneth told him.

'Then let's set aside the following week for rehearsals, and I'll get the fellow I've asked to be our agent to look for a booking the week afterwards. Can you let Mr Bliss know you'll be leaving the troupe?'

Kitty and Gwyneth had gone shopping for materials. They'd already designed some costumes for the new act, but decided they needed more, and were looking for something spectacular for their final number, something in silver or gold which would be a contrast to the dark suits of the men. Nell was in Kitty's sitting room stitching ribbons on to the half-finished costumes when Paul walked in unannounced.

'Kitty said I'd find you here.'

'Paul! Sit down. Would you like some tea? It's almost time and I can ask Meggy to bring another cup.'

'Not for me, thanks. Nell, you're not appearing this week, for once, so I want to take you out to dinner one evening. How about tonight?'

She looked astonished, then couldn't prevent a smile of delight. 'I'd love that. Tonight's fine. Thank you.'

'Good. I'll book a table at Endersby's. I'll call for you at seven.'

Gwyneth pleaded exhaustion and retired to bed, and Kitty left some time earlier on one of her mysterious excursions. Nell was waiting alone when Paul arrived, and Meggy, with a grim smile, showed him into the sitting room.

'You look lovely, as always. White suits you,' Paul said as he came towards her.

He looked splendid himself, tall and distinguished in a beautifully tailored dinner jacket, sporting a white gardenia buttonhole. Nell wanted to return the compliment, but knew it wasn't done. Besides, she felt unusually shy, and when he came to pin the spray of delicately hued orchids on the shoulder of her dress she trembled slightly.

'You are rather like an orchid, rare and shy and lovely,' he said, holding her chin so that she was forced to look up at him. She blushed faintly, and her lips quivered. She could never get used to the extravagant compliments Kitty's friends used. Paul dropped his hand and turned away. 'Come, we mustn't be late.'

It was only a short drive to the hotel, and they didn't speak again until they were seated in the restaurant. Mrs Endersby was on duty tonight, and smiled brightly at them as they went in. Then Paul chatted easily, asking about the new act, the places they were going to, and the success Nell had had with her first solo performance. By the end of the meal they were laughing easily together as Paul described some of the foibles of his patients and Nell told him about amusing incidents during the shows, outrageously mimicking distracted stage managers or splutteringly furious performers.

Paul laughed most at the story of the escaping monkey who had snatched off the magician's wig, and fed it to the singing parrot, sabotaging at one go three entire acts and reducing three grown men to tears of fury. He wiped tears from his own eyes.

'Let's have coffee in the lounge.'

They were shown to chairs set in a corner of the lounge, partly screened from the rest of the room by a huge bank of flowers and greenery. When they'd finished Paul took Nell's cup out of her hands and put it down.

'Nell, I know how much the dancing matters to you, and I have no wish to drag you away from it yet, but you must know how I feel about you. Darling Nell, I love you, I have from the moment I saw you, I think, and I do so want to marry you.'

Nell gaped at him. Never in her wildest imaginings had she ever expected one of Kitty's wealthy friends, who lived in a huge house and was a respected professional man, to want to marry her. They might have made other propositions, but none had, and somehow she had never expected Paul to offer a casual affair. Even less had she imagined he would stoop to offering marriage to someone like her. He must have gone mad.

Paul laughed at her bemused expression. 'Nell, my dear, you must have had some idea how I felt!'

She shook her head. 'You can't!' was all she could say.

'What makes it so impossible to believe? I know I'm ten years or so older than you, and you are still very young, only just seventeen, and perhaps you haven't thought about marriage yet. I'm willing to wait for you, Nell. Not happy to, no man could contemplate being apart from you if you loved him, but I know how much your dancing means to you. If you can promise one day to marry me I'll try to be patient.'

Nell had recovered her breath. 'I've never even thought about it. But it just isn't suitable,' she added in a low voice, recalling Mrs Mandeville's hopes that he would find a girl to make him an appropriate wife. She almost giggled hysterically. How his mother would be horrified if she knew!

'Why not?'

'Can't you see why not? Paul, you're rich, well known in Birmingham, you have a position to keep up. Your wife must be the same class and be able to help you. I'm just a nobody, I come from one of the worst slums in Ladywood. My father's a drunken bully, and so are some of my brothers! You'd soon grow ashamed of me. Your family and friends would be shocked. Your mother would be horrified.'

'Nell, it's my life, and I'm the only one who can say what sort of wife I want. Do you care for me at all?'

Nell sighed. For a few moments while she put forward all the arguments against such an astounding marriage, she had allowed herself to glimpse what it could be like, and found the picture conjured up alluring beyond her dreams. Paul wasn't like her father. He'd never hurt her, she was convinced. But she'd never contemplated marriage with anyone like him. The best she could have hoped for in Ladywood was someone like Tom, and she didn't want that. She'd been determined for so long that she would never marry she couldn't adjust to admitting the possibility. She caught at her straying thoughts. It wasn't remotely possible.

'I like you enormously,' she said quietly. 'But it just wouldn't do. Besides, I don't ever wish to marry.'

For a moment he didn't speak, and when Nell nervously glanced up at him she was startled at the look of desolation in his eyes.

'I won't attempt to persuade you, Nell,' he said at last. 'Can we be friends still?'

'Please, yes, please,' she whispered.

'Perhaps, in the future, you'll change your mind. I shall continue to hope. I don't say I'll never ask you again, but I won't make myself a nuisance, I promise. Now would you like some more coffee, or prefer to go home?'

Chapter Sixteen

Paul sat in his library, a glass of brandy in his hand, and stared at the girl in the portrait. She was honey-blonde, small and plump, her vivid beauty startling in its impact. She was as unlike Nell, with her elusive charm, as possible. Even at seventeen Victoria's feminine attractions had been abundantly evident. She had been energetic, always laughing, wilful, and damnably enticing. Even from the grave she had the power to fascinate him.

He silently berated himself. What the devil had he been thinking of, prosing on to Nell in that boring, reasonable manner? No wonder she had rejected him. How had he ever imagined that a young girl, and Nell was very young still, could possibly find a pompous fellow of his advanced age remotely exciting? He wondered ruefully if she'd have accepted him if she'd known him years ago, when he was impulsive and devil-may-care.

What he should have done, he told himself angrily as he drained the glass, instead of taking her to a formal meal in quiet, elegant surroundings, and making what sounded like a business proposition, was sweep her off her feet. He should have found some wildly romantic spot, hired a couple of violins, organized an alfresco picnic, then thrown himself at her feet while the violins played soft, seductive music from behind a bank of roses. Or perhaps he should have paid a couple of villainous-looking ruffians to kidnap her, with him swooping to the rescue and carrying her off in his arms.

He rose abruptly to his feet. He was being ridiculous. But what the *hell* could he do? This, at least, he thought as he hurled the brandy glass at the seductively smiling lips and mocking eyes which stared down at him.

Nell tossed and turned, unable to sleep despite her physical weariness. They had rehearsed endlessly all week, and when they weren't dancing or singing, or planning improvements to the act, she had sat up late sewing the new costumes.

Outside work Gwyneth had been subdued. She was still shaken from the accident and Paul, when he came to see her, ordered her to sleep as much as possible. Kitty was withdrawn, slipping out every evening on her mysterious forays, and inclined to be snappish if spoken to.

Nell had no one she could confide in. Gwyneth had her own problems, and Kitty wouldn't understand. Besides, Nell was beginning to wonder if she hadn't imagined the whole episode. When she saw him Paul was cool, calm and friendly, the same as he always had been. Surely he had never made her that impassioned proposal? A man like him could never lose control of himself to the extent of asking a girl from a slum to marry him!

Her thoughts ran on. When it was time to get up she rose thankfully, though heavy eyed. For brief moments during the daytime bustle she could forget. When she couldn't forget she could often force her tired brain to concentrate on other matters. But in the endless hours of darkness her mind was uncontrollable. She wavered from incredulity and disbelief to a passionate craving for the bliss that might have been. Then, peeping hesitantly into the future, she would encounter despair. If it had been true, if she had believed him and they had actually married, it would have destroyed him. She could never mould herself into a suitable wife for Paul Mandeville. He would have known that, in the end. Yet being honourable he would have had to make the best of it. And that would have been unbearable. The alternative, not being free to love him, was worse.

She hadn't known her own feelings before he said he loved her. The very idea would have seemed laughable, incredibly presumptuous, had she even thought about it. In merely contemplating marriage with Tom Simmons she had raised her eyes far above what a girl in her position could reasonably expect. To go hundreds of steps further and imagine marrying a man like Paul was as unlikely as marrying the Prince of Wales.

Yet she knew now she loved Paul. Why had it taken her so long to understand her feelings? She hadn't loved Tom. At the time Tom proposed she hadn't known what love was, hadn't known she could abandon everything else for it, but had instinctively rejected accepting that she might love him. Now she shuddered at the thought that in her ignorance and desperation to make a better life she might have allowed Tom to persuade her. Marriage with him would be like drinking muddy pond water compared to the champagne of life with Paul.

The first performance of the new act was a triumph. The girls had never before experienced the thrill of having an ecstatic audience calling them back on stage for encores. Andrew, grinning broadly, pushed them back on in front of him, and signalled that they should repeat the last number. They hadn't dared tempt fate by rehearsing special encores, but would remedy that first thing in the morning.

'Darlings, you were wonderful! We have to celebrate!' Andrew exclaimed.

They smiled, and for a moment forgot their own concerns, but before she had finished the first glass of champagne Nell felt the familiar blanket of misery descend on her.

She sat down on the stool before her mirror. Even the fact of having one of the best dressing rooms, the three of them sharing but having a dressing-table and mirror apiece and good lighting, did no more than vaguely surprise her. She began to cream off her stage make-up, ignoring the excitement behind her. Then she realized that Gwyneth was doing the same thing. She glanced sideways, and met Gwyneth's eye.

'I shall be so glad to get back to the lodgings,' Gwyneth said abruptly.

'Are you tired?' Nell asked with quick sympathy. Gwyneth looked so pale, and ever since she had crashed Timothy's car had been unusually subdued, though her dancing had been the same as ever.

'Yes, and I don't really feel like this,' Gwyneth said quietly. 'Let's slip out and go back on our own.'

'What about Kitty?'

'Kitty? She'll find someone to bring her back, even if Andrew doesn't,' Gwyneth said with a note of bitterness in her voice.

'She looks as if she's enjoying it,' Nell commented, glancing through her mirror to where Kitty, still in her stage costume, was surrounded by men and talking eagerly to the theatre manager.

They finished with the make-up, then slipped behind the screen to change into their street clothes. It had been a very hot day, so neither of them had brought coats to the theatre. They were not conspicuous as they emerged and gradually edged their way towards the door. By now most of the other performers had crowded into the room, together with many unknown people. The noise level was increasing, and little notice was paid to them as they smiled their thanks at the congratulations and eventually, with sighs of relief, gained the passageway outside.

'Come on!' Gwyneth said, and with a laugh ran swiftly towards the stage door. 'Let's hope there aren't too many stage-door johnnies waiting!'

There were a couple of very young men sitting nervously in open-topped cars in the street outside, but Nell and Gwyneth linked arms and pretended absorption in their own conversation, and beyond a hopeful 'Doing anything tonight, luv?' from one of the men, reached the main street unmolested.

There was a tram coming and, laughing with relief at their escape, they ran to scramble aboard. It was only a couple of stops to the end of the street where they had found rooms for the week, but by the time they arrived their brief lightness of mood had faded. In silence they walked the hundred yards to the tall, terraced house where they were staying. They let themselves in and, suddenly weary, began to climb the stairs.

'Come and have some cocoa,' Gwyneth suggested, and Nell, not really wanting to be alone with her private devils, listlessly followed Gwyneth into her room.

Nell sat on the bed while Gwyneth lit the small spirit stove and set milk to heat. They didn't speak until they were clasping the hot, comforting mugs. Then they chatted desultorily about the show, their success, and the plans for the forthcoming tour Andrew had arranged. Finally these topics were exhausted and Nell reluctantly rose to her feet.

'I'd better go to bed,' she said quietly.

'No. Nell, don't go.' Gwyneth looked up at her, pleadingly. 'Nell, there's something I ought to tell you, but I don't know how to.'

'Gwyneth?' Nell sat down again, and impulsively reached out her hand towards the other girl. 'What is it? Are you in trouble somehow?' she asked quickly.

Gwyneth laughed shakily. 'No. No, Nell, it's not me. I — well, I don't want to be impertinent, but I couldn't help noticing how quiet you've been for the last week. I wondered if you knew?'

'Knew? Knew what?' Nell asked. For a dreadful moment she imagined Gwyneth was going to say she knew about Paul, and even to her best friend she couldn't bear to speak of that agony.

'It's difficult. I feel like a traitor, yet you were my friend first. It's about Tom Simmons. I don't know how much you like him.'

'Tom?' was all Nell could reply, startled. 'What about him?'

'He and Kitty. Oh, Nell, I didn't know if you knew, but Kitty's been keeping so quiet about it I decided she didn't want to tell you. She's been seeing him regularly. I found out while we were shopping in New Street. She'd arranged to have lunch with him at the Queen's Hotel. That's why she went out every evening last week; she was with him.'

Nell suppressed an urge to begin laughing. She knew that if she started she might not be able to stop. But the thought of the aristocratic Kitty enamoured of a trade-union officer, especially the rather stodgy Tom, was hysterically funny.

'Oh, Gwyneth, is that why you've seemed preoccupied? But I really don't care for Tom! Even before I met you, before you helped me escape from home, I couldn't bring myself to marry him. At the time it would have been a marvellous opportunity, I'd have been able to get away and live comfortably, but I didn't want to! I didn't ever want to marry anyone! I still don't!' she added vehemently.

'Then what's been keeping you awake this past week? If you didn't know about Kitty and Tom, and didn't care anyway, why have you got such dark shadows under your eyes?'

'I don't know,' Nell lied. 'I haven't been able to sleep. I suppose it was worrying about the new act. You know how I used to worry about finding lodgings? It's the same sort of thing, not knowing what's going to happen, worrying in case things go wrong. It was safe, dancing with The Bliss Beauties, I didn't have to cope with changes.'

Gwyneth looked keenly at her, and Nell tried to smile confidently back. Then the older girl shrugged.

'I hope that's all it is. I'm thankful you weren't hurt about Tom. You can do a lot better. What has me absolutely puzzled is what Kitty sees in him when she has Andrew and Timothy and Paul, and dozens of others clamouring after her. Whatever it is, she should have told you she was seeing him. It wasn't very straight to go sneaking off without a word.'

Somehow Nell escaped to her room. Gwyneth was a good friend, worrying about her feelings for Tom. But she was thankful Gwyneth had no idea about Paul, and imagined he was simply showing a friendly interest in teaching Nell to drive. She just could not endure sympathy for her loss of him.

Then she berated herself fiercely. What she'd just said to Gwyneth was true. She didn't want to marry. Marriage meant children, and the sort of drudgery and poverty her mother had to endure. It flickered through her mind that Paul was wealthy, had servants, and would no doubt employ nurses and governesses for his children, but the idea of him having some other girl as wife, and children that weren't hers, was so painful that she rejected it in a panic. She did not, in any circumstances, ever want to get married. She had to cling to this belief in order to suppress the agony of loss.

Tom sighed, and began at the top of the page yet again. It was important he knew the exact details, and yet twice he'd come to the end of the sheet and realized he hadn't taken in a word. Firmly he tried to push all thoughts of Kitty away. The enigma of why she had pursued him, demanded that he take her out every single evening the previous week, and showed him very plainly that despite his excuses about not being able to spend a weekend with her she wanted their acquaintance to progress much further, could not be resolved. He knew he was a well-favoured young man, with good prospects and a comfortable home to offer any girl he might honour with his attentions, but even his self-esteem boggled at the idea of Kitty regarding what he could offer as a magnificent prize.

He hadn't even been able to face a weekend with her. Frowning, he knew he'd been afraid. He'd never had a girl, and the very idea that he might not know what was expected of him, or be able to go through with it with sufficient poise, terrified him. Briefly he'd contemplated buying the information with one of the professionals who haunted the back streets near New Street station, but he shrank from the dreadful possibility that he might be recognized. Somehow he had to educate himself to be ready for Kitty, but as yet he couldn't think how.

Grimly he set about mastering the document, and had managed to grasp the main import before his father returned from a meeting.

During the next few days Tom was too busy to think much about Kitty. But he'd planned to take a few days' holiday in August, during the week Kitty would be in Blackpool. He'd been afraid the threatened miners' strike would prevent him from going to Blackpool, but now that was averted and he could go to be with her. And, he thought with rising excitement, once there he would surely be able to find a girl willing to initiate him into the mysteries of sex, a girl he would never see again. Then when he presented himself once more to Kitty he would not be petrified of disappointing her with his inexperience.

At the end of the first week, filled with triumph at their success, Andrew organized a party after the last show. Declaring that the theatre wasn't big enough he booked a room at a nearby hotel, where he had stayed that week, and invited all the artistes, the management and the backstage staff.

'I've asked the theatre critics on all the local papers in Manchester and Liverpool and all the towns round about,' he said, grinning. 'We've already had good reviews, but this should make them eager to come and see us when we get to their towns.'

Nell had no desire to go. Each night she'd crept back to her room and huddled into bed, clasping her misery to her. Somehow she'd found the courage to move through the day without breaking down, and give of her best at each performance, and she prayed no one else had an inkling of her true feelings. But if she refused to go there would be comments and questions, and they would be worse than enduring the party.

By now she had several party dresses, but she pulled out the first to hand and took it with her to the theatre ready to change after the show. It was a delicate green silk, reflecting the colour of her eyes and emphasizing them against the pallor of her face. She couldn't find enough interest to apply even a slight touch of colour to her lips, or powder her nose, and watched listlessly as

Kitty fussed with her black eyebrow pencil, and dabbed on the new shade of rouge powder she'd bought that morning.

At the party she forced herself to smile and listen to the other guests. Luckily they were all so eager to talk her own silence passed unremarked until one of the band sat down at the piano and everyone began to dance. Andrew had been standing nearby. He turned to reach for her. 'Nell, I hardly ever have the chance to dance with you.'

It was a slow foxtrot, and it was some time before Andrew, who had been enthusing over the success of his ploy to invite the theatre critics, several of whom had appeared, noticed silent tears forcing their way out from behind Nell's tightly closed eyelids. He looked round swiftly. No one else seemed to be paying them any attention. There was a door nearby, and without a word he whisked Nell through it.

'Come on, let's find somewhere private,' he whispered, and led her, unresisting, up a wide flight of stairs and along a corridor to the room at the end. 'Sit down while I get you a drink of brandy,' he said, pushing her gently so that she subsided on to the bed.

For some time, as she struggled to control her sobs, he sat beside her and held her hands, persuading her to sip the brandy.

'I'm sorry,' Nell whispered.

'Are you feeling ill?' he asked anxiously.

She shook her head, and sniffed. 'No, thank you. It was that tune. They played it when – when Paul – when he took me to Endersby's.'

He glanced down at her in surprise. 'You and Paul?' he asked sharply. Nell gulped and nodded. 'At Endersby's? I didn't think the virtuous Mrs Endersby catered for that sort of client,' he murmured to himself, and Nell, with a shuddering sigh, looked up at him enquiringly. 'Did he hurt you?' he asked suddenly.

'Oh, no, nothing like that, it was my fault – I didn't expect it,' Nell tried to explain. 'Andrew, please don't say anything! I couldn't bear it if Kitty or Gwyneth knew! Promise you won't tell them!'

'Of course I won't,' he reassured her, looking thoughtful. 'Here, drink some more. It's making you feel better.'

Obediently Nell drank, and then tried to struggle to her feet. 'I mustn't stay here, Andrew. Do you think I could slip away, go back to our lodgings? I really can't face going back to the party.'

'There's no need to go back yet. Look, they always leave me some sandwiches for after the show,' he said, moving to where a laden tray was sitting on a table. 'Let's have some. You're probably hungry.'

To please him Nell tried to eat, but the food tasted like sawdust, and she couldn't even manage one sandwich. She did drink the wine he opened, though, and gradually began to feel less despairing. Andrew chatted encouragingly about the theatres they were appearing in during the following few weeks, and she tried to pretend an interest. At last, however, he fell silent, and once more she rose to go.

'You know, I thought old Paul was irretrievably wedded to the memory of his darling Victoria,' Andrew said suddenly, and Nell sat down again, startled.

'Victoria?' she whispered.

'Yes, his fiancée. I'm sure you've heard about her. She was really something, a peach of a girl, and great fun. We, all the men who knew her, were utterly devastated when they announced their engagement. We'd all had hopes, I think, no one like her had ever been seen in Edgbaston before! She was only seventeen, but he'd been crazy for her for ages. Some people thought he'd kill himself when she died, he was a changed man. He had no spirit any more. He'd been quite a Don Juan before they became engaged. He never looked at another girl afterwards, so it's a great coup for you to have caught his interest. If you play your cards right you could do quite well out of him. He's a lot richer than I am.'

'I don't want his money!' Nell declared, and suddenly another sob erupted.

'Here, Nell, I'm sorry! I've been thoughtless, talking about her,' Andrew exclaimed. 'Have some more brandy. Nell,' he went on as she struggled again to contain her sobs, 'no man's worth this agony. Come here, sweetheart.'

He put his arm round her, and it was so comforting to be held tightly Nell didn't resist. When he began to kiss away the tears she shook her head, but that made her feel dizzy and she collapsed back against his chest.

'Look, Nell, lie down for a moment. Have a sleep while I go back to the party. I can't desert them all evening. Relax now, it'll do you good. Let me take off your shoes. You look utterly exhausted. Have you been sleeping badly?'

She was so weary she only half-heartedly protested when he lifted her up to slip off her dress. His bed was so comfortable, and she craved oblivion. Besides, she was feeling strangely lightheaded. It must be the lack of sleep, combined with the wine and brandy she had drunk. She didn't hear the door close as he slipped quietly from the room.

Some time later she dreamed she was lying in Paul's arms. He was kissing her, so gently and expertly that she pressed her lips eagerly against his, and snuggled closer to absorb the warmth of his body. Strange sensations, tinglings in all her nerve endings, a craving for some kind of fulfilment, overwhelmed her, and when he began to stroke her body she responded instinctively.

It wasn't until she felt the weight of a heavy body on top of hers, and a hard knee forcing apart her legs, that she knew it was no dream. Terrified, she opened her eyes and in the moonlight seeping through the curtains, recognized Andrew's face close above her own. He looked different, she thought wildly, he was intense and at the same time triumphant, like he sometimes was when he was playing his music, not at all like the easy-going man she knew.

'No, Andrew! Don't, you're hurting me!' she gasped, but he just smiled. Before she could turn away her face, for the odd lassitude still restricted her movements, his mouth came down hard on hers. With a grunt of triumph he entered her and the entire world seemed to explode as Nell's scream was stifled and her body ruthlessly pounded, sending her spiralling down into welcome darkness.

Chapter Seventeen

'Gwyneth! I've been driving along the whole Promenade trying to find you! Hello, Nell, how are you? Where's Kitty?'

Timothy brought his car to a screeching halt and leapt out. He bounded across the tram lines, beaming delightedly at the two girls.

'Timothy! Is the car mended? Is it all right?' Gwyneth asked urgently, and he nodded.

'Of course, only a few scratches and a couple of dents. I thought I'd come and get a few lungfuls of the jolly old sea air and watch you at the Winter Gardens. It must be something to be appearing in Blackpool, and at the same theatre as the Tiller Girls. Are they better than The Bliss Beauties?'

'They're very good, and have given me lots of ideas,' Gwyneth replied enthusiastically. 'I'm beginning to wish I could get back with a troupe and try them out.'

'Deserting dear old Andrew? But how is the new act going?'

'We've had good reviews, but – I don't know, there's something wrong and I can't decide what it is,' Gwyneth said, a frown crossing her face. 'It may not have been such a good idea to combine all the different types of entertainment in one act. It seems to confuse some of the audiences, and the other acts don't like it, they sometimes think we are encroaching on their specialities.'

'And what do you think, Nell?' Timothy turned towards her.

Nell glanced up at him, and laughed harshly. 'I think Gwyneth worries too much about the other acts,' she said curtly. 'What does it matter about them so long as we're a success?'

He gave her a puzzled look, but turned back to Gwyneth, and after a few minutes during which they continued to walk towards the Tower, Nell muttered an excuse and turned back. Timothy looked after her for a moment.

'Nell looks different. Her face is thinner,' he said.

Gwyneth nodded. 'I don't know what on earth's the matter with her. She's been like this, withdrawn and as if she's in her own world, ever since we left Birmingham. I can't explain it. It's not homesickness, I'm sure. At first I thought she was upset about Kitty and Tom Simmons.'

'Kitty and that dreadful little union man? What about them?'

'Oh, I don't suppose you know. For some reason Kitty was encouraging the poor fool. He was slavering at her feet for the whole week just before we started the tour. I thought Nell minded, he used to be her boyfriend, but she said she didn't particularly like him, ever.'

'I can't imagine Kitty falling for someone as common as that,' he said, his lips curling in contempt.

'I don't think she has. She's making eyes at the drummer now, and the silly fellow doesn't know if he's on his head or his heels. She's showing no sign of missing Tom. But after the first week, Nell suddenly changed. She was no longer so quiet, but she'd have spells of frantic activity, and then she'd go quiet again, and afterwards she'd make unpleasant remarks about people. That's just not like her, she's usually so gentle. And she won't speak to Andrew if she can avoid it. She refused to go to the party he threw after our first night here, and has even said she wants to leave the act.'

'Odd. But that's enough of her. Do you think you can face another driving lesson?'

'No! I don't think I can ever drive again!' Gwyneth exclaimed. 'I dreamt for weeks about that child and what might have happened. Even going in Kitty's car terrifies me.'

'The way she drives I'm not surprised! But at least come out for a drive with me.'

'It's too late now,' Gwyneth said hastily. 'There's a matinée, and I ought to be going back soon.'

'Shall I be able to get a ticket for the show?'

'I expect so, there aren't so many people here as usual, they say. It's the unemployment, and lots of miners used to come to Blackpool for holidays or day-trips from the pits in the north, but now there's the threat their wages will be cut they can't afford it. Or else they're trying to save money.'

'Can we have supper together after this evening's show?'

Gwyneth looked up at him. He had promised never to try and make love to her, after that disastrous visit to Manor Farm, and on the occasions they'd met since he'd behaved impeccably. She knew she could never have Paul, so why not accept invitations from other men?

'Thank you, I'd like that.'

'Will you let her come out with us? In a different place she might change – have more confidence, I suppose.'

'We take the children out occasionally, Miss Dawson, and of course if they have families or friends who can visit they sometimes go out with them.'

'That poor child has no one but us. We promised to keep in touch when we sent her to the home at Moseley. We could take her to a cinema, perhaps, if there is something suitable showing. I doubt if she has ever been to one, and it might surprise her into some reaction. She has been seriously ill, I understand?'

'Yes, but we couldn't find any physical cause.'

Amy recognized the visitors as soon as she was fetched into the room. She flashed them a quick glance, and then bent her head. They'd betrayed her once, she couldn't trust them again. And however much she wanted to, she couldn't speak. Her throat seemed to swell whenever she tried, and nothing, no sounds, would come out.

The visit to the cinema did intrigue her though. She watched the antics of the figures on the screen, even smiling a little as they danced to the accompaniment of a small cinema orchestra. When two of the men began to fight, however, she turned away and buried her head in the back of the seat, and dry sobs shook her body. Only when the sisters led her from the auditorium and into a huge café behind, ordering tea and cakes, did she stop shivering.

'Whatever she's suffered, it seems likely to be connected with violence,' the doctor to whom they reported this afterwards mused. 'Yet there were no marks of violence on her when you found her?'

'A few old bruises, and a cut on her leg, but no more than one might expect any active child to acquire normally. We were always falling over or banging into things at her age. There was nothing to make us suspicious.'

'Poor child. However, you did your Christian duty in rescuing her, and bringing her to us when no family could be found. We can still train her for a useful occupation even if she never recovers her power of speech – if she ever could speak, that is, though the experts all tell us there is no physical impediment.'

Tom spent most of his first day in Blackpool walking about, trying to find a suitable girl who would introduce him to that one aspect of life his schoolteachers had neglected. But the ones he felt confident enough to approach either hurried away with frightened glances over their shoulders, or told him indignantly that they weren't that sort of girl. He'd been puzzled. He hadn't even got as far as explaining why he wanted to scrape acquaintance. He sat in a deckchair and watched. He saw plenty of fellows, dressed as he was in flannels and sports jacket, begin to talk to girls and after a while link arms and stroll on. On the huge sandy beach there were several groups of men in shirt sleeves playing cricket, who were watched by admiring bevies of girls. When the games ended couples formed, and they went off to buy ice cream or rock or sit in cafés and drink tea or eat fish and chips.

Eventually Tom began to perceive a certain liveliness in these girls, a saucy look in their eyes, which had been absent in the ones he'd ventured to approach. He sneered. Trollops! His own taste was clearly superior to that of most of these yokels sporting in their state of undress. He would never dream of taking off his jacket and rolling up his shirt sleeves. Belatedly it occurred to him that only with such a girl, a trollop no less, could he improve his education.

The thought sent him hurrying back towards the small boarding house where he'd found the cheapest room he could. He recalled the leers from some girls waiting outside Central Station when he'd arrived the previous night, and shivered. With reluctance he accepted that he would not have the nerve to deal with a prostitute, and did not know how to get what he wanted from any other sort of girl.

He had a ticket for the show at the Winter Gardens, and after high tea at his boarding house, sausages and chips, made his way there. It was a cheap seat and he was too far away from the stage to be able to feast his eyes on Kitty as he'd anticipated. He could, however, see the outrageous costumes she and the other girls wore, and he drew in his breath in shocked disapproval.

'Cor, they'm a bit o' crumpet!' the man beside him exclaimed, and leaned forward, watching the minuscule skirts and long bare legs displayed, and the tight bodices which, Tom was horrified to see, left absolutely nothing to the imagination.

Tom turned away. He could not bear to listen to the lewd comments of the men around him. To think that once he'd been foolish enough to offer marriage to Nell, up there showing herself to all and sundry with total disregard for decorum! And even worse, to think that but for his stupid fears, he might have been treated to a private display of even more than Kitty was presently revealing.

At last the show was over, and — with some difficulty, for the Winter Gardens was a vast and confusing complex — he found the stage door. He joined the milling crowd of hopeful young swains just as Kitty was emerging on the arm of a dark, saturnine-looking man at least twenty years older than she was.

'Kitty!' he exclaimed, and she turned round with a smile. It faded slightly as he pushed his way towards her and she recognized him.

'Tom? What are you doing here?'

'I came to see you – your act,' he stuttered.

'How sweet! Isn't that sweet, darling?' she turned to her escort, who looked on sardonically.

'Kitty! Can't we go and talk somewhere?' Tom muttered, desperate.

'Oh, Tom, I'd love to, but not tonight. Pierre is taking me to supper.'

'Tomorrow, then?'

'Tom, I'm sorry, but that's not possible.'

Tom watched with increasing dismay as Kitty turned to smile intimately up at the man. She reached up her hand and with a soft whisper and a giggle smoothed his pencil-thin moustache with a red-tipped finger. She turned back to Tom, unable to conceal the triumph in her eyes.

'I do hope you enjoy your day-trip to Blackpool. Perhaps Nell would take pity on you and let you take her for a cup of tea in Lyons. I don't think she's having supper with anyone tonight.'

Their return to Birmingham began with a performance at Endersby's Hotel. Andrew had arranged it, as he did all their bookings, and Nell, who seemed to go through the days oblivious of everything except her work, didn't know what was planned until the Sunday they returned to Edgbaston.

'Well, a few days to rest, and then the gala evening on Saturday,' Andrew said gloatingly. He was having a late breakfast, tucking into a plateful of Meggy's best cooking, while Kitty toyed with a piece of dry toast and Nell looked down into her coffee, unheeding.

Gwyneth nodded. 'I want to go and see Mr Bliss today, some

of his new girls are appearing in the same show. Perhaps we can arrange to have a joint rehearsal sometime this week.'

'OK, I'll speak to Richard Endersby if Bliss hasn't already organized something.'

'Endersby's?' Nell asked, suddenly alert.

'Oh, Nell, don't you ever take in anything these days?' Kitty said impatiently. 'We're performing there on Saturday. We told you last week.'

'Oh, yes, I'd forgotten.'

She escaped as soon as she could and ran up to her room. She did not know how she could endure to go back to the place where Paul had proposed to her. It would revive all the agony of loss, and the recollection of the shame she felt every time she thought of what had happened between her and Andrew.

She locked the door and went to kneel beside the chest of drawers under the window. Carefully she opened the bottom drawer and lifted up the clothes folded inside. Beneath was her patch-box. She hadn't worn it in the belt round her waist since soon after she came to live with Kitty. She knew that no one would steal it from her room, and besides, it had been difficult to conceal once she began dancing and had to wear skimpy clothes on stage. She still took the precaution of hiding it beneath the scented paper with which Meggy lined the drawers.

Clutching the box Nell threw herself down on the bed. It was her one remaining tangible link with the happy life she'd known with her grandparents. She'd always regarded it as a talisman, believing that so long as she possessed it no real harm could come to her. She should have taken it on the tour. She should have risked the possibility of losing it, having it stolen from unfamiliar lodgings. If it had been with her she wouldn't have let Andrew make love to her. The memory made her feel defiled. Even if, to begin with, in her dreamlike state she had believed it was Paul kissing her, she should not have been so abandoned as to kiss him back so eagerly. She was by now no longer clear when she'd known it was not Paul, when she'd begun to protest.

'Darling, every girl panics at the final moment, but it was worth it, wasn't it?' Andrew had said when, recovering her senses, she had berated him for what he had done. 'You were enjoying it,' he went on. 'I wouldn't have made love to you if you'd said no, I'm not such a cad, but by that time it was too late to stop. I can understand it, if you didn't enjoy it with Paul, if that was your first time –'

'I didn't!'

'– but it would have been far more difficult for you next time if you'd given way to your fear and stopped at that point.'

'There won't be a next time!' she'd raged at him, and he had shrugged, and suggested it would be better if she allowed him to drive them to their next town rather than arouse Kitty's suspicions by returning in her present distraught state.

She had complied, and she still could not decide what the truth had been. She'd had a frightful headache, and suspected she'd drunk far too much. Dimly she recalled Andrew giving her brandy and wine, but she had no idea how much. That didn't excuse her wanton behaviour. Even if it had been Paul she should not have behaved in that way. If it had been Paul he wouldn't have wanted her to, she told herself, but it didn't help. Nothing helped. Nothing could take away the feeling of disgust at herself and fury with Andrew. The only consolation was that she was not pregnant.

She wanted to leave the act, but was too nervous of the future to know whether she could return to one of the Bliss troupes. She did her best to ignore Andrew and appear normal, and knew she made a dismal failure of this attempt. She could not, however, return to Endersby's where she had experienced that brief time of enchantment listening to Paul, however deranged he might have been for that moment, asking her to be his wife.

In the end, she realized it would be impossible to explain. Andrew would give her the amused, triumphant look he had used ever since that night, and she could not endure the questions Kitty and Gwyneth would ask. It had been difficult enough to fend off their anxious enquiries about her health during the past few weeks. She would have to grit her teeth and go through with it. At least Paul wouldn't be there.

He was. Nell saw him the moment they danced into the ballroom. He was with Mrs Mandeville and a middle-aged couple she did not know. She missed her step and Gwyneth glanced at her anxiously. Recovering, Nell tried to smile back and concentrate totally on the dancing. She succeeded so well that the burst of applause which greeted them at the end was, as Andrew, waiting offstage, enthusiastically informed her, mainly due to her.

'You were absolutely marvellous, Nell,' he exclaimed.

'I agree.'

It was Paul's deep voice, and Nell gasped. She turned slowly to face him and her heart fluttered so wildly she could not speak.

'Aren't you going to congratulate the rest of us too,' Kitty demanded, her voice brittle. She went across to link her hand in Paul's arm.

'Of course, Kitty. You were all wonderful, and so much better than you were before you went away. But for some reason Nell seemed inspired tonight. I've never seen her dance so well.'

Andrew strolled across and put his arm round Nell's waist. He pulled her close. 'Maybe there's a special reason for that, eh, Nell darling?' he said, in a low voice but quite clear enough for Paul to hear. 'We had a fantastic tour, Paul,' he went on, releasing Nell and turning to talk to the other man, somehow getting between them so that Nell drew back. 'There were marvellous notices in all the local papers, and some of the big ones too. Now we have a few weeks round the Midlands' theatres, and then we're off to take London by storm. After that, who knows? Maybe we'll be going to America.'

Pale, with a bleak look in his eyes, Paul excused himself when Kitty announced that the after-show party would be at her house.

She smiled up at him. 'Paul, darling, surely you won't let me down. These days Andrew can't pay attention to anyone but Nell,' she said, an edge to her voice. 'Timothy will be there for you to talk to if you don't want me. Did you know he actually stirred himself to drive all the way to Blackpool to see Gwyneth dancing? Of course he pretended it was to see all of us, but he didn't take us all to intimate little suppers at the Norbreck.'

'I have my own guests, Kitty,' Paul said, firmly removing her hand from his arm. She stared angrily, then shrugged and flounced away. 'Thank you,' he said to her retreating back, 'but I must now go back to them. I've been away long enough.'

Abruptly he left the room and Nell, suppressing the anguish which seeing him had revived in all its intensity, retreated into the small private parlour Mrs Endersby had provided as a dressing room. By the time Gwyneth and Kitty came in she was busy creaming her face, and the concentration enabled her to avoid looking at her friends.

She spent the next hour trying to avoid Andrew. Since he had made love to her she had been constantly trying to do so. While they were touring, and living in different lodgings, it had not been difficult. He was too busy during their times at the theatres, and after they had performed she could elude him and leave swiftly. Her pallor and lack of spirits made her excuses not to attend parties believable, but she could not avoid one in Kitty's house.

He cornered her in Kitty's small sitting room, between a table and the large settee which Kitty had re-covered in a tweed material, to replace the white Nell had seen that first visit so long ago, so that she could not move away without physically pushing past him. He was reproachful.

'Nell, sweetheart, why are you taking such pains never to speak to me?'

'You should know why,' she replied, struggling to keep calm.

'Oh, come, you make too much of a friendly little romp,' he said, trying to catch her hand.

'Is that all it meant to you?' she demanded, suddenly furious, no longer caring about the other people in the room, who looked startled and discreetly began to edge away.

'Nell, you were perfectly willing to begin with,' he said softly.

'I —' She stopped. How could she tell him that in her muzzy state after too much wine she'd thought it had been Paul making love to her? 'I was asleep to begin with,' she substituted tiredly, her anger evaporating as it was replaced with grief for her loss. It should have been Paul loving her. She could never have married him, but she had come to know by now that she would have gone to him willingly as his mistress. Now he wouldn't want her.

Andrew laughed. 'Is that your excuse?' he asked. 'Nell, you are beautiful and desirable. Forget how it happened, or why, just remember that you enjoyed it and can enjoy it again. It may not have been as good as it can be, the first time we were together. Paul's rather stuffy anyway, so you probably didn't enjoy it with him, but I can show you how to make love. Why won't you let me?'

'Because I despise you!' she said tautly. She suddenly realized that all the other people had left the room, closing the door, and they were alone. Seeing the expression that came into Andrew's eyes she began to tremble.

At first Andrew stared in amazement at her words. Then he stepped close to her and she couldn't get away. The table pressed into her legs, and she was almost sitting on it when Andrew jerked her into his arms. 'You dare say that?' he demanded incredulously. 'A slut from the gutter, and you have the impertinence to say such a thing? Where do you think you'd be if Kitty and I hadn't helped you? Not living in luxury and fêted by your audiences!'

She struggled, but he'd captured her hands and she could only turn her face away as he tried to kiss her. Then the door was opened sharply and Kitty swept into the room. Andrew swiftly released Nell and turned to face Kitty, who was eyeing them suspiciously.

'I've been trying to persuade Nell to come back to the party,' he said smoothly.

Nell seized the excuse. 'I'm exhausted. Do you mind if I go to bed, Kitty?' she asked.

'It depends who with,' Kitty said curtly. 'Oh, don't look so shocked, Nell! Take Andrew to bed if you want to! Paul as well! Both of them! What do I care?'

It was true, she was exhausted, but she couldn't sleep. The party continued long after Nell crept into bed. In a while the sounds of Andrew's tenor saxophone penetrated her room and she tried to cover her ears. Even in his playing he conveyed his anger. Instead of the piercingly pure, exuberant richness he normally produced the notes were harsh and strained, teetering on the edge of disharmony, and even more powerful than normal as they bewailed both hostility and torment.

At last the guests departed, and Nell heard Kitty banging about in her room, apparently not caring who might be asleep, slamming doors and singing loudly as she went to the bathroom. It was late morning when Gwyneth brought a cup of tea into Nell's room.

'I wondered if you were ill,' she said, quietly closing the door behind her. 'Have this, it'll help.'

'You're an angel,' Nell said gratefully. 'I couldn't sleep for ages, and I've a dreadful headache.'

'Shall I fetch an aspirin?'

'No, thanks, I have some here.'

Gwyneth perched on the end of the bed. 'You haven't looked well for weeks. Is there anything I can do?'

'I'm quite all right, Gwyneth.'

'You aren't. Perhaps you're overworked, too tired. Why don't you ask Paul for a tonic?'

Before Nell could think of a reply her door opened again, this time noisily. Kitty stood there in her new satin dressing gown. It was scarlet, the fashionable colour since Noël Coward had worn one in *The Vortex*, and the normally pale Kitty sported cheeks which flamed to match.

'I am absolutely fed up with being woken up hours before I want to be!' she said viciously.

Gwyneth stared in amazement. 'We weren't making a noise, Kitty, I just brought Nell a cup of tea,' she began to explain, but Kitty cut her short.

'You are both ungrateful little tarts! Not only do you wake me up, you behave disgracefully with my guests! I saw you last night, Nell, making up to Andrew when you thought you had him alone. Are you trying to play him off against Paul? I don't know why you bother, you might know neither of them would ever dream of being serious about someone like you! Their girlfriends come from good families.'

Gwyneth, at first startled, leapt furiously to her feet. 'Kitty Denver! What in the world do you think you're saying? Have you run mad? How dare you say such untruthful, hurtful things to Nell? I thought you were her friend, I thought it didn't matter what families we came from! Just because you have money you can ignore the fact that your mother was, and still is from what you say, an upper-class whore. You are a bastard in more senses than one!'

'Gwyneth!' Nell breathed, aghast.

Kitty turned on her. 'Don't bleat!' she almost screamed. 'As for you, with your stupid middle-class Welsh preaching morality, why should I be friends with a jumped-up shopgirl just because we can both dance and sing? I could laugh to see the way you try to entice Timothy with your simpering and pretended fear of stupid little motor cars! He'll never take someone like you seriously. He'll marry a girl from his own class.'

'Like you, I suppose?' Gwyneth retorted angrily. 'Don't hope too much, Kitty! Timothy will choose a lady, not a pampered harpy!' She turned to Nell. 'Pack your clothes, we're leaving here now.'

'I was about to suggest you'd outstayed your welcome,' Kitty said bitingly. 'After all I've done for the pair of you, you could be a little more grateful, and behave in a manner that doesn't offend my better-class guests.'

Chapter Eighteen

'Where have they gone?' Andrew demanded on Monday morning.

Kitty shrugged. 'How should I know?' They sent for a taxi, and I certainly wasn't eavesdropping when they told the man where to go. I was glad to see the back of them.'

'But why? What on earth induced them to leave? How can I get in touch with them about our next performances?'

'They didn't say,' Kitty replied, tossing her head. 'The ungrateful bitches just walked out. After all I'd done for them, too, giving them a free home with bedrooms better than either of them had ever seen before, as well as taking them everywhere in my car. But that's the trouble with that class of person, they don't know how to be grateful and begin to take advantage. It's as well they've gone.'

'Did you throw them out?' Andrew demanded. 'I know you, Kitty, and you can be a jealous little cat at times. You were spitting mad when you found Nell with me last night, even though there was nothing wrong happening. And you've been in an odd mood ever since Timothy began to teach Gwyneth to drive. What's the matter, can you see your admirers being attracted to girls who have more pleasant natures?'

'If all you intend to do is insult me and defend them, you can get out too!'

'I will. Don't forget we have a·rehearsal tomorrow.'

'I won't forget, and I won't be there! I never want to set eyes on either of those little trollops again. Nor do I want to appear on the same stage as them. Find someone else, Andrew dear, who can endure dreadful dingy lodgings and filthy backstage dressing rooms, and who's not so particular about the sort of girls she dances with. I have other plans.'

Gwyneth's shoulders drooped, but she managed to smile at the receptionist. 'I see. Thank you. If you're full here we'll have to try somewhere else.'

Nell was waiting on the other side of the hall, beside a pile of hastily packed cases. Seeing Gwyneth's slight shake of the head she sighed. It was all her fault they had lost their home. Then she rallied herself. It was in no way her fault and she must stop feeling guilty for what others did. Despite herself her voice wavered as she spoke. 'We ought to have kept the taxi. We'll have to find another one and try somewhere else.'

'Can I help?'

Neither of them had seen Mrs Endersby emerging from her small office and crossing towards the stairs. They swung round as she approached them, and Gwyneth managed to smile.

'We need rooms for a few nights, but your hotel is full. We can try elsewhere.'

'You both look terrible. Come and have some coffee with me, and perhaps we can do something. Go into my room, I'll be back in a moment.'

When she followed them into the small but elegantly furnished room, more like a sitting room than an office with its comfortable chairs arranged about a fireplace, she waved them to seats. 'Please, sit down and be comfortable. The coffee will be here in a moment. I thought you both lived with Kitty Denver. So why do you need rooms?'

'We – er – we decided to move out,' Gwyneth said hesitantly. Her anger had cooled and she was feeling ashamed of the way in which she and Kitty had hurled bitter accusations at one another. When it was too late she wondered how such bad feeling would affect the way in which they had to work together. If only they could prevent speculation amongst their friends it might be possible to heal the rift sufficiently for it not to damage the act.

Marigold Endersby was not deceived. 'What you really mean is that Kitty threw you out, without giving you time to make other arrangements,' she said drily. 'Here's the coffee. Thank you, Jenny.' She poured the coffee and handed it to them.

'We'll find rooms soon enough,' Gwyneth assured her. 'It just seemed simpler to go to an hotel for a night or so and give ourselves time to look round. We can try some in the centre of the city, they're bound to have rooms available.'

'When do you go on tour again?'

'In two weeks. We're in Leicester and Nottingham then. Luckily we have no bookings for this week, and the next one is in Walsall, so we don't have to stay away. We've plenty of time to find somewhere just to leave our belongings. It's amazing how much one acquires without realizing.'

'It's Sunday, not a good day for trying to find rooms. And neither of you look fit enough to start searching. You're very pale, Nell. Are you ill?'

'Just a headache,' Nell said, but winced. It had intensified from the moment Kitty began her accusations, and she'd had no thought for aspirins, all her energy reserved for packing as rapidly as possible.

'How fortunate I was here. I came just for a few minutes to sort out a problem. Now I'm taking you home with me. Just for a couple of nights. The hotel is full for the next few days, and if you haven't found anywhere more suitable by then you will be assured of a room here after Wednesday. Don't argue,' she added as Gwyneth opened her mouth. 'Nell ought to be in bed. And it's only for a short while. I always keep rooms ready for Richard's parents when they visit, but they are in America at the moment, they won't need them. Finish your coffee while I have your luggage put in my car.'

*

'You shouldn't have done it, Miss Kitty. It wasn't kind or ladylike. And if it hadn't been my day off I'd have told you so to your face.'

'Oh, shut up, Meggy, and mind your own business! I was quite bored with sharing my home, and they were a pair of ungrateful little sluts.'

'They were well mannered and polite, and always did what they could to help me,' Meggy retorted.

'They may have crawled into your good graces, but they outstayed my welcome.'

'What you mean is that you were afraid they might steal the men you thought you owned.'

'You're as impertinent as they were. I wish I could get rid of you too.'

'You can't. It's your mother pays my wages, and here I stay, though there's times I'd like to be free of your tantrums.'

Kitty glared at her. 'I'm going shopping. See that you turn out their rooms and get rid of every single trace of them before I come back!'

Meggy sniffed, and watched balefully as Kitty flounced out of the room. Then she collected her mops and dusters and went slowly upstairs. Three hours later the rooms Nell and Gwyneth had occupied were once more lifeless and sterile. In the middle of the dining-room table, where Meggy, as she did when she was angry with Kitty, had laid out a coldly formal lunch, sat Nell's patch-box.

'What's this?' Kitty demanded as she sat down.

'I found it in Miss Nell's room. It had slipped under the paper in one of the drawers, and I expect she had to pack in such a rush she missed it. Where can you send it? Shall I ask Mr Andrew to give it to her?'

'I'll ask him. Now do go away, Meggy, this room's gloomy enough without having your miserable face hanging over me while I eat.'

When Meggy's grumbles became inaudible as she closed the door with a snap, Kitty picked up the patch-box and looked curiously at it. It was delightfully pretty: oval in shape, about two inches long and half an inch deep. The lid, which was slightly raised, had a border of deep royal blue, as did the sides. On the lid, on a white background, a spray of delicately painted flowers was being inspected by a pair of blue tits, and the flowers were reproduced on the sides. Kitty looked closely, and discovered that this was a free design, not the cheaper transfer prints which were more common. She raised the lid and found a tiny mirror inside it. Her eyes widened, for the interior, though tarnished, was silver. Most of these boxes, she knew, were made of copper or even cheaper metals. Then she noticed the inscription and carried it over to the light to read it.

'"To my true love Nell",' she repeated, astonished.

How on earth had someone like Nell, who had been destitute when Kitty first met her, acquired such a beautiful object? Kitty frowned. It was possible either Andrew or Paul had given it to her, in which case they were more seriously attracted than she'd imagined. The thought made Kitty furious. It was not comforting to imagine that either of them liked Nell enough to spend a lot of money on such an unlikely present. Yet the engraving was old, it hadn't been done recently. Could Nell have bought it with her earnings from dancing? Kitty shook her head. Even with the free accommodation and transport Kitty had provided, it would have been far too expensive. Nell had, Kitty knew, spent a lot of money on clothes, since she'd possessed virtually nothing to begin with.

Could she have stolen it? Despite her need to think badly of Nell, who had filched the affections of both Andrew and Paul, Kitty could not believe this. Besides, when would Nell have had an opportunity? It wasn't new, these boxes were not produced now. Besides, there was a slight scratch on it. It would have been too much of a coincidence if she had stolen a box bearing her own name. Unless she had somehow seen the inscription and been tempted because it *was* her name? To Kitty's knowledge Nell did not show any interest in shops selling such antiques, and had never been inside a house where it might have been carelessly displayed, a temptation for someone as poor as Nell. Perhaps she'd had it all the time. Kitty frowned. If she had, apart from the puzzle of where it had come from and how she had acquired it, she had never been as poor as she'd claimed. It could have been sold for a great deal of money, certainly enough to have kept Nell in comfort had she left home and looked for another job away from her family. And that meant she had been sponging on Kitty's good nature while she could have afforded to support herself.

Conveniently forgetting that by the second time she and Nell had met, Nell had a job and was paying her own way, Kitty stoked the fires of her jealousy with resentment. However Nell had come to own the patch-box, she didn't deserve to have it returned to her. Losing it would serve her right for being so secretive.

Forgetting the lunch she hadn't even started, Kitty went hastily to her sitting room and thrust the patch-box out of sight in one of her bureau drawers, behind some embroidery she had started a year ago and grown tired of. Then, a satisfied smile on her lips, she decided to go shopping for another hat.

Marigold calmly insisted that Nell go straight to bed in one of the communicating rooms overlooking the back garden of her house. She was thankful to sink down into a deliciously comfortable feather mattress and rest her throbbing head on the soft, lavender-scented pillows. Within minutes she was fast asleep. It was dusk when she awoke, blessedly free from pain, and lay remembering her new hostess's kindness.

'Would you like some soup?'

It was Gwyneth. She'd been sitting quietly in an armchair beside the fireplace. Now she was in a condition to notice her surroundings Nell saw that the room was furnished as a sitting room as well as bedroom. She suddenly knew she was ravenous.

'That would be lovely.'

Gwyneth rose and tugged at a bellpull beside the fireplace.

'Marigold — she told us to call her that, she's not very much older than we are — said to ring down when you were ready.'

'This is a lovely room. I'm not even sure where we are. It's not near Kitty's, is it?'

'No, her house is much closer to the Hagley Road, on the north side of the Botanical Gardens. This is just off Richmond Hill Road, where Paul lives.'

Nell busied herself pleating the sheets. 'Does he? I didn't know where he lived, precisely.'

'Marigold told me. Isn't she fantastically kind, to bring us to her home? She insisted I had lunch with them all. At least, with the older boy, Dick, who's just ten. The two little ones are in the nursery.'

'She doesn't look old enough herself to have a son of ten.'

'She explained he was born when she was still only seventeen. Richard was a pilot in the war, and he was lost in Germany for years, terribly injured. It sounded so romantic. While everyone else thought he was dead she opened the hotel and made a great success of it; and he thought she was dead too, but eventually came home and found her. They are still terribly in love,' Gwyneth added almost to herself. 'It can't happen in many marriages. It's too great a risk, compared with dancing!'

Marigold herself brought a tray with soup, some cold meat and salad, and a bowl of late raspberries. 'Do you feel better now, Nell?'

'Much, and thank you for helping us! It was so kind.'

'I can't let my most popular dancers be homeless! We didn't want to wake you for dinner, so I hope this is enough. If you stay in bed you'll be quite fit in the morning. You can take it easy tomorrow. Gwyneth says you have a rehearsal on Tuesday. Then you can begin looking for rooms. If you want anything else, ring for it.'

'And I'll be in the room next door, with the door open,' Gwyneth added.

*

Andrew had booked Frank Bliss's studio for the rehearsal, and on Tuesday Nell and Gwyneth were there early.

'I heard how successful you were on your tour,' Edwina said while they were waiting for the others to arrive. 'I still wish you were dancing with us though.'

'It was very good of you both not to mind when we left. We did feel disloyal after all you'd done to get us started.'

'You mustn't, Gwyneth. We were sorry to lose you, but you have to take every opportunity. You are both too good to stay in a chorus line for ever, and anyway dancers have very short professional lives, they're finished at thirty. If you can develop other specialities, like the singing you're doing now, you'd be able to stay in the music halls for much longer if you wanted to.'

'I enjoy the variety, but I still much prefer the dancing,' Gwyneth said. 'We hope you'll help us to devise some new routines. Will you have time? Are you busy with your classes?'

'It's easier now we have an assistant teacher. I am helping Frank more with the paperwork, as he travels a great deal looking after the troupes and finding bookings for them. We have four troupes out now and another almost ready to start. They occasionally dance at charity shows, too. And we've sent one girl, who came to us after you left, she could already dance, to the Folies-Bergère to John Tiller's girls there.'

They couldn't ask any more. Andrew arrived with two of the musicians, and after greeting Edwina briefly began to lay out some sheets of music he'd brought. 'Kitty isn't coming,' he announced abruptly. 'We'll have to reorganize the routines she was in.'

The men clearly knew this, there were no exclamations or questions. They immediately began to offer suggestions for cutting out some of the songs and substituting others where Kitty's absence would not be noticed. Gwyneth waited for a pause.

'We can alter the songs,' she said slowly. 'It won't be so easy to change the dancing. We haven't many routines for just the two of us as we wanted to include Kitty as much as possible.'

'Can't you simply change them for two dancers?'

'Of course not! They depend a lot on pattern and interaction. You can't get the same effect with a third of a team missing!'

'Get another girl,' Andrew said dismissively. 'Surely Mrs Bliss has someone capable.'

'Not someone able to learn several complicated routines in less than a week!' Gwyneth snapped. 'The three of us spent far longer doing it, and we'd had the advantage of working together for some time, and knowing some of the basic parts of the routines beforehand. We adapted them to make them look better.'

'Then adapt these. The dancing is your problem, Gwyneth. I have enough to think about with the music. Let's begin with deciding what we definitely have to drop, and see how much is left. Then we can try out some of the new stuff.'

'And we still have no help deciding what we are going to do!' Gwyneth fumed after they had finished the rehearsal and gone to have something to eat in a teashop in New Street. 'We'd better revive some of the speciality dances we did with The Bliss Beauties. At least Kitty wasn't involved in many of those.'

'And Marigold said we could use the ballroom at the hotel for practising. It's free tonight.'

'We also have to look for rooms! Sometimes I feel I could kill Kitty!'

Nell grinned at her. She felt so much better, she could face her problems with much greater equanimity. 'I know it makes it awkward for the act,' she said slowly, 'but it was never very easy living with Kitty. In some ways I think I'll prefer being independent. She always expected us to show how grateful we were, and though I was, of course, it felt uncomfortable.'

Gwyneth nodded. 'I know what you mean. She was so unpredictable. She could be kind and generous but she had a nasty mean streak. Not with money, she was generous enough with that, but with her friends.'

'Let's forget it. We need to find rooms.'

'Timothy, you shouldn't have come here!'

'Why the devil not? Andrew told me where you were. The Endersbys are good friends of mine and I wanted to see you. I went to The Firs and Meggy told me what Kitty had done. Kitty wasn't there, or I really think I'd have wrung her neck!'

Gwyneth chuckled. 'I can't imagine you summoning up the energy,' she said. 'Marigold offered us rooms here in her house for a few days, but we can't abuse her hospitality. We have to find somewhere to live soon.'

'And have you?'

'No, we saw some we liked, but there was always just one, and we want to be together. We'll try again tomorrow.'

'Come and live with me.' She stared at him, utterly astounded. Timothy shrugged, and a wry smile twisted his lips. 'Yes, I know I was less than subtle when I enticed you into my wicked lair, but I thought you had partly forgiven me.'

'Yes, on the understanding that you never tried anything again!'

'I won't, without your full agreement. If you insist we can have a proper document setting out how far I can go, and on what terms.'

'Don't be idiotic!'

'I mean it, Gwyneth. I want you, and if you came to live with me you'd be treated like a queen. I've been kicking myself ever since it happened for being so crass, so impatient, and ruining my chances with you. Haven't I shown you that I've reformed?'

'I won't give up dancing for anyone. And I don't want to marry you, Timothy.'

'Ah. I haven't explained myself properly. I didn't mean we would get married ... It isn't that I wouldn't prefer to,' he added swiftly, seeing her expression. 'My family wouldn't stand for it, you see. They expect me to marry a girl from – well, from amongst our set. Not that I have any intention of complying for years yet, and in the meantime we could have fun together.'

Gwyneth, with a tremendous effort, suppressed the urge to

pick up all the ornaments in Marigold's drawing room and throw them, one after the other, at Timothy's head.

'That is almost as insulting as what you tried to do before,' she said, her voice taut with fury. 'I would not have accepted marriage, from you or anyone, and I certainly have no desire to become your mistress just to enable you to while away a few idle hours when you have nothing better to do.'

'Gwyneth, it wouldn't be like that, believe me! We'd be together, we could travel, I'd take you to all the places you could go to as my wife! It's just that it wouldn't be — suitable to marry you.'

'Everywhere but to meet your family, I suppose? Or your superior friends? I think you'd better go before I really lose my temper. Get out! Go! And I never want to see your silly simpering superior face again!'

'It's getting farcical, everyone throwing people out,' she said ruefully to Nell later that night, when they were sitting in Nell's room. 'I was so furious, but I wanted to laugh and cry at the same time. I didn't know which to do first.'

'Is it because of your upbringing that you won't go and live with him?' Nell asked curiously. 'Do you think it's wrong?' If it had been Paul suggesting it to her she would have gone without a second thought, and gladly.

Gwyneth shook her head. 'Oh, yes, I've always been taught it was one of the worst sins. But I don't think that was my main reason. I just don't want to. And it was so insulting, the way he told me I was fit to go to bed with him, but not to be his wife. And I want to dance,' she added firmly.

As Gwyneth prepared for bed she allowed herself to wonder what her response would have been if it had been Paul making the suggestion. Then she shrugged. It was impossible to imagine. Paul wasn't that sort of man, and even if Nell couldn't see it it was obvious to Gwyneth that he had no time for anyone else. If it had been otherwise, she might have been tempted. As it was, her dancing must be sufficient.

*

Andrew called rehearsals every morning, and Edwina offered to help Nell and Gwyneth as they struggled to prepare different routines.

'If you are interested, by the way,' she said as they were taking a short rest, 'there are a couple of ground-floor rooms available in a house on the other side of the road. They aren't cheap, but I think you could afford them.'

'Really? That would be ideal!'

'Go and see them when we've finished. It would certainly be convenient for rehearsals here.'

The rooms were large and bright, and well furnished, although by no means as elegant as either The Firs or the Endersby home. Nell and Gwyneth were relieved to have found somewhere and arranged to move in the following day.

All week they were so busy rehearsing they did no more than unpack what they needed immediately. It was not until Sunday, when they were trying to decide which costumes they would need for the next week's show, that Nell missed her patch-box. She searched in all her cases, and through every possible place where it might have been concealed. Then she sat and tried to recall that dreadful morning when they had been packing in frantic haste so as to get out of Kitty's house. She'd been slow, too much in pain to hurry, and Gwyneth had helped her. Gwyneth may have taken the other things out of the drawer where she'd kept the patch-box, and missed it. She hadn't thought to look herself.

She remained amidst the chaos of the room, desperately trying to convince herself she'd put the patch-box in some other place, where so far she hadn't thought to search. Gradually, as the realization that it was lost penetrated her brain, blind panic overwhelmed her. Her thoughts whirled. It was her talisman, and she'd always had the feeling that while she had it there was hope for a better life. Without it, how would she sustain her memory of her happiest years with her grandparents?

*

Andrew came into the dressing room with only a perfunctory knock. Nell and Gwyneth turned from the mirror in surprise.

'Have you seen Pierre?' he demanded.

'Didn't he drive here with you?'

'No, he said he didn't need a lift.' Andrew pushed his hands through his already disordered hair. 'We're on in half an hour. He implied he had a car, or someone to bring him. Did he say anything to you?'

'No. He didn't seem to have time for anyone last week. He was off the moment we finished rehearsing.'

'And not very interested in the rehearsals,' Andrew replied slowly. 'Was he ill?'

Gwyneth shrugged. 'He'll turn up. Maybe they — whoever it is bringing him — have had a puncture. He won't let us down.'

Every five minutes Andrew, looking more and more distraught, came to see whether Pierre had arrived, but no one had seen him.

'You'll have to change the order of the acts,' Andrew said desperately to the stage manager as the rest of them were waiting in the wings.

'There's only two more before the top man. You can't shift 'im.'

'But please can we have a few more minutes? Something dreadful must have happened.'

Reluctantly, and with the displaced artistes complaining bitterly, the programme was rearranged. Still Pierre did not arrive. With three minutes to go before they had to appear, the stage-door keeper shuffled up.

'Note fer Mr Denver,' he said lugubriously.

Andrew snatched it. 'Thanks,' he muttered as he tore open the pale blue envelope. Gwyneth narrowed her eyes. She had seen that sort of envelope before. And encountered the flowery perfume which wafted up from it, for a second overwhelming the mingled backstage aromas. 'Damn her to hell!' Andrew exploded.

'Be quiet!' hissed the stage manager. 'You'll be heard on stage!'

'What is it?' Nell whispered.

'That damned cousin of mine!' Andrew said bitterly, lowering his voice. 'This note is to say she and Pierre have left for a short holiday in London. She hopes the sudden decision will not greatly inconvenience us! The feeble milksop! He daren't tell me himself, but they must have been plotting this all last week!'

'What can we do?' Gwyneth asked. 'We can't get the right rhythm without the drums!'

'You'll 'ave ter do the best yer can, mates!' the stage manager, who had been listening to the exchanges, intervened. 'The show must go on! An' 'ere come the great opera duo,' he added contemptuously as the previous act, receiving little applause, bowed themselves off stage.

Before they knew what was happening, the curtains parted and Nell and Gwyneth were in the full glare of the footlights. A panic-stricken glance showed them that Andrew and his depleted group of musicians were ready to play, and on the first ragged notes from the saxophone they began to dance.

'It was a bloody shambles!' the manager complained afterwards. 'That's the last time you amateurs appear in my theatre! And you needn't think you'll get paid for tonight, either. You didn't provide what you promised, and I was lucky no more of the audience walked out.'

'Look, it wasn't exactly our fault!' Andrew tried to bluster. 'We didn't know the blasted man was going to let us down without warning.'

'That's your problem. Did you see old Jimmy's look as he went on? If you've killed his act too he'll be after your blood. Take my advice and scarper, fast!'

'Come on, Gwyneth, let's go,' Nell urged. As they walked towards the station she was shivering.

'I don't think I've ever been so humiliated, or so terrified,' Gwyneth confessed. 'It wasn't so bad when they were just shouting, but when they started laughing, and Andrew stopped playing and shouted back at them, I wanted to run!'

'So did I! Do you think Kitty did it on purpose?'

'Of course she did, to spite us. I think she and Pierre were up to something while we were in Blackpool, but I didn't think it was any more than pique on Kitty's part, to show us she didn't care that Timothy and Andrew were paying us more attention than they gave her.'

'How can anyone be so mean? It's wrecked all the reputation we've worked so hard to build. Even if she's no longer interested, does she have to ruin it for us?'

'People as spoilt as Kitty Denver don't care a scrap about anyone else so long as they get what they want, whether it's admiration or revenge. Cheer up, Nell, at least we won't starve. Edwina will be glad to have us back, and you know in many ways I prefer dancing.'

Nell thought she did too, but all the way back to Birmingham on the train she was wondering whether this was the first piece of bad luck to assail her now she had lost her patch-box.

Frank and Edwina were pleased to welcome them back, but to Nell's dismay they didn't have places for both of them together.

'In a few weeks there may be another place, or I can move the girls around, but I don't want to disturb the line-up now, they've only just begun performances,' Frank explained.

'We can put Gwyneth back in the first Beauties, they need someone and she knows most of the routines already. They go on tour to Oxford and Gloucester and Bristol next week,' Edwina suggested. 'Nell can stay with the second Beauties in Birmingham for a few weeks. They need someone with experience, and we could introduce a solo spot for her.'

It was better than nothing, and they had to accept. Andrew, after the débâcle of the Walsall performance, had angrily disbanded the group and was making plans to set off on his own tour.

'I've had enough of slaving for the benefit of others,' he

announced bitterly. 'I'm looking after me in future. But I do wish you luck, you did nothing to cause the problems,' he said to Gwyneth and Nell.

'I should think not!' Gwyneth exploded when they were out of earshot. 'If anyone caused it, apart from Kitty, it was Andrew trying to kiss you and making her jealous!' She started to laugh. 'Don't worry, Nell, we'll be even better off now, and we'll soon be back in the same troupe. Edwina has promised, and have you noticed that she has far more say in running things than she used to?'

It was unbelievably lonely when Gwyneth had gone. The other girls in Nell's troupe were either shy or resentful because she had more experience and was promoted at once to doing solo spots. Their first few engagements were in Birmingham, so she didn't have to try and share lodgings with them, and they were happy enough to travel back with her to the city centre from whichever theatre they appeared in.

The advantage was that Nell had time to go and see her mother frequently. Mrs Baxter was pathetically grateful for these visits, and assured her daughter that Pa wasn't in the least suspicious about the extra luxuries Nell's money provided.

'It ain't as if 'e cared,' she said tiredly. 'So long as little 'uns don't fuss 'im, 'e don't notice what they 'as ter eat. Our Ned came ter see me last week, an' said 'e'd seen yer Pa wi' that Janie Pritchard, near 'er 'ouse. 'E don't allus come 'ome nights now.'

'Ma, that's awful!'

Her mother shrugged. 'Why should I want 'im in me bed? It's a damn sight better without 'im snorin' an' kickin' me.'

Nell shuddered, and hugged her mother close.

'It ain't as if we needs 'is money. 'E never gave us much anyroad. We can buy food on what me an' Eth gets, what you gives us, an' the coppers Benjy an' Fanny bring in.' She smiled, her face softening with love. 'Benjy's found an old bucket an' shovel, an' 'e collects 'oss muck from road, an' sells it fer 'a'penny a bucket. 'E's a good lad.'

'Have you heard any more — about Amy?' Nell asked hesitantly.

Mrs Baxter shook her head. 'I think the lass is dead. At first, I felt as if 'er was callin' me. 'Er don't no more. Better off dead, p'raps. Not all on us can get out of slums like you did.'

'Ma, if I can help any more, I will,' Nell promised.

As she walked back along Broad Street to her room, culling her brains for ways in which she could help her mother escape from a hopeless existence, she heard her name called. 'Nell, I thought it was you!'

'Kitty!'

Kitty smiled as though they had never quarrelled. 'I hear you're dancing with The Bliss Beauties again. God, you can't know how divine it is not to feel tied any more. It was fun while it lasted, but it was enough for me, traipsing all over the country and all those dreadful lodgings. I'm looking for something more exciting now, more glamorous.'

'I hope you discover it! Kitty, when we — left The Firs, I must have missed a little patch-box. Did you find it?'

'A patch-box? One of those old-fashioned things?'

'It was in one of the drawers of the chest. It could have slipped under the paper.'

'I don't go grubbing about under drawer linings,' Kitty said with a slight shudder. 'I didn't find it.'

'Meggy might have done. Please, would you ask her to look?'

'If it means so much to you. Though if she did find it, she might not admit it.'

Nell was shocked. 'Meggy would never steal anything!' she said indignantly.

'You have more faith in her than I do,' Kitty drawled. 'I must dash, Nell, I'm meeting a new man for tea at the Grand. He's a grubby manufacturer, but he's fabulously rich, and a fantastic lover. Far better than Andrew. Give my dear cousin my love, won't you?'

Nell was rehearsing the next morning in Endersby's ballroom

when Marigold came into the room and spoke briefly to Edwina. When the dance had finished Edwina called Nell over to her.

'Mrs Endersby needs you, Nell,' she said gently. 'We'll be finishing soon, so don't bother to come back.'

'Nell, come into my office, please.'

She led the way through the hotel and towards the room Nell had seen before. She ushered Nell in, then closed the door gently and indicated for Nell to sit down. Nell, however, was standing in the centre of the room, puzzled, facing Paul who had risen from his chair and taken a step towards her.

'Nell, my dear,' he said, 'I'd give anything not to have to tell you this. It's bad news.'

Chapter Nineteen

HE reached out for her, hesitated, and then took her hands firmly in his. 'Come and sit down.'

Marigold moved to a small cupboard and quietly busied herself with pouring two glasses of brandy as Paul drew Nell to sit beside him on the settee.

'What is it?' Through her churning fear she was conscious of his hard, comforting grasp, and his eyes, full of sympathy, close to her own.

'It's your mother,' he began, but Nell interrupted.

'Is she ill? Has Pa – What's happened?'

'It's nothing to do with your pa, Nell. He wasn't there. There was a fire. No one knows how it started. It was the middle of the night. People heard an explosion, but before they could do anything the entire house was burning. I'm sorry, darling, but they all died.'

Marigold came and held the brandy to Nell's lips. Without thought Nell sipped, coughed, and with her gaze fixed on Paul's face, uttered a dry sob. 'Ma? The little ones? You're saying they're all – dead?'

'I'm so sorry, Nell. They'd have been suffocated by the smoke before the fire reached them. It would not have been painful, not like burning.'

'Not painful? You think death isn't painful!' She struggled to free her hands, but he forced her to be still.

'We none of us know what death is like, Nell, but I've watched people dying, and at the end any pain they feel seems to leave them. Suffocation is quick, not like the agony of burning flesh.'

He looked up as Marigold, with an odd choking noise, hastily set the brandy glasses down on a table beside him, and then, her glance apologetic, swiftly left the room. He turned his attention back to Nell and went on talking, gently yet firmly, until her rigidity left her and she began to weep. He gathered her in his arms and stroked her hair away from her forehead, and after a while persuaded her to sip more brandy.

Nell sat up, took a deep breath, and gratefully accepted the handkerchief he proffered. 'I'm sorry. I'm all right now. Please tell me what happened.'

Paul sipped his own brandy. 'We aren't sure. From what people nearby said it seemed like a gas explosion. There may have been a leak, or the gas mantle could have been left on, and the light for some reason blown out. Before anyone could help the house was on fire. No one could get in, and they couldn't hear anyone inside calling or crying. That's why I'm sure they would have been overcome by smoke or even gas before they knew anything about it. The houses on either side were damaged, though no one else was hurt.'

'All the little ones? They all – died?'

He nodded. 'When the fire was out, they found all their bodies.'

She shuddered, and turned away her head. 'Where's Pa?'

'He seems to have been drunk, and hadn't gone home. He was with some friends,' Paul told her.

'If I hadn't given Ma money he wouldn't have had enough to go drinking, he'd have had to give her some,' she said bitterly.

'Then he'd have been killed too,' Paul pointed out softly.

Nell turned to him, her eyes blazing. 'That might have been a good thing! Rather than all those innocent little babies! And Ma, he never made her happy, never helped her, just used her until her poor body was worn out with having so many children!'

He thought she would collapse into tears once more, and tried to put his arms round her, but she shook her head, took a deep breath, and looked up at him from tear-drenched eyes.

'I'd like to go and see. Please will you come with me?' Her voice shook, but she controlled it. When he nodded she managed a brief smile of gratitude. 'I'll go and change.'

He suddenly recognized why she looked strange. She was wearing the rehearsal costume Edwina had introduced, neat grey bloomers and a loose, white shirt tied with a narrow bow of ribbon at the neck. Her legs were bare, apart from short white socks, and suddenly she looked no more than a child.

'I'll wait for you here,' he said, rising to his feet and turning away towards the window. He wanted her so much. He wanted the right to comfort and protect her. But she didn't want any man, and from what he was discovering about her father, and the life her mother had led, he could understand why she might reject all thoughts of marriage.

Marigold slipped back into the room. Her eyes looked suspiciously bright but she was calm and businesslike.

'Gwyneth's away on tour. Nell can't be left alone in her lodgings, so bring her back to me. I'm going home now, and she must stay with me until Gwyneth gets back.'

'Thanks, Marigold! I was worried what to do.'

'And she wouldn't have agreed to go to your house,' she said, with a sympathetic smile. 'Oh, don't try and hide from me, Paul. I can see how it is with you, however much you try to appear calm and uninvolved. And I wish you luck, she's strong, though so young, and a delightful person. I'm very fond of her.'

He wondered whether to confide in Marigold. Then he decided it wouldn't be fair on Nell. Sensible though Marigold Endersby was, she might try and influence Nell in his favour. He didn't want Nell to be under any pressure. Nor did he want her, out of perversity, to turn against him. One day, he believed, she would come to him freely. It was fiendishly difficult being patient, but he was prepared to wait.

*

The house, and the ones to either side, was little more than a heap of debris. The roof had collapsed and bare, burn-streaked walls reared up, grotesque silhouettes against a cerulean blue sky. Much of the rubble had been shifted as men searched for the bodies, and was piled in the middle of the court. It reeked of smoke and dust.

People stood gossiping at their doors. Older children crowded excitedly as near as they were allowed to the wreckage, while their toddler brothers and sisters clung to their mothers' skirts, thumbs in mouths, sensing the fear as well as the fascination of some dramatic event touching their lives.

There was a ripple of comment as Nell approached, then a watchful silence. Many of the people recognized Paul as one of the doctors from the clinic. A few called greetings to him and words of sympathy to Nell, but most were speechless. Nell, in her fine clothes, with her handsome, attentive escort, had moved beyond their lives and understanding. There had been varied and ingenious rumours about Nell's change of fortune, many of them scurrilous, but since few of them had the means to visit music halls they didn't know the truth. They had to be content with imagining the unmentionable depravity pretty young women might indulge in.

'There's nothing left!' Nell gasped, halting abruptly at the entrance to the court. She stared into the shell of what had been her home, and saw some twisted metal which, she realized with a shock, was the bedstead she had once slept on. Another twisted heap was, on closer inspection, recognizable as the zinc bath tub which had hung on a nail outside the kitchen.

She let her gaze wander. They'd had wallpaper in the house next door, she noticed inconsequentially. A piece of it was hanging from the top of the far wall. She hadn't known they were rich enough to wallpaper their bedrooms. Her gaze swept on, and came to rest with a jolt.

'Look! Up there, on the top of that chimney!' She caught at Paul's arm and pointed.

'That piece of rag? What is it?'

'It was — it was a doll's dress. I gave the doll to little Joan for her fourth birthday, just a few weeks ago. None of us had ever had proper dolls. She used to undress it every night before she went to bed, and hang the clothes over the knob of the bedstead. Paul, take me away, please!'

Swiftly he led her to his car, which was parked at the entrance to the alley. She sat with head bowed as he drove away and didn't look up until he halted.

'Where — this is Marigold's house!'

'She asked me to bring you here. You mustn't be alone. Besides, there will be arrangements to make. Marigold will help you.'

'I mustn't presume! She was so good before.'

'She is, and wants to help. Let her do this.'

'Where's Pa?'

It was the first time Nell had mentioned him after her bitter outburst.

'He didn't know about the fire until he got to work this morning. He hadn't been home all night. He's been taken to your brother Ned's house, near Commercial Street. I have the address. Do you want to see him? This afternoon, perhaps, when you've had a rest?'

Nell was shaking her head. 'I don't want to see him! Paul, I don't have to, do I? I can't help blaming him for not being there. And — I know I shouldn't, it's wicked, but I can't help wishing it had been him and not Ma!'

'You needn't do anything you don't want to do,' he reassured her. 'Now go in and let Marigold look after you.'

Albert Baxter stood looking down at the nine coffins. They were like a set of those silly boxes that had no purpose except to fit inside one another, he thought with a spurt of anger. Take the smallest, for little Ronny, not yet two years old, fit it into Joan's, then Betty's, and so on until they were all enclosed by the one which held his Emily. Back into the womb from which they had sprung, he thought fancifully. He began to weep, and didn't hear any more of the burial service which the Reverend Wragge Morley, Vicar of St John's, was conducting.

He and Ned had wanted the ceremony to be conducted by their mentor, Pastor Wiseman. Ned and Florence had become members of his fundamentalist religious sect some time before, and Pa, under the joint influence of an unusual twinge of guilt and pointed innuendoes from Florence that only if he reformed his ways would he be welcome in her home, had embraced the same faith. But Bert, the next oldest son, and Nell, supported by a very pretty but implacably formidable young lady from Edgbaston, had insisted that Emily and her children should be buried with a Church of England ceremony.

'Ma was christened and married in church, not chapel,' Nell declared, 'and she'll be buried by it too!'

As Nell was paying they had to submit to her wishes. Albert, wiping his nose on the sleeve of his jacket, glanced to where she stood. She was unrecognizable as his daughter in her smart black costume, and her black hat which managed to look saucy even with a deep veil attached. To either side of her stood the doctor who worked at the Ladywood clinic and the lady who had helped make the arrangements.

He resented their presence. This was a family do. And he resented their fine clothes and air of wealth. He glanced down at his own shabby clothes, all he had, and mourned that he hadn't been wearing his best suit and new waistcoat on the night of the fire. If Nell had the money to waste on the sort of flowers she'd sent, she could at least have bought him some respectable clothes. As soon as this was over he'd mention it to her. They would still come in useful after the funeral.

He had no chance to mention it. The moment the last coffin had been lowered into the big grave, the pretty golden-haired woman took Nell's arm and guided her away. Danny tried to speak to Nell as she passed, but she turned her head away and walked steadily on. Albert and his four eldest sons watched as they got into a large chauffeur-driven Bentley saloon and drove away.

'Bleedin' toffs!' Danny exclaimed.

'Never mind. Florence's got some grub ready, come an' 'ave – have some,' Ned suggested.

Danny and Sam glanced at one another. 'Any booze?' Danny asked.

'No. Yer knows we don't drink no more. It's agin the Good Book.'

'It were the demon drink ruined me 'ole life,' Pa informed them seriously.

'If Pa hadn'ta got drunk 'e – he'd 'ave bin 'ome – home that night,' Ned said, stumbling crossly over his aspirates. It was difficult, trying to speak like Florence wanted. It wasn't too bad at home, but when he got with his workmates or his brothers he forgot the lessons she'd given him.

Danny looked at Sam and sniggered. Clearly Ned didn't know about Janie Pritchard. They wondered whether that was against Pa's new chapel morality too.

'Er . . . We'd better get back ter work,' Danny said, and he and Sam, followed swiftly by Bert, escaped.

'Paul's mother has invited us to tea,' Marigold said a few days later.

'In Kenilworth?' Nell asked, surprised.

'No, at Paul's house. She's staying with him for a few days and said she'd love to see you again. She does like you, Nell, there's no need to be afraid of her. She was worried it might be too soon after the funeral, but I told her you needed some distraction. It's – destructive to brood on things that can't be helped. I know that too well.'

Nell looked at her curiously. 'You seem to be so calm and happy,' she said softly. 'You've been so good to me.'

'I wasn't always happy or calm. I feel for you so much, since my youngest sister was once badly burned.'

'Was she seriously hurt?'

'She was scarred. But that was a long time ago. I wanted you to know I understand a little of what you're going through. Shall we accept the invitation?'

Nell nodded. Marigold was right, she knew. She had to keep busy to suppress her anger and regret at the pointless tragedy of Ma's life and death. She'd seen Paul's house from the outside, and the opportunity to visit it was too tempting to miss. It wasn't likely he'd be there, he'd be working or visiting patients.

It was bigger than she'd expected, on the crest of the rise and set well back from the road. The main door was at one corner, with a large lobby full, it seemed to Nell, of umbrella stands and fleshy-leaved plants. The entrance hall led off to the left, and a woman Marigold introduced as Mrs Williamson, Paul's house-keeper, showed them into the main drawing room. This was a big, high-ceilinged room stretching right across the front of the house, with three bay windows overlooking a long, sloping lawn surrounded by mature trees.

Mrs Mandeville made them welcome, expressed sincere regrets for Nell's bereavement, and then turned to Mrs Williamson. 'We'll have tea in half an hour. I want to show Miss Baxter round the house.'

Nell followed, marvelling at this opportunity to see Paul's home, determined to remember everything she could, so that she could think of him in his own surroundings. It was better than thinking of her own family, though it brought a different kind of pain, emphasizing how far apart they would always be.

'We'd better not invade the kitchens, but this is the dining room. It looks out over the back garden, which Mr Williamson cultivates mainly for vegetables. Rather old fashioned, I'm afraid, with this heavy Victorian furniture. Paul hasn't bothered to change anything since I left. I think he spends most of his time in the study, beyond the stairs.' She led the way past a gracefully curving flight of stairs which rose off the hall to the right, overlooked by a wide, deep window with panes of coloured glass through which the sun cast many-hued diamonds of light. There was a passage leading to a door to a conservatory, which contained, Mrs Mandeville explained, two productive vines. 'We will have some of the grapes for tea, they are still delicious, and I am so proud of them! My husband planted them when we moved here thirty years ago. But it's too cold to spend time there, and this is Paul's sanctum. It's really the library, but he has made it his own special place.'

Nell gazed round. It was a welcoming, informal and comfortable room, with deep leather armchairs, solid-looking tables mostly covered with books and papers, a wide fireplace where she could imagine roaring log fires, and a big desk set near a window overlooking a formal rose garden where the roses still bloomed.

Above the fireplace was a portrait of a girl. Nell stared at it, fascinated despite herself. That must be Victoria, and she was incredibly lovely! No wonder Paul could not forget her.

'We'll have a quick look upstairs, the first floor, anyway. There are several rooms in the attic, and the Williamsons prefer to use that as a flat rather than have the sitting room off the kitchen. Paul put in a bathroom for them. When we used it as a nursery there wasn't one up there.'

Nell lost count of the bedrooms she was shown. There must have been six or seven, and a big bathroom even more luxurious than Kitty's. They were well furnished, but cold and empty. All except the largest, at one corner to the front, with a small dressing room off it, which was clearly Paul's. Nell glanced surreptitiously at the large bed, and felt her cheeks glow with embarrassment. It was too intimate, looking at his bed. She turned away and left the room swiftly, thankful when the others followed her and Mrs Mandeville led the way back downstairs. She was relieved Paul was not at home, she could not have concealed her emotions from him.

It was a month before Gwyneth returned to Birmingham, and Nell moved back into her lodgings. 'I was so sorry I couldn't be here with you,' Gwyneth said as they sat drinking cocoa the first night back.

'You came every Sunday, that helped. Let's forget it. There are odd hours when I can manage to think about other things. It does no good to keep remembering, and wishing. Where do you go next?'

'A week in Solihull, then Frank says there may be changes. He was very mysterious when I spoke to him last night.'

'He wouldn't send me with the troupe when they went off to Manchester, said he wanted to have me in Birmingham. I'm only rehearsing, though he's paying me performing wages. I think that's Edwina being kind.'

'I have a feeling we'll be dancing together again. I do hope so, it's not the same without you to share digs with.' She was silent for a while, then spoke hesitantly. 'Frank told me something else. Andrew has formed another dance band and will be playing at Endersby's again next week. Have you seen him?'

'No. Well, I don't expect we'll be there, so we needn't see him. Gwyneth, I'm so tired, I must go to bed.'

A few days later, when Nell was rehearsing some new steps with Edwina, Frank Bliss burst into the studio waving a telegram.

'It's come! They want six girls! They go next week. The Bliss dancers are established, recognized!'

'Frank, that's wonderful,' Edwina replied, and glanced with a smile at Nell. 'Can we tell Nell now? I assume you want her to go?'

'Of course. That's why I didn't send her to Manchester. Nell,' he went on portentously, 'the Bliss School of Dancing has been asked to supply six of their best dancers to — the Folies-Bergère! What do you think of that?'

'Paris? The Folies-Bergère? With the Tiller Girls? And you want me to go?'

'Of course! Derval left the selection to me, on the understanding that if any are unsuitable they will be sent back. You and Gwyneth are our star dancers, and we have to show them in Paris what Birmingham and the Bliss School can produce!'

'They will provide costumes,' Edwina said practically. 'Max Weldy is a brilliant designer, so we need not do anything about

262

that. You will stay, at least until you find your way round Paris, in the hostel in the rue Duperre, near the Place Pigalle.'

Frank interrupted, full of excitement. 'Ah, the Place Pigalle! The memories it brings back! Gay Paree! The boulevards, the cafés, the girls! Yes. Well, I will leave you to discuss arrangements with Edwina. Tell Gwyneth to come on Sunday, and I must be telling the other girls I have chosen to go.'

Nell went straight to Endersby's. There was no one else to tell, and during the weeks she had spent in Marigold's home they had developed a real friendship. She knew Marigold would be pleased for her. She'd been recommending a total change to help Nell forget.

'I'd like to tell Paul, too,' she said hesitantly. 'I haven't seen him for over a week, though, since I left you. I expect he's been busy. He was so helpful, and spent such a lot of time finding things out for me, getting me Pa's address, dealing with the Vicar.'

'Telephone him,' Marigold suggested, indicating the instrument which sat on her desk.

Nell drew back. 'I daren't! It would seem too presumptuous.'

'Why? Paul's a friend, and he would be hurt if you left without telling him.'

'Couldn't you tell him? Please, Marigold, I would feel too awkward.'

'I'll telephone, but only if you promise you'll speak to him too.'

A few minutes later Nell replaced the receiver, a smile trembling on her lips. 'He's asked me to have dinner at the Grand,' she said, slightly breathless.

'When?'

'Tomorrow. Saturday.'

'Then we haven't much time. You need a new dress.'

'But I have plenty of dresses, more than I ever dreamt of having.'

'And they are mainly white, or pale colours, or the black

263

you've been wearing lately. They make you look so young. It's time you discarded mourning anyway, to help you put the whole tragedy behind you. I've had a fancy to see you in something sophisticated. Besides, you will need a really good gown for Paris. The best-dressed women in the world live there. Come, we're going to visit the best shops in the city. And before you say you can't afford it, it's an early Christmas present to you.'

Bemused, Nell allowed herself to be swept along. Marigold seemed to know exactly what was wanted, and though Nell would have been happy with almost any of the gowns she was shown, Marigold unhesitatingly rejected them. 'No, it's not good enough.'

'But we've been in a dozen shops already!'

'And we'll go in a dozen more until we find the one that's just right. Here is one that might have something suitable.' She was inside the shop before Nell recognized it. Miss Fremling, sensing a wealthy customer, stepped forward, and Nell blushed vividly as she recalled the days when she had scrubbed this floor. Then Miss Fremling paused, glancing from Nell to Marigold, and looking confused.

'Surely, it's Nell Baxter?' she asked hesitantly.

'Yes. Good morning, Miss Fremling. How are you?'

Nell, sensing the older woman's embarrassment, turned to Marigold and explained. Marigold laughed.

'Then surely you'll be delighted to see how beautiful she can look, now she's properly fed and not so overworked,' she said briskly, and explained what she was looking for.

Lizzie, who had been hovering nearby, smiled nervously, and while Marigold inspected the gowns Miss Fremling displayed, Nell spoke to her. 'Hello. You're Gwyneth's friend Lizzie, aren't you? I saw you once or twice.'

'How is she? Still dancing?' Lizzie asked shyly. She raised her hand to smooth down her hair, and Nell saw that she was wearing a ring with a tiny diamond.

'She's doing very well. We're going to Paris next week,' Nell said, at the last moment deciding not to say precisely where. People had the wrong impression of the Folies-Bergère, she'd discovered. 'Are you engaged?' she added quickly, and Lizzie's attention was diverted.

'Yes,' she smiled. 'Tell Gwyneth George and I got together again. He was ever so sorry about the quarrel,' she added, colouring slightly. 'We're getting married next year, or maybe the one afterwards. It depends how quickly we can save enough money. George says he won't start in anything but his own house.'

'Nell, this looks perfect!' Marigold called, and Nell turned back. She gasped. Marigold was holding up the most gorgeous dress she had ever seen. It was a deep ruby red silk tunic dress, with slightly paler red and silver fringes. The neck was modestly high in front, daringly low at the back, edged with delicate silver thread and bead embroidery.

'It would have been disastrous to use gold thread, but the silver enhances it, and when you move, the different shades produce a fascinating effect,' Miss Fremling said enthusiastically. 'With Nell's dark hair it will be perfect!'

Nell tried it on, and knew their search was ended. She would have bought it, despite the price being so high it would have taken all the savings she had, even if Marigold had rejected it. Fortunately Marigold nodded, and she and Miss Fremling decided that it fitted perfectly and didn't need any alterations.

'We'll be unlikely to find shoes to match,' Marigold said as they waited for the gown to be wrapped in layers and layers of tissue. 'I think silver will be best, not too heavy as black would be. And I have a pair of ruby earrings which have never suited me, I'm too blonde. Even Richard said they were a mistake after he bought them for me, and went out straight away to get sapphires instead. I shall give them to you.'

Overwhelmed, Nell stammered her thanks. 'I don't know why you should be so generous,' she exclaimed.

'I was poor too, once. Think of it as an investment,' she added, reflecting that if Paul didn't make another attempt to propose to Nell when he saw her looking so sophisticated he didn't deserve to win her.

'Kitty, please let me talk to you!'

'Tom, you're being an utter bore! Do you have to waylay me whenever I come out of the house? We had fun, darling, but it's over. Can't you understand?'

'But — the things you said, I thought you meant them!' he muttered, walking beside her as she set off along the road.

'Don't you ever say things you don't mean? In the excitement of the moment? Maybe even mean them a little then, but afterwards you realize you've been silly and allowed yourself to be carried away.'

He was hurt. 'Then when you said you'd marry me you didn't mean it?'

Kitty laughed, a brittle sound. 'Tom, I don't want to be cruel. I never actually said I would marry you, just that I'd think about it. I did. For about two minutes. Can you really imagine us being married? We're so unsuited.'

'I don't see why,' he said stubbornly. 'OK, you've got more money than I have but in these days surely that's not what's important.'

'Really, darling, you do have some odd ideas. Can you imagine me even contemplating marrying a man who can't provide me with everything I want?'

'Money isn't everything.'

'No, and you haven't provided any proof that you can give me anything else!'

He flushed. 'Just because I wouldn't organize a dirty weekend? Kitty, I want to respect my wife. I couldn't do that if — if we'd been to bed together before our union was sanctified!'

She grinned knowingly, and he was certain she was quite aware of his dilemma. If he'd been more experienced, her glance seemed to say, he wouldn't have been so fussy about his future wife's virginity.

'It's more than that, Tom. Not just sex. I couldn't bear to be

266

married to someone who came from the wrong background. It would be too demeaning to have a plebeian husband.'

They walked along in silence while Tom digested this. It was more painful than anything else. Until he'd met Kitty he had been satisfied with his lot, content to know that he had been privileged with a better education than the neighbouring children, and any girl he wished to marry would regard it as a favour. Both he and his father had white-collar office jobs, even if it was working for a blue-collar union. At least it was one of the élite unions. The railwaymen had always been at the top of the tree.

'Goodbye, Tom,' Kitty said sweetly as she stopped by Endersby's Hotel. 'I won't see you again, I'm leaving Birmingham.'

'Where are you going?' he demanded, startled.

'To Paris,' she said with a brilliant smile. 'I'm going back into the dancing troupe, and we're going to dance at the Folies-Bergère.'

'What! In the – without any clothes on?' he gasped, appalled.

'Dancers wear clothes,' she corrected him gently. 'Nell's going too. Wish us luck!'

'I can't, Paul! Please don't ask me!'

He hadn't meant to, just yet, but she'd looked so delectable in the gorgeous dress he'd been suppressing the urge all evening. As he'd driven Nell home and they stopped outside her lodgings, the proposal came out of its own accord. It was no wonder she'd refused such an inept, gauche declaration. Why did he choose places where he was unable to take her in his arms and kiss her into acceptance?

Nell clenched her hands into fists, the nails biting into her palms, but she was unaware of the pain. She must not weaken, for both their sakes. And if he kept asking her she would, one day, she knew it. And he would regret it ever after, and she couldn't bear to make him unhappy.

'I'm sorry, Nell. I was a fool. Of course you want to go to Paris, it's a marvellous opportunity.'

She wanted to scream at him that it had nothing to do with Paris. What would she care about that, if she were suited to be his wife? How could anything compare with the joy of being married to him, provided always that he could never feel she had cheated him, caught him in some unwary moment that he would deplore for the rest of his life. She thought of the unknown Victoria who would have been such a perfect wife, with whom she could not compare. And she thought of her mother, old before her time with constant childbearing. She didn't want to marry, but she was beginning to understand the temptations that led girls into that trap.

He stepped out of the car. 'Come to me if ever you change your mind,' he said softly as he helped her out, and dropped a light kiss on her brow.

Chapter Twenty

'MR Bliss, please.'

Patsy looked nervously at the young man on the doorstep. 'He ain't 'ere.'

'I have to see him or Mrs Bliss. Urgently. It's a legal matter.'

Patsy retreated, startled, and Tom followed her through into the hall. The strains of a dance tune played on a rather ancient gramophone came from the room to the right, accompanied by the thuds of dancers' feet pounding the bare boards.

'The class'll be over in a couple of minutes. Can yer wait?' she asked, and when he nodded led the way into a small office towards the back of the house.

Tom looked round, and nodded in reluctant approval. It was neat and businesslike, not at all like the shambles he had somehow expected a theatrical business to be. The table which served as a desk had several piles of papers – letters and bills, Tom saw on closer inspection – each pile held down by heavy paperweights. Two spikes held receipted bills and invoices, while a large ledger lying open was made up as far as the previous day. The inkwells in the heavy stand were full, and pens lay neatly beside them, divided into red and blue. A small pile of clean blotting paper stood handily by.

He wandered over to the wall on which was pinned a large timetable for the classes. Tom whistled in surprise when he saw how busy the school was. Next to it was another sheet of paper divided into columns, showing the bookings for each troupe, where they would be and when. Mentally he began to reckon how much the Blisses must be receiving in fees from students, and percentages from the working girls. He had just come to the conclusion that even though he did not know what they charged for each class, their income must be enviably large, when Edwina came into the room.

'May I help you?' she asked, seating herself behind the desk and waving him to the small wooden chair in front. 'Patsy tells me it is a legal matter. Do you represent the police or a solicitor?'

Faced with her air of confidence Tom stammered, coughed, and started again. 'Neither, precisely,' he managed. 'That is, I understand that you are sending some dancing girls to Paris?'

'Yes, we are.'

He struggled on. 'Are you aware that girls under the age of twenty-one have to have a document signed by their fathers, giving permission for them to work abroad?'

For a moment she stared at him. 'My husband is dealing with all that,' she said calmly. 'I am sure he will be obtaining the documents.'

'Nell, Nell Baxter, is she going?'

'What is that to you? I really think you should tell me your name and by what authority you are here before I discuss particular girls with you.'

Tom glowered at her. 'Nell's father is a friend of the family,' he said finally, stretching the truth considerably. 'I believe you may not know that she has a father. He — since the tragedy he has moved in with his son, and you may not know his present address. But you still need his permission before Nell can go abroad, and as her friend I hoped to save possible trouble if she hadn't told you, or you thought she had no parents.'

'My husband will have it all under control, Mr . . . You still haven't told me your name.'

'Simmons,' Tom muttered. He'd hoped to leave without disclosing who he was, in case it got back to Nell's ears that he had interfered, but Mrs Bliss so clearly expected it he didn't know how to refuse to answer her.

She rose and moved to the door. 'Thank you for your concern, Mr Simmons. Now I must ask you to excuse me, there is another class waiting. Goodbye.'

He was glad to leave, taking time only to lay the sheet of paper with Mr Baxter's name and address on it down on the desk. Edwina stared after him, a frown on her face. She hoped Frank knew about these signatures. He hadn't mentioned them, but surely he would know? She would have to tell him, for she sensed that Mr Simmons could mean big trouble.

Nell sat on the bed and looked in despair at the clothes spread about her. What on earth would she need for Paris? Was it worth taking all her party dresses? She wouldn't feel at all like parties, she would be missing Paul too much. She had seen him on almost every occasion she had worn one of these dresses, and each time she saw them she recalled everything they had talked about.

She sighed. It was foolish to allow her thoughts to dwell on Paul. She must forget him. She must remember that she didn't want to marry. She must, when she thought of him and felt that overwhelming sense of longing, remind herself of the disaster it would be for him to marry a girl like her. She would take all her new clothes. She would welcome parties and make herself so busy that she would, in time, forget what she had lost.

Before she could change her mind she began to pack her clothes. She and Gwyneth had both bought large trunks. 'I shall buy lots and lots of clothes, so even if they are not full going they certainly will be when I come back,' Gwyneth had declared excitedly.

They still had a few days before setting off, and Nell had borrowed a book about Paris from the municipal library. She puzzled over the rather small street map until she found the Place Pigalle, then traced the way from there to the theatre, and round to the rue Saulnier where, Edwina had told them, the stage door was. At the back of the book there was a list of useful phrases, and she and Gwyneth giggled as they tried out the strange words in the phonetic spelling provided.

On Wednesday Frank called them together. Gwyneth and Nell looked startled to see Kitty, for they had not known she was to be included.

'Darlings, how divine to see you, and how absolutely scrumptious fun it will be to dance together again!'

'I thought you'd given up stage dancing,' Gwyneth said curtly. The memory of the fiasco on the occasion when Kitty had seduced the drummer was still fresh, still hurtful to her professional pride.

Kitty laughed. 'Oh, yes, I had, but I was so bored! I would never have expected it, I thought I would relish my freedom, but I missed it all. So I decided to come back, and Mr Bliss was an angel, he let me join this troupe.' She flashed a brilliant smile towards Frank, and he turned away hastily, fumbling with a sheaf of papers.

'Girls, may I have your attention please,' he said briskly. 'I have here forms which you must ask your parents to sign. If you are under twenty-one, that is. To be specific, your fathers have to sign them to say they permit you to work abroad. Will you each take one and bring it back tomorrow. If your fathers live outside Birmingham, will you please send the forms today with a letter asking for them to be returned at once. That should take no more than two days, so I will collect them here on Friday before you leave on Saturday.'

'I never thought I'd be pleased to be so old,' Kitty said cheerfully. 'How fortunate, as my mother is unavailable and heaven knows where my unknown father is!'

Nell and Gwyneth were looking at one another in consternation. 'What can we do?' Gwyneth demanded as they walked the short distance to their rooms. 'It would be quite useless asking my father, and yours would refuse just to spite you.'

'Forge their signatures,' a voice behind them said cheerfully. 'No one will ask.'

'We can't do that, Kitty,' Gwyneth said in exasperation, turning round. 'It's probably illegal.'

'Pooh! What on earth does a piffling little thing like that matter? Look, you two, I've wanted to apologize for my utterly evil temper, and say I'm sorry I threw you out of The Firs. Can we be friends again? And if you don't want to forge the silly signatures I'll do them for you.'

Instinctively Gwyneth shook her head. 'If that's what I have to do, I will, but I'll do it myself, Kitty. I couldn't ask you in case you got into trouble.'

'The offer is there if you need it. Now, please say you forgive me, and we'll go and have dinner together to celebrate. I planned this, and in the hope you would be kind I've already booked a table at Endersby's.'

They were dubious, but it would be churlish to refuse. And they would have to work together in Paris. In the end it was an enjoyable evening since Kitty put herself out to be charming. Nell was so tired when she got back to her room that she put off the decision about whether she would risk going to ask Pa for his signature or do as Gwyneth had decided, and forge it herself.

Early the following day, before it was properly light, she was woken by a fierce hammering on the door of the house. Startled, she heard the landlady go to open it, grumbling that some folk hadn't the consideration to leave decent people in peace at six o'clock in the morning.

'I wants me daughter!' a loud voice announced, and Nell shrank down under the blankets. How on earth had Pa discovered where she was living?

He blustered his way into the house, and Nell knew she could not hide from him. She scrambled out of bed and into her sensible woollen dressing gown. No satin ones for her, she thought ruefully. Then she opened the door and looked at her father.

'What's this I hears about yer goin' ter bleedin' Paris ter sit about on the stage in yer birthday suit?' he shouted. Nell's heart sank. He would never understand. But before she could reply he started again. 'I'm not 'avin' it, see! I'm goin' ter see that 'orrible pimp what's corruptin' me daughter, an' I'll tell 'im what ter do with 'is dratted dancin' classes! I won't 'ave me blessed Emily's precious memory soiled by lettin' 'er poor child be dragged inter a sink of iniquity!'

'Pa, listen —' Nell began, but he gave her a look of triumph and turned to thrust his way past the indignant landlady and out into the street. Nell went back into her room and sank down on to the bed. The dream was over. She would not be going to Paris.

Gwyneth looked round at the girls. They were a varied bunch, dark and blonde, even a couple of redheads, and of widely differing heights. Clearly there was no attempt to have a matching troupe like the Bliss dancers or the American ones like the Ziegfeld girls, who, it was said, were even measured to ensure they matched in every detail. It must be true that Monsieur Derval selected the girls for personality rather than looks. She hoped she would meet his very exacting standards. She wished vehemently that Nell were there. It had been hard leaving her behind, so despondent. It seemed as though nothing could go right for her at the moment. First there had been the fire, and the deaths of most of her family, leaving — from what Gwyneth could tell — the least attractive ones alive. Hastily she caught at her wayward thoughts. It was wicked to wish anyone dead. Just as it was wicked to forge her father's permission for her to work in Paris, the voice of conscience whispered. Gwyneth thrust it away. That action hadn't hurt anyone. She concentrated on the rehearsal about to begin in a basement room at the theatre.

First there were exercises, then simple steps practised alone. Then the girls were divided into small groups, matched for height, and each practised in turn. This was when the stage director really pounced on any sign of awkwardness. A girl who was not in time, or didn't kick precisely the same height as the others, or moved without the amount of grace required, was told of her faults in a loud, caustic tone. Not understanding French, Gwyneth found, was no advantage. He was as fluent with damning epithets in English as French, and many of the girls were English.

When they were finally asked to form a single line Gwyneth wondered how they would manage. There were over twice as many dancers as she was used to. They were at that point matched for height, the tallest in the centre, and she was half way down one side, between Kitty and Bertha, a girl from Liverpool. With several new girls joining the line the first few attempts were ragged, and their instructor seemed about to tear out his hair. He screamed imprecations at them, faulted almost every step, and only after several hours of the most intensive practising Gwyneth had ever experienced declared that there was no more he could do that day to make such a motley crew into anything like a respectable chorus line.

Gwyneth thought she would never reach the hostel. She and Kitty were sharing a room with two other English girls, and they all flopped down on their beds and moaned in agony.

'I cannot endure this!' Kitty declared. 'I've never been so exhausted in my life!'

'He's a slavedriver!' Sophie, from Bradford, agreed.

'They told me it was hard, but I didn't know what they meant!' This was the fourth girl, Betty, from Manchester.

'And we have to start again tomorrow,' Gwyneth groaned.

'What will it be like when we have performances as well as just rehearsals?'

'Unbearable! God, I need a drink,' Kitty exclaimed, and reached over to her night table where she had assembled an array of bottles and a cocktail shaker. 'Anyone else want a White Lady? No lemon or ice, so it will be strong — just what I need. So long as they never run out of drink I'll survive!'

'I chose the wrong time again. Though I wonder if any time is the right one,' Paul confided, his tone dispirited.

'You might stand a chance now she's alone in Birmingham,' Richard said encouragingly. 'Marigold said she was devastated when that dreadful father refused to let her go with the others.'

They were in Paul's library, sipping brandy after dinner. They dined together occasionally, when Marigold was on duty at the hotel, or away inspecting one of the other hotels they owned.

'I don't want her to accept me because there's no other option,' Paul said, shaking his head.

'Has she indicated she likes you?'

'That's what makes it so damnable. She has said she does. At first she was shy, uncertain, but natural and friendly. I thought I had a chance. She says she doesn't want to marry, she wants to dance.'

'She's very young. But now she's been prevented from going to Paris perhaps she'll change her mind.'

Paul sighed. 'I wish I thought so. The second reason was that she was unsuitable, from the wrong background. How can I overcome that?'

'People said the same about us. I was rich, Marigold's father was a miner. But I can't imagine marriage to anyone else.'

'Nell is the right girl for me, the only girl,' Paul said quietly, and glanced up at the portrait.

Richard watched him then suddenly sat up. 'Has she seen that?' he demanded.

'The portrait? Of Victoria? She came here once with Marigold, but how could she know who it is?'

'She might have heard how you keep a portrait of your dead fiancée in your room. She might believe you still want her, and she could never compete.'

Paul laughed, a harsh sound. 'Have I ever told you why I keep it here? Guilt.'

'Guilt?' Richard looked startled. 'You don't mean you blame yourself over her death? It was a riding accident, wasn't it? I know you were there, but you weren't involved in any way?

Had you had an argument? Do you think that made her reckless?'

'We were always having arguments. As it happens we hadn't, that day, so it's not what you think. I was young and infatuated, and she was very lovely. But within weeks of becoming engaged I knew it was a mistake. The families were both so pleased I couldn't face jilting her, though I suspect that in the end I would not have been able to go through with it. No, my guilt stems from the relief I felt when she died. Her tragedy was my escape. When I first saw her injuries I knew that if she lived she'd be a cripple, and how could I have deserted her then? I've felt guilty ever since.'

'My dear fellow, how appalling for you. But it's been years now, surely you can forgive yourself for very natural feelings? If you got rid of that portrait you could go to Nell without reserve. Then she couldn't help knowing you loved her.'

'Nell, wait for me.'

She turned, and sighed. It was bad enough being here in Birmingham when the others were experiencing the pinnacle of excitement at what was the most famous music hall in the world, without having Tom pestering her.

'Tom, it's no use. I've told you every day this week, I don't want to go out with you.'

'Nell, dear, I can understand your disappointment at not going to Paris, but won't you spend a little time with me? After all, in a few weeks you'll be traipsing all over the country again, touring in these wretched shows, and I won't see you at all.'

'You weren't exactly eager to see me when you were going out with Kitty Denver,' she pointed out sharply, and he had the grace to blush.

'I – well, that was a mistake. She was so persistent,' he muttered.

Nell laughed. 'Kitty was always enchanting when she wanted something. I don't suppose I can blame you. It must have seemed as though a princess had come out of a fairy tale.'

'Then you forgive me?' he asked eagerly.

'There's nothing to forgive. You are as free as I am to have what friends you choose. I just don't want to be one of them.'

'But, Nell, we got on so well when you were working at the factory. I thought you'd be happy to marry me. It's only since you began to get ideas above your station that you turned against me.'

'No, that's not quite true. I began to know you better, Tom, and also I met other people, I saw what there could be to life. Surely you don't wish me back in the factory, living in a slum?'

'You wouldn't have been spoilt then. But I wanted to take you out of it. I was improving myself, I'm getting to know a lot about the regulations on employment, I might begin to make that my speciality. But that isn't the main point. I thought if you didn't go to Paris I had a chance to get you back.'

Nell looked at him suspiciously. 'You knew I was asked to go to Paris? How?'

'I met Kitty and she told me,' he said impatiently. 'What does that matter?'

'It matters if it was you who told Pa and persuaded him to make a fuss! You know a lot about employment rules, do you? More than Mr Bliss? It was odd how he suddenly produced the letters for our fathers to sign. Did you by any chance tell him he needed them?'

'What if I did?' he blustered.

'If you did, and if you told Pa, then you've wrecked my life, Tom Simmons, and I will never forgive you! Go away! I don't ever want to speak to you or see you again!'

'You are simply not good enough. I cannot think why Mr Bliss recommended you to us. Oh, you have a certain amount of competence, a natural ability, you move well, but you have not that extra something which we demand of all our dancers. You are mediocre.'

Kitty was bright red with fury. She had never before had to endure this kind of criticism. She had thought herself so clever when she contrived to find Frank Bliss alone, tempted him into certain indiscretions, and then made use of his weakness. Her threat to expose him to Edwina had persuaded him to include her in the group he sent to Paris. She knew she was good when she bothered. She knew she had talent. And now, to be told by this obnoxious little man that he didn't want her with his dancers was an unbelievable insult. She opened her mouth to blast him with invective, but he forestalled her.

'If you have no blemishes, then you could perhaps join the tableaux.'

Kitty closed her mouth. She narrowed her eyes and thought rapidly. This would save her from the humiliation of being rejected. She could say she preferred it to the dancing. Besides, the dancing was proving much harder work than she had expected, even while just rehearsing. The girls in the tableaux just posed. 'You mean become a nude?' she asked cautiously.

'We have a couple of vacancies to fill. You are pretty, and seem to have a good figure, but the nudes have to be utterly flawless. They must have no scars, no moles. Their figures must be superb, and their skin perfectly smooth. Do you think you might be suitable?'

It would be galling to be inspected for flaws, but Kitty had confidence in her own body. She could endure that. And the tableaux she had seen had been graceful; there was nothing unpleasant about them. She would not be lowering herself except in the eyes of prissy old straightlaced spinsters, for whose opinion she didn't care a jot. 'I'm prepared to try it,' she said.

Gwyneth felt sick with anticipation. Years ago, when she had been dancing secretly in the small cove below the house, where she escaped from the censure of her father, she had tried to imagine what it would be like to be the centre of attention, admired by everyone as she danced. Then her dreams had been vague and uninformed. Sometimes she was dancing with an incredibly handsome man, in a ballroom where the ornate painted ceiling and elaborately carved pillars competed with the glitter of the gowns and the sparkling jewels. Everyone would stand back in astonishment, whispering excitedly about this wonderful new dancer who had miraculously appeared in their midst. Alternatively she was the prima ballerina astounding everyone by her skill in a remarkable new ballet.

She had never seen herself as a chorus girl, in a show where girls clad only in discreetly glued patches and almost transparent body stockings were arranged in tasteful, and sometimes excruciatingly difficult-to-hold poses or paraded draped in provocative or minimal costumes. She had at first been shocked at the reality of this near-nudity. It was very different from what she had imagined, but then she chided herself for being naïve. She hadn't forced herself to think of the practicality, preferring to ignore it and concentrate instead on the dancing and the marvellous settings and costumes she'd heard about, and had very soon become accustomed both to wearing revealing costumes herself and mingling with bevies of nude beauties backstage.

It was very different from Cinderella, she thought, grinning at the memory of her youthful fantasies. Ballrooms were not in the least as she'd envisaged them, and when they were crowded the possibility of anyone, however brilliant, being able to move freely through the throng and display their expertise, was remote. Ballet was out of her reach; she had started serious dancing far too late. But stage dancing of the sort she now did was immensely satisfying. Mastering any skill and performing it to the best of her ability had a fascination she hadn't previously understood. The steps were not at all complicated; the effect came largely from the timing, and the fabulous, gloriously imaginative costumes. If only she could gather together a group of girls and experiment with more difficult steps!

First, she reminded herself, she had to prove she could hold her place in the Folies line. It had been too difficult for Kitty, but the older girl seemed happier with her less demanding role. For Gwyneth the professionalism of her new colleagues and teachers had been a revelation, and she gloried in it. It took ten months to devise and prepare for a new show, she'd been told, and everything, down to the last sequin on over a thousand individually designed costumes, had to be exactly right. Monsieur Derval and his team were perfectionists of a sort she had never before encountered.

'Ready?' the stage manager asked, and Gwyneth tensed. She forced herself to breathe deeply, to relax. And then they were on stage.

'Wasn't it fantastic?' Bertha asked as they climbed for the final time, out of breath, up several flights of stairs to their dressing rooms.

'This is the best revue yet,' one of the old hands told them. 'The Baron de Meyer actually came to photograph us. They say the sequence "The Chastity Belt" was the best we've ever done.'

'Some people prefer "The Perpetual Adoration",' another put in.

'It's all utterly marvellous! And I didn't freeze with terror,' Gwyneth said with relief.

'I'm exhausted. Are you coming back to the hostel?' Bertha asked.

'I ought to wait for Kitty. You go on.'

Kitty was grumbling when Gwyneth went to find her, but quietly. 'My feet are perpetually stretched,' she complained as they went towards the stage door. 'I have to reach out so hard and make sure I touch that ledge all the time. I know I shall get cramp and have to move.'

'Don't the straps you're tied with help?'

'They just cut into me,' Kitty said petulantly. Then they passed through the stage door and she halted so abruptly that Gwyneth bumped into her. 'Just look at that!'

Outside, in the narrow street, a row of large and expensive motor cars waited. In the light of the gas lamps they could see a solitary man in each. Some were young, but the majority were well past middle age. Many puffed at huge cigars, and one even sipped at a glass of champagne, the bottle propped up on the dashboard.

'Come on!' Gwyneth urged, embarrassed. 'They'll think you're looking for someone.'

'If anyone with a car like that is looking for me, I might accept an invitation,' Kitty replied with a laugh. 'I've never seen so many expensive cars all together, not even outside the Ritz!'

Chapter Twenty-One

TOURING on her own was far less enjoyable than when she was with Gwyneth. Nell even missed Kitty, having forgiven her for throwing them out and recalling only the fun she had been. She made friends with some of the other girls in her troupe, but it wasn't the same. Besides, she was by far the best dancer and did the solo spots, so there was a certain amount of jealousy. She was thankful to be working hard over Christmas, but after the end of the pantomime season there was a gap in bookings. Some of the girls found work with other troupes, a few left to take other jobs, and a few had to be dismissed. Nell had several offers to join other troupes, but as most of them were likely to be going abroad it was impossible to accept. Frank Bliss had no suitable vacancies, because Nell insisted she would not take the place of any girl he dismissed in order to make room for her.

'Why don't we ask Nell to teach for us?' Edwina asked.

Frank eyed her thoughtfully. Deep down he knew that his venture would not have been the success it was without Edwina. She was good at devising routines, and had an excellent eye for costumes, knowing what was just right. She had also taken over much of the paperwork. But she had only been able to spare the time for this when he engaged another teacher to do the simple work, and teach the ballroom-dancing classes. That had been the beginning of her emancipation, and he had mixed feelings. Nevertheless he respected her judgement.

'It would be a waste for Nell to teach,' he said now.

'It would if it were something permanent. But if we don't use her she will eventually leave us. It might be only a few weeks before there is a suitable vacancy, you know girls leave all the time. Miss Carstairs wants to have a holiday, Nell could take her classes, and it would be sensible for us to take a break while times are slack.'

And so Nell found herself training the new students, being in complete charge when Edwina was away. Edwina insisted she had an appropriate salary, more even than she had earned as a dancer. She was busy and beginning to look to the future once more.

'Are you coming back to the hostel?' Gwyneth asked, as she and Kitty prepared to leave the theatre.

'Not tonight, Josephine! Remember that man we met at the party on Sunday? The one who was an Austrian baron, or count or something? I'm going to supper with him.'

'You don't know him,' Gwyneth warned.

'Of course I do. I met him in perfectly respectable circumstances, at one of the best houses in Paris, in the rue du Faubourg Saint Honoré. Besides, I can take care of myself.'

That was probably true, Gwyneth thought, and shrugged. She wasn't Kitty's keeper, thank goodness, and if Kitty wanted to be foolish and take risks that was her choice. She knew that several of the girls had found admirers, and she had received many invitations, of varying sorts, herself. Occasionally she went to a party, but she resolutely refused all invitations to intimate little suppers or weekends in the country châteaux which all the men who haunted the Folies seemed to own. She'd only ever been tempted by one man. If Paul Mandeville had shown the slightest interest in her, she thought as she left Kitty and, smilingly shaking her head at an importunate young man, walked back to the hostel, she could have contemplated giving up dancing. But he had eyes only for Nell, and no one else could distract her from the joy and satisfaction of what she was doing now.

*

'I wants ter see yer boss!'

'He's busy,' Patsy said crossly. She was fed up with this job, answering the door all day long.

'Tell 'im it's Nell's Pa.'

Patsy shrugged. Why should she have the bother of arguing with callers? Let Mr Bliss send them away. Silently she gestured to him to come in, and opened the door of the office. Then she went upstairs where she knew Mr Bliss was indulging in an after-dinner brandy.

'So I put 'im in the office,' she said and slid behind the door before he could give her any other instructions.

Frank suddenly recollected that there was a large sum of money in the drawer of his desk, and from what he'd seen of Mr Baxter he wouldn't trust him not to investigate and help himself to anything which tempted him. He went swiftly downstairs.

Mr Baxter was slumped in the more comfortable chair behind the desk. He sat up when Frank entered, but did not offer to rise. Short of physically heaving him out — and that, Frank judged, would be an impossibility for anyone as slight as he was — Frank must either stand or sit in the smaller chair. He chose to stand. At least then he could look down on Mr Baxter.

'Well? What do you want? I'm an exceedingly busy man.'

'I wants me rights!'

'What does that mean?'

'You give me daughter a job at this 'ere prance shop.'

'Nell teaches at my academy of dance, yes! But I employ her, not you. So what is your business with me?'

'I wants 'er wages.'

Frank stared, incredulous. 'You want me to give Nell's money, money she has earned, to you?'

'That's what I said.'

'That's monstrous!'

'No it ain't. What's 'er done fer us, 'cept cause trouble? 'Er owes me. I used ter get 'er wages when 'er worked fer old man Forster, so why not now?'

'I am not responsible for what her previous employer did, but while Nell works for me I will give her the wages she earns. Now please leave, Mr Baxter, we have nothing more to discuss.'

'Oh, ain't we? We gorra lot ter bleedin' discuss! I ain't leavin' till yer does what I want!'

Frank crossed to lift the telephone and began to wind it. 'If you don't go, I'll call the police,' he said calmly, though he felt anything but calm. 'Operator? Is that the operator? Good, please can you —'

'I'm goin', yer poncy little twat!' Mr Baxter said hurriedly, heaving himself out of the chair. 'But you ain't 'eard the last on it. I'll mek sure I gets me rights!'

'No, thank you, I don't want to make a call,' Frank said as the front door banged. Shaking, he replaced the receiver. He needed another brandy.

'They're from Timothy. He's in Paris,' Gwyneth said excitedly as she read the note accompanying the huge bouquet of flowers. 'He wants to take me to supper after the show.'

'Timothy? Here? I didn't know he was coming to Paris,' Kitty said with a frown.

'He doesn't explain why, it's quite short. Perhaps he's visiting friends.'

Kitty was thoughtful. 'Perhaps. I must go and change now — though change is hardly the word when all I do is undress!'

Gwyneth laughed. 'Hardly. But it must take a lot of time sticking those patches on in just the right places!'

'Painful, too, when you pull them off again!' Kitty replied. 'At least I don't have dozens of changes like you do. I don't know how you manage, running up and down hundreds of stairs every night,' she added, and with a cheerful wave went along to her own dressing room.

How nice it would be to see someone from home, Gwyneth was thinking as she changed into her street clothes afterwards. Nell wrote every week, and she sometimes had letters from the other girls they'd danced with, but none of them ever mentioned

Paul, and she craved news of him. She could ask Timothy in a casual manner about both Paul and Andrew, and it would not seem odd.

She assumed Kitty was supping with one of her admirers. The Austrian baron had been largely supplanted by an Italian prince, though he was still good enough for Kitty when the prince was unavailable. At the moment the prince's attractions were being tested against those of an exiled Russian count, but Gwyneth cynically judged that if it were a question of marriage, Kitty would prefer the title of *principessa* to either of the others, even though Italian *principi* were two a penny.

She emerged through the stage door and looked round for Timothy. She saw him eventually in a car parked at the end of the street. He obviously hadn't been aware of the parking problems in the rue Saulnier, and come early enough to get close to the stage door. She began to walk towards him, taking no notice of the tapping heels behind her. There were dozens of girls emerging from the stage door, going home or walking to meet their escorts.

'Gwyneth! Lovely to see you again! And Kitty, too.'

Gwyneth swung round, to find Kitty flinging herself with abandon into Timothy's rather surprised embrace. Kitty couldn't have stopped to take off the *cache-sexe*, she thought with a mixture of irritation and amusement. Presumably she calculated that even if she succeeded in muscling in on Gwyneth's supper invitation, she would not succeed in detaching Timothy from her tonight.

'It's so nice of you to take us out for supper,' Kitty said, tucking her arm into Timothy's.

Gwyneth glanced over her shoulder to see the baron, looking offended, retreating backwards. Kitty must have decided that the loss of him was worth the chance of trying her luck with Timothy once more. There was nothing Timothy could do. When they reached the restaurant there was a discreet shuffle as the table he had booked was hastily relaid for three, and then they were seated, in an almost totally screened alcove, with a waiter who had difficulty in concealing his amusement as he took their order.

'Would there be a Mr Bliss in this establishment, or is the name a cheap ruse to entrap the unwary?'

The voice boomed through the hall and echoed up the stairwell. Patsy glanced nervously behind her and Nell, coming down the stairs, gave her a reassuring smile.

'Can I help?' she asked, coming forward. 'Both Mr and Mrs Bliss are away for a few days.'

'And who might you be, miss?'

'I teach here.' Nell spoke curtly. She took an instant dislike to this man, with his bristling black moustache, aggressively jutting eyebrows, and loud voice. Then she realized that behind him, peering round at her rather like an inquisitive bird, was a tall, slender woman.

'Then you can give me the information I seek.'

He marched in, and Nell, despite herself, found she was backing along the hall. If she hadn't she'd have been mown down. She resisted the temptation to show him into the office, though. Such bad manners would be punished and he needed taking down a peg or two. Making him stand in the hall while he stated his business might serve. As the woman, whom Nell had forgotten, came in nervously behind him, Nell felt a moment's doubt, but she suppressed it. A woman attached to such a man must put up with any hostility he aroused. She must be used to it anyway.

'That depends on what you want to know,' she replied firmly.

'I'll ask you not to be impertinent, miss. My daughter has been seduced into this den of iniquity and I demand that she be returned to me at once.'

Nell bristled. 'This is a perfectly respectable dancing school and no one has been seduced into it against their will!'

'No dancing school, as you call it, can be respectable. All forms of dancing are the snares of the devil!'

Nell was beginning to have horrid suspicions about the identity of her caller. Although he spoke with the normal upper-class accent of the minor public schools, she could detect a slight Welsh intonation. She stole a glance at the woman and her suspicions hardened. She was well into her fifties and her hair was white, her face lined, but she had Gwyneth's nose and eyes.

'Please, I want my daughter back,' the woman said. 'Is Gwyneth – Gwyneth Davis, that is, here?'

Nell was about to reassure her that Gwyneth was well and happy, and successful, when Mr Davis intervened.

'If she is she'll pack her bags and return to our protection at once! I am not having my daughter contaminated by further contact with sinners!'

His tone made Nell change her mind. She might wish to reassure Gwyneth's mother, but she knew Gwyneth had written to her several times when she was safely far away from Birmingham and could post the letters without fear of discovery, so at least she would know how her daughter was.

'I cannot give information about our dancers without Mr Bliss's permission,' she said briskly. 'You must understand that we can have undesirable people making enquiries, people who believe all dancers are immoral whores, and against whom we have to protect our girls.'

'All dancers *are* immoral whores!' he bellowed, his face growing red with fury.

'If you believe that you must see why I cannot tell you where any of them are,' Nell went on calmly. She was beginning to enjoy herself. 'Men searching for whores usually have one purpose in mind, and whatever you may believe we do not run a bawdy house, nor do we supply girls just to satisfy the lusts of intemperate men. Now please leave. If you care to call again next week Mr Bliss will tell you the same. Goodbye.'

She endured a good ten minutes while he ranted and bullied her, but eventually he gave in to the anxious persuasions of his wife. That, or he accepted that Nell was not going to be moved. Flinging fearful imprecations over his shoulder as he went, he at last stormed out of the door, Mrs Davis almost running to keep up with him.

'Cor!' Patsy breathed. 'I thought 'e was going ter hit yer, Miss Nell!'

Nell laughed shakily. 'So did I! Patsy, let's have a pot of strong tea! I'll come down into the kitchen and have it with you.'

'It seems like all the dads are coming after the daughters,' Patsy remarked a few minutes later. 'Why all of a sudden?'

'What do you mean?'

'Didn't yer know? Miss Nell, yer own dad came a while back.'

'No one told me! What did he want? Was anything wrong?'

'No. Mr Bliss gave him a right flea in 'is ear! He didn't shut the door of the office, see, and I was dusting the hall. I couldn't help 'earing it, miss.'

'Of course not,' Nell said, too anxious to discover what her father had wanted to worry about Patsy eavesdropping.

'Yer dad wanted Mr Bliss ter give him yer wages,' Patsy said with a sniff. 'Cheek! Why, it's not as if yer lives with him. I used ter give Mom my wages from my first job, and she gave me pocket money, but when I came here, livin' in, I just used ter send some home. How could I have managed else? But I wish I'd given her more when she was alive.'

She sniffed again, and Nell smiled at her abstractedly. 'We all wish we'd been better after people die, Patsy. I'm sure you did as much as she wanted. What happened?'

'Mr Bliss started ter ring fer police, and yer pa went.'

'And he hasn't been back?'

'Don't suppose he'd dare.'

No, Nell thought as she went back upstairs, her father would not want the police involved. But she was concerned. She didn't know what he could do, but being her pa she knew he wouldn't be satisfied until he'd tried everything he could to get his own way, and if at the moment that meant he wanted her wages, she would have to take care.

*

For two weeks nothing happened and Nell relaxed. They heard no more from Gwyneth's father and Nell hoped he had gone back to his Welsh valley. Then when one of Frank's best solo dancers broke her leg he swiftly moved Nell into her place, and once more she began touring and dancing with a troupe. After a month they were to go to Walsall, the first time Nell had appeared at that theatre since the collapse of Andrew's act.

'I'm nervous,' she confessed to Edwina. 'It's superstition, I know, but it feels like my unlucky theatre.'

'One of us will come and be there,' Edwina promised. 'If I can't come I'll make sure Frank does. He wants to see the troupe dance anyway.'

To Nell's relief the first performance went well, and Frank came round to the dressing room afterwards to congratulate them.

'Nell, I'll drive you back to Birmingham, there are things I need to discuss, some changes I'm thinking of making, and you are involved.'

It was a freezing cold night, and the trains were badly heated. Nell thanked him gratefully and they sat for a while in the empty dressing room after the others had left, discussing the performance and what could be done to improve it. Then the stage manager poked in his head to say everyone else had gone and would they be away soon? Hastily they stood up and apologized for keeping him. He followed them to the stage door, wished them a cheery goodnight, and bolted it after them. They could hear his footsteps retreating as he went to lock up the other doors. Frank's car, another Austin Seven like Kitty's, was parked a little way from the theatre. They had to pass though a narrow alley from the stage door and then along a slightly wider one to get to the street. It was as they turned the corner into the second alley that the attack came.

'Pimp! I'll learn yer ter mess wi' my gel!'

That was all he said but Nell recognized her father's voice. Before she could move, however, she was pushed violently aside and it seemed as though a whirlwind had attacked Frank. Mr

Baxter, abstemious for months, had finally given in to the old temptation. Nell could smell the whisky on his breath as she fell, but she was dazed from hitting her head against the wall and unable to get to her feet.

Frank attempted to dodge but Mr Baxter had cornered him where the two alley walls met, and was battering him mercilessly. Then Mr Baxter's foot skidded on a patch of ice and he almost went down. Frank seized the opportunity and slid past his opponent's outstretched hands, but then he stopped to help Nell to her feet.

'Come on, run,' he gasped, but it was too late. Mr Baxter rushed towards them, kneed Frank in the groin, and as he doubled up in agony swung a powerful left hook which connected with Frank's chin.

Nell heard the bones snap as Frank fell. With a sob she flung herself down beside him and touched his face. Then she shuddered as Frank's head, his neck broken, lolled helplessly away from her. By the time she absorbed this and looked up, she was alone with his body.

Chapter Twenty-Two

'The show must go on. Frank always said that was the most important thing. We must keep on. He'd want it.'

It was long after midnight. Nell wanted to scream, but she had to sit in the bare room and listen to Edwina's monotonous voice. After she'd run from the alley, distraught, and eventually found a policeman on The Bridge, the nightmare had continued. She had been taken to the police station in Goodall Street, Edwina had been fetched from Birmingham, and the theatre manager roused from the bed of the magician's assistant.

Frank's body had been removed, and Nell had explained how they had been set on as they left the theatre. At first they had listened to her with some suspicion, but the extent and severity of Frank's bruises, plus her own injuries, convinced them it was no lovers' quarrel. The only thing she didn't reveal was the identity of their assailant. 'A big man,' was all she could say, and shook her head when they asked if she could recall any other detail.

She could not betray her father. However badly he had treated her and the rest of the family, he was her father. She could not endure the thought that she might send him to be hanged. He might deserve it, and his demands from Frank had been totally unreasonable, but she could not be responsible for putting the hangman's noose about his neck. After all, surely he couldn't have meant to kill Frank. It was the drink, making him unaware of what he did. She said as little as she could, and because she was so obviously shocked they did not press her.

'You must do the show tonight,' Edwina suddenly said, and the manager looked at Nell anxiously.

'I couldn't!' she exclaimed, shuddering.

'But without you the act is nothing! Ordinary! And everyone will come to see you when the news gets round,' said the manager.

Nell looked at him in amazed disgust. How could he even think about his profits and want to use the death of someone connected to the theatre in order to boost them? To her astonishment Edwina supported him.

'You must, Nell, for me. Frank would have wanted it. And now he is gone I have to manage everything alone. Besides, what else would you do but sit and brood?'

Nell sighed. It was worse than they knew. She would never forget the glare of hatred and avarice in her pa's eyes or the viciousness of his sudden attack. Perhaps it would be better to try and forget with work.

'If you wish it,' she said. 'But I cannot bear to travel on the train with the others every night. They will ask endless questions. I'll find a room here for the week, when I've fetched some clothes.'

'We will pay for a room at the George Hotel,' the manager offered, generous in his relief.

'Thank you, Nell. Now I suppose we must go home.'

'What about the deceased's car?' They had forgotten the police sergeant sitting with them until this brutal reminder. 'It was parked near the theatre,' he went on stolidly. 'Can either of you ladies drive?'

Edwina nodded. 'Yes, I can. Nell, you could have the car for the week if you preferred to stay at home. You learned to drive, didn't you?'

Nell shuddered. Driving would be too painful a reminder of her happy days with Paul. Besides, she could think more clearly if she were in an impersonal room, and decide what she should do about her father.

'You may need it, there will be so much to do,' she told Edwina gently. 'But I'll drive it back to Birmingham now if you don't feel able to.'

The rest of that week passed in a blur. Nell was conscious of much fuller houses than was normal, but to her relief the other girls in the troupe did not press questions on her. Edwina must have spoken to them. And on Saturday evening Paul appeared, sending her flowers and a note that if she wished he would drive her home after the show.

'Edwina thought it would help,' he explained when Nell, too weary to protest, accepted his offer. 'Do you have to get anything from the George?'

'I have a case there, it was too heavy to carry all the way to the theatre and back to the station,' she said.

Without a word he drove to The Bridge, drew up before the porticoed entrance of the hotel, and went in to collect her case. Then he drove round the statue of Sister Dora and towards the Birmingham Road. They did not speak more than a few words. Nell had forced herself to dance, to try and appear normal, although the horror of what her father had done had been even more overwhelming in the past few days than at the time. Now she felt in danger of collapsing, and Paul's medical intuition warned him that there was something more affecting her than just the horror of what had happened.

'Will you be all right tomorrow?' he asked gently as they arrived outside her lodgings. 'Would you like me to come, or perhaps Marigold?'

Nell tried to smile. 'You've already done more than I could expect. And I can't always be running to Marigold for help! I mean to spend the day with Edwina, there must be so much for her to do and perhaps I can help.'

'You know where I am if you need me,' he said, and the moment her landlady opened the door he was gone.

Nell stared after him for a long time, standing in the open doorway, then heaved a deep sigh and went inside.

'Yer pa's bin 'ere ev'ry day, wantin' ter know when yer'd be back,' her landlady said, her eyes bright with curiosity.

Nell controlled her expression and tried to speak normally. 'Has he? What did you say?'

'Told 'im ter come Sunday, o' course.'

Nell resolved to be gone as early as possible the next morning. She could not face her father yet. All week she had vacillated between her distaste at betraying him, and fury at his behaviour. Whatever she did, she felt, she would always regret.

Edwina greeted her calmly. Patsy had a new uniform, Nell noticed, a dark blue woollen dress and a paler blue, lace-trimmed apron more like the ones hostesses wore for afternoon tea than a servant's practical apron. The office had been rearranged, a new rolltop desk placed at an angle to the window, and either side of a small table there were two armless but upholstered chairs.

'Sit down, Patsy will bring coffee,' Edwina said, and took one of the chairs. She wasn't wearing black, although it normally suited her and she often wore a black gown for dancing exhibitions. Today she wore a pale green dress, one Nell had never seen before. Edwina noticed her glance and smiled thinly. 'I wear black when I'm on public display,' she said calmly, 'to satisfy the proprieties. Ours was mainly a business partnership, and as I don't mourn him it seems hypocritical to wear black in private.'

'Didn't you love him at all?' Nell asked.

'I don't think I ever did. At first I was dazzled. He seemed so far superior to me, yet he wanted me. He promised me fine gowns and jewels and luxury. I was a lowly kitchen maid when we met,' she explained. 'I soon realized it was my ability to dance that he wanted, and someone who would adore him and always be ready to tell him how wonderful he was. Oh, I had the gowns and the luxury, but nothing else. I had such dreams of love, too, but I suppose that is how life will always be.'

'I'm . . . sorry.' It seemed inadequate, but then, how many marriages were happy? Her parents had not been happy. And

Edwina's dreams of a wonderful life with a man who'd been far above her showed how unsuitable such marriages were. She thrust aside the tempting thought that Paul would be different. In so many ways she wasn't fit to be his wife, even less so now than when they had first met. As well as everything else she was now the daughter of a murderer. She dragged her thoughts back to what Edwina was saying.

'I don't want to keep on just the same as we were. I've some ideas, but I need help, someone to discuss them with, talk over the possibilities and problems.'

Nell began to forget her worries. She needed hard work to distract her, and the past week had shown her that dancing, though physically tiring, did not prevent her mind from endless speculation. This might be something she could do, which would occupy her brain.

'Will you keep on the ballroom?' she asked. 'You'll have to take over doing the bookings, so will you be able to manage all the classes at both places?'

'That's one main worry. I don't think I could deal with all the people in the theatres. I may have to employ someone, but whom could I trust?'

Nell's thoughts were racing. 'I wonder? It might work! One of the original Beauties, Kathy, was planning to marry another dancer she met. He was with his sister but she wanted to leave and I think he and Kathy thought they could team up, but then he broke his leg. He won't be able to dance again, but he knows the theatre people, he'd been his own manager for several years.'

'She's not good enough except in a line. That would be ideal! Kathy can ask him to come and see me. Then I can carry on teaching from here, but I don't know what to do about the ballroom.'

Nell was becoming enthusiastic. 'Edwina, I don't know how much money you have, but could you reorganize the school completely? It isn't satisfactory using the hotel ballroom only when it's free, and making do in these small rooms at other times. Would it be possible to build a special hall, where we might have several classes at once, and big enough for social dances as well as performances? Then we could put on shows whenever we wanted to, not just when the ballroom was free? We could have tea-dances too.'

Edwina nodded slowly. 'I have all Frank put by. He was very careful with money, and he charged high fees. Fair, but high. And I own this house. I could sell it and raise more money that way, since I wouldn't need a big house if I had a hall. But we might be competing with the shows Marigold puts on.'

'We could do those too, and she wouldn't mind, she'd encourage you. In fact she could probably help with advice, she founded and ran Endersby's Hotels by herself, while Richard was away in the war.'

'It sounds possible. Oh, Nell, if you help me I know we can do it!'

'How about some classes for acting and elocution? We both know how important it is to speak well. And with our own premises people will be able to find us easily, as all the classes would be there rather than in two places.'

'That sounds exciting!'

'We could try training larger troupes too, more like the ones at the Folies-Bergère. We could call them the Edwina Girls.'

They discussed ideas all day, and Nell's head was full of plans as she walked back to her room. She let herself in and stopped short. Pa was sitting on the bed, his head sunk into his hands.

'I didn't mean ter clobber 'im so 'ard! Nell, you didn't tell 'em it were me?' He was pleading, his eyes bloodshot and terrified, his lips slack. Nell had never before seen her father afraid, and the sight sickened her.

'You killed him,' she accused. 'He'd done nothing to you, and because of your greed for my wages, *mine*, which I've earned and I'm entitled to,' she went on, her voice rising and becoming passionate, 'you killed him!'

'I needs the money,' he complained. 'That dratted Florence

'as threatened ter kick me out, wants the room fer 'er bleedin' kid, an' the brat's not six months old!'

'You killed him,' she repeated tonelessly.

'It weren't my fault! I'd been drinkin', an' the dratted beer were doctored, must 'a' been! I can drink twice as much at Ryland Arms. It were just a friendly punch-up! I didn't know the daft chump 'adn't the guts ter put up 'is fists!'

Nell stared at him, not comprehending such ridiculous excuses. 'If you'd let me go to Paris it wouldn't have happened,' she said at last.

'But you'm my gal, Nell, an' I won't 'ave yer flauntin' yer legs in front o' randy old men! 'Tain't dacent!'

'Neither is murder!'

Suddenly the bombast left him. He cringed, and Nell decided that was worse. 'Nell, fer the sake o' yer ma, bless 'er soul, don't tell police! It won't bring 'im back, an' yer can't live with yersen if yer gives yer old pa up to them lot!'

'I won't say anything – on one condition.'

'What? Anythin' yer wants, Nell, anythin'!'

'Get out of here and keep away from me. I don't want to see you again, ever. I don't want to be reminded I'm the daughter of a murderer! If you keep away from me I'll forget I saw you that night. I won't give you up.'

For a moment he stared at her, assessing whether she meant it. Then he grinned, straightened his shoulders, and rose to his feet. 'You allus were the best o' the bunch!' he said jauntily. 'I knew I could trust me little Nell!'

He stepped across towards her, his arms outstretched, but she backed away behind a chair. 'Go, now, or I'll change my mind! And if you come pestering me or Mrs Bliss, I'll go straight to the police!'

He hesitated, and then shrugged. 'Won't even give yer old pa a farewell kiss! Too la-di-da now! It's yer loss, me little beauty!'

It was Timothy's last evening in Paris. 'I hate leaving you,

Gwyneth,' he said. 'Are you absolutely sure you won't come with me?'

'I've no particular desire to go to South Africa,' she replied. 'Besides, you'll be back in a few weeks. Now your uncle has decided to make you his heir, you just have some papers to sign, I thought?'

'Yes, but then I have to go home to England and sort things out there. No more delectable little suppers in Paris for us! I have to be prepared to spend at least half the year in South Africa.'

'Where no doubt your uncle will have a suitable girl ready for your inspection. You say he wants you to marry soon.'

Timothy groaned. 'Gwyneth, don't! You know I don't want to marry. Especially I don't want to marry some prim child the family considers suitable. Not for years yet, anyway. Life's too much fun. Or at least it would be if you came with me to South Africa!'

'Where you would have to keep me hidden from your uncle? No thank you, Timothy!'

'Darling, you know how it is with me! I can't marry you, but the way you refuse to move in with me, even to have a weekend in Monte Carlo, makes it look as though you're playing hard to get, with marriage the price!'

Gwyneth laughed. 'Oh, Timothy! Why do you imagine every girl wants nothing else except marriage? I want to dance, that's why I won't leave Paris. And I won't come to bed with you because, much as I enjoy being with you, and we have had fun, I don't love you!'

Reorganizing the dancing school occupied Nell completely for the next few weeks, and she found that gradually the horror of Frank's murder receded. It wasn't that she forgot it, or excused her father's part in it, more that she was so busy she had no time to dwell on it.

'I've found the perfect site for the new building, on the Hagley Road,' Nell announced. 'Come with me and look at it, then we can talk to the builders.' Another time it was 'How do you like this design for a new rehearsal uniform?' and again, 'How many more classes should we aim for if we employ another teacher?'

Gradually, as she and Edwina became closer, Nell's sense of fun returned, and she frequently reduced Edwina to tears of laughter as she aped some of the people they dealt with, especially those who seemed to believe that women were incapable of doing business.

In between teaching existing classes, training the new, extended line of girls for two charity shows they had planned, and talking over her plans with an energetic, increasingly confident Edwina, Nell had no time to brood. She was brusque with Tom when he appeared on her doorstep offended she was not ready to drop everything and go with him on a Sunday picnic.

'I've bought a car,' he said, aggrieved. 'I thought you would like to have a drive in it.'

Nell sighed. 'I would, Tom,' she said untruthfully, 'but I really don't have time. Besides, it's only March and a really cold day.'

'But Mother put up the picnic basket specially!'

'You should have asked me first to make sure I could go,' she snapped, irritated at his complacent assumption that he had only to appear and she would at once fall in with his wishes.

'When will you have time?' he asked, rather sulkily. 'Nell, I know I behaved badly about Kitty, but surely you knew what she was like? It didn't mean anything. It was nothing to what I feel for you. I was hoping we could start again.'

She shook her head. 'I'm sorry, Tom. It's no good.'

'I won't give up,' he promised, turning away. 'I know what I want, and it's what you want deep down. One day you'll recognize it, and then we shall forget all this nonsense about dancing.'

A week later he came again. 'Nell, I need to talk to you about your father. Have you time just for a short ride in my car?'

She was suspicious, but she did not dare refuse. If he had

somehow discovered anything about her father's part in Frank's murder she had to know. 'Just for a short while, then. I'll fetch my coat, it's still cold.'

'Your brother Ned, he's joined an odd sort of religious brotherhood,' he began, after solicitously helping her into the car. He steered carefully into the Hagley Road and headed towards Bearwood.

'Yes, I know. It's Florence, his wife. She joined it first. What's that to do with Pa?'

'This brotherhood' – Tom was not to be hurried – 'they disapprove of all alcohol and tobacco and bright clothing. They don't sing, they have no worship as such, just go round in the streets preaching and begging for alms.'

'How do they use them?' Nell asked, intrigued in spite of herself. 'Do they run homes or a charity?'

'No one is really sure. But your father has been seen with them.'

Nell shrugged. 'I can't imagine him doing without his beer! I'm sure he has relapses.' In fact she knew he did, she thought, shuddering, as he had on the night he'd killed Frank.

'He doesn't seem to be drunk. But he's collecting money, and last night he came to our house and said you'd sent him, told him I'd give him a big donation.'

'I did nothing of the kind! Tom, surely you wouldn't believe I'd do that? Besides, I haven't seen him for weeks!'

'I thought it wasn't true.'

'Did you give him anything?'

'Of course not. He was abusive, but when I threatened to call the police he calmed down at once and went away.' He would, Nell thought. Of course he would. And joining his sect was probably the price he had to pay for his room in Florence's home. 'Nell, now we've come this far, I want to show you something.'

They were passing the junction with Lordswood Road, and soon afterwards he turned left and drew up in front of a neat terraced house with deep square bay windows.

'What is it? You know someone who lives here?' she asked, bewildered.

'I'm planning to buy it,' he told her proudly. 'Mother wants to go further out into the country, and she's looking for a house in Moseley or Yardley. She suggested that you might have refused me because you didn't want to live in another woman's house, and the answer was for me to buy a house of my own. I can afford it. I'm earning good money with the union, and Father will help me. Well, would you like to see inside?'

'No! Tom, I don't want to marry you, even if you have a dozen houses! Why don't you listen?'

'You don't know what you want,' he replied calmly. 'Women never do. That's why they need husbands to guide them.'

'That's utter rot! I am managing perfectly well without a husband, Tom, and I intend to go on doing so! Now take me back or I will get out of this car and walk home!'

'Er, *excusez-moi, mademoiselle, mais je cherche* Miss Davis, Miss Gwyneth Davis.'

Kitty glanced round, pausing on the step. 'Can I help you?'

'Oh, you speak English! How convenient! My French is a little rusty, I haven't had much opportunity to travel of late years – the cares of a family, you know. I am looking for Miss Davis. Is this the hostel where the – dancers – live?'

'Yes,' she replied slowly. She wondered what he wanted. He didn't look the usual prosperous middle-aged swain who haunted the stage door, and anyway Gwyneth was boringly devoted to her work; she didn't have swains. You couldn't count Timothy, who was merely amusing himself with her until such time as he looked seriously for a girl of whom his family would approve.

'I wonder if you could tell her someone wishes to see her?'

'We are not permitted gentlemen visitors,' she informed him primly, and smiled inwardly as he coloured. 'She'll be back from rehearsal soon, though. If you wait here you're bound to catch her.'

She nodded affably and passed through the door. She would

have been interested to wait and watch the encounter, but she was going out with a new admirer, and he was so rich he'd even offered to buy her an apartment in the Champs-Elysées, so she did not want to risk offending him by keeping him waiting. Perhaps she ought to go back and warn Gwyneth? It was only a very short distance. Then she looked at her new watch, gold encrusted with diamonds, a present tucked into the first bouquet her admirer had sent to the dressing room together with his invitation to supper, and decided she didn't have time.

Ten minutes later Gwyneth walked towards the hostel. The man stepped forward, and without speaking grasped her fiercely by the arm.

'What the – Father!'

'Yes, my dear, though I am ashamed to call you daughter. I have tracked you down at last, and you are coming home with me today.'

Gwyneth was pale, almost incapable of speech, but at this she shook her head vehemently. 'I can't! I won't!'

'It's no use being defiant, girl! You are under age and you need my permission to work here. If you can call such vile, disgraceful exhibitionism working!'

'I am dancing here, nothing more wicked than that!' she protested, but her heart had sunk and she knew that only a miracle would save her. Her father had the law on his side and he would never give in. It wouldn't be possible for her to continue working at the Folies even if she could elude him now. She would have to wait for her twenty-first birthday, when he would have no more power over her. 'You ought to come and see us dance before you condemn us!' she tried. 'It's unjust to say we are bad without knowing what we do!'

'I do not have to wallow in filth to know that it is filth! I've seen the harlots parading in the rue Richer, I don't need to see the ones inside! You have betrayed your upbringing and caused your mother unbearable pain and shame, but there is still time for sinners to repent, and I mean to wrest the devil from your soul!'

304

'The hostel where we live is run by an English minister,' she said desperately. 'Surely you cannot accuse him of being a sinner?'

'More shame for a man of the cloth to bring such infamy on the Church!'

'You are uncharitable!'

'I do what is right, and you have shown you are not fitted to distinguish good from evil. Now go and pack your trunks, I have tickets on the late train.'

Nell was puzzled when weeks passed and she received no more letters from Gwyneth, even though she made time to write at least a page every week. She felt isolated and quite out of touch, despite the pressures of reorganizing the dancing school. Kitty had never bothered to write, all the news Nell had of her came from Gwyneth. She'd seen Timothy briefly in the centre of the city and he'd said he was off to South Africa again. She'd never been especially friendly with him, but as one of the crowd he was a familiar face and she would miss him. Andrew was on tour having formed another dance band. Even Marigold had taken her children to stay with their grandmother during the Easter holidays, when Dick was home from school. There was Tom, increasingly persistent, but she was determined to avoid him. And although she saw Paul occasionally, at Endersby's or as they met walking along the street, she could not persuade herself he would want to spend time with her. Even if he did she would feel too uncomfortable, knowing how unworthy she was.

Then Andrew suddenly reappeared in Birmingham. If she hadn't hoped he might have some news she would not have given him so warm a welcome, but it was well over six months since he had made love to her. He had never again attempted to be alone with her and she decided lunch with him at the Grand would do no harm.

'I'm off to London next week to discuss a new project,' he told her, full of enthusiasm.

'Tell me.' Andrew had the most amazing capacity to start

afresh, she thought. In the short time she'd known him he had been involved in so many different schemes she had lost count. When one failed, or he got bored, he simply shrugged his shoulders and went on to something else. She suspected he had the same attitude towards women.

'I've been invited to do a tour in America,' he announced proudly.

'Andrew, that's marvellous!'

'It is rather exciting. It's not finalized yet, there are lots of details to sort out. I have to find out whether the programme and venues are acceptable. That's what I'm going to discuss. I don't suppose you feel like a few days in London? Can't you forgive me and be friends?'

She shook her head. 'I thought I had forgiven you, but I don't want to go to bed with you, Andrew! I've never been to London, but I'm far too busy to go now.'

'What with? Just dancing?'

'Lots more. I'm helping Edwina. We have so many plans, and I'm involved with all of them. We want to train a big troupe, but so far we haven't got all the right girls, and we need to keep the ones we have got working.'

'It must be tricky fitting in their engagements and the first rehearsals.'

'Yes, it is. We have to keep them near Birmingham and some of the touring troupes resent it.'

'I was sorry to hear about Frank, by the way. You were with him, I understand? That must have been ghastly for you.'

'It was. I'd rather not talk about it, please.'

'Fine. What dancing are you doing? You seem to be doing a lot of organizing now.'

'I'm getting quite out of practice, but I can't go away for long tours. We're planning to do some charity shows, and while it won't pay it will advertise us.'

'Nell, why don't you come with me to America? I love you, you know, and I'd wait until you were willing to trust me again.'

She stared at him in astonishment. 'America?'

'Don't look so disbelieving! Why not? If you want to dance you would be bound to get taken on by the Ziegfeld Follies in New York, and most of my appearances would be in New York and New England. We could be together for much of the time.'

For a few minutes she was tempted. She could get away from Tom, try to forget Paul, start afresh. She would still need Pa's permission but now she could force him to sign the letter by threatening to inform the police about his killing Frank. The school was running well and Edwina didn't really need her, she had many excellent dancers who could take her place. Then she knew she could not cheat Andrew. It was clear he expected them to live together, but she could not love him. Even though he had made a whore of her she would go to no man without love. Insidiously the thought crossed her mind that she did not need Andrew. Why had she not thought before about her hold over Pa? If they wanted her still at the Folies-Bergère there was no barrier to her getting his permission. She would ask Edwina to make enquiries straight away.

The next charity performance took place at Endersby's. Marigold organized the event as soon as she returned from her holiday with the children and their grandparents, inviting her wealthiest customers to a reception followed by the performance. Andrew was back in Birmingham, having completed the arrangements for his tour of America later in the year, and offered to play as well. The tickets were all sold within days, and they were sure of raising a very respectable sum for the city's children.

'There's still time to come to America with me,' Andrew said to Nell as they waited to go on stage. 'I'm going in the autumn now.'

Nell shushed him impatiently. 'It's my cue! Be quiet!'

For the first number the girls, dressed in floating white dresses, danced an introduction. Nell, wearing a circular black velvet cloak lined with white silk, the corners looped to her wrists, which opened to reveal a flame-red costume clinging tightly to her body, would burst on to the stage and do her solo dance against the swaying background of the white. It was a spectacular vision, one of Edwina's innovations, simple but effective. Nell listened intently, knowing she had to time it precisely for greatest effect, and then she was on doing a series of cartwheels across the floor with the cloak revolving round behind her, then whirling horizontal to the floor as she spun in a dizzying sequence of steps before flinging the cloak aside to do some more elaborate acrobatic dancing.

There was a spontaneous eruption of applause which died as the audience concentrated, then the dance was over when Nell sank to the ground, the girls bringing the cloak to spread about her.

Instead of high kicking their way off stage as they usually did, they drew Nell to her feet and formed a line which she led round the edge of the ballroom floor. She hesitated infinitesimally as she saw Paul smiling at her, and then passed on, blaming her rapidly beating heart on her exertions, not the sudden unexpected sight of him.

She hadn't expected him to be there. He had not made any attempt to contact her since the night he had driven her home, and in her irrationally guilty state she had wondered whether he knew her secrets. She had been glad he kept out of her way, she told herself, but she wanted to see him. It was all too confusing and she must change quickly for the next number.

The entire show was a great success but Nell hesitated before she went into the ballroom afterwards to join the guests and receive their congratulations. She needed to compose herself before she met Paul. The rest of the girls were eager to go, and soon Nell was alone. When a light tap came on the door she started to her feet, suddenly aware that she had not changed from her final costume, which had a short skirt sewn with feathers, and feathers wired to form a high collar or ruff.

The door opened and Andrew came in. 'Good, I thought you might be alone, darling. I came to congratulate you. You must take that costume to New York, you'll be sensational. The red one too, that's even more enticing!'

Before Nell could move he had pulled her into his arms. 'Why the devil have you kept away from me?' he demanded.

'Andrew, let me go!' There was panic in her voice as she struggled, but he had her at a disadvantage and she could hardly move.

'I'll never let you go again! I was a fool to lose you before.'

As he bent to kiss her the door closed sharply. Andrew cursed, looked up, and then swung Nell round so that they both faced the door. Paul was standing inside it.

'I believe Nell asked you to release her, Andrew,' he said evenly.

Andrew, his face flushed, grinned and hugged Nell closer. 'You needn't worry, old man! She likes it rough. It's a pose to pretend she's reluctant. Were you taken in? Is that why she turned to me? When you overcome that sham modesty she's a real hot little piece of flesh!'

Nell was never certain exactly what happened next. She didn't know whether Paul pushed her aside as he stepped forward, or whether Andrew did. She heard Andrew's laugh turn into a choking gasp, as Paul's fist shot out and connected with Andrew's jaw. She screamed as Andrew, stepping back, tripped on a costume draped carelessly across a chair. Then he was lying on the floor, cursing and muttering, while Paul stood menacingly over him.

'You'll sign the letter or I go to the police!'

Pa complained and resisted, but Nell was implacable. She had come to her brother's house at a time when she knew Ned and Florence paid their weekly Sunday visit to her family, and discovered Pa nursing a bottle which smelled strongly of whisky.

'I thought you'd signed the pledge?' she asked scornfully.

'I did, but 'ow's a man ter keep 'is spirits up when 'is daughter turns agin 'im? Shames 'im afore 'is mates showing off 'er legs, an' more. No better'n a drab, though yer wears fine feathers.'

'Sign the letter, or as well as going to the police I'll tell Florence about this. Then she'd certainly throw you out, if the police didn't come for you first!'

Clutching the precious permission she went gleefully back to tell Edwina. She hadn't seen Paul or Andrew after the previous evening's fracas. Paul had thrown her coat round her and bundled her out of the room with a hasty apology, and she had avoided the guests and gone straight home. When she went to collect her abandoned clothes the next morning Edwina told her she'd heard there was a vacancy in the Folies troupe which Nell could have as long as she reached France by the following Saturday.

She wanted to go, and that way she would avoid both Andrew and Paul. Edwina, pleased for her, had made light of finding other girls to take her place.

'Of course it won't be the same, but you deserve your chance after the last disappointment. If you think your father will relent you mustn't consider me. But I do hope you can do the big charity show in London on Monday first. You can take the boat train on Tuesday and give yourself a few days in Paris before starting work. I want you to do the cloak dance once more. No one else is remotely capable of doing it well enough.'

'Of course, and I've never been to London. It will be easier to travel with the troupe than find my way alone.'

Now all she had to do was tell Edwina she had the letter, and pack her trunk. She was thankful she didn't have time to think. Within days she would be with Gwyneth, and discover why her friend had not written for so long.

The show was in a huge theatre in the East End of London. Several dancing troupes were taking part, as well as other artistes. Nell's troupe, with the cloak dance routine, were to conclude the first half.

'Those children, they make such a noise!' Edwina muttered as she checked that the girls were all prepared.

'I wonder how many of them go to dancing classes and want to become dancers?' Nell mused.

'They aren't all from classes,' Edwina explained. 'It was decided to invite some of the poor children whom the charity supports. I think it was to fill up the unsold seats,' she added softly. 'Now girls, after the juggler finishes you're on. Are you ready?'

They nodded nervously. They were fairly new, most of them, and mainly provided the simple backing for Nell. When they had more experience they could be moved to other troupes as appropriate. None of them had performed in such a large theatre before, but the rehearsal had been good and Edwina and Nell inspired confidence.

The juggler came off to loud applause, the dance music began, and the dancers were on stage. Nell concentrated on her cue, and then she was on, doing her cartwheels then whirling around with her cloak spinning too. In the excitement of this no one noticed a disturbance in the auditorium until there was a shrill scream.

'Nell! Nell!'

Nell halted abruptly, and as the dancers and the orchestra came to a ragged halt, she peered through the footlights.

'Nell! It's me, Amy!'

Chapter Twenty-Three

NELL flew down the steps at the side of the stage and gathered Amy to her. 'Amy! Is it really you? Let me look at you! Where've you been? How on earth did you get here?'

The child was sobbing and hiccuping, unable to speak, and clinging so fiercely to Nell that her rough, bitten nails dug deep into Nell's shoulders.

'Bring her through here,' a quiet voice interposed, and Nell looked up, dazed, coming back to reality. Seeing row upon row of faces turned towards her, avid with either curiosity or disapproval, she flushed, hastily picked Amy up, and allowed herself to be guided by the stage manager through the pass door into the blessed obscurity of backstage.

'It's my sister,' she explained breathlessly. 'My sister, Amy. She disappeared in Birmingham, over a year ago. No one knew what had happened to her.'

Edwina was beside her. 'Can we find a room where this can be sorted out?' she asked. 'And what about the dancing?'

The stage manager glanced at Nell. 'Will you be able to dance if we have the interval now?'

She was shaking, but with happiness. 'I – yes, in a few minutes,' she assured him. 'The show must go on. Edwina, I'm so sorry! I just didn't know what I was doing, hearing Amy like that!'

'Then I'll explain to the audience and hope they will be

understanding,' said the stage-manager. 'Here, this room is empty, take the child in there for a few moments, and then I'm sure she'll want to see you dance.'

'Please stay, Edwina,' Nell asked as Edwina stepped back. 'Now, Amy, tell me what happened to you.'

Amy spoke, hesitantly, in a hoarse voice. 'Pa – was mad at me. Said 'e'd make me tell 'im where yer was. I ran off an' two ladies found me. Stayed wi' them, then they went away an' took me ter big 'ouse with lots o' kids. Then another 'ouse.'

There was a hesitant knock on the door and Edwina went to open it.

'Excuse me, is the child in here? I'm Matron of the Barnardo's home which has been looking after her.'

Nell smiled at her, her eyes glistening. 'Please come in! She's just been telling me how she was lost. None of us knew where she was. Why didn't she tell you where she lived?'

The woman, dressed in grey, came further into the room. 'For some reason she wouldn't, or couldn't, speak. The doctors could find nothing wrong, and decided it was the result of some sort of shock. It seems they were right if she's been talking to you. And I heard her. Her name is Amy, I think she said?'

'Yes, Amy Baxter. I'm her oldest sister, Nell. Thank you all so much for looking after her, I'm so relieved she's been all right. We thought – thought she was dead.'

The stage manager came back in. 'That's that. The audience seem to be enjoying the sensation, rather than being annoyed. I think it would be best if the child goes into one of the boxes. Maybe you, madam, would go with her?' he suggested, looking at the matron.

Amy shook her head vehemently. 'Want ter stay with Nell.'

'Darling, I must get ready to do the dance. Don't you want to see it? Afterwards I'll come straight to you, or you'll come back here, and you can come back to Birmingham with me.'

Edwina looked up sharply and the matron began to shake her head, but before either of them could speak the stage manager cut in.

'We've only a few minutes, it's a short interval and we must get the child settled and warn the dancers.'

'Please, Amy? Afterwards we can be together all the time.'

A reluctant Amy was led away and Nell, her cloak restored to her from where she had dropped it on the stage, rejoined the troupe, all eager to ask what had happened.

'It was my sister, she's been missing for over a year,' Nell said briefly. 'Now please, let me concentrate! I can't think about the dance, but I must! I've forgotten all the steps!'

The dancers received warm applause at the start of their act, and Nell, seemingly inspired, danced better than ever before. When she sank into the final crumpled heap the applause was deafening and continued long after they had left the stage.

'They want an encore,' the stage manager whispered, but Nell shook her head.

'I must go to my sister. I'll change first, then we'll be ready to go.'

It was only then that she realized and turned a stricken face to Edwina. 'I was going to Paris tomorrow,' she whispered.

'I wondered when you would remember it,' Edwina said drily. 'Come on, let's go back to the hotel and we'll talk about it.'

Feverishly eager to be reunited with Amy, to be sure it wasn't a dream, Nell changed in haste. Amy and the matron were waiting for her in the same backstage room, the child having insisted she didn't want to watch the rest of the show. Nell hugged Amy close.

'You'll soon be back home with me,' she reassured her, wondering how Amy would receive the news of the deaths of her mother and all the younger children.

The matron coughed. 'I'm sorry, but she is in our care. We cannot permit her to be removed until we are satisfied that there is a suitable home for her to go to.'

'I have to be with the men,' Mr Davis proclaimed. 'Their cause is just, wages are deplorably low, and they must be supported.

A strike is the only possible way of making their grievances known, and forcing the Government to take action.'

'But what will happen? During the strike? If all the trains stop, I mean? Won't that inconvenience everyone?' his wife asked hesitantly.

'We must all make sacrifices. The workers will be protected. Somehow we shall distribute food. In any case people have known about the strike for months, they have been buying a little more food each week.'

'So a few extra tins of salmon will feed the workers until we get the pack ponies organized?' Gwyneth queried sardonically.

'You know nothing about it, miss, and I'll thank you to remain silent. While all this has been going on you were shamelessly flaunting your body before men whose only thought was to defile you! What can you, or they, know about the real world of hardship and poverty such as our miners endure? I could tell you tales of affliction, men horrifically injured, left to beg in the streets while your depraved friends fornicate and guzzle caviar and champagne. We are fighting for a fairer world! I shall continue to do my duty and pray on my knees that you will repent of your evil ways, see the light, and earn forgiveness.'

Gwyneth shut her ears. Her father had always been a pompous bore filled with evangelical fervour, and uncompromisingly narrow minded. Since she had been forced home from Paris he never lost an opportunity of fulminating about her supposed transgressions. This was now mixed with zeal for the miners' cause, and plans he was helping to coordinate in the area for the proposed general strike. She let her thoughts wander back to her schemes for escape.

This was amazingly difficult. She had been expecting to be treated harshly ever since he found her in Paris, but not literally to be a prisoner. He had locked her into the old nursery on the attic floor, high up and with barred windows. There could be no escape from there. She was permitted to come downstairs only when he was at home, for an hour or so each evening. She ate dinner with her parents, the only good meal of the day, and afterwards walked in the garden, screened by thick hedges, accompanied by her father. It was her only opportunity to be outside so she endured in silence the sermons on her moral corruption, ingratitude, and the dreadful fate which awaited an unregenerate sinner.

During this hour her room was cleaned, a jug of water and some slices of bread placed there, then she was once more incarcerated for the next night and day. All she had for entertainment was a Bible and the household linen which needed mending.

At first she had been too shattered by the abrupt ending of her dreams to care. After wallowing in misery for a week she forced herself to try and make plans, first for escape, and then for how she could hide until her twenty-first birthday in October, when her father could no longer control her. She had no idea how she might escape, but she had to be prepared to take whatever opportunity offered. Remembering the belt Nell had worn, in which she kept her precious patch-box, Gwyneth made a similar one from a strip of linen cut from the sheet she was turning. She didn't think even her father would notice if it was narrower than it ought to be. Fortunately he had not searched her cases when they finally reached home, declaring he had no intention of contaminating himself with the indecent garments she now appeared to prefer. In the confusion of their arrival, her father's denunciations mingling with his triumph at having snared her, her mother's lamentations and futile protests when she learned of Gwyneth's proposed imprisonment, Gwyneth had been able to abstract and conceal the small box which held her savings.

Now she could always carry her money with her. She also began exercising each day to keep her limbs supple and her body healthy. She had thoughts of simply breaking away from her father in the garden and running, but it would be fruitless. She would have to go eastwards eventually, there was nowhere to hide for more than a few days in the Pembroke peninsula. The villagers knew her and would be too afraid of her father to help.

The railwaymen and the bus drivers would recognize her and tell him if she tried to leave on either train or bus. Besides, she could not reach them and get away before her escape was known, for her father could follow her in his car immediately. One day, however, he would relax his guard and she must be prepared for it.

'You must go to Paris.'

'Edwina, I can't!' Nell swung round from staring out of the window in their small hotel sitting room. She had been pacing restlessly for hours, ever since they had returned from talking to the authorities at the Barnardo's home in Barkingside. 'I have to stay here and get Amy out of that dreadful place, she hates it so much!'

Edwina sighed. 'I know, Nell dear. But there's nothing you can do. You have a father and four older brothers, and one of them is married. The matron was adamant that they would never release Amy into your care alone. They insist the children go back to their parents, and houses where they will be cared for in conditions at least as good as the Barkingside home.'

'How can they think an orphanage with so many children is better than being with someone who loves them!'

'They mean things like proper food and clothing. And good treatment. Amy was not well dressed when she was found, and clearly terrified. Would Ned and his wife take her? He's got a safe job on the railway. Could that be the answer?'

Nell's shoulders drooped. 'He was never interested once he got away from home. And I don't think Florence is the sort to be kind to Amy. Besides, Pa's living with them.'

'And Amy would be terrified.'

'I can't leave her. At least I can find a job near the orphanage and visit her as often as possible.'

'You could visit just as easily from Birmingham, Nell. You are only allowed to visit once a month, on Saturday afternoons. If you are quite sure you won't go to Paris then stay with me. At least you'll have friends to help.'

At last Edwina persuaded her to go to bed, but for the second night Nell tossed restlessly. How different, though, from last night when she had been full of excitement at finding Amy, feverishly making plans about providing a home for the child, and making it up to her for the long year of separation and misery. Now it seemed as though Amy was not to be released. A slow, burning anger began to consume Nell. How dare they do this to her little sister! She would fight them with every weapon she had until Amy was given into her care.

'They won't negotiate. It's all been a sham since last year,' Mr Simmons declared. 'The Samuelson Report said nothing to help, and there's only just over a week to go.'

'So you're going to London, to the special conference next week?' Tom asked.

'Of course. I'm going later today, there are other meetings. I know you'll be here looking after the office.'

Tom nodded. When his father had departed he took out the letter which had come for him that morning and read it once more. What ought he to do? He still wanted Nell, despite her present way of life. His infatuation with Kitty had been a madness, and though at times he dreamed of what might have come of it, in his sober moments he recognized she was not the sort of girl who would ever have made a suitable wife. Nell, if she could be reclaimed from her obsession with dancing, would be far more suitable to a rising young union official. And now she had written to him for help. The providential reappearance of Amy seemed to have put a stop to her mad scheme to dance at the Folies-Bergère.

He could easily do as she asked, and find out whether her father was still living with Ned. It was years since he'd been friends with Ned but it wouldn't be difficult to meet him again. Ned had always been rather simple, grateful for any attention. And he worked on the railways so Tom could pretend he sought him out to discover the real opinion of the less influential railway workers. Ned would be flattered and a few casual questions would provide the information Nell wanted. He could do it today and she would receive the answer tomorrow as she had asked. She would be grateful to him, Tom, and if he helped her now the gratitude might develop into something warmer. He reached for his hat, a new and, he felt, rather dashing grey trilby, and left the office.

'You must go to Paris.'

Nell sighed with frustration. It was now Friday. She had spent all day Tuesday arguing with the people at the orphanage; all day Wednesday writing to people she hoped might help, such as Tom who could tell her quickly how her father was, so that she might devise schemes to include him or not in the rescue of Amy; and all day Thursday arguing with Edwina again about going to Paris. Now Paul had come to bully her.

Briefly she wondered why he had come and how he had known. But the matter was too urgent for irrelevant speculation. 'If I go to Paris I won't be able to see Amy. I won't be able to plan to make a home for her,' she explained again as if she were talking to a child.

'Come and sit down,' he said calmly, and as she impatiently shook her head he took both her hands in his and drew her to sit on the settee beside him. 'Nell, it will take time to deal with all the formalities – weeks, probably months – and to begin with there is little you can do. You could come home frequently to see Amy.'

'I couldn't afford to! I have to save every penny now towards getting a proper home for her.'

'You would resent her later.'

She stared at him, aghast. 'How can you say that? I could never resent Amy!'

'Listen, Nell. This is what you've wanted to do for a long time. It's the summit of any dancer's ambition to be chosen for the Folies-Bergère troupe. You were prevented from going before, and you were terribly disappointed then. Go for a few weeks, fulfil your contract with them, give them chance to find a suitable replacement. Then when you come back you will at least always be able to look on your time there with satisfaction; you'll have danced in Paris. If you give that up for Amy now, and discover it wasn't necessary and it didn't help her, you'd feel some chagrin. It would be bound to influence how you felt about her, whether you knew it or not. And there won't be another chance. Even though you are the best dancer Edwina has ever seen, better even than Gwyneth, she says, they wouldn't forgive you if you let them down.'

'I'm not better than Gwyneth! She's marvellous.'

'So are you. But do you understand? You wouldn't mean to blame Amy, but deep down you couldn't help but wish, sometimes, that you'd had at least a taste of Paris.'

Nell knew he was right. It had been an instant, unthinking decision to forget all about Paris, but later, when she had realized what that meant, she had been forced to stifle many pangs of regret.

'Would they ever let her go if they thought she was to live with an immoral dancer?' she asked bitterly.

'Nell, not everyone is prejudiced like that. They brought the children to see dancers, after all. They are sensible, careful people. They know you are not immoral.'

She thought with agony of that night with Andrew. What would Paul say if he knew how easily she had succumbed to him? Then he would call her immoral; he would despise her, refuse to help her.

'Someone has to be here to try and sort things out.'

'Will you let me do it?'

'You? Why should you help me?' she asked, genuinely puzzled.

'I have the authority of being a doctor, they will listen to me. I also knew your family, at least some of them, slightly, and I have helped once before in a similar case to reunite a child with its mother. Nell, it will take several weeks to organize the preliminary details. Remember, they had no idea who Amy was. They'll have to contact the ladies who found her and check records. While they are doing this there is nothing you can do.'

'No, but I don't feel I should be too far away.'

Paul gave a silent word of thanks. She was weakening. 'Paris is not the other side of the world. It would not take many hours for you to return to London. Besides, your salary at the Folies-Bergère would be much more than you get in England. You could save more than you can here — it might help persuade them you can look after Amy.'

Nell looked at him as if seeing him for the first time. 'Why are you helping me like this?'

He wanted to say he loved her, enough to let her leave him and follow this driving ambition to dance. He wanted to say he still hoped she might one day agree to marry him. But that would disturb her, make her worried, might even make her feel he expected more in return than simple gratitude, and he would never try to buy her love.

'I'm sorry for Amy,' he said at last.

'Nell! How wonderful!' Kitty exclaimed, and ran across to hug Nell fiercely.

They were in the hostel, and Nell had just been shown into the dormitory she was to share with three other girls. To her astonishment one of these was Kitty.

'Where's Gwyneth?' she asked. 'I haven't heard from her for weeks. Oh, I'm so tired!' The last week had been exhausting, and when she had finally agreed to come to Paris they had all been very busy organizing trains and tickets, sending telegrams, and promising to keep in touch about Amy.

'Gwyneth? Oh, Nell, it was funny! That dreadful man!'

'What man? Kitty, what happened?'

'Her father. He came here, he'd discovered where she was, but I don't know how. He was utterly foul! The way he ranted and raved about us you'd think we were all the whores of Babylon!'

'She always said he was a fanatic. But where is she?'

'He took her home. She's under twenty-one and she'd forged his permission. Stupid fuss!'

'So that's why she didn't write. Have you heard from her, Kitty?'

'No, as it happens I wasn't here when she left, I was out with a friend. I believe he hauled her off to the train, saying he wouldn't let her out of his sight until he had her safely back in Wales. I expect she's there now, being preached at about her iniquities.'

'Poor Gwyneth. I don't even have that address, I just know it's near Saundersfoot. Do you think a letter could possibly find her?'

'Addressed to Davis, in Wales? There's no chance.'

'I suppose you're right. Perhaps she'll write to one of us soon.'

'Perhaps. But Nell, tell me all your news. Have you seen Andrew? Or Paul? Neither of them has written for absolutely ages. Timothy was here, but he went off to South Africa again weeks ago.'

'Andrew's going to America and Paul's trying to help Amy. Oh, yes, and Frank was killed.' Nell explained everything once Kitty paused in her excited exclamations. 'Nothing has gone well for me since I lost my patch-box,' she said tiredly. 'I used to think it was a sort of talisman, and it seems I was right.'

There was an uncomfortable silence. Then Kitty smiled brightly. 'I'm not dancing now,' she told Nell. 'It was too much like hard work, besides giving me muscles I don't want! Do you realize you'll have a dozen costume changes, and it's five flights of stairs up to the dressing rooms we have? Talking of which, you have a rehearsal tomorrow afternoon, so you'd better go to bed. I'm going out for a late supper with a friend. I'll see you in the morning.'

Gwyneth knew she would have to leave as soon as she could. Her father would be in Cardiff for a few days, helping to organize the South Wales strikers, but he might be back at any time. The one piece of good fortune was that he was travelling with a man from Pembroke, so had left his car at home. She had only to get out of her room.

She knew her mother would be sympathetic and not try to stop her, but she would not disobey her husband to the extent of unlocking Gwyneth's door. It had been Mr Davis's instructions that Gwyneth should not be permitted out of her room while he was away, and all food should be taken up to her by the odd-job man, Dai, who was a little simple-minded and in such fear of hellfire that he obeyed Mr Davis unwaveringly. He would guard her while the maid did what was necessary.

It might be possible to induce her mother to open the door if she thought Gwyneth was ill. On the day her father left Gwyneth packed a small valise with essentials and refused all food, complaining that she felt sick. When she knew Dai would be occupied in the garden the next morning, and her mother sorting the linen on the floor beneath, Gwyneth began to emit loud groans. Soon her mother's hesitant voice could be heard on the landing.

'Gwyneth, darling, what is it? Are you ill?'

Gwyneth moaned again, and replied in a feeble voice: 'I'm feeling so sick! My stomach! And my head!'

Her mother, after a slight pause, went away. Soon she could be heard climbing the stairs once more and fitting the key into the lock.

'Darling, let me see,' she began, but Gwyneth had slipped past her and before Mrs Davis knew what was happening pushed her into the room and slammed the door shut.

'Mother, I'm sorry,' she said, feeling wretched. 'I love you but I won't endure this treatment. Father's a monster! He's kept me locked up for over two months! It was the only way I could think of to escape. Dai will be up here soon with my food and he'll let you out. If I don't lock you in Father will blame you. Don't worry about me, I'll write soon.'

'But Gwyneth, how will you get away? There are no trains!'

Gwyneth laughed, shakily. 'I know how to drive, Mother! I'll write and tell you where I've left the car.'

*

Timothy tapped his foot restlessly. 'Come on, Andrew, stop that endless practising. We have to do something to help! Besides, it will be fun!'

'You need to go back to Paris and find Gwyneth,' Andrew responded, breaking off the jazz tune he was trying out.

'We'll both go, I'll find out why she hasn't replied to my letter, and you can have another go at the little Nell.'

'I don't know why you call her little! She's as tall as Kitty and Gwyneth,' Andrew replied.

'But we can't go while there's a general strike and almost no trains and boats. Let's go and drive a couple of buses, at least we could do that. It would be something to do while we wait, and if I don't do something I shall go mad with frustration.'

'You never used to be like this. At one time you could sleep all day. Is it the prospect of being even more filthy rich and covered in your own diamonds?'

'Gold, Andrew, not diamonds. Will you come?'

'No, but please go yourself. I want to get this phrasing right and you're being a hell of a hindrance, old fellow.'

Timothy shrugged, and took himself off. He spent the whole of that day and the next driving a bus between the city centre and Longbridge. The strike, while a nuisance, did not seem to be having a great deal of effect on most people. Volunteers drove trains and buses, and to start with there was almost a holiday mood. He had just begun the last journey of the day back to the city centre when he saw a woman waving down the bus. He stopped obligingly, and then stared in delight. He neither knew nor cared how she came to be here, but he was overwhelmed when he saw Gwyneth. For the first time he knew that the attraction she had for him was no passing fancy. He had to have her.

Once she could thrust the thoughts of Amy from her mind Nell was enchanted with Paris. The professionalism of the dancing girls was a revelation. She and Gwyneth had possessed it, and a few of the others in the troupes they had led had had the same urge for perfection as did Edwina, but in a different way. Here, however, everyone in the theatre had it, from the top management to the solo performers, the designers and costume makers, and every dancing girl and showgirl. Everything had to be perfect, the amazing technical effects, the stunning tableaux, the cheeky banana skirt worn by the brilliant new star from America, Josephine Baker, known as the Black Pearl, and the last feather and inch of ribbon and sequin on the dancers' legendary clothes.

Like Gwyneth, she had at first been embarrassed at the virtual nudity about her, but as everyone appeared to treat it as perfectly normal she was soon able to do so herself, and also became accustomed to her own costumes, which were much more revealing than any she had previously worn. When everyone else took them for granted, regarding them only as a part of the entire spectacle, it seemed silly to let a false sense of prudery bother her.

Paris itself, when she could be persuaded to look at it, was delightful. The trees were by now in full leaf, the flowers in window boxes blooming, and the pavements alive with beautifully dressed people. Kitty showed her all her own favourite places, and they often sat drinking coffee or wine in small cafés, observing the world.

Occasionally Kitty persuaded her to go to parties with the new friends she had made. 'You mustn't fret about Amy,' she chided. 'Paul will arrange for her release. He always gets what he wants. Look at how women all fall for him, and his mother moves out and leaves him to his own devices. He got you to come here; he can surely get Amy out of that place.'

So Nell attended suppers after the performances, picnics in the Bois de Boulogne, and drove out on Sundays to the châteaux of Kitty's male admirers. She was taken to see the Palaces of Versailles and Fontainebleau, went to the races, and firmly refused all the many invitations for more private excursions. She insisted on going with other girls.

At one time, with a particularly persistent young Spanish duke, who was good company and reminded her a little of Paul with his deep-set eyes and beautiful mouth, she was tempted. Why not, she asked herself, sighing dejectedly. Wasn't she a whore? Hadn't Andrew robbed her of the only thing she could have given to Paul, if he'd ever wanted her? And so she agreed to have supper with him.

He was ecstatic and escorted her proudly to the Ritz. He was at first furiously angry, then cringingly apologetic when Nell refused to eat the supper he had ordered in his suite.

'We eat in public or I go straight back to the hostel,' she told him. She was cross, yet remorseful. She might have known that by accepting his invitation she had given him the wrong impression. A tiny part of her wondered whether she had meant to go to bed with him as he so ardently desired, but in the end she could not force herself to comply. He bore a faint resemblance to Paul, but he wasn't Paul, and she would never willingly allow any other man to make love to her.

Every day Nell watched for letters. Edwina wrote with news of the school and what they were doing about Amy. Marigold wrote to say she was sure Nell was doing the right thing, and she could not be of any help in England. There was a long letter from Tom, which had missed her at the London hotel, to say that Pa was still living with Ned, but was looking for a room somewhere because they only had two bedrooms and Florence was hoping to have another child soon. Then he passed on to his own doings, enthusing about how well he was progressing in his career and their plans to support the miners during the national strike. Finally Tom sent his love and suggested that if Nell were to marry him he would be prepared to offer Amy a home until she was old enough to go into service.

Paul did not write. It was only from Edwina's later letters that Nell discovered how much he had been doing, travelling to London almost every week to talk to the people at Dr Barnardo's, to insist on visiting Amy on the grounds that he had once treated her family, pointing out that her terrible experience, plus the loss of her mother, necessitated some continuous contact with her former life.

Then there was a letter from Gwyneth. It was short, with no address, just to say she had escaped from home and her father.

I am helping Edwina for a while, but she doesn't know where I live. It's safest until my father has promised not to try and drag me back home. I've written to him through a solicitor Marigold took me to, and he believes I am in London. I daren't risk him coming here. If the Folies management will forgive me, and want me back when I am twenty-one and don't need his permission, I will happily return then. Please, Nell, will you ask them, and write to me when you next write to Edwina?

Finally, a small packet arrived for Nell. There was no covering note although it was postmarked Birmingham. She opened it, puzzled, and inside a small metal tea caddy, carefully wrapped in cotton wool, found her patch-box.

Chapter Twenty-Four

'Tell me everything,' Timothy had demanded.

He and Gwyneth were sitting in a small café drinking mugs of strong tea. She'd needed little persuasion to wait while he handed over the bus. The journey – first the long drive and then finding her way to Birmingham – had left her wilting and numb. She was happy to let someone else make decisions for her.

'Did you know my father hauled me back to Wales?' she asked, and he nodded.

'Kitty wrote to me. She said he was frightful.'

Gwyneth shuddered. 'It was much worse than she knew. He's kept me a prisoner since, only allowed out of my room in his company. I tricked my mother while he was away helping the miners, and stole his car. There was no other way to leave the village, no one would have helped me. They're all too afraid of him.'

'You drove?' Timothy chuckled. 'I knew you could do it if you had the incentive.'

Gwyneth grinned back at him. The tea was reviving her and she felt safer than she had all day.

'So what are you going to do now? Nell's in Paris – '

'Nell? At the Folies? Oh, how wonderful for her! I wonder how she managed to get her father's permission?'

'Were you hoping to stay with her?'

Gwyneth frowned. 'Yes, I was.'

'And your father would look for you at Edwina's.'

'I can't go to Edwina's, not to stay, though I hope she'll find me some work. I'll have to go to a small hotel until I find lodgings again. I'll just have to hope I can avoid my father when he comes after me.'

'You could always come and stay with me,' Timothy said diffidently. 'No strings. I won't be at Manor Farm all the time anyway.' Perhaps, he thought optimistically, she would accept his overtures if he made them slowly.

'Really? You'd let me live there? That would help enormously,' Gwyneth said slowly. 'I could come into Birmingham by train to see Edwina.'

'Then let's go. My car is just round the corner. There's so much to tell you. I couldn't believe it when I saw you running for the bus,' Timothy said, laughing triumphantly. The first hurdle had been cleared. In time Gwyneth would relax her defences.

On the drive home he told her about how Nell's sister had been found, and she exclaimed in surprise.

'Where is she living then? With one of her brothers?'

'It's not so simple. Apparently the orphanages won't allow the children out until they have satisfactory homes to go to. Paul made Nell go to Paris because he said it takes months to sort out. He's dealing with it, from what I understand, though I can't see why he should concern himself.'

Gwyneth could. He still loved Nell and in this way might help her. For a brief, betraying moment when she learned that Nell was in Paris she had wondered whether she might now have a chance to win Paul for herself, but this information forced her to accept the hopelessness of it. Paul still loved Nell and always would. Yet Nell had left him to go to Paris. Didn't she love him? Surely Nell wasn't so dedicated to dancing as she used to be? For Paul Gwyneth knew she would be prepared to give up her ambitions.

'And Andrew is soon off to America.'

It was ironic, she thought as he gave her all the news, that she and Paul would soon be the only ones left in Birmingham. Suddenly she felt very lonely, much more so than when she had first run away from home. Perhaps she wasn't as independent as she thought. When they reached Manor Farm and Timothy showed her to a small bedroom several doors away from his own, she turned in the doorway and held his arms. 'You're so kind,' she whispered, and reached up to kiss him on the lips.

Then she chuckled, for Timothy had backed away, startled, and was looking at her in consternation. 'Were all those attempted seductions just teasing?' she asked. 'Don't you want me after all?'

'But – I said no strings!' he exclaimed.

'And it was very sweet of you. Timothy, I've been awfully silly, refusing you for so long. Can I change my mind – or don't you want me any more?'

Then she gasped as he crushed her to him, kicked the door shut, and with trembling hands began to remove her clothes.

'Marigold, it's Paul. I need your advice. Can we meet at the hotel?'

'Of course. I shall be there this evening. Come in for a cocktail.'

As she put down the telephone Marigold wondered what Paul had to say. He'd sounded abrupt and oddly uncertain. When he was shown into her office later he was restless, pacing the floor while she prepared cocktails.

'Here, drink this and tell me what is bothering you.'

He sighed, and then smiled ruefully. 'Marigold, does everyone come to you for help and advice? You look so young and fragile yourself, and yet I know life hasn't been easy for you. Is it that strength people instinctively recognize?'

'I've made plenty of mistakes myself,' she replied gently. 'What is it? Nell?'

'Yes. You know she keeps refusing me. She has this foolish notion she isn't good enough for me because she was born in a slum. I've tried to be patient, I haven't even written to her in Paris, but I wondered . . . Well, now Amy has been found and Nell wants to make a home for her, things have changed.'

'How? So far as you and Nell are concerned?'

'Don't you see? Someone has to provide a home for Amy, and I can't see the Dr Barnardo's people being happy with Mr Baxter's guardianship if they see him in his normal state! If Nell married me they would look on our home as much more suitable.'

'And you are thinking of suggesting this to Nell? Oh, Paul!'

'Why not? It would solve her problems.'

'But don't you see, even if she agreed, and I doubt if she would, she would always feel a sense of obligation to you. There could never be the sort of equality, the partnership, which is necessary for a good marriage. I've watched Nell and I'm fairly certain she does love you. But she could never express that love freely if she thought she'd married you for Amy's sake. She would think you wouldn't believe her. She has to come to you without any coercion or persuasion other than the fact that she loves you. You must be even more patient, Paul.'

He pushed his hand through his hair. 'In a way I thought you'd say something like this. I hadn't worked it out so clearly, but you are right, as usual. I'm in such a turmoil I must have hoped you might persuade me differently.'

'Poor Paul, I do understand. But go on supporting her when she comes home from Paris. One day she will realize that the differences between you don't matter.'

'You were wonderful! Nell, you were so good tonight! I've never seen you dance better!' Kitty enthused.

'I didn't know you could see us,' Nell said, laughing.

Kitty grinned. 'I'm stuck there, unable to move, and all I can do is gaze into the mirror behind me! It isn't as good a view as from a box, but it's enough!'

'I think it's all because my patch-box turned up so oddly. I wonder how it could have got to me? Do you suppose Meggy found it somewhere and sent it on? But if so why didn't she enclose a note?'

'Perhaps she forgot,' Kitty said hastily. 'I shouldn't say anything, Nell, it would embarrass her. She can't write very well. I'll tell her it arrived safely and you're grateful when I write to her.'

'You're writing to her? I didn't know you did.'

'I have to let her know I'm moving away from Paris. I don't have my mother's address, she's somewhere in California now, but Meggy can tell her when dear Mama suddenly decides she has to get in touch with me.'

'You're moving from Paris? Leaving the Folies? Kitty, why? When did you decide this?'

Kitty shrugged. 'A few days ago. I'm bored with all this, it's tedious having to be on stage every night. The dancing was hard work but at least it was interesting. Not like this posing, having to stay still even if your nose itches or you get cramp in your leg. Besides,' she added petulantly, 'I get so many black marks for being late for rehearsals or losing earrings or silly things like that I've already had four of their damned warning letters. One more and I'll be dismissed. I'd rather go first.'

'But what will you do? You don't sound as if you're going home.'

'No, I want to stay in France for a while. Don't tell the others, Nell, or they'll scratch my eyes out. I know I can trust you not to be envious. I'm going to the south of France, to Nice, with the prince.'

'Your Italian? But Kitty, he's old! He's in his fifties!'

'Does that matter? It's all the better, perhaps. If I play my cards right he'll marry me. He's a widower. I'll wear him out in a few years and be left a rich widow while I'm still young enough to enjoy it.'

'But you've got plenty of money already, surely?' Nell asked, rather disturbed by Kitty's attitude.

'Nell, don't be bourgeois! You can never have enough money, and in any case mine belongs to dear Mama. I don't relish being dependent on her charity for the rest of her life! And after she dies the trust money stops, and I'll have a big house and no way of running it! And Timothy is no longer interested, he couldn't take his eyes off Gwyneth when he was here. I had hopes of him, I admit, but he's besotted. Not that he'll ever marry her.'

'When are you going?'

'At the end of the week. But I'll keep in touch. Perhaps I'll send you an invitation to the wedding!'

'I shall miss you.' Nell knew it was true. Despite Kitty's tantrums and her occasional unpleasant moods, she had been a friend. It was Kitty who had first helped her escape from her home. She could never forget that or cease to be grateful.

Paul waited in the rue Saulnier, feeling uncomfortably conspicuous. The usual line of mainly elderly men driving the latest model cars filled the narrow street. He was on foot, having arrived in Paris just in time to catch the show. He thought about Nell. With such a good troupe of girls and the training she received here her dancing was exceptional, and he had a twinge of regret that his news would mean the end of Paris for her. Then he saw her emerge from the stage door with Kitty.

Kitty hesitated for a second, then waved and walked elegantly across to one of the parked cars. A uniformed chauffeur opened the door for her and she slid into the back seat. As the car pulled away Paul saw a man beside Kitty, an oldish man, thin faced and narrow shouldered, with a hawk-like nose.

'Nell,' Paul called, realizing that in watching Kitty he had allowed Nell to move away. He strode along the street and Nell turned, almost colliding with him. He caught her in his arms and, suddenly breathless, she stared up at him.

'Paul? It's really you? What are you doing here? Is Amy – Is she all right?'

'She's well, and so is everyone else. I wanted to see you, to explain in person. Let's go and have supper.'

Soon they were seated in a small but expensive restaurant

nearby, and Paul shook his head when she demanded to be told his news. 'Let's order first,' he said calmly, and Nell subsided. Her heart was beating uncomfortably fast and she was apprehensive, but Paul didn't seem concerned. Surely he would look different if he had bad news. At last the orders were given and Paul turned to her.

'What is it?' she asked again.

'Good news in one sense. The authorities have agreed to let Amy go provided you live at home with her.'

'But that's what I wanted in the first place! When? I must give in my notice at once.'

'Steady, that isn't all.' He was silent, then took a deep breath. 'They have other conditions. They will only permit Amy to go if she is living with her father.'

'But – she's terrified of him!'

'I know, and I tried to explain. Two of the Barnardo's people went to see him, however, and they also saw Ned and his wife. They were impressed with Florence, and she promised to keep an eye on Amy although she could not have the child to live with them. Your father must have been very much on his best behaviour for they didn't see any reason why he should not have his daughter back, provided he could find a good house to rent and you kept house for him.'

Paul shook his head when Nell began to make plans for returning to England immediately. 'There's no haste. You can't do anything for a few days. I've arranged to take you to the Barkingside home to see the authorities there next week. You must see Monsieur Derval and ask him to release you from your contract. For Edwina's sake,' he added when she began to protest. 'He's already had Gwyneth dragged away without the opportunity of explaining, and if you left too he'd never employ any of Edwina's girls again. He'd say they were all unreliable.'

Nell bit her lip. It was worse than he imagined, for she did not expect Kitty would bother with details like contracts, and she was going at the end of the week too. 'When can I go?'

'On Monday. I mean to take a few days off and stay in Paris, then I'll travel back with you. Do you have time to show me some of the sights? It's several years since I was here.'

Nell's emotions were in utter confusion. She wanted to be back home with Amy, yet it would be a wrench leaving all the friends she had made amongst the Folies girls. The prospect of living with Pa again filled her with dread, yet here was Paul proposing to spend time with her in this city which was so wonderful. Since there seemed nothing she could do about it, she was determined to make the most of her time with him.

She had to see Monsieur Derval in the morning, and he was flatteringly sorry to lose her. 'If you can ever come back,' he said in his attractively broken English, 'we shall be delighted to find a place for you. Many of our girls have moved on to perform individual acts, and I could see that as a possibility for you. But I honour you for your duty towards your little sister.'

'He's an amazing man,' she said to Paul later as they had lunch together. 'He's been here for just a few years, yet he's done so much. He's got rid of the girls who used to haunt the Promenoir. Do you know they used to have a ticket system, and if they misbehaved they didn't have their tickets renewed, and they weren't admitted without?'

Paul laughed. 'When I first came here I was a very young student. Where they have the new foyer there used to be a winter garden, and it was a regular meeting place. I found it most embarrassing! Those women were extremely hard to deter!'

'You did deter them?' she asked, laughing, and then blushed at her temerity.

'Indeed I did! They frightened me to death! But tell me, why is there a plain wall just inside where the old façade used to be?'

'That's part of the reconstruction. Monsieur Derval is determined to do it all without closing the theatre. It will be knocked down when the new entrance is built. The walls are being covered again too, and the new walls are being made somewhere else and brought in in sections. The same with the ceiling.' She chuckled. 'A couple of workmen went to sleep on the false ceiling they built, and found the ladders had been taken away! There was a tremendous panic when they were heard banging.'

'Will you miss it all very much?' he asked suddenly.

'Yes, of course, but Amy is more important. And thank you for persuading me to come. You were right, I can look back on it now with some satisfaction.'

'And pride. I thought the show was superb. Derval has made it all so much more spectacular than it was before. Does he always use that enormous staircase?'

'Yes, he says it helps to get lots of people on the stage, which is less than twenty feet deep. That's very shallow compared even to some of the small Birmingham theatres. It seemed very odd at first entering down steps.'

'I shall think of that tonight. I'd like to see Josephine Baker again. I've booked a box in the circle.'

'She's good, isn't she? I've heard she's unreliable, but she's always been so kind to all of us. Why don't you come and see her tonight after the show?' she suggested impulsively.

'I couldn't intrude.'

'Why not? Her dressing room is always crammed full of people. And animals!'

'Animals? You mean dogs? Derval uses dogs a lot, doesn't he, on stage?'

'There may be dogs, but she has cats and rabbits and mice and birds! She even brought in a boa-constrictor one day.'

Paul laughed in delight. 'Then I must meet her.'

The next few days were enchanting for Nell. If she could forget everything else she could revel in the joy of Paul's company. Instead of lying in bed in the mornings, recovering from the late-night show, she was up early and out with Paul. She had no rehearsals and they were able to spend all day together until she had to be at the theatre.

After the show she went for supper with Paul, and together they found small hidden cafés where they sampled real French cooking rather than the fare provided for the many foreigners who came to visit the Folies-Bergère. On their last day they took a train to Fontainebleau and wandered in the forest, ate in the small village of Barbizon, and arrived back at the hostel at midnight.

'Goodnight, Paul,' Nell said with a sigh. Tomorrow they'd be leaving Paris. Never again would she have such a magical time. Never again would she be with Paul in the same companionable way of the past few days.

'Nell.' He turned her towards him, and gently drew her into his arms. The kiss was sweet and gentle, but Nell felt as though she was drowning as she surrendered to her fever of desire and clung unashamedly to him. Then she drew away and without a word ran into the hostel.

'Let's get a couple of things straight!' Nell said firmly. 'You are not having any of the money Edwina pays me, I am keeping it for the rent and coal and our food. I've used my savings to buy furniture and cooking things for the kitchen and beds for me and Amy. If you want a bed and blankets and food you can buy them with your own money. You still have a job, unlike many. And you can do your own washing, too, I'm not messing about with your filthy clothes.'

'I'm yer pa, I've a right ter yer money!' he blustered.

'No, you haven't! You are only here because the people at the orphanage wouldn't let Amy come to me on my own. And it's a better house than the one you provided for us,' she added.

'Yer thinks a lot o' yersen,' he jeered. 'You an' yer fancy talkin'. It's still a dratted back-ter-back 'ovel.'

'With a little garden in front, and not opening into a smelly court.'

'Yer'll be laughin' stock o' Ladywood, mekin' yer old pa do 'is own washin',' he grumbled.

'I'd rather all Birmingham laughed at me than have to touch anything of yours!'

He changed tack. 'I want the big bedroom.'

'You can't have it. We need more space, and besides, there's a lock and a bolt on the door, which I need. I'm not having you rummaging through our things when we're out. The little one's clean and empty, and you've got a couple of hours to find some bedding before they bring Amy.'

'It ain't right, treatin' yer old pa like dirt!'

'If you'd treated us properly I wouldn't. And I'm warning you, if you lay a finger on either of us I'm going straight round to the police and I'll tell them you killed Frank.'

'An' then they'd tek Amy back ter Barkingside!'

He glared at her, then strode out of the kitchen and away along the path which led between the tiny front gardens. Nell heaved a sigh of relief. She'd known it would be difficult meeting him again, but had forced herself to lay down the law, state the conditions under which she would live in the same house. Ever since Paul had told her in Paris that she could get Amy back, she'd accepted the necessity of sacrificing her own ambitions and returning to Ladywood. It was a hateful prospect, to be once more in the same house as her father, but the only way. Fortunately for her she had the truth about Frank's death to threaten him with. Whether she ever could bring herself to betray him, for he was her father after all, she did not know, and prayed it would not come to that.

It had been so difficult leaving the Folies-Bergère. At least in the years to come she could look back on it with the satisfaction of having achieved so much. She could still dance. She would help Edwina and even dance in local theatres. She would not be able to go on tour, but in many ways that would be no loss. She hadn't enjoyed going to different lodgings every week, never getting to know a town properly before having to move on. With her solo dances she could fit into almost any troupe's routine with very little rehearsal. And for a few months, until she was twenty-one, Gwyneth was in Birmingham too. She refused to mull over the time she and Paul had had together in Paris. That was too precious for everyday thoughts. She allowed herself to dwell on the ecstasy only at night, when she was alone.

As Nell tidied the kitchen, arranging the pretty china she had bought in the Bull Ring Market on the small pine dresser, she tried hard not to think of Paul. He'd been so kind, so helpful, and she knew he would come sometimes to make sure they were all right. If she didn't see him too often perhaps the longing for him would eventually diminish. Seeing him frequently would simply keep her craving at fever pitch, and she knew there was no future for herself with him.

She sighed, and began to scrape potatoes. The stew was simmering in the big iron pot she'd found on a stall in the nearby market, and the appetizing smell pervaded the kitchen. She had insisted on looking for a decent house, one with an inside tap and an oven in the range, even though it was more rent. She'd be able to cook properly, for she could still remember the lessons her grandmother had given her. Perhaps they could afford roasting meat occasionally, and she could bake cakes, maybe even bread. Amy would not have to endure stale crusts spread with a scrape of dripping, and watery stew, her only taste of fruit or vegetables the half-rotten discards scavenged from behind the shops.

Restlessly she prowled around the tiny house, rearranging the things she had assembled during the past two weeks. Would it be better to have the beds against the other wall, facing the window? Would Amy like the flowered chintz curtains she'd made? She plumped up the feather mattress on Amy's bed again, and straightened the pillow with the lace-edged slip. Back in the kitchen she began to lay the table, using the tablecloth Marigold had given her from the hotel. She'd bought a secondhand set of four Windsor chairs, though she hoped Pa would rarely want to sit down with them. Gwyneth and Edwina might visit, come to tea on Sundays perhaps. Even Paul might come and sit down for a meal.

She thrust the thought away. It was too intimate, too painful to think of him sitting down with her, eating food she had

339

prepared. Then she heard the sound of a car drawing up at the end of the terrace. Amy was here at last!

Tom, on his way home, paused. Surely that was Nell's father just emerging from the Turk's Head? The figure staggered slightly, paused, then set off at a slow, careful pace along Ladywood Road. Odd, hadn't Ned told him his father had signed the pledge? Tom walked faster and soon caught up with the man. It was Nell's father, and as he turned to see who was beside him the beer fumes wafted into Tom's face.

'Mr Baxter. It's a long time since we met. How are you?' Tom asked, stepping out of range of the alcoholic miasma.

'Who are yer? Want summat?'

'Just to know how you are. Are you living back in Ladywood now?'

' 'Ere, I knows yer! Yer was sweet on me little Nell once.'

'I used to work at the same factory,' Tom explained. 'Tom Simmons, remember me? Where is Nell now?'

'Why d'yer want ter know?'

'I'd like to pay my respects,' he replied stiffly. What a dreadful old man. Yet he wasn't all that old, he couldn't be much more than mid-forties, but he was sodden with drink, his eyes bloodshot, and his hands unsteady.

Mr Baxter guffawed, wheezed, and clutched at Tom's arm to steady himself. 'That's a laugh!' he chortled. 'Our Nell, respectable? 'Er's a pesky whore!' he snarled, his mood suddenly changing. 'I'd like ter know what 'er got up to in them foreign parts! Or what got up 'er! 'Er's a bitch! D'you know, 'er won't even cook fer 'er old pa? Meks me do me own washin', an' never cleans me bedroom.'

'She's living with you?' Tom asked, surprised.

Mr Baxter's mood swung again and he winked at Tom. ' 'Er 'as ter, else 'er can't 'ave Amy with 'er. Them folks knows a gal needs 'er pa ter look after 'er. But Nell's spiteful, 'er teks all me wages, gives me 'alf a crown fer meself. Tom, lad, 'ow about a couple of bob? Jus' 'til Saturday?'

'I don't think you need it if you've been drinking in the Turk's Head,' Tom said curtly and turned away. He walked on, trying to shut his ears to the imprecations hurled after him. He could find out Nell's address from the factory and arrange to call round there when her father would be at work. Why hadn't she let him know she was back in Birmingham? It was the least she could have done after the help he had given her discovering what she wanted to know about her brother and father, even more after he'd offered to marry her and provide a home for Amy. Perhaps she was waiting until they could meet. Well, he'd be considerate and make that easy for her.

Gwyneth drew to a halt and waved. Nell broke into a run and scrambled into the car beside her.

'I know it's not far, but I wanted to show off my new car!' Gwyneth said, with a self-conscious laugh. 'It's a Singer. Do you like it? Somehow I didn't fancy an Austin!'

'It's divine!' Nell drawled, and they laughed.

'I've hardly had time to talk to you in the last few days since you came back to Edwina's.'

'It's been busy. But what made you buy a car? You were terrified of driving before you went away.'

'Yes, but it seemed so ridiculous only ever to drive when I was running away from people, and then discovering I could do it when I really wanted to, that I bought this little car. I'm quite used to it now, and it's the only sensible way to get to — to where I'm staying — after a day at the school.'

'We haven't had time to talk. I don't know much at all about what happened.'

'We'll treat ourselves to tea at the Kardomah and catch up with one another's news,' Gwyneth suggested.

Later, sitting over tea and cream cakes, she told Nell about her humiliating departure from Paris. 'He dragged me off, insisting on sitting in the dormitory while I packed, and even stood outside the ladies at the station while I went to the lavatory. Then back at home I was locked in all day. I tricked

Mother when he was away helping the local miners during the General Strike, and stole his car. It was the only way I could travel while the trains were mostly not running. I left the car at Oxford station, and made a fuss about getting to London. I hoped someone would remember me when he went asking. Luckily I managed to beg a lift to Longbridge, and then met Timothy driving a bus. I'm staying with him now, that's why I need a car.'

'You're staying with Timothy?'

'Don't look at me like that! I know I said all sorts of things, but he was so kind, so helpful, and I do like him a lot, really.'

'Then are you staying with him permanently?'

'Not after my birthday. I'm going back to Paris, they said they'd have me back. Besides, after Christmas Timothy is going back to South Africa.'

'Would you go with him if he asked you?'

'I won't give up dancing, not even if he asked me to marry him, and he's made it clear he won't do that.'

'I wonder if Kitty will persuade her Italian to marry her?'

'Or if he'll tire of her before she goes on to someone else! What about you, Nell? Is Amy settling down?'

'Yes, she's so thankful to be out of that orphanage. She's still scared of Pa, though. He isn't at home much, fortunately, and I make sure she isn't ever there alone. Edwina's being so helpful. Amy comes to the dance studio every day for her dinner, and after school. Edwina's starting a stage school, and her teacher for that is giving Amy elocution lessons. She's a good mimic, like me. She talks like I do now. She wants to join the acting class as well as a dancing one, and I think she could be good.'

'She's very pretty, with that gorgeous red hair. Almost as pretty as you.'

Nell laughed. 'I'm still too skinny, even though I gorge myself on cream cakes. Have another?'

Gwyneth shook her head. 'No thanks, I have to watch it.'

'Gwyneth, you know Edwina's plan is for us to work locally, doing solos and dancing together just some of the time along with whichever troupe happens to be in Birmingham? Well, I've had an idea.'

'You always did have plenty.'

'We form our own troupe, a specialist one. There are a couple of other girls, both good dancers, who can't easily leave Birmingham to tour, and probably some I don't know about who'd prefer to stay at home. We'll call it The Nell Gwyn Girls.'

'Nell Gwyn?' Gwyneth chuckled. 'I like that. And we wear orange costumes? I don't think strings of oranges round our waists would be quite the same as Josephine Baker's bananas, though.'

'And it would be expensive throwing them out into the audience!' Nell signalled to the waitress. 'Let's go and talk about it to Edwina.'

By September The Nell Gwyn Girls was established, and performing in many local theatres.

'I know it's only for a couple of months, until I go back to Paris,' Gwyneth said. 'You can replace me afterwards, and who knows, one day I might tire of the Folies and we could start touring with it, our own act.'

During the day both Nell and Gwyneth trained dancers at Edwina's new studio on the Hagley Road. Edwina had moved to a smaller house nearby. Amy had joined a dancing class and was already doing small solo parts in the charity shows which were now an established part of Edwina's programme.

Amy had settled down in the new house, and after the first few weeks, when she had trembled every time she saw her father, she began to ignore him. He wasn't often at home, for which Nell was thankful. She suspected he had a woman somewhere, but so long as he didn't bother them she didn't care. When she was dancing in the evenings Amy slept either at Edwina's or with her best school friend, Phyllis, who lived a few doors away and also came to Amy's dancing classes. Nell told herself that it was all working out in a very satisfactory way. She wished she could believe herself.

She began to doubt whenever she saw Paul. He was always friendly, always asked how Amy was, offered to help if she needed him, but the former warmth which she had unconsciously come to depend on was missing. It was even missing, she felt, when he drove them out occasionally on Sunday afternoons.

He'd suggested it one day when they met outside Edwina's school.

'I'd love to go to Sutton Park,' Amy exclaimed. 'Nell's told me a lot, but I haven't been for years and I can't remember much about it. Ma took us once, when you lived with Gran, Nell, but I'd only just started school and I can't remember much, just lots of green grass and trees.'

'If it's still warm enough we'll spend all day there on Sunday. I'll bring a picnic,' he suggested, and Nell couldn't bring herself to refuse. She'd shown them the cottage where she'd spent such a happy childhood, then they walked through the Park, admiring the pools and finding a shady spot under the trees near Bracebridge Pool for their picnic. Afterwards Nell pulled the patch-box out of her pocket and showed it to Amy.

'Gramps gave me this,' she explained softly. 'I never let anyone at home know, because I was sure Pa would take it and sell it. Gramps's grandfather, our Great-great-grandfather Perry, helped to make it. They lived in Wednesbury which is famous for them. He was an enameller.'

Amy exclaimed in delight, and took the tiny box carefully. 'Look, it opens, and there's a mirror inside the lid,' she said, showing it to Paul. 'Oh, there's a message inside.' She twisted the box round to catch the light, and slowly read out the tiny inscription. 'It says "To my true love Nell". Nell, it can't mean you!'

Nell laughed. 'No, it was made about a hundred and forty years ago. He was married to an Eleanor and made it specially for her when they married, and as my name is really Eleanor even though I've always been called Nell too, Gramps thought it would be appropriate for me to have it. I've always thought of it as my lucky box. When I lost it everything went wrong, and then it was sent to me in Paris, and soon afterwards they said you could leave Barkingside.'

Reverently Amy closed the box and handed it back to Nell. 'Is it valuable?'

'Yes, I think so, but I would never sell it.'

'Tell me more about when you lived here.'

'There's so much! During the war there were soldiers in a big camp in the Park. We used to go picking blackberries in the fields, and Gran always seemed to be making jam or preserving the vegetables Gramps grew in the garden. She kept chickens and I used to collect the eggs. Gramps had a pig too, but I hated it when the poor thing was killed, it seemed like eating a friend.'

'And you went to school here. Was that different from in Ladywood?'

'I suppose so. We used to go for walks, looking at flowers and grasses and things. If the pools froze over in winter we skated, and we went swimming in summer in Keeper's Pool. The Park is very old. That pool's named after a man called John Holte who used to be King Henry VI's Keeper of Sutton Park.'

'I remember you ran away after Pa fetched you home. You ran to your schoolteacher. I can't imagine running away to Miss Porter!'

Nell laughed. 'My teacher was the only person I knew here who I thought would help me after Gran died. I'd been back in Birmingham for a year or so, and felt I couldn't bear it any longer. It was a difficult time. There had been a terrible thunderstorm and the dam of Longmoor Pool had burst; it overflowed into the other pools and all the shops in the Parade were flooded. But she couldn't very well hide me when Pa came. I had to come back.'

Amy nodded. 'I'm glad you did, Nell,' she said shyly, taking her sister's hand. 'You won't ever leave me, will you?'

Involuntarily Nell's glance flew to Paul's face. He looked cold, his lips compressed into a straight, narrow line. 'No, Amy,' she said gently. 'I won't ever leave you again.'

Chapter Twenty-Five

It was late on Friday night when Tom left his office, carefully locking the door. His father had gone long ago. It was already dark, cold for late October, and he was tired. The journey from his new house was more than he'd expected, crowded on to the buses in the morning. He didn't care to take his car into the city for fear it would be damaged. To make matters worse he had to do his own cooking when he got back at night. A woman came in to clean and do his washing, but she wouldn't stay long enough to cook a meal, though she did sometimes prepare a stew or a pie he could heat up on his new gas cooker. It was a blessing he didn't have to wait for an old-fashioned range to be lit and get hot. The sooner he could persuade Nell to marry him the better.

Thinking of Nell, he wasn't especially surprised to see Mr Baxter hovering on the doorstep of the office building. He'd had the impression the man had been loitering there once or twice lately.

'Tom Simmons? I wants a word with you.'

'Mr Baxter? What is it?'

Mr Baxter shuffled his feet. 'I'm desperate,' he said, lowering his gaze. His first aggressive words seemed to have abashed him. 'Nell, 'er won't give me any spendin' money. 'Er won't even buy me food.'

'Why should Nell support you? You have a job and earn your

own money. I don't suppose Nell has much left over by the time she's paid the rent and bought things for herself and Amy.'

'You don't understand! I've been given the push! Old Forster med up lies an' chucked me out. 'E said I weren't doin' me job proper. Bleedin' liar!'

'I'm not giving you money to spend in the Turk's Head!' Tom said indignantly. 'Nell pays your rent and you've got four sons left. Go to them for help.'

'But you wants ter wed our Nell, don't yer? I could 'elp yer.'

Tom eyed him suspiciously. He couldn't imagine how the old reprobate might have any influence over Nell, but it was becoming imperative that he should have a wife, and he didn't want anyone but Nell. He wasn't making a great deal of progress himself, for he was hardly ever able to see her. It might be worth at least considering what Mr Baxter had in view.

'How?' he demanded brusquely.

Mr Baxter's eyes took on a crafty expression. 'It'll cost yer. Ten bob,' he added hurriedly.

Tom hesitated. The thought crossed his mind that marriage to Nell would mean being repeatedly approached by Mr Baxter for money. He wouldn't let it. Once they were safely married he'd make sure the wretched man never came near them again. He'd do it now, except that he would need Mr Baxter's permission to marry Nell. He had to put up with him in the meantime. Sighing, he reached into his pocket.

'Half a crown.'

'Ten bob!'

They compromised at five. Tom handed over two half-crowns and in return was told, with many winks and salacious nods, to present himself at their home on Sunday afternoon.

'Then it'll be up ter you, if you'm man enough!'

'Nell, I want you to marry me! I'm sorry for what happened before, I was drunk, a fool, and I wanted you so much. I'm off to the States in a couple of weeks, and I want you to come with me as my wife'

'Andrew, I can't. I have to stay with Amy. And anyway, I don't want to marry you. It's got nothing to do with — what you did. If nothing had happened I still wouldn't want to marry you.'

'Are you still hankering after Paul Mandeville? He'll never marry a dancer, Nell, he's far too conscious of his position in society. Not like me, I'm a strolling player and we'd suit each other in every way. You could try for the Ziegfeld Follies, they'd be pleased to have you with your experience in Paris. Or you could start singing with me, we could develop our own act.'

'No, Andrew. I can't desert Amy.'

'Bring her too. See how much I want you, Nell?'

She shook her head. 'I'm sorry, it's impossible, and it wouldn't work anyway. Oh yes, you're charming and handsome, but you're not what I want. I don't want to get married.'

'Come without! I thought it was your sense of decorum that would insist on marriage, but I'd be happy either way.'

'I wish you luck in America, Andrew, and one day I'd like to see it myself. But it's no good.'

He smiled, and before she could move away, bent forward and kissed her on the lips.

'Marriage is in the air,' he said lightly. 'But it seems as though I'm not to be lucky. I had a letter from Kitty yesterday, she married her prince a week ago. If you change your mind, write and tell me. Meggy will have my address. There won't ever be another girl like you, Nell.'

'I can't 'elp gettin' sack!' Pa grumbled.

'Can't you? You could at least try and find another job instead of sitting round moaning all the time, except when you can cadge drinks. You've been in the pub this morning, so you've had some money to spend. What happened to your signing the pledge?' Nell asked, exasperated. She brushed her hair back from off her forehead and sat back on her heels. Scrubbing the tiled kitchen floor was not her favourite job, but it was worse when Pa sat around moaning about his own lot.

'That were just ter keep that dratted Florence 'appy. 'Er wouldn't 'a' give me 'ouseroom if I 'adn't.'

'Sensible Florence! I wish I could do the same!' She moved the bucket. 'At least keep out of my way while I wash the floor. It isn't easy having it all to do on Sundays.'

'Nell, luv, you was allus the best. I knows I didn't allus treat yer right, but now we'm on our own, let bygones be bygones, eh?'

'It's too late. I can't forgive you the things you did. Not just the beatings you gave me, and the others, and the way you terrified poor Amy so that she ran away. It was how you treated Ma. I suppose she loved you once, but I don't know how she could have done unless you were very different when you were young.'

'We'm all different when we'm young. Yer ma were real lovin', and 'er were as pretty as you am now. Then 'er changed, 'ad no time fer me.'

'Can you wonder at it, with sixteen children to look after?' Nell exclaimed. She still trembled with fury whenever she thought of the treatment he'd subjected them to.

He grew defensive. ''Tweren't my doin'! We teks the kids the good Lord sends.'

'And try to provide for them! Which you didn't, most of the time. You spent your money on drink and whores like Janie Pritchard. If you hadn't been with her the night of the fire you might have been able to save them.'

''Ow d'you know where I was?'

'Everybody knew. You hadn't been near home that night.'

'Yes I 'ad! I come 'ome when they was all abed.'

'You did? You never said! Then why didn't you smell the gas? It must have been leaking for hours before the explosion.'

'It weren't leaking when I was there, 'cause I turned it on. Was lookin' fer more matches. Used me last one ter see me way across room. Fire was almost out. It were perishin' cold, and that's why I went out again, find me a bit o' comfort!'

A dreadful suspicion crossed Nell's mind. 'Did you find them? The matches?' she demanded.

'Yes, course I did. They was on table.'

'Did you light the mantle?'

'Must 'a' done.'

'Did you turn it out when you went?'

''Ow should I know? Ain't yer gonna finish that floor? Young Tom'll be 'ere soon.'

'Tom? What do you mean?'

'I told 'im ter come this afternoon. Nell, I mayn't 'ave been a good pa sometimes, but now I'm gonna insist yer does what's right. Fer yer own good, mind. An' poor little Amy's. Tom's a good lad, an' 'e's gorra good position. An' 'e's just bought a big new 'ouse out Bearwood way. Plenty o' room, I went ter look at it. 'E'd look after all on us. So yer's ter say yer'll wed 'im when 'e asks.'

Nell rose slowly to her feet. She was tempted to tip the bucket of dirty water all over him. Only the thought that she'd then have to mop it all up again stopped her.

'Pa, listen to me! I will not marry Tom Simmons! I don't even like him, let alone love him. And I certainly won't marry him just to provide you with a nice comfortable home! I can keep myself and Amy better than you ever did, but if you don't get a job you'll have to go and find somewhere else to live! I mean it!'

'Yer can't throw me out, me gal! If yer tried it the Barnardo's folk 'ud tek Amy back!'

'I don't think so. Not when they heard what you've just told me. About leaving the gas on the night of the fire. And being so drunk you forgot to light it before going off to visit your trollop! It was you killed Ma and all the little ones! As well as Frank! I had to have you here when they came and inspected us, to see whether we were fit to look after Amy, but they won't take her back now. I don't need you any more. You can stay because you're my father, but only as long as you behave yourself!'

*

Kitty glared out of the window at the wonderful view of mountains and forest, the sea glinting silver in the far distance. Her gaze swung to the foreground, where old Jacques was opening the massive iron gates to let her husband's Fiat out of the high-walled compound in which the villa was set. At least she wouldn't have to endure his increasingly ineffective love-making for a while, nor his complaints that respectability seemed to have stifled her flair for inventive provocativeness. She was tired of doing all the work, and saw no point now she was the *principessa*.

She turned back to the elegant writing table, and the partly written letter. Although he insisted on reading them first, he didn't forbid her to write letters.

It's a magnificent view, and we are miles from the nearest town. Wonderful solitude! We don't go out much, or entertain as yet. Cesare insists we are still on our honeymoon. He says that when we go to Rome later in the winter I will be prostrate from meeting his family and the constant round of pleasure. He is very protective of me, won't permit me to lift a hand for myself, and showers gifts of clothes and jewels on me.

She paused. Of late she'd had suspicions that he never really intended to introduce her to his family. It was true that he provided her with magnificent jewels, but he made it plain they were heirlooms to be passed on in time to the next prince. And when she could never show them off to anyone there wasn't much point in having them, or the gowns. She would have preferred to go shopping to choose her own clothes, rather than have a dozen dresses sent up from Nice every month. In fact if she didn't soon escape from this luxurious prison, where the only people to talk to were Jacques and his equally ancient wife Marietta, she would go stark, raving mad.

Italian husbands are deliciously jealous, Nell dear. It is so comforting to feel cherished, to have no decisions to make other than what to wear or eat. Give my fond wishes to everyone, and say I long for the time when they can come and visit me, either here or in one of our Italian homes, though I have yet to see them!

Tom was furious. The old rogue, he'd deliberately caused him to come all this way, and Nell wasn't here. Neither was her father. He hammered on the door again until a neighbour put his head out of his own door.

'Give over, mate! Can't us 'ave a kip Sunday afternoons?'

'Where are they? I was expected. Has anything happened to them?' Tom asked quickly.

The man shrugged. 'Saw little gal with 'er friend, young Phyllis. They was goin' off somewhere, hour or more ago. 'Aven't seen t'others, but there was a right lot o' shoutin' ten minutes since, both on 'em yellin' fit ter bust!'

Tom trampled on the herbs Nell had planted in the small front garden in his frantic eagerness to get to the window. He peered through. Everything looked normal, the table had been cleared after dinner, the fire in the grate was banked down, and the chairs were set neatly under the table. His shoulders drooped. They must have gone out after all. Mr Baxter had been having him on. If Nell had known he was coming she'd have waited. The shouting was probably normal; he'd heard the old man had a vicious temper when he was drunk, and if he had to live with the old devil he'd shout too, so he could hardly blame Nell for unladylike behaviour.

He turned away. He'd go and visit one or two friends in the neighbourhood, perhaps be invited to tea, and come back later on when someone would be at home.

It had been a splendid party. Many of the former dancers, girls who had been in the first troupes but who had now married, came, bringing their husbands. Gwyneth had been toasted for her birthday, and her future at the Folies-Bergère.

'It doesn't seem real,' she said to Edwina and Nell as they

353

cleared away the glasses afterwards. 'It's not my birthday until tomorrow, I hope it won't be bad luck celebrating early.'

'We had to have it today if you're going to Paris tomorrow,' Edwina said briskly.

Gwyneth smiled. 'I don't mean to be ungrateful, Edwina, I've enjoyed being back here. But the Folies-Bergère is so special!'

'And you can't wait to get back. I understand. Now who can that be at the door?' Edwina went to open it and almost immediately came back, her face white. 'Gwyneth, it's your father, he says.'

'You dare doubt my word? What sort of vile establishment do I find you in? Though I suppose as you've lied to me since May I would expect you to look on all men as corrupt. I came here,' he ranted, looming over Edwina, 'and you swore to me my daughter had not been here! I went all the way to Paris again, and spent weeks searching for her in London. You were guilty of deception, and fraud, and unlawfully depriving me of my daughter! I have a good mind to lay charges against you!'

'It wouldn't do you the slightest bit of good, my man.'

They all swung round at this intervention, in Timothy's most condescending, upper-class drawl.

Gwyneth spoke first. 'I thought you'd gone home?'

'I came back, fortunately. The door was on the latch so I let myself in. So this deplorable specimen is your father? You may as well know now, Mr Davis, that Gwyneth has been with me since she escaped your clutches.'

'But — that can't be true! A friend — from Cardiff — was in Birmingham and saw her at the theatre! Dancing! Almost naked!'

'My girls are respectably dressed!' Edwina said indignantly.

'Gwyneth has been staying at my house, respectably chaperoned by my housekeeper and her family, who will swear to that, because she was terrified of what you might do if you found her unprotected. What do you think a court would say to a minister who beat and imprisoned his own daughter and took a malicious delight in starving her?'

'I didn't beat her, or starve her! And a man has the right to control his daughter and punish her if she's defiant and rebellious!'

'It will be your word against ours.' He let the threat hang in the air, then Gwyneth spoke.

She looked at Mr Davis, her expression grim. 'You're too late, Father. I'm free of you tomorrow. You have no power over me then. I can go to Paris without your permission, and I intend to do so.'

'Or you can get married.'

Gwyneth looked at Timothy and opened her mouth, but no words came. He gave her a brief smile and took Mr Davis by the arm.

'I think you should go,' he suggested gently but inexorably, steering the minister to the door. 'I'll ask Gwyneth to write to her mother. And don't worry, I'll look after her.'

When he came back into the big dance studio where the party had been he found Gwyneth standing where he had left her. Nell and Edwina had vanished, and he smiled at their tactfulness.

'Gwyneth, darling, I couldn't leave you. I know we agreed you would stay with Edwina tonight, ready for the train tomorrow, but I couldn't go home without you. Don't leave me. Come with me to South Africa.'

Slowly Gwyneth shook her head. 'I'm very fond of you, Timothy, but I can't.'

'Don't you understand? I love you! These past few months I've seen what it could be like if you were always with me, and I thought you loved me too!'

She sighed. 'Yes, I think I do –'

'Then you'll come?'

'– but I can't give up the dancing.'

'Darling, you can dance, start your own dancing school out there, I'm sure there's a place for it. All I want is for you to be with me.'

She shook her head. 'I had so little time at the Folies-Bergère, which was so wonderful. When I was a child, and dreamed of being a dancer, I never thought I could be anything but a moderately good one. To actually be there, on that stage, a part of the thrill of performing with the best chorus in the world, one of them, one of a team – it's impossible to describe! I won't give that up just to become another dancing teacher in some country far away, one I might not even like.'

'Not even to be with me?'

'With you?' she asked, suddenly angry. 'You've made it very plain how it would be, me hidden away in a discreet little love nest, not offending your uncle and his friends! Well, Timothy, it's been fun while it lasted, and I've been grateful for the place to stay, but –'

'Be quiet! I want to marry you, Gwyneth! I'm not suggesting anything else!'

'Marry? But – you always said –'

'What I always said is beside the point! It isn't what I'm saying now. Now I know I can't do without you, and be damned to what my family and friends will say! I want you, and I want you as my wife.'

For a long moment Gwyneth looked at him, neither of them moving, then he stepped forward, arms outstretched. Suddenly she moved, warding him off.

'No, Timothy. I'm sorry, truly sorry. I think I love you too, but I have to dance. Dancing is my life. It's what I must do.'

Nell and Amy walked home, Amy chattering excitedly about her first grown-up party, and what people had said to her. Nell didn't hear. She had been so shocked at Gwyneth's devastated face when finally Timothy had gone.

'I wanted to, but I couldn't,' Gwyneth had sobbed to them later, and after a while Edwina had taken her upstairs.

'I'll put her to bed, Nell. Amy's in the kitchen with Patsy, you'd best get her home.'

'I'll come in the morning before she leaves. If she's fit to go.'

'I think I'll telephone Paul. She's so distraught, she needs something to calm her.'

It was a moment before Nell became aware of someone else at her side. Then Tom spoke.

'It was good of Gwyneth to ask me to her party,' he said stiffly. 'I've been trying to speak to you for weeks, Nell, but you are always so busy.'

'Have you been hanging around outside?' she asked, astonished.

'I wasn't hanging around, as you put it!' He was indignant. 'I wanted to offer to walk you home, but first that older man stormed in, then Timothy, so I didn't want to interrupt.'

'It was kind of you,' she tried to mollify him, 'but we really are just round the corner. The new house is much closer to the Hagley Road, only a few minutes' walk along Francis Road and I'm almost home.'

'And most of the way along Friston Street, too.'

'Tell me about your work,' she said hastily. 'What's been happening since the General Strike?'

The subject lasted all the way to her door. 'The miners didn't appreciate the sacrifices all the rest of the workers made, they wouldn't agree to end the strike on the best terms we could get for them. At the TUC Conference in Bournemouth in September there was such a lot of disagreement. I don't think such a concerted action will ever happen again, even though it was so well organized. The miners have been drifting back to work, especially here in the Midlands, in Warwickshire and Cannock Chase, though the rest of them are still discussing terms.'

'Where's Amy?' Nell asked suddenly. As soon as Tom had joined them she had skipped ahead. 'Oh, the door's open, she must be inside. Thank you for walking home with me, Tom. It was kind of you. But it's late, long past Amy's bedtime, and she has to be up for school tomorrow. You'll have to be at work too.'

He began to speak again, but she smiled and firmly shut the door, leaving him outside.

*

Amy ran ahead. Tom was a pompous old bore and she hoped Nell wouldn't marry him. As she started along the path between the small front gardens she realized their light was on. Pa was home early. Then she recollected that they were much later than usual, it must be nearly midnight. The pubs would have closed long since.

She pushed open the door and went into the kitchen. He wasn't there, but she could hear sounds above. Then she frowned. Those sounds were coming from their bedroom, not his. How could he have got in? Nell always locked the door and took the key with her. If Pa was messing about with their things she'd hate him worse than she did now!

She crept cautiously up the stairs, her eyes widening as she saw their door sagging open. It looked as though Pa had taken an axe to it, breaking it near the lock. Inside he was bending over the chest of drawers, and then he straightened, uttering a grunt of satisfaction. He held something up which gleamed and shone, reflecting the light and sending back sparks of brilliant colour.

'That's Nell's box!' Amy shouted, forgetting her fear of him as she leapt forward, snatching at his hand. 'You were stealing it!' she accused him as she seized the patch-box, which in his surprise he let go.

'Give it 'ere!' he ordered, but Amy backed away, and then suddenly turned and hurled herself down the stairs. She heard his heavy footsteps lumbering after her and panic took over. She didn't even notice Nell standing by the hooks on the wall, her arms raised as she hung up her coat and hat. Clutching the patch-box to her Amy fled through the door and along the path, Pa yelling and running after her.

'Amy! Pa! What is it?' Nell demanded, and as neither of them took any notice grabbed her coat. She was dragging it back on as she ran along the path after them, just in time to see Amy, with Pa in hot pursuit, turn the corner into a deserted Ledham Street.

Amy knew only that she had to get away. He was gaining on

her. She was so tired, it was late, but she forced her legs to carry her along Ledham Street, round the corner, and across another road. Then she saw they were approaching the canal, and on the wharf there would be places to hide, to dodge him while she got her breath back and tried to think. She darted down an alley but he was close behind her and followed. She could hear him panting, swearing and calling her name. If he caught her he'd kill her!

He almost grabbed her, but she dodged and dived for the shelter of some barrels. They were right on the edge of the wharf and she managed to squeeze into a small space between two piles. Then, her heart beating painfully, she realized she was trapped. He had only to drag the barrels aside and he could get at her.

Nell saved her breath for running. She hadn't known Pa could run so fast, and she was terrified he would catch Amy. She had no idea why he was chasing the child, but the memory of what had happened the last time he'd driven her in panic from the house kept her running. The streets were deserted, there was no one to call to for help. Suddenly she realized they had vanished and she stopped, listening. She heard his shouts and after a moment discerned they came from an alley to the side. Dimly she recalled it led down to the canal wharf, and she searched wildly for the narrow opening. Here it was! She sped along it, and as she came out into the open saw her father heaving at a pile of barrels, swearing viciously as he struggled with them.

'Pa! Let Amy be!'

He swung round, startled, and the barrel he'd been tugging at slipped. Slowly it began to fall, and as Nell screamed a warning her father saw it and tried to move aside. He staggered as his foot caught on a rope stretched taut between two posts, and the barrel caught him full in the chest, and both fell with one mighty splash into the murky water several feet beneath.

Fearful of what she might see, Nell peered over the side. Pa had vanished. The barrel, heavy with its load, had sunk, and it appeared he had been taken with it. She watched for what seemed like hours, but he didn't come to the surface. There was nothing she could do.

'Amy,' she called softly. 'You can come out now. He's gone, it's safe.'

'He was stealing your patch-box!' Amy cried as she scrambled out from her hiding place and Nell turned to clasp her sister to her. 'Where's Pa gone?' she asked warily.

'He fell in, but he's vanished. I think it's too late. He may have been trapped by something under the water. There's nothing we can do,' she said quietly. 'Let's go home, Amy.'

Chapter Twenty-Six

Nᴇʟʟ sat huddled beside the fire all night. She'd piled on coal, and it roared away, but still she shivered. Amy, hysterical, had finally agreed to sleep in front of the fire on the mattress Nell brought downstairs. She couldn't bear to go back into the room where she'd last seen Pa.

'He – he was stealing your patch-box, your lucky box!' she sobbed as Nell half carried her home. 'Look, I got it from him,' she said, handing it to Nell.

Nell sat in the firelight, looking at the bright enamel, and thought about the man who had crafted such fine work. It had been her talisman, but could she bear to own something which had indirectly brought about the death of her father?

'I didn't love him,' she whispered to herself, but that made it worse. If she had felt anything but disgust and contempt for him she might have been able to mourn. As it was she knew only an enormous relief, as if a burden had been lifted. It had, of course. Now he could no longer terrorize Amy. It was his greed which had caused his death. Yet there was guilt too, that she didn't feel more sorrow. 'I ought to tell Ned,' she said wearily, but on the thought her head drooped, and the next thing she knew she was lying half on the mattress, cold and stiff, while someone hammered on the door.

Nell rubbed her eyes as she struggled to her feet. 'I'm coming,' she called, and went to open the door.

Paul stood outside, and at the sight of her he frowned. 'You look dreadful,' he said, stepping into the kitchen. 'And what's this? Why is Amy sleeping down here? Is she ill? Nell, what's happened?'

Nell heaved a shuddering sigh. 'Pa's dead,' she said baldly. 'He – he fell into the canal last night.'

Paul's eyes widened, then he stepped towards her and she relaxed when he drew her into the comfort of his embrace. He stood quietly as, shaking and sobbing, she told him all that had happened. After a while he sat down in the only comfortable chair the room possessed, and pulled Nell on to his lap, cradling her to him.

'Hush, darling, it wasn't your fault. There was nothing you could have done.'

'I should have tried to help. I should have fetched someone. Maybe if I'd not been so stupid they could have saved him.'

'I doubt it, Nell. People drown quickly, and you couldn't see him. He might have been knocked unconscious as he fell, or been caught on something underneath the water. Were there boats there?'

'I think so, a barge a little way up the wharf.'

'Then there would probably have been ropes under the water. Nell, he wouldn't have suffered a great deal. It would have been too late by the time you could have fetched help.'

'But I shouldn't have just left him there, alone, and come back here as though nothing had happened!'

'You had Amy to care for. How is she?'

'She cried a lot, then went to sleep. But – why are you here, Paul?'

Suddenly realizing she was sitting on his lap with his arms about her, Nell blushed and scrambled off.

'You didn't come to see Gwyneth off at the station,' he said. 'Edwina thought you might have overslept after last night, but I thought that would be unlikely, so I came to check.'

'Gwyneth has gone! And I wasn't there to say goodbye!'

'She said to tell you she'd write when she got there, and you were to go and see them all as soon as you could. Now I think you had better wake Amy — is she down here because she is too frightened to be left alone? You ought to make her eat some breakfast. And pack a few clothes. I mean to take you both to stay for a while with Edwina.'

'Amy wouldn't sleep upstairs. Pa broke down the door of our room. But can Edwina manage?'

'Of course, and if she can't I'll take you to Marigold.'

'No, Marigold has already been so good to me, I can't impose. Besides, she's having another baby soon.'

'Go and pack the clothes first. Then we can leave without Amy having to go upstairs. It will be easier for her not to have to go back into that room and be reminded.'

Ned and Florence stood to one side of the grave, with Nell's other brothers. She faced them, trying not to think of that other funeral, when Ma and the children had been buried. Edwina was beside her, and behind them Tom and Paul. Amy, suffering from shock, had developed a severe cold and was being cared for at Edwina's house by Patsy.

As the ceremony ended Nell turned away, and found Tom in front of her.

'Nell, I must have a word with you,' he said urgently, taking her arm.

'Please, Tom, not now,' she replied wearily, and smiled thankfully at Edwina as the latter stepped forward.

'Tom, Nell has to go straight back to bed. Come and see her tomorrow if she feels well enough.'

Tom looked as though he wanted to argue, but Paul was there too and between them he and Edwina shepherded Nell away. Ned came across to him.

'Our Nell's too stuck up fer likes of us now,' he said resentfully. ' 'Er won't even come back ter tek a cuppa tea with us. Will yer come, Tom? Florence got in a nice bit of ham, and a pork pie.'

Tom wanted to follow Nell, but while she had her guardians

about her he knew there was no chance of speaking to her. He nodded at Ned, and they began the long walk towards the latter's house behind New Street Station. Florence bustled about when they got there, boiling kettles and setting out daintily cut sandwiches on doily-covered plates.

'Nell Baxter's too good fer us, Tom,' she said with a sniff. 'She never once came here, heven when her pa was livin' wi' us. Hit's not as if we live in the sort o' squalor she did when her was a kid. Hi've got some nice stuff, I have, me ma and me aunties saw I had a proper trusso when I married Ned. Do yer like me cups and saucers? A full dozen, Hi've got. And plates ter match, and a sandwich plate too. Don't see many o' them in Ladywood!'

Tom hastily admired the cups and saucers, took a sandwich which was too small to make two bites, and wondered if he was supposed to take more. But Florence had replaced the plate on the table, too far away for him to reach.

'There were summat funny 'bout Pa's death, I say!' Danny said belligerently. ' 'E'd bin in water hours afore they found 'im. Must 'ave fell in durin' night.'

'They said he fell in 'cause he was drunk,' Ned put in, 'but he'd signed the pledge, he wouldn't 'ave — have gone back on that. Besides, why should he 'ave been down on wharf? 'E'd no call ter go there any time, let alone at night.'

Sam sniggered. 'I can think of a good enough reason,' he muttered, but Ned swiftly told him to shut his dirty mouth in front of ladies.

'But — he was at home that night. I saw him,' Tom exclaimed.

'You did? 'Ow?' Danny demanded.

'I walked Nell home. We'd been to a birthday party for one of her friends, one of the dancers, and it was late. Your father was already home, though . . .' He stopped, frowning.

'What?' Ned asked. 'If yer knows summat, yer ought ter tell us, Tom.'

'I'm not sure. I was walking away and there was a noise. When I turned round I was sure I saw Amy running along the

364

street, with a man running after her. It must have been your pa. Then Nell came out too. At least, I thought it was Nell, but I wasn't really sure until later. I went back to the house, but the door wasn't bolted and no one was there. I called up the stairs, but no one came. I couldn't follow them, I hadn't seen which way they went. But I hung around a bit, and some time afterwards Nell and Amy came back, and Nell bolted the door. I've only just thought of it, but she must have known her father wouldn't be coming back.'

Ned eyed him thoughtfully. 'I'm gonna 'ave a word with our Nell. Tom, like some more tea? An' what about a sensible piece of pork pie, instead of these bits o' birdfood?'

Tom paced up and down his small parlour. Ned had said he believed him, though he'd made it plain he felt sure Tom knew more than he'd told them.

'We know yer'd want ter protect Nell,' he'd said with what was almost a leer. The others had left and Florence had gone to bed. 'Yer wouldn't split on 'er, would yer? If yer just happened ter see 'er by the canal? It'd be easy ter push an old man in, especially if 'e'd had a few drinks when 'e weren't used to it. And it's only her word 'e never come ter surface. Wouldn't a proper daughter 'ave gone fer help? Pa could swim, and though the water was low and probably 'e couldn't 'ave climbed up by himself, he could 'ave been saved if she'd fetched help.'

'Nell wouldn't have deliberately left him to die.' Tom was still shocked at the very idea.

Ned had winked at him. 'Yer's sweet on 'er, ain't yer? And yer can't give evidence against yer wife.'

He was making so little progress with Nell. Even before this dreadful thing had happened, she'd had no time for him. Now he'd be expected to treat her carefully for months. But Ned had shown him how he might persuade her to agree to marry him. Would it work? Suddenly Tom made up his mind. He would at least attempt it, put his luck to the test.

*

'I'll be fine, I can teach this week, Edwina,' Nell insisted. 'And we can't give performances until we've reorganized The Nell Gwyn troupe. We said we'd give that a break after Gwyneth left, start again after Christmas.'

'As you wish. But don't you need time to look for a new house? If you really won't come and share this one.'

'Edwina, it's marvellous of you to offer, and it would make life much easier, but I'm afraid to accept. If I did, I might never want to go back to my own place, and you'd get fed up with us in the end.'

'You know you can stay for as long as necessary, and come back whenever you wish.'

'You're a good friend. We can't go back to that house, and now perhaps I can afford a through house with a garden. There are plenty for rent. I've been thinking I could offer lodgings to some of the dancers if I had somewhere bigger. It would do Amy good to be with other girls, especially now she's as mad on dancing as I am! I'll go and look this afternoon.'

None of the houses she saw were suitable, and she was making her way rather dispiritedly down the Ladywood Road when Ned caught up with her. 'Nell, we've got to talk.'

She looked at him and smiled faintly. 'Hello, Ned. How are you? And Florence?'

'As well as can be expected. Look, let's go in here and have a cuppa tea.'

He led the way into a small café, and sat silently until the tea was brought and Nell had poured two cups. Then he looked worriedly at her. 'Tom knows summat,' he said abruptly.

'Tom? Knows what? What do you mean, Ned?'

'Look, Nell, I'm not blamin' yer fer anythin', I know well enough Pa were no saint. Both you and Amy 'ad a lot ter put up with.'

'Why should I be blamed for — what are you saying, Ned?'

'Tom. Tom Simmons. 'E saw yer, the night Pa — fell in canal. *If* 'e fell in, and from what Tom said 'e seemed ter think there was summat fishy goin' on.'

'Pa fell in when he was chasing Amy! I told you exactly how it happened, the next day.'

'Yes, I know what yer said, but Tom, he could say different. It stands ter reason, Nell, summat odd were goin' on, the three on yer chasin' out the 'ouse — house like that at midnight.'

'Tom wasn't there! He'd left us before we went in.'

'It didn't take yer long ter come out again, an' Friston Street's long and straight, he'd 'ave seen yer all right.'

'But — even if he followed us, he'd have seen nothing apart from what I've said.'

'Perhaps yer thinks yer protectin' young Amy? If Tom said she pushed Pa, don't yer think they'd believe 'im? After all, 'e's a very respected trade-union official.'

'He couldn't say that! It would be lies!'

'Oh, I wouldn't suggest he'd tell a deliberate untruth, but it were dark. Lots o' shadows. Perhaps 'e didn't see properly?'

Nell stood up abruptly. 'Go and take your lies somewhere else, Ned! Neither Amy nor I pushed Pa, and no one can make us say we did!'

It was a Sunday morning, a few weeks later, and Nell still hadn't found anywhere to live. Amy had departed to visit her friend Phyllis for the day, while Nell and Edwina relaxed over cups of coffee and desultorily talked about plans for the new year. They heard the doorbell ring, and a moment later Patsy came in to announce there was someone to see Nell.

'It's that Mr Simmons,' she said, and Edwina hastily hid a smile at her tone. Tom tended to patronize Patsy, and the girl resented it bitterly.

'I'll see him in the office,' Nell said quickly. She hadn't seen Tom for some weeks, not in fact since her father's funeral, and she did not wish to encourage him. The office would be businesslike and he would not have to be invited to share their coffee.

'I'll go along to the studio, I have to fetch those sketches for the new costumes,' Edwina said as Nell rose. 'It's a nuisance I forgot them last night, but I'll be back in a few minutes if you want a diversion.'

Nell grinned at her. 'I imagine I'll be able to get rid of him quite quickly.'

The office was a small room to the side of the front door. Edwina preferred to keep her papers at home rather than at the studio, since it was easier to work here in the evenings. There were, however, a pair of easy chairs set beside a small table inside the large bay. When Nell went in Tom was sitting in one of these, and rather to her surprise did not offer to rise. She decided to be as formal as possible and sat in the upright chair behind the desk.

'Tom, good morning.'

'Nell, my dear, I hope you are recovered by now?'

'Yes, thank you. It has been several weeks.'

'Indeed, I know that full well. It has been a long time, but I have curbed my impatience. I decided it was only right to allow you to get over your tragedy before renewing my proposal.'

Nell began to feel angry at his persistence. She did wish he would accept her refusal. 'Tom,' she began, but he raised his hand to silence her.

'Don't be hasty, my dear. Things have changed. As you know, I have been very patient, I have loved you for a long time, and not many men would have permitted their future wives to behave as you have done –'

'In the first place, I am not your "future wife", and in the second, you have no right either to control or criticize my behaviour!' Nell broke in furiously, her eyes flashing. 'I have told you until I am tired of saying it, Tom, I do not love you, I will not marry you, and I don't ever want to see you again! Do you hear me?'

He smiled, a superior, complacent smile. 'I hear you. You are shouting, my dear. Now please permit me to speak. You will regret it if you don't.'

Suddenly Nell recalled Ned's doleful hints. At the time she

had been angry, then for a while concerned. Could Tom possibly tell lies about her? She didn't think he'd been there on the canal bank, but perhaps he had. He could have hidden. But if he said either she or Amy had pushed Pa, he lied, and she would tell everyone so. She was tense with fury. What would it do to Amy, whose confidence was so fragile since she'd been taken to the orphanage, if the child were accused of murdering her father? Even if she, Nell, were accused, it would destroy Amy.

'Go on then,' she said curtly. 'Say what you have to, and then go.'

'I see you have some idea of what I mean to say,' he replied, sitting back in the chair and crossing one leg negligently over the other. 'You know, of course, that husbands and wives cannot testify against one another in Court. To marry me would be the safest way of preventing me from telling what I saw the night your father died. I was down by the canal. I'd followed you, you see.'

'You didn't see anything,' Nell declared firmly, gripping her hands together to prevent them from shaking. 'You didn't see anything, other than what I told the police, because there was nothing different to see.'

'I could tell them different.'

'Will they believe you?' she demanded. 'Why should you tell them something like this weeks afterwards?'

'Oh, that's easy. I wanted to protect your sister. I knew how much she'd suffered, how your father frightened her. It would do no good to accuse her of murder. But then . . . what shall we say? She tried to stick a knife in me? I came to realize she was ill, her problems had caused her to lose her reason, and for everyone's sake she would be better off locked up. But if you were to marry me, Nell, I would forget all this. What do you say?'

'I say you are a monster!' She took a deep breath. 'I'll fight you every inch! I'll kill you rather than let you harm Amy any more! But before I did it I'd ruin your precious reputation!

You're not the only one who can tell lies! And as for marrying you, I'd rather get into bed with a slimy snake! Now get out!'

The door was pushed open and Paul walked in. 'How fortunate I heard all that. Mr Simmons, blackmail and threats and perjury are criminal offences. When you make threats against my future wife you make me very angry. It is going to give me great pleasure to throw you out of here. But before I do, be warned. If you even try to speak to Nell again, ever, I will lay information about this conversation. And don't think I won't be believed! Several of my patients are barristers and judges!'

With that he advanced purposefully towards Tom, who belatedly attempted to struggle to his feet. Paul grasped the back of Tom's collar, twisted it so that Tom went puce, and jerked him forwards. Then he pushed him contemptuously towards the door. Nell, bemused, followed, and saw a grinning Patsy holding the front door wide open. Paul marched Tom to the top of the steps, down them and along the path. With deliberate precision he pushed the hapless Tom, releasing him to send him sprawling into one of the largest heaps of horse droppings ever seen on the Hagley Road.

'He won't dare speak to you again, Nell.'

Edwina laughed. 'His face! When he realized what you were going to do, and that he couldn't do a thing to prevent you, he looked as though he'd collapse from mortification.'

'I merely put him where he belonged. And I haven't enjoyed myself so much for months!'

'Get yourselves drinks,' Edwina suggested. 'I'd better go and help Patsy with lunch. You will stay, won't you, Paul?'

Before he could answer she left the room, and he turned to Nell, sitting silently on a small chair beside the fire.

'Was there any need to humiliate him like that?' she asked, her voice taut with anger. 'I know he's abominable, and he was trying to threaten me, but can you imagine what he'll feel, to have one of the swells of Edgbaston toss him into a load of horse manure, as though he's got no dignity?'

'Nell!' He was utterly taken aback, dismayed by what she said. 'He was threatening you!'

She stood up and faced him, her eyes bright with unshed tears. 'I'd dealt with him! He couldn't have hurt me, whatever he thought! Any threat to his position, his reputation, would be enough to stop him.'

'I wanted to protect you!'

'Tom will never forget the shame of what you did! Just because Tom comes from Ladywood you think he's beneath you, and you can treat him like muck, toss him into it! For all your fine words, and the hours you spend in the clinic, you don't really care about us, do you? It salves your conscience, that's all! Makes you feel good for all the money you've inherited, not had to work for!'

'You don't know anything about my money! And I do more good with my work than that pompous little bore does with his pious preaching! Are you suddenly finding you're in love with him after all?'

'Of course I'm not! You just wouldn't have done it to one of your own kind – to Andrew, for example!'

'That, my dear Nell, is precisely where you're wrong!' he snapped, by now as angry as she was. 'I chucked Andrew into a pile of muck years ago, when I found him and Victoria –' He stopped abruptly, took a deep breath and then turned away. 'I apologize, Nell. Do you wish me to apologize to your friend?'

'He is *not* my *friend*! I detest him! I never want to see him again in my life!'

'Then why are we fighting?'

'I'm not fighting! It's just that – there's no need to be so contemptuous of Tom just because he's poor!'

'If that's what you think of me it's no wonder you've refused to marry me all this time!'

She turned away, and stood with her back towards him, her hands clenched hard together.

'How could I marry you when you would despise me as much as you do Tom? I'm just a girl from a slum, not at all fit for the wife of a smart doctor! You'd better go and find someone more like Victoria, someone your mother would approve of!'

'Victoria was a slut!' he snapped. 'Within months she'd have been in someone else's bed, probably Andrew's!'

'He does seem to succeed with your women!'

'What?'

'Nothing.' She was aghast at what she'd said. 'You'd better go.' Suddenly she found his hands on her shoulders, biting into the soft flesh so fiercely that she cried out in pain. 'Paul, let me go! You're hurting me!'

He relaxed his grip, but only to turn her round so that she was forced to face him. 'I didn't mean to hurt you, but you're not going, Nell, until we've sorted some things out! What's Andrew to you?'

She was suddenly weary, longing only for him to leave her. 'Nothing! And if he is, you've no right to protest. You don't own me.'

'If I thought – Nell, if he's hurt you I'll break every bone in his body!'

'Well, at least you'd be able to set them for him!'

For a second his grip relaxed, and then he pulled her to him. As she was held, imprisoned, against his chest, she could feel him shaking. For a moment she was alarmed, and then the laughter he'd been trying to suppress escaped him.

'Nell! Oh, Nell, what are you doing to me? I can't even be angry with you for long, before you make me laugh!'

'I'm not doing anything except trying to get away, you big bully!'

'You have the oddest effect on me! I thought I'd become a sober, upright citizen before I met you! Instead I sneak in disguise into fleapit music halls to watch you dance –'

'What do you mean?' she demanded, but he ignored her.

' – and then I not only knock poor Andrew down because I'm

jealous of him, I assault your latest suitor and hurl him out in to the street. Why are we quarrelling?'

'I'm not! I wish you'd go away!'

Suddenly he was serious. 'Do you, Nell? I know I've been inept, making the crassest attempts at proposals I've ever heard of, because I was terrified of losing you, but if you really want me to stop asking you to marry me then I'll go.'

He released her and moved a few steps away from her. Nell closed her eyes tightly and bent her head, fighting to remain calm. She didn't know why she'd flown out at him like that. She didn't care what happened to Tom. He'd deserved it, and yet she'd felt sorry for him.

'Well?' Paul asked softly, and Nell shook her head.

The soft click of the door closing made her raise her head abruptly. She was alone in the room. Suddenly she knew she'd never again see Paul, and a torrent of desolation swamped her. The next moment she was tearing open the door and flinging herself down the steps into the street.

'Paul! Wait!'

He was sitting in his motor, the engine already running. Nell scrambled up beside him, her words tumbling out incoherently.

'Paul, you can't! I'm not suitable! I'm not your sort! Your mother wouldn't want me, she wants someone like Victoria! I'm just a girl from a slum, I'm not fit to marry you, and – and Andrew, when we were on tour, I – I – but I can't marry you, but if you want me, there's no need! Oh *hell*, Paul, I love you so much!'

'Then I think we'd better go somewhere quiet where we can sort it all out, don't you? I'm kidnapping you, Nell.'

She looked round. She hadn't been aware they'd been moving, but already they had reached Richmond Hill Road. Paul turned in through the narrow gateway and drew up outside his house. She permitted him to help her down and meekly followed him into the house and along the hall to his library.

'Would you prefer to come to me without marriage?' he asked.

She nodded. 'It's the only way.'

'Are you married already?'

'No! Of course I'm not!'

'Then there's no reason why you should deprive me of getting married and having legitimate children.'

'But I'm just –' she began, but he put his fingers on her lips.

'I don't care who or what you are, Nell. I never did want Victoria, and I don't care a damn what my mother wants – as it happens, she's been singing your praises ever since she invited you here. Why do you think she wanted to see you then if not to look you over in your future home? She thinks I'm slower than a snail. Nor do I care if you let Andrew make love to you.'

'You don't?' She twisted her head away from his hand and managed to speak. 'But –'

'I do wish you'd find something else to say!'

'You said you'd break every bone in his body!'

'If he hurt you. Did he? Were you willing?'

'Of course I wasn't! It was only once. I'd drunk too much, I was half asleep and I didn't know it was – I thought it was –' She stopped, and blushed furiously.

'Are you awake now?'

'Of course I am!'

'Then perhaps we could continue this discussion somewhere more comfortable, such as upstairs?'

Nell's eyes widened. 'But it's Sunday morning!'

'Do you object to the time of day or the actual day?' She giggled. 'We'll be late for lunch, but I'm sure Edwina will understand. And afterwards I think you'd better marry me as quickly as possible to stop this madness.' When she opened her mouth to protest he silenced her by the most effective method available to him, then swept her into his arms and carried her swiftly upstairs. 'I love you, Nell,' he murmured as he set her gently down on the bed. 'I have since I first saw you, and I need you, sweetheart. I'm incomplete without you. But unless you agree to marry me as soon as possible I'm leaving you now. I won't have you on any other terms.'

It was more than she could bear, the appeal in his eyes. He saw her answer and pulled her close again.

'I'll have to marry you now, won't I,' she whispered some time later. 'You're a respectable doctor, aren't you?'